WATCHMAN
TELL US OF THE NIGHT

WATCHMAN
TELL US OF THE NIGHT

A NOVEL BY

A. B. PAULSON

VIKING

VIKING
Viking Penguin Inc., 40 West 23rd Street,
New York, New York 10010, U.S.A.
Penguin Books Ltd. Harmondsworth,
Middlesex, England
Penguin Books Australia Ltd, Ringwood,
Victoria, Australia
Penguin Books Canada Limited, 2801 John Street,
Markham, Ontario, Canada L3R 1B4
Penguin Books (N.Z.) Ltd, 182–190 Wairau Road,
Auckland 10, New Zealand

First published in 1987 by Viking Penguin Inc.
Published simultaneously in Canada

LIBRARY OF CONGRESS CATALOGING IN PUBLICATION DATA
Paulson, A. B.
Watchman tell us of the night.
I. Title.
PS3566.A835W38 1987   813'.54   86-15713
ISBN 0-670-80323-5

Printed in the United States of America by
R. R. Donnelly & Sons Company, Harrisonburg, Virginia
Set in Janson

Designed by Ann Gold

FOR IRENE

ACKNOWLEDGMENTS

Grateful acknowledgment is made to the editor of *The Georgia Review*, where a section of this novel appeared under the title "Olaf's Calling"; to the Blue Mountain Center, Blue Mountain, New York, where portions of the original manuscript were written during a generous residency; and to the Augsburg Publishing House for advice about reprinting material from *The Lutheran Service Book and Hymnal*.

JANUARY 1981. THE SUBURBS.

Lᴉɴᴅꜱᴀʏ ᴡʏᴀᴛᴛ ꜱᴍɪᴛʜ looks out over the wooden shutters in the dining room, looks past the bare birch tree to the corner where the yellow school bus has stopped—red lights flashing through a cloud of exhaust. She watches her son, Alex, clamber aboard behind his third-grade friend. The bus door eases shut and the vehicle pulls away. Lindsay, touching fingertips to her mouth, wonders at this impulse that urged her to the window—this sense, hovering in the cold morning air, that *something is wrong*. Today, she senses, some terrible thing will happen.

In the kitchen she sets her notebook on the table, rinses out her coffee cup, and stacks it in the dishwasher. What could go wrong today? Yesterday it was the dishwasher. With her husband gone for the week to Houston, she'd had to call a repairman. The day before it had been glassware. Unaccountably, anything glass—tumblers, a favorite vase, a cold jar of pickles—had slipped from her fingers. She'd spent the day on her knees, it seemed, with a whisk broom and dustpan methodically gathering the debris. And each time, standing up to survey the floor, came the old fear: with broken glass *you can never be sure you've gotten it all.* Worse, there's always that thin ridge of glittering dust that won't sweep over the edge of the dustpan—that last bit you whisk into the corner thinking, *good enough.*

Lindsay looks down at her notebook on the kitchen table.

It's her poetry she ought to be writing. It's the work she's chosen—this sitting home, this silence of an empty house. But now her attention wanders from the page. She imagines a poem about a woman forced to walk barefoot over broken glass. A kind of medieval peasant type—full-skirted, haggard, lugging some terrible burden: a dead pig, a wicker basket of heavy black bread, a big bag of bones, shopping bags stuffed with old Manhattan telephone directories. Or stuffed with the really heavy varieties of garbage: wet coffee grounds, orange rinds and banana peels, the mossy leftovers you find forgotten on the back shelves of the refrigerator, the ones you ask your husband to dump because it's too awful to even look, to lift the Tupperware lid—awful because you can't even recognize the stuff beneath the mold that's grown magenta fluff in the cold metal darkness.

Lately, trying to daydream herself into a poem, it's been this strange trip into images of garbage and rot, or a kind of blank test pattern in the mind, or the other thing. *Men.* Lately she's been daydreaming about men. Encounters with men, glances exchanged, men who might drop over for a drink just the day her husband is out of town.

> *A woman studies the ads for men's cologne,*
> *trenchcoats, leather belts, and rugby shirts—*
> *She considers the heft of muscle under pin-stripe*
> *lapels, the taut thighs in western jeans,*
> *the bulge at the crotch in double-knit slacks . . .*

Her conscience doesn't like this kind of poetry. Just remember what men are like, says her conscience. Remember what happened four years ago. At this Lindsay winces. Her conscience is a snide sadist. What happened four years ago isn't related logically to these recent romantic fantasies. But it involved men.

It was late March 1977—the day after two 747s collided on a runway in the Canary Islands. Five hundred seventy-

2

seven passengers were killed. Her son, Alex, was at nursery school. Two men came in the back door. They were wearing ski masks. Lindsay dropped a plate to the floor, where it shattered. She backed against the refrigerator and pressed her hands to her cheeks. One had a gun. She stared at it thinking how small the hole was where the bullet came out. She'd seen such men on TV during the Winter Olympics in Munich.

They ordered her into the living room. She slumped, trembling, onto the couch, then tried to sit erect—posture perfect. She pressed her thighs together but still shook all over. They explained that in fifteen minutes she would place a phone call to her husband at the bank. One of them pulled the drapes shut.

She looked at them in disbelief. Tears welled up in her eyes. She blinked them back and shook her head. "No," she said, a little too loud.

Eyeholes in the masks turned to stare at her.

"He doesn't work in a bank," she insisted. Her mind was racing. She tried to think of what Richard's job was called. "Marketing," she said. "He supervises sales representatives." A wave of something dark washed over her as the two men approached the couch. My God, she thought. They think I'm fibbing.

She saw now that the men's hands were trembling. So far they'd been rather polite—as if they were unaccustomed to walking on thick carpeting.

"You've made a mistake," she declared. It was nearly a joke—the way the two of them exchanged a worried look. But the instant passed and Lindsay broke down, weeping into her hands. At some level she'd considered a dash to the door, to the telephone, a cry for help. These not-so-bright thoughts drained away as she hid behind her palms. And only then did it strike her: that *other* Richard Smith, over on Larchmont Circle. They often got his mail by mistake.

She looked up at the two figures, blurred now through tears. "Please!" she cried, wanting to call them idiots. "Look in the telephone book."

The men retreated. There was a conference. Wiping her eyes, she saw one consult a stopwatch. The other one went into the kitchen. She heard voices. The third one came in now. The one they'd been waiting for. The leader. He walked straight at her and stared down through round eyeholes. Slowly he peeled off his mask and said, "Hello." Then he crouched down before her. "Tell me," he said.

She looked at his face, his blond mustache, the acne scars on either side of his nose. "My husband doesn't work in a bank," she repeated. "There's another Richard Smith." She pointed west, toward the pulled drapes.

He kept staring at her. Finally he said, "She's telling the truth. Somebody fucked up. Let's get out of here." But he didn't move when the other two left. His eyes kept drilling into her. In his look was menace but also something else. Perhaps he admired her courage. At last he straightened up and put a finger to his lips. "Nobody," he said. Just that one word. Then he said it again softer, almost whispered it: *Nobody*.

She understood. Don't tell, he was saying. She was to tell no one. Not her husband. Not the police. Nobody. Lindsay took a breath and nodded and nearly crossed her heart, so sincere was her promise to this stranger. Then he was gone.

Lindsay's word was good. She didn't tell anyone about the men in ski masks or their blond leader. Especially him. It wasn't so bad, she told herself. Spells of anxiety melted away ten pounds of flab and made her look like a slim college girl again—the timid one who had stood at the edge of anti-war demonstrations and, in English classes, who had pointed out odd details in long novels. In late April, the nightmares stopped. A year later, looking into the bowl of her Cuisinart, she broke into abrupt laughter, thinking of the men's incompetence. Those dumb guys, she thought. You plan a bank robbery, keep a house under surveillance for maybe a week, time everything down to the second, and it turns out that to begin with some dumbbell looked up the wrong address in the phone book.

Eventually Lindsay met the other Mrs. Richard Smith at

a cocktail party. She was a small dark woman intensely concerned about dolphin meat in cans of Japanese tuna. Lindsay flashed her warm smile, but declined a lengthy chat. She mustn't risk letting out the terrible secret, decided Lindsay. This other woman—this double of herself —was safe, in a way, because of what Lindsay knew. Those three men would have to choose some other banker's wife for their hostage, probably in another city. Unwittingly she had been keeping a distant watch over this other small person, as the woman had been keeping her own loony watch—over unknowable aquatic creatures out in the blue Pacific. After this, Lindsay examined the cans of tuna in the supermarket with new curiosity. Who, she wondered, were the dolphins looking after? Maybe swimmers drawn out beyond their depth?

The only lasting effect of her brush with violence was a guilty sense of having survived it so easily. It had been a mistake, an accident. After the men left, Lindsay turned on the TV and saw the news of the terrible plane collision in the Canary Islands. Apparently a handful had survived even this—had clambered from the burning wreckage. Or was this some older memory, this image of tiny figures crawling out from a monstrous ball of flame? The Hindenburg, perhaps. She'd first seen it as a girl through one of those antique machines that flipped a stack of still photos into motion. Her father had turned the crank.

It terrified her to think that people were allowed to take photographs of such things: catastrophes, corpses, atrocities, the rotting dead. When the pictures appeared a year later of the bloated Jonestown victims, she refused to look. She hurried by the newsstands. The omens—the signs of what we were up to—seemed so obvious. These images of mass death transfixed the Republic. It was some terrible discipline of the spirit, a preparation to gaze across a landscape of mutilation so vast that only eyes of stone could look, take it in, refuse entry. Next came the nuclear accident at Three Mile Island. Lindsay considered whether the horror was already within our midst, something breeding at the core, in the marrow. Then came the DC-10 crash in Chicago. Accidents. Mistakes. Men and machines. There seemed to be some pattern, but not one that offered explanations beyond the easy one. Things were flying apart. Centers were not holding. Or else the center was something awful, like the bright flash on the horizon of her dreams. Some nights she found herself sitting upright, trembling, in the dark bed.

Beneath this series of catastrophes in the news, she felt something else—a current, a counter-force perhaps—welling up from below. She sensed it whenever Richard borrowed her blow-dryer to style his hair before the bathroom mirror. She especially sensed it shopping for panty hose, shoes, a new bra. Everything was getting sexier. Again, the signs had been obvious for years—on TV, in magazine ads, in the advice Ann Landers gave. But none of it had ever touched her before. She'd kept it at a distance. Now she felt it buoying her up. She felt willing even—in her own prim way—to flaunt her body. But lately these feelings seem urged upon her from without, like some new additive in an old brand of breakfast cereal. Yet she drifts along with this current anyway to see where it will carry her. Recently, with men, she feels mildly swept into *episodes*.

Last week in the bank, for example, she'd spoken with a young vice president who had explained the interest on certificates of deposit. He had sandy hair that he brushed back now and then a little boyishly from his forehead. And she knew she looked pretty good—well, smart—in her tweed jacket and the Saks wool skirt with pleats. After some terribly earnest talk about penalties for early withdrawal, they both stood up and shook hands. The thing lasted for only an instant. She felt a subtle change in pressure as he held on a moment too long. Their eyes locked, and up her arm surged a flood of information—as if some vessel had broken, some dike she'd been shoring up over the years had finally given way. The message carried on this tide didn't surprise her. Men often gave you these intense looks. They were often good-looking men. Debbie, her neighbor down the block, is a connoisseur of such looks. "The roving eye," she calls it, putting on her sly smile. But there in the bank, hand in hand with a boyish man, what surprised Lindsay was her matter-of-fact willingness (surely it wasn't yet an eagerness) to send back a reply of equal intensity. "Yes," the two of them silently agreed. "We could do that, couldn't we?"

Lindsay had felt giddy all afternoon. The next day she found herself making an unnecessary trip to the bank to cash a check. From the cashier's window she finally spotted him. Toward the rear, behind a long row of desks, he stood with his back turned, joking with a secretary. The young woman (the kind with gorgeously thick hair) had glanced up at him slyly from her typewriter. At that moment, something caught in Lindsay's throat. She heard the cashier counting out the bills, snapping them crisply on the counter. The next thing she knew she was pushing out the glass doors, taking a breath as part of her—the snide, wisecracking part—looked on and said, "Tut-tut, you dumb cluck." And there in the parking lot, traffic roaring by on Commercial Drive, she really had felt a stab of pain, as if a sharp instrument had found its mark, had pierced the throbbing place she calls her heart.

Lindsay sits down and smoothes the page of her notebook. "A Poem About Women Who Work in Banks," she announces aloud, looking for her Bic pen and her coffee cup. Lindsay needs lots of coffee to write poetry. Anything to induce a little madness. Sometimes singing helps. Opening the dishwasher—no need to dirty another cup—she sings:

Crown him with man - y crowns! The Lamb up - on his throne!

Lindsay is the assistant organist at the Good Shepherd Lutheran Church. She used to be religious. Now the Spirit has withdrawn, gone into hiding—perhaps into pure melody. So, playing the organ is a purely financial arrangement that pays sixteen-fifty for an early communion service. Pastor Ekdahl is strapped for cash. Last year his choir quit. His congregation keeps dying. Lindsay's husband, Richard, sometimes goes for the ten o'clock sermon by himself, dropping Alex off at Sunday School. Richard's attendance has something to do with the Rotary Club, some of whose older members are in the congregation. He seems to know which Sundays the men will assemble at the golf course instead of on the church lawn.

Richard also worries about men. Last year, when she declared that she was going to work full-time, his objections finally came around to the world's erotic peril. First he asked, "What about Alex?"

"The school bus will drop him off at Mrs. Appleby's."

"But the house," he complained next. "The house will be empty all day."

"You're not really worried about the house?"

"I'm worried about *you.*"

"I'm a big girl now."

"Yeah. There are guys out there who like big girls."

"So that's it!" she laughed.

"It's not funny. Things go on in offices."

"Oh, really?" She made a goofy face.

"Aw, you win," he said. "We'd better stock up on TV dinners, huh?"

Last month, Richard wasn't prepared for her latest surprise: she was quitting her job to stay home, cook dinner, and wait for the school bus.

"You can't quit your job!" he insisted.

"Yes, I can," she said. "Because I did."

"You did?" He looked bewildered.

"It was getting pretty boring."

"But—the car payments. The VISA bill! What'll we do?"

"You mean, what will *I* do? Alone all day in an empty house with the whole day free?"

Richard nodded dumbly at her words. "Yeah. What about that?"

"I'm going to write poetry."

"Aw, Linz," he groaned. "Come on! You're not serious?" He looked to see if she was putting him on. "Oh, God, you're serious. Okay," he sighed. "At least I won't worry about guys taking you out to lunch."

Lindsay closes the dishwasher and tries not to think about yesterday's episode. Another man. The one who came to fix the dishwasher. He'd arrived with his toolbox —looking like a young, unemployed actor—to twist the timer dial, to listen as the machine strained to go through its cycle. In Levi's he kneeled on her kitchen floor and removed the screws that held the bottom panel. When he pulled it away, Lindsay stared at what it had hidden: fat rubber tubes and colored wires, gray flufs of dust, coffee grounds, specks of detergent caught in spiderwebs, the shell of a beetle on its back, scattered popcorn kernels, dirty crumbs—all the debris that unaccountably filters down and collects in the most secret place of every kitchen.

"Where's the fuse box, ma'am?"

"Oh. I know that," she said, wanting to help and thinking that the vacuum was in the same closet.

"You'd better show me."

"No. I can do it. You want the current off." She pointed. "Under there. Those wires."

In the closet she ran a finger down a list her husband has taped next to the circuit breakers. When she was in the second grade, she'd brought home a Fire Prevention Checklist, and her father had shown her how to change a fuse: the old kind with little windows that blurred over when the wire tab inside burned through. It was a quick memory from way back—the basement smell of damp, of potatoes near at hand putting out those terrible feelers, of her father breathing behind her in the darkness as she stood, trembling a little, on a wooden crate. He'd insisted she do it all herself: pull the big main switch, hold the flashlight in one hand, strain up with the other to screw the stubby plug into place. It had been a lesson for a girl in self-reliance, but wherever she'd lived, someone else (boyfriends, roommates, a lover, then her husband) had always gotten to the fuse box first.

Lindsay jabbed at the dishwasher's circuit breaker. She half-expected the light in the utility closet to go out, half-expected to find the repairman standing behind her—the two of them together in a small space made suddenly intimate by darkness. But no one stood at her elbow, and the light overhead still glared brightly off broom handles and the dustpan, glinted off that nameless chrome thing on the mop that you squeezed down against the sponge.

Back in the kitchen, the young man had set her best glass fruit bowl on the floor—under the open door of the washer. He was siphoning out the water that wouldn't drain from the interior. She noticed he wore cowboy boots. She was certain her glass bowl had never touched the floor. A plastic tube now curled at its bottom beneath dirty water that rose slowly toward the rim. He wasn't *that* young—twenty-nine maybe. He kneeled in his jeans and boots and watched the water rise. She wasn't entirely sure how siphons worked. Something to do with "water seeking its own level." Now and then, she found, you had only these slogans to go on.

"I know what's wrong," he said, finally looking at her. His eyes—a fine shade of blue—moved over her face. His mouth was pursed a little like the young Steve McQueen. What was that look? Brashness. Innocence. She couldn't decide.

"How do you know what's wrong so fast?" she asked.

"It's a bone," he said. "I'll show you."

The bowl was full. He pulled out the plastic tubing and lifted the glass vessel slowly toward the sink. Her bowl was enormous and fragile in his broad, wet hands. He poured out the water in one smooth splash. Then he returned it to

the floor with astonishing gentleness—even swept the linoleum free of grit before setting it down. This delicacy was
something she hadn't expected. And there was, she noticed
now, something fine about his features: an Ivy League clarity to the line of his mouth and jaw. He'd been an athlete,
she guessed. A pole-vaulter.

He was ready to siphon out more water. If she watched
now, she would learn the secret of these tubes that urged
fluids unnaturally above their own level. When she saw it,
she made a face and said, "Yuk." He had sucked on the
thing. That was how he had drawn dirty water over the rim
of the open door so that it flowed down, pulling the rest
after it. She felt a little sheepish for not having figured it
out before. At the same time, there was a queasy disgust at
the blunt fact of it. The real secret was whether or not
you'd risk sucking dirty water through a tube. To put the
thing in your mouth.

Eventually he showed her the bit of chicken bone that
had stuck in a valve. "If this ever happens again," he said,
"you could fix it yourself." He pressed with his thumb and
the blade of a screwdriver on something in the machine.
"See? You lever this little clip off the end of this thing."

Lindsay, alone in the house with this clever stranger,
leaned closer to look. It was the poet in her that made her
curious about the names of things. "What do you call it?"
she asked.

"This? That's the retaining ring on the solenoid shaft."

"And that part, what's the name of that?" With some
vague notion of later impressing her husband, she squatted
down in her old mauve Cacherel slacks and repeated aloud
as he named machine parts and tools: *solenoid shaft, flange,
allen wrench.* She peered in at an awkward angle, her thigh
pressed against his. *Ground-terminal adjustment screw, leveler-
lock nuts, elbow-reducer adapter.* More than once her hair
must have brushed his face. She felt the heat of his forearm
less than an inch from her cheek. "Tut-tut," said that voice
in her head. Eventually she wondered if he was simply
inventing the names, stringing out the words just to pro-

long the intimacy of the moment: *motor-mount-gimbal-bracket-guide-assembly*. He said it nonchalantly and touched her wrist as if pointing out an exquisite detail on a piece of fine porcelain. She felt a little faint. *Axel-free-play-compensation-receptor*, he murmured. My God! she thought. What dumb thing am I allowing to happen here?

Abruptly she stood up, flushed, then folded her arms and looked down. He knelt there, still at her feet. She went to the stove with a sponge and rubbed vigorously at a stain by the front burner. Neither spoke now. She heard him fastening the dishwasher panel back into place, heard the clank of tools being put away, the toolbox snap shut. When she looked again he was standing, head cocked to one side, peering at her expensive fruit bowl as if to catch the light from one special angle.

"It's hand-blown glass," he said.

"I know."

"It's very lovely."

She didn't answer.

"If it was mine," he mused, "I'd find a way to use it every day."

"Well, it's not yours."

For some reason, this struck them both as funny.

He smiled, a little shyly, and rubbed a finger in his ear. Then he headed for the door.

"Will someone send me a bill?" she called after him.

"Someone always does." He opened the door. "So long." And that was the end of it.

In just the past week, there had been these two: the fellow at the bank and the athletic young repairman. Nothing terribly serious. Yet, she understood that she'd brushed the edge of something here, an unexplored region of tangled arrangements through which some women moved with furtive self-confidence. Her neighbor Debbie would shrug and say, "That's modern marriage for you." Even on her quiet suburban street, Lindsay feels the boundaries of this dark zone widening, spreading out like some spilled fluid. How much longer, she wonders, can she make her prim way past it, like a good girl taught not to slosh through puddles.

Job or no job, in or out of the house, Lindsay doesn't feel safe from the allure of other men. When she went back to pick up her last check at Thurston, Owens, & Bradley, Dave Fanshaw, who'd had the desk behind hers, joined her in the little elevator. His good-bye hug was so warm and extended that by the time the doors opened again at the lobby, her shoe had come off. It was another gesture of fondness from a decent, intelligent guy—good looking and roughly her age. These men—they merely wanted to tell her that she was bright, and charming, and—a little special. Now, didn't she—a thirty-three-year-old suburban woman with lines appearing about the eyes—didn't she deserve at least that?

But lately she's been aware of these little jabs of pain. She felt one again when the young repairman had said "So long" from the kitchen door. These pangs are something new. Or rather, they're so old that she has to search back through the years all the way to high school to touch their tender agony. She thinks of all those melancholy partings in rock-and-roll songs—the lyrics they'd sung along with and believed in enough to hum in the dark, hugging a pillow that, by morning, was still damp with tears. She ought to write a poem about it.

Lindsay smoothes back her hair and looks at the kitchen clock. It's still early. Ten to eight. Closing her notebook on the blank page, it hits her all at once. If something terrible is going to happen today, then she'd better take control and do it herself. Just now, the worst thing she can think of is having all her hair cut off. Really short this time. There's a new place in the mall where they don't know her, where no one will tell her to think twice, to come back tomorrow. Afterwards, she decides, it will be something out of Peter Pan. Leotards around the house. For accessories, just a belt. And poems about—what? "The Poetry of Human Flight!" she announces and dramatically flings her notebook in the general direction of the bathroom.

2

IN THE FALL OF 1957 Lindsay's father, John Wyatt, disappeared. He left his Pittsburgh insurance office during a heavy storm that had closed the airport. Three days later his car was found northeast of Harrisburg, at the bottom of a ravine where a bridge had washed out. The state police decided he must have missed the turn at Indiantown Gap, took 343 as far as Licksdale, and was circling back to U.S. 22 over Mad Mountain. His body was never recovered.

Lindsay was ten years old. She recalls the night the police came to their house. Her mother had stayed up late ironing her husband's shirts, pressing his pants and neckties—as if getting his entire wardrobe in order might bring him back. After midnight, Lindsay heard muffled voices downstairs and the sound of her mother weeping. Lindsay lay huddled in bed. Heavy footsteps mounted the stairs. A police officer beamed a flashlight into her face. She pretended to be asleep.

The next day, Harriet cleared out the closets and delivered nine cartons of neatly pressed men's clothing to the Salvation Army. Dumped in the trash were toiletries, socks past darning, old letters, and photos. Lindsay snatched a few items as the garbagemen heaved the debris of her father's life into their truck.

They listed her father as a missing person. Her Uncle Alfred arrived from California and arranged a memorial service. Lindsay, a fifth-grader, gravely shook hands with a man who had known her father in 1944.

"But what did my daddy do in the war?" she asked.

"He helped us look for Hitler's atom bomb," explained the man.

"Did you find it?"

"No."

After the service, an attorney from the insurance company came to the house and explained that, legally, John Wyatt wasn't exactly dead.

Uncle Alfred got all red in the face. "That's preposterous," he declared.

The attorney waved a sheaf of papers. "The court, as herein provided, shall adjudge and decree said party to be an Absentee Under the Law."

"Can't you speak English?"

The attorney sighed and pushed up his glasses. "The procedure is substantially the same with prisoners of war," he said. "Mrs. Wyatt's counsel has offered to act as receiver of the estate. It might take years to settle this."

"But what if he comes back?" said Lindsay.

The lawyer rested his gaze upon her. He put on a gruesome fatherly smile. As she sat on the couch, her knees were bare. She decided he was trying to peek up her skirt. Then light from a window caught his glasses and turned them into blank disks. She suddenly understood that a man with nasty thoughts has no eyes in his face.

3

AT THIS HOUR of the morning, the parking lots surrounding the Heathersford Shopping Mall stretch out flat and vacant, swept dry of last week's snowfall. They have piled the slush and salt out in the overflow parking areas—where the employees are supposed to leave their vehicles. Bucket loaders have heaped up ten-foot mounds of the stuff. In a month or two the sun will bore into these piles from low in the southern sky. Around specks of grit hollows will melt, forming crystalline grottoes—like one of those Chinese mountain landscapes where tiny ivory figures sit meditating on the transparency of the world.

Garth Erikson stops his 1957 Plymouth Belvedere beside one of the snow mounds and gets out. It takes him two or three glances to figure out what these weird piles signify. It's the artist in him. He wonders if this is some new school of sculpture that he hasn't kept up with. Finally he decides that they are pretty impressive, these piles. Of course, they would be equally impressive fashioned from reinforced concrete. Garth scratches his beard. But then they wouldn't melt in the spring, would they? Suddenly he yells out these last words into the clear morning air. "WOULD THEY!" Faintly, his words return off the walls of the distant, looming mall. In their echo rings something unspeakable—the voice of some other self: enraged, astonished, an ogre seeing himself for the first time in a mirror.

Lately Garth has been yelling a lot. This morning he

hollered all the way through rush-hour traffic—suburban maniacs roaring past his vintage 1957 Plymouth (the model with Torsion-Aire Ride and the big fins in back: "Flight-Sweep Styling," they called it). "Slow down, you lunatics!" he shouted. A Trans Am sped past on the right and whipped into the lane ahead of him. "Nitwit! Bourgeois oaf!" Garth didn't realize it, but he was grinning with the excitement of it, this rush of zealous commuters, his own adrenaline surging through his late-thirties veins, reflexes sharpened up like a teenager's, the view ahead gleaming with sharp lines of chrome, the white stripes on the highway whizzing past like some upbeat and linear mantra.

At least the drive out distracted him from his agony, this clutching tightness in the chest, this pitiful melancholy. It's the same old story. Una has moved out again. She claimed it was her progressed Venus entering Aquarius.

Una has straight blond hair she recently got frizzed. This makes her look like a wild woman who's been wandering the moors around Stonehenge. But anything Una does to herself only makes her look more provocative.

The day she moved out, Garth had a suggestion. "Maybe Venus in Aquarius means you're going to make some kind of breakthrough. Computers maybe. A new synthesis." Over the years he'd had to read a lot of trash about orbs and transits just to carry on a conversation.

"Bullshit," said Una. "It's in my seventh house."

There was a long silence as it sank in. "What's his name?" he finally asked.

Una was pulling underwear out of a drawer and stuffing it into a shopping bag. These days she had her pack-up-and-leave routine down to ten minutes flat. "It doesn't matter. Look, you've got to accept me as the person I am. Flow with it. You know what I mean?"

Garth put his hands in his pockets and looked at the dirty dishes in the sink. They'd been through this before. The worst part of it was that he was getting used to these other men: jerks with Mars trine her sun, the one with Pluto conjunct her midheaven, that dumb jock with Scorpio rising. Together, they comprised a starry pantheon of stiff pricks, lascivious satyrs, goat-men with huge genitalia a-dangle. All of them calling to her on some frequency that he wasn't tuned into.

Gray light came in the big windows of the loft apartment. He walked over and looked down into the street. A Jeep was parked by the curb.

"That his car?"

"Yeah. A CJ-5. He's going to take me out driving on back roads once the snow clears."

Garth looked at the Jeep. Somewhat desperately, he remarked, "The Sierra Club doesn't like people tearing around the woods in off-the-road vehicles."

"Fuck the Sierra Club."

He watched her strip half the closet bare. The empty wire hangers clanged like a wind chime for the insane. He noticed that she was putting on weight. A new puffiness filled out her face.

Idly he asked, "Why not a snowmobile?"

"He's got one of those, too. Hey, have you seen that plastic thing I keep my makeup in?" She bustled into the bathroom without waiting for an answer. Five minutes later she was standing at the door holding a suitcase and three shopping bags. Did she expect him to help carry the stuff downstairs? He didn't ask why she'd left her paints set up in her corner of the loft. It seemed less a promise of a return than a sign that this time she was putting everything behind her.

Garth put on a bitter look and prepared to holler something loud. But then the gray light spilled onto her crazy hair and creamy cheek like something from a Vermeer painting and he wanted to take her in his arms and hold her until that impatient CJ-5 honking downstairs screeched off without her—off into the woods, across the frontier, over a hill, gone. Dear Una: blond fortuneteller, delicate poise in each mute gesture, frazzle of Naples yellow in her hair. Why had she chosen him for this unfathomable agony?

Wind gusts across the parking lot. Garth wonders if there's a shop in the mall called the Jealous Lover. If there were, it would be stocked with weapons, voodoo dolls, shelves of malign potions. He'd fill a shopping cart with revolvers, blowguns, and medieval devices for flaying the flesh. Actually, an old army surplus store would do—with its machetes and coils of strong, thin rope. He'd truss up Una's new lover and hammer tent pegs into his eardrums. Or a hardware store where every bright new Stanley tool concealed murderous possibilities: hacksaws, ripping chisels, wood rasps— Garth pictures himself leading a mob of peasants whose garden rakes and battery-powered hedge trimmers glint in the light of midnight torches. The rage is up in him now, and he bellows at the monolithic mall. It's this strange other self within him, the ogre. Has he lived thirty-nine years of cheerful goofiness only to discover, in an empty suburban parking lot, that he's a homicidal maniac?

Actually, Garth has heard that inside the mall—buried in concrete when the place was constructed—is a work of Hidden Art. He heard the rumor in a New York bar in 1974. That's when Rumor Art was a pretty big thing, an offshoot of Secret Art. Garth belongs to an older school. He still publishes his works of art, usually in the classified ads of *The New York Times*. But the general idea is the same: subvert the dominance of the Art Establishment. That is, get it past the museums and the museum directors. Slip it by the critics and the wealthy patrons. On his part, Garth left the art object behind in 1972. Now, for him, it's all in the mind. There aren't many revolutionaries like him left in 1981. Maybe he's the only one.

Garth trudges toward the mall under a high, overcast sky, sensing the vastness of this flat space, and half-knowing that something unpleasant is going to happen in there, up ahead, across the asphalt. He had a friend who did Parking Lot Art in the late sixties. Actually it was Detonation Art, a branch of Earth Sculpture. His friend got commissions to set off explosives in parking lots. He made some pretty big craters which the art critics came out to see. It was quite the big thing for a while. You could hardly get near those holes in the asphalt, there were so many art critics standing around the edges, nodding to themselves, taking notes, pointing out one thing or another. But then Garth's friend got a bad review in one of the art journals. Some guy decided that the craters "had become obsessively rationalized by the very process of allowing materiality access to articulation; had in fact allowed an abject and sentimental Romanticism to corrode the purity of gestural statement." Well, the word went out and it was all over for Parking Lot Detonations. That's how the old art game went. You took your chances.

Garth thrusts his hands deep into the pockets of his army greatcoat. He's leaning into the wind, looking down at the lines painted on the asphalt. He knew a guy in New Mexico who used to come out at night with big brushes and cans of black and yellow paint. He'd redo the lines on the parking lots. The next morning the cars would obediently arrange themselves along those new lines—slightly askew at first, then becoming curves, odd angles and loops, spirals, hieroglyphics perhaps, strange messages spelled out to passing aircraft. His friend would have gotten in trouble with the police if it hadn't been for all that time he spent at night on his knees. They gave out. The last Garth heard, the guy was doing Footprint Art in hospital corridors.

Garth scratches his beard and swings one foot in an arc. He's got a bad knee, too. If it goes out of joint, he knows just how to smack it so that it pops back into place. As he heads for the mall entrance, the joint clicks ominously. He mulls over his latest work of art.

Situation Wanted

A line in space
From the ground
Four feet.

Usually Garth doesn't sign them. He just sends them in
to the classified ads. But today, feeling a little angry and
depressed, he's tempted to tinker, to make this latest crea-
tion a regular Baroque piece. He starts over:

Personal

An oblique line
In air
Pass through it.

"Jeez," he says, making a serious face. His art claims to
be stripped clean of personal references. But this piece
reminds him of his parents, who went down in a small
plane somewhere near the border between Honduras and
Guatemala. It was a line they didn't pass through. In
1962, both were in their mid-fifties, but the Peace Corps
had valued their skills. Garth's father was a high school
shop teacher. His mother cultivated a half-acre vegetable
garden. At the time of their death, Garth was in art
school. There were no insurance policies, although the
government coughed up some mysterious payments a
year later. The money went for the institutional care of
Garth's brother.

Garth jogs the last few yards to the mall entrance, grimacing. Pushing back memories of his parents' death sometimes requires strenuous physical activity. He's
concentrating on his high school track team and all those
hurdles he knocked down just to come in fifth or sixth, long
after someone had broken the string they stretched out at
the finish line. A custodian is unlocking the glass doors of

the mall. He looks startled to see a large bearded man racing toward him. But he holds the door open, and Garth trots through in triumph, one knee joint clacking like a Halloween cricket.

"Morning," puffs Garth, slowing to a walk inside. Shopping malls give him the creeps, but there's no avoiding them these days. The corridor is lined with those out-of-the-way shops you'd never patronize except under duress: Tuxedo World (in the window, powder blue shirts with ruffles), The Visual Connection (one wall plastered with glamorous-looking people, all wearing glasses), and Star Cutters (a unisex beauty parlor with swivel chairs facing trapezoidal consoles). Garth strolls down to the window display at Travel Your World. The window is full of brochures ("Florida . . . Your Way!" "Las Vegas Westward HO!") except for a cardboard Canadian Mountie with one gloved hand cupped to his mouth, calling out "Canada . . . So Much to Go For!" Garth especially likes the Mountie, because in this cardboard version he stands only four feet tall—as if in the wilds of Saskatchewan there's a whole barracks full of little Mounties who didn't meet the official height requirements. Shipped off, far from the cameras of tourists, they spend their days parading on ponies, making their little beds, and polishing size-five boots.

Garth heads down the wide deserted corridor. At the corner of Florsheim and Radio Shack, the ceiling opens up into a high atrium. Daylight filters down through high windows, and from beside a fountain, almond trees grow up—pale new growth at the top reaching for light, trembling in the breeze of the air conditioning system. A merchant rolls down the awning over the Hallmark Card Shop. His place is hung thick with red valentine hearts, suspended from the ceiling. Next door, a guy still wearing his parka, sets out chairs at the Café Coffee. Slowly the place is coming alive with morning activity. The other stores are all locked up—grilles pulled down across their wide entrances. But inside all the lights are on. In the windows, neon signs blink. Overhead, bright letters spell out Thom McAn in red. The Bathtique in lime green. Garth, in his drab greatcoat and gray janitor-style pants, feels stunned by it all. He squints at track lighting that glares on stark white plaster. He passes by ruddy walnut paneling and deep green walls with magenta trim, bricks of sienna and peach mortared with umber, swaths of orange and electric blue the color of detergent bottles. He wonders if he's lived in decaying downtowns too long, where the grit, exhaust fumes, and airborne garbage have abraded the flesh, laid bare the nerves, left him too open, too vulnerable, to these sensory assaults. It's enough to give you a hard-on. Soon the restless suburban souls will arrive, and he's curious to see how they will handle it: these Technicolor highs every ten yards, this harsh turquoise and raspberry-sherbet red. And these lights—hundreds of clear glass bulbs in overhead rows, the filaments glowing like needles that invite you to stare into brightness just this side of retinal damage.

His boots pound the parquet floor. The place is getting to him. He brushes past a guy delivering milk to the café. He hurries past A.S. Beck (why so many shoe stores?), past The Tie Racket, The Fabric Mill, The Tobacco Gallery, Board 'n' Barrel, Bits 'n' Pieces, The Cheese Brigade. He's made a circle and come back to Radio Shack. The scary light-headedness of an anxiety attack is weakening his knees. He's had a glimpse of the soul of this place: a vast interior bombed out and charred black.

They've turned on the Muzak. Garth heads back the way he came in, wading through a dense current of sound. He makes it all the way to a stone bench facing the interplanetary beauty parlor. Real daylight comes in the glass doors. And actually, as Muzak goes, this tune is okay. In fact, it's the old Art Van Dam quintet playing. Feeling better, Garth eases himself down on the bench, swings up his boots, and stretches out to listen.

"*Uff da*," he mutters, a Scandinavian expression— roughly the equivalent of *Oy veh*. This time they've really done it, he thinks. They've arranged an out-of-the-body vision for him. Straight overhead he sees himself in the mirrors on the ceiling. Hands gripping cold stone, he's certain the corridor has tipped. It's a huge vertical shaft the architects have borrowed from the United Mine Workers. If he lets go, he'll slide, feet first, down the shaft, boots crashing through glass doors, and then the long mutilated skid down a sheer asphalt cliff, a plummet past his Plymouth's deadly tail fins. Garth nearly hollers, but he halts in midflight to scratch his beard. Something presses him flat onto the cold stone slab. Mere gravity couldn't do it, he decides. Rather, it's the force of the old sadness. At this hour, Una probably lolls in the sack with her new boyfriend, or fiddles with dirty dishes at the sink —that lovely ass of hers hitched to one side on account of her hip trouble, and the guy is sitting at the kitchen table eyeing all that sweetness. Against these agonizing visions, there's no defense for Garth except to take a little nap. That's it, he thinks, as heavy-lidded eyes close on that other self clinging to the ceiling. Just for a minute or two, he'll rest his eyes.

When Lindsay turns off the ignition of her VW Rabbit outside the mall, she's humming one of the alleluias from the hymn "Christ the Lord Is Risen Today," and her watch says 8:45. If she's there when the haircutters open at nine, she won't need an appointment. Lindsay paces toward the mall with a look of breezy disdain for the world. Her skin seems unnaturally white since last summer, when, hearing stories about skin cancer, she decided to give up baking in the sun. She never did get very tan, anyway. But it's her walk, and her taste in clothes, that make a haughty first impression. She learned this chin-up posture taking voice lessons at Smith College. It's the eyebrows she's conscious of keeping elevated. Sopranos employ this technique to keep from singing flat.

Inside, she's surprised to see a large bearded man stretched out on a bench. Eventually it had to happen, she thinks. The skid row bums have found their way out to the suburbs. There's another bench in front of the travel bureau. Lindsay turns her back on the snoring figure and sits down. What tune, she wonders, is that cardboard Canadian Mountie belting out:

Al - - le - lu - ia ?

At the other end of the mall, the minibus from the senior citizen center pulls to a stop. Out steps Mr. Maynard Manard, age seventy-eight, retired salesman of business forms and commercial novelties. Not many old folks take the morning bus from Maynard's building—a high-rise co-op that won't rent to anyone under sixty—but all neighbors are up at the crack of dawn. Passing down the long carpeted hallways, Maynard hears them puttering around, vacuuming, washing the dishes, tuning in the TV, as the sky lightens along the eastern horizon.

On mild days, the cardiac club is out on the sidewalk before breakfast—old geezers in jogging suits, determined to outlive the mass of blue-haired ladies who run the place by majority vote. One jogs. A few others trot. But mostly they're brisk walkers. They stretch out in a line around the building, colorful in their outfits, each with his own distinctive style: long, loping strides, or quick, deft shuffles; fists clenched tight against the chest, or palms flopped loose; heads down, or up to the wind; cheeks puffed, flaccid, or tense—each of them a marvel of the human machine in splendid, astonishing motion.

But not Maynard Manard. His doctor told him last month that he had the heart of a teenage jitterbug. After hearing this, Maynard decided, at the age of seventy-eight, to take up smoking cigarettes. The only difficulty here, he realizes, given his Social Security budget, is their expense. He's figured the trade-offs involved in buying them at eighty cents a pack. In 1981, that kind of money will buy a can of Spam or a box of Pop Tarts. And this explains his early arrival at the mall. Mr. Manard has come to scout the big sand-filled ashtrays before the janitors can clean them out.

Cane crooked smartly over one arm—wearing his gray Hart Schaffner & Marx pinstripe, his eighteen-dollar necktie, and his late brother's Rolex watch—Maynard walks his regular route, pausing now and then to grope among bristling arrays of half-smoked Marlboros and Winstons. By the time he reaches the garden court, the Baggie in his coat pocket is bulging.

He pauses next to a stainless-steel trash container. He prods the crumpled paper cups aside and peers into the trash. His fingers snake in to retrieve something printed in color on glossy paper. The brochure slides into a side pocket—he'll examine it later, perhaps take it home for his elaborate, cross-referenced collection. Poking through trash excites him. Perhaps it's the next, inevitable step after tobacco in a series of degrading addictions. Who knows where it will lead? Probably to extramarital sex. His wife passed away five years ago. Now, as far as getting by goes, women in his building still give him the eye.

Maynard adjusts his fancy necktie and makes an elaborate show of checking the time on his wristwatch. He's spotted something else in there—under a crumpled wad of napkins sticky with ketchup. And he's denied himself this sort of thing for an entire month. Dr. Grinstein strictly forbade it.

"Verboten," stated the doctor. "At your age? Don't be a dummy. Listen, I know what I'm talking about. You should be glad I'm telling you."

But Maynard is already leaning into the trash up to his elbow. He's got it now. It's the comics section of last Sunday's newspaper—the one with Blondie and Dagwood on the front page. Maynard's hand visibly trembles as he stuffs it into his breast pocket and strides off.

Mr. Manard, it turns out, is a narcoleptic. The spells, for
Maynard, began about Thanksgiving. Since then—oh, two
or three times a week—his knees have buckled in the midst
of conversations, and he's slumped to the floor apparently
unconscious. After a few moments of dozing, he springs up
again feeling oddly refreshed. "Nothing to it, as far as that
goes!" he declares, leaving behind a cluster of perplexed
onlookers.

Last month at a senior citizen banquet, he slumped forward and dozed for ten minutes with his forehead in a bowl
of chocolate pudding. No one at his table seemed to notice
the attack until it was over and he was sitting up straight
in his chair again. Then Mildred Gustavson said, "What's
that on his forehead?"

"Hush up," said her sister.

"There's something terribly wrong with his forehead."

"Shhh. You're making a scene."

"Oh, Mr. Maynard. Yoo-hoo."

"Hush."

The major glanced over. He'd seen some nasty wounds
in the South Pacific. "Why, it's pudding," he announced,
and whispered something in Maynard's ear.

The next day Mr. Manard went to the clinic. Dr. Grinstein made him confess that the attack had followed the
after-dinner speaker's impersonation of Arthur Godfrey.

"So what?" asked Maynard.

"So you're a cataplexic narcoleptic. That's what." The
doctor explained that cataplexy (a temporary paralysis of
the cranial muscles and limbs) was often brought on by
hearty laughter. In turn, these attacks triggered the narcoleptic episodes. "So you've been collapsing. Falling down?"
he asked.

Maynard shrugged. "Sometimes I fall asleep standing
up. If there's a chair I'll sit down. It's not like passing out,
as far as that goes."

The doctor frowned at him.

"Okay," smiled Maynard. "A couple of times I stretched
out on the floor. What's the cure?"

Grinstein shook his head. "It's a mystery. There's no cure. Except"— Grinstein rubbed his brow—"if I were you, I'd avoid laughing. Seriously." There was something ludicrous about this advice. "So tell me something funny"—a smile flickered on the doctor's face—"and I'll tell you to avoid it."

"That's easy," smiled Maynard. "Blondie and Dagwood."

Grinstein looked at him. "That's *funny?*" He reached for his pen. "Okay. Number one: Blondie and Dagwood. Verboten." The doctor made a little cough to disguise a chuckle. "Okay. What's next? Somebody on TV?" The doctor grinned across the desk at his patient.

"My TV fritzed out," said Maynard.

"Fritzed out?"

"I spilled some liquid on it—knocked a glass over."

"What a shame."

"Metamucil, actually," frowned Maynard. "It gooped up the inside."

"Oh, dear," said Grinstein, then snorted into his hand. He'd never thought of administering a bulking agent to a television set. "So, when it spilled it was—"

"Just starting to thicken up."

"Oh!" cried the doctor. Then he abruptly stiffened his expression. Such talk might trigger a narcoleptic attack— and a bizarre malpractice suit.

"Something sizzled inside," added Maynard.

"Enough," cautioned Grinstein, putting up his hands. To keep from laughing outright, he'd contorted his face into a frightful grimace.

"I'm serious," said Maynard glumly.

"Of course!" cried the doctor, wiping his eyes. But now he wore a helpless look. Suddenly he plunged toward his desk blotter and buried his face in his arms. For a whole minute he hunched there, convulsed. He seemed to be repeating his patient's name to himself. Finally a weak hand went up, as in surrender.

Mr. Manard got up as Grinstein wheezed and snorted in a heap. "Go!" had come the doctor's muffled cry. "That's enough for today, Maynard Manard!"

Mr. Manard follows his regular route through the largely deserted mall, and turns the corner at Radio Shack. Up ahead, he sees two figures: a woman sitting on a bench and a man stretched out on another. The woman gives him a bright good-morning smile as he takes a seat at the other end of her bench. Ignoring the fellow sprawled out across the way, he returns a polite nod, and then feels the forbidden bulge of newsprint in his breast pocket. Better to delay a private chuckle, he decides, and examines the glossy brochure first. The front cover says, "Important Free Gift Offer Inside!" But the inside pages disappoint him. The thing is filled with photos of near-naked women wearing odd undergarments. They ogle and wink at the camera as they adjust peculiar leather straps on their brassieres. Disgusting, thinks Maynard, and lets the pamphlet fall to the floor. Now, at last, he draws out Blondie and Dagwood.

"You dropped this, sir." The young woman, handing him the brochure, has glanced at the photos. She gives him a look of tense embarrassment.

"Thank you," he mutters, stuffing the brochure back in his pocket.

Lindsay slides a few inches farther away from the old gentleman. Wouldn't you know it, she thinks. A big place like this and she's chosen the spot where the bums and perverts hang out. A glance over her shoulder at the sprawled-out wino makes her sigh. What a shame. He's not old. And if he cleaned himself up, trimmed that beard, he'd probably look okay. Well, obviously the haircutters are not going to open until nine-thirty. She considers walking around for the remaining quarter of an hour, then decides to stay put, with a melody annoyingly stuck in her mind.

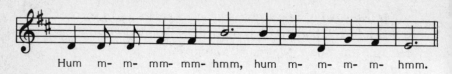

Hum m- m- mm- mm- hmm, hum m- m- m- m- hmm.

Garth has been watching her in the ceiling mirror since she came in. At once his other self despised what he saw— her clean-cut, expensive suburban look. He figures she's wearing about eight hundred dollars worth of clothing, not counting the jewelry. On the other hand, he's grown a little tired of the arty women he's typically been involved with. Aging hippies, most of them. Their lives a mess. So gradually, while observing Lindsay in the ceiling, he's begun to recover the old allure of her type: dazzling white teeth, posture like teatime, and that look of just having stepped out of the shower.

Who is this haughty, unattainable woman? he wonders. And what does she look like—right side up? The Muzak has hit a long blank in its tape. And faintly, as if across a misty landscape, he hears her voice, a clear soprano head-tone. She was humming to herself until the old guy arrived. Now she's started again. Garth strains to identify the melody. Good grief, he thinks. It's a hymn. Maybe she's one of those awful concoctions from Texas, born again and wealthy.

Meanwhile, Mr. Manard has worked halfway through Blondie and Dagwood. A rare smile creases his usually glum face. Here comes Dagwood back from the neighbors'. He's still wearing that frilly housedress—the one Blondie forced him to put on so she could pin up the hem. Dagwood looks mad. Next door, Tootsie asked him to answer the doorbell. It was one of those hick salesmen, holding a gizmo. Wearing that housedress, Dagwood yelled, "Beat it!" Now he's back in his own living room. Mr. Manard examines the davenport where Dag-

wood takes his naps, then looks up from the page, distracted.

   Lindsay has drifted into the lyrics of the hymn, mouth-
ing them in a musical whisper. Now the old guy has
glanced up. But heck, she thinks. These guys do whatever
they feel like doing. Before she married Richard, Lindsay
did a lot of zany things—even on the street. So she repeats
the last bar, a little louder:

A - wake, my soul, and sing--

She stops again, head cocked, listening for a moment. She
goes on:

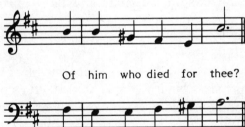

Of him who died for thee?

   Oh-oh, she thinks, having sorted out a baritone voice that
has joined hers in harmony.

   Without meaning to intrude, Garth has been singing
along with Lindsay. The tune took him all the way back to
the Lutheran boys' choir. He was a soprano himself until
his voice changed. But phooey, he thinks—now she's heard
him. The romantic moment has been ruined, just as they
were headed for a coy duet.
   He steals a glance at her. She's on her feet, looking

haughty and indignant. This is their first good look at each other. Garth squints and decides that her eyes are lovely and her lips—ah, a connoisseur of women's mouths, this man—her mouth is perfect. He springs up with easy nonchalance, a clatter of coins and car keys falling from his pockets. It's not precisely the charming gesture Garth had in mind, but he's committed himself now to something dramatic. Lindsay is blushing so furiously that she puts a hand to her hot cheek.

Dagwood stands in his living room, looking sour. Blondie kneels demurely at his feet, pinning up the hem of the dress her husband is wearing. The telephone rings. Mr. Manard chuckles as Blondie—except for her left heel— leaves the frame to answer it. But now another ring hangs in the air, this one from the direction of the front door. Maynard begins to chuckle, recalling the thousand doorbells he rang as a Fuller Brush salesman. Next, Dagwood —wearing the dress—glares out the front door. A confused expression appears on the salesman's face. This just happened next door. What nightmare is the salesman trapped in, condemned to visit endlessly this same horrid household? "SCRAM!" yells Dagwood. Now there's a terrible tussle on the front walk: stars, bared teeth, and lots of eye-gouging. Mr. Manard laughs now about as heartily as he ever does. Hunched over, he bobs his head and lets out muffled grunts—in waltz time. He's keeping the last frame of the comic covered so he won't peek ahead.

Garth glances over at him and finally says to Lindsay, "He's not the tenor we need, but I bet he plays the marimba."

Mr. Manard isn't listening. He's eating up the comic's last view of the hick salesman. Lying on his back all bunged up, the fellow blinks at the reader through one blackened eye. "Boy!" he exclaims. "I wouldn't want to be married to that Amazon!" This crack sends Mr. Manard over some new threshold of hilarity. And he'd better enjoy the moment while he can, because it's coming. Like a terrific wall of water darkening the horizon, one of those spells is going to hit.

Garth is gazing at Lindsay, pleased with himself, certain they can now share a good laugh together. But something else—a sudden vacuity of sound and movement in the direction of the old gentleman—draws their attention.

Mr. Manard sits open-mouthed, eyes wide, in total paralysis. As they watch, he tilts slowly forward and rolls in a kind of somersault right onto the floor.

Garth is already in motion. He kneels beside the body, feeling for a pulse at the neck, listening for breath at the open mouth. His friend Wally has vaguely told him the routine for cardio-pulmonary resuscitation. But Garth has never actually had to do it. His mind is a blur of nervous terror. "Help!" he shouts into the empty corridor. "You!" he roars at Lindsay. "Get down here!"

Suddenly she finds herself kneeling beside the old man's head, watching Garth angle the body's chin upward. "Now each time I get to five," he instructs her, "pinch his nostrils and blow." She watches, horrified, as he covers the wrinkled, gaping mouth with his own. She's not sure she can do it. In the distance—dreamlike—she hears the sound of feet pounding the corridor in a run, jingling keys, and the crackle of a walkie-talkie. "Oh, God!" she whispers.

Garth has laced his fingers together on the man's chest. "Shit," he says. "Do you know the right way to do this?"

Lindsay looks at him in terror. She'd thought that he knew what he was doing. "Feel for the sternum. Don't press there. Up a little farther. Hurry!" She heard this advice on TV a year ago.

As Garth, arms stiff, begins thrusting down rhythmically on the man's chest, Lindsay hovers over the mouth of what might be a corpse. She observes a particle of food lodged between two yellow teeth and wonders how much time has passed. A minute? Thirty seconds? Her hands are trembling. Then she does it—plants her lips wide open on the old man's mouth and exhales a long breath into him. She's forgotten to plug his nose, so she does it again.

". . . 3-AND! 4-AND BLOW!" chants Garth.

Meanwhile, Mr. Manard is semiconscious, though a bit disoriented. Everything looks dim. His pupils have contracted, as in deep sleep, but he's certain that someone is pushing him in the chest. It's not an entirely unpleasant sensation, a rough jouncing. But there's something else. A woman has just kissed him on the mouth. It was an odd kiss. Vapory, he decides. And look here. Someone—a cop —is looking down at him.

The security guard stares down at the three of them and says "Ten-four" into his walkie-talkie. Garth keeps pumping on the chest of the victim. "Are we doing this right?" he asks. His voice is a little hysterical.

"Beats me," says the guard.

"Christ," says Garth, out of breath.

Lindsay raises her head. "There's something wrong," she says.

"Don't stop!" shouts Garth.

"Look at his eyes," says the guard and folds his arms.

Lindsay is shaking her head. "It feels like he's blowing back."

"What's the matter?" It's the voice of a woman. Onlookers have arrived.

"What happened to him?" asks a custodian.

"Stop a sec," says the guard. He squats and feels for a pulse at the wrist.

A small crowd now circles the scene. Everyone looks down at Mr. Manard. The old man lets out a long blubbering snore. There follows a tense silence.

"Nothing wrong with him," says the guard.

As if on cue, Mr. Manard sits up. "Well!" he says. "As far as that goes!"

The cluster of people begins to disperse. Lindsay and Garth remain there on their knees, breasts heaving with shaky exhaustion. They look up dumbly at the old man brushing off his suit. He says to them, "I'm sorry. I must have given you two a fright." The guard hands him his cane and leads him off down the corridor.

Lindsay and Garth are left alone together. The floor is cold and smooth between them. They avoid each other's eyes. But finally, still kneeling, they do it. They exchange a look—the one they will remember. If there is any meaning in what they now silently exchange, it is too opaque to register consciously.

As Lindsay slowly gets to her feet, the glass doors fly open. Two men in white rattle a chrome stretcher through the entrance.

"I can't get up," says Garth. "There's something wrong with my knee."

The ambulance attendants stop the stretcher next to Garth. One of them hunkers down and yanks on Garth's leg. "Ow!" he says. "Who asked for your help?"

The other attendant stands with his hands on his hips. "Meniscus?"

"Right. You grab him under the arms."

"Wait a minute!" cries Garth as they fling him onto the stretcher.

"Take it easy, fella." One of them pushes Garth down on his back.

"You've got the wrong person!" yells Garth as they wheel him away.

"Think I ought to slug him?" says one attendant.

"This is ridiculous," protests Garth. "Help!" he calls to Lindsay.

She doesn't know what to do. The glass doors slam. She stoops to gather up the coins and car keys Garth had dropped earlier. Snatching them she runs out. But the ambulance is already squealing away, red lights flashing.

Back inside, a young man wearing a glossy black shirt unbuttoned to his navel is unlocking the door of the Star Cutters hair salon. Dropping the keys of the bearded stranger into her purse, she senses there is still time to back out of this thing. The young man is waiting, actually holding the door open for her, like he's been expecting her all along. She wants to pretend that this morning has never happened. But it has. She throws back her shoulders bravely. The morning—it just keeps on happening.

4

THIS MONTH THE wide yard behind Lindsay's house is a plane of snow, a hard crust that will bear a man's weight without leaving footprints. One level lower the earth is frozen, deep enough this dry winter to kill the bulbs of jonquils and tulips that she planted in the fall.

On the deck sits the Weber grill her husband never wheeled into the garage, its shiny black dome reflecting sky and whiteness—and now also reflecting a figure moving quietly on the cold, bare boards. There's a distant roar of traffic on Commercial Drive and the sound of the easy sweep of wind through the bare lilacs.

The Thermopane door glides open at his touch. He knows that no one is home. He steps out of his boots, stoops to move a house plant, and pads across tile to the thick carpeted stairway. Upstairs in the bedroom, his eyes scan the clutter of makeup before a mirror. He stands there for a moment, touching his clean-shaven face, examining his own reflection. In the woods, he shaves without a mirror. In the left pocket of his jacket he carries a nineteenth-century, pearl-handled straight-edge razor. He can shave in the dark—and often does. Mirrors make him uneasy. His eyes dart to the bed, where the covers are pulled back on just one side. He knows that Lindsay's husband is out of town. He knows a lot of things. Without pausing, he opens a certain drawer in the dresser. How many times has he entered this room in her absence? His hand moves over the yellow lamb's-wool sweater he saw her wearing once on the street. In the closet, he roves through paisley patterns, touching plaids, summer cottons, and liquid silks. He draws in one last lungful of her scent and looks again at the half-made bed. A notebook lies closed on the night stand. He knows what's in it, so ignores it. He moves down the stairs and walks out the way he came in.

5

Near the Air New England desk at La Guardia, Lindsay's husband, Richard, sits with his face in his hands. He's waiting for a standby seat on a connecting flight home. His suit is rumpled, and he looks like a man whose septic tank has just backed up. "Oh, God," he groans. In Houston he met two women at the convention. That's why he's coming home a day early.

They'd picked him up last night in the bar of the Hyatt Regency. Kathy had dark hair and wore lots of eye makeup. Mona seemed more conservative—big tortoiseshell glasses and a tweedy outfit—but her neckline dipped to reveal a deep cleavage. They were both bright, funny, and had MBAs. Within ten minutes they'd dragged him off grinning to a French restaurant in an adjacent hotel. Richard felt ready to oblige certain impulses that the good Boy Scout within him had knotted into a tight mass of reluctance.

The rest of the evening is not very clear in his mind. Drunk, in a hot hotel room, he fears that he performed a cowhand's strip-tease in front of two half-naked women. He'd slipped off his necktie and tied some fancy knots in it. The tautline hitch with an adjacent sheepshank was a big hit. Then he whipped out his belt and whirled it like a lariat, but they didn't seem impressed until he coyly slid down his zipper and dropped his pants. There was an enormous bulge in his Jockey shorts. Facing them like a gunslinger, he felt his pecker come free. It twanged stiffly in the direction of Mona's breasts. She made a big appreciative *O* with her mouth. And then a hot wave rose up and he knew something was wrong. Houston! Mission Control! It was too late. He came in three quick bursts—the semen spurting precisely into the cleft of Mona's bosom. She looked startled. Richard swung toward Kathy with a helpless look on his face. The thing was still ramrod stiff. "Don't shoot," she said, putting up her hands. Then it went down like a garden hose when you shut off the faucet. On his naked body, Richard felt the icy blast from the air conditioning system. He was fumbling for his clothes. The women no longer looked amused. Slipping out the door, he thought he heard their muffled laughter behind him.

That was last night. This morning he'd run into Mona on the exhibit floor. She gave him a big wink and slid her arm through his to walk beside him.

"We think you show real promise, Richard."

"You do?"

"Kathy and I are both very understanding. We've decided we're going to help you. With your P.E."

He didn't follow this. Physical Education?

"See you then. Six o'clock in the bar?" She smiled at him.

"You're very sweet," he told her. After she walked off, he'd gone straight to his room, called the airlines, and started packing.

Now at La Guardia Richard sits slumped, mired up to his neck in a sludge of humiliation. It occurs to him that "P.E." must stand for "premature ejaculation." Maybe he should have stayed for some therapy. The idea makes him cringe.

He reaches into his pockets for cigarettes, but finds instead an old brochure from Scotts about how to have a greener, healthier lawn. That was one January surprise about Texas. The grass was green. Lindsay has told him that Easter will come late this year. He wishes it were spring now, wishes he were going home to spread Turf-Builder on the back lawn.

Lindsay feels her hair falling in wet clumps onto her shoulders. It's too late to stop now. The sound of metal shearing hair in eager snips comes from high on the back of her head. The comb, meeting no resistance, bites down in quick strokes to scalp level. Against the scarecrow facing her in the mirror, a plastic smock tight about its throat, she shuts her eyes.

The tide of morning events congeals about her. Another clump of hair falls to the floor. Why aren't there more customers in this place? She squints at a placard taped to the mirror. It bears the hairdresser's name: "Manni." He dots the final *i* with a tiny, have-a-good-day face. Evidently he's mistaken her for a regular. That, at least, would explain why she can't understand this story he's telling her.

"Anyway," says Manni, "I wasn't really close to Ken— if you know what I mean. But he was a really terrific guy."

Lindsay is only half-listening. My God, she thinks. My ears are sticking out!

"So maybe you remember?" Manni is saying. "He developed this mad crush on Jules. Even though Jules is practically married to Robert, this resident at the hospital— proctology or something like that. I'm parting this on the side where your cowlick is, okay? But I was going to tell you about this wacko girl, Pauline, who started hanging around the bar."

Lindsay has lost the thread of Manni's story. She's going over the scene she endured out in the corridor. She can't erase the image of those yellowing teeth in the old man's mouth. She shudders, recalling the hollow crack of a skull on concrete. She considers all the chances in the world that someone might die within arm's reach, and you'd be helpless to do anything but watch.

Richard, she decides, would have done something. At

41

least, he was like that when they first met—stopping on the street to help staggering drunks, to reason with the come-ons of panhandlers. In Chicago she'd had to tug him past sidewalk vendors, street musicians, and con-men hustling watches.

In Waukegan, where Richard Smith grew up, he had been an Eagle Scout and once saved a child's life. It was during a bad wind storm. Using a fallen branch, he pushed a live wire away from the kid. Then he gave her artificial respiration. Richard's picture was in the *Chicago Tribune*. "Quick Scout Saves Tot," said the headline.

Richard told her this story on their first date. They were on a bus coming home from dinner and a movie on Randolph Street in downtown Chicago. In August of 1972, she was twenty-five. Both of them had dropped out of graduate school with the idea of working on McGovern's presidential campaign.

"If the branch had been wet with rain," he explained, "I would have electrocuted myself."

Lindsay gazed across the aisle at their reflection in the bus window. Richard seemed large. It was night and the streets were dark.

"You must have been a very brave young man," she said.

"I didn't feel brave," he confessed. "And anyway, the kid suffered brain damage. It turned out sort of rotten. They didn't put that part in the newspaper."

The fall of '72 would seem terribly romantic when Lindsay and Richard looked back on it. They'd work their fingers raw stuffing envelopes until four in the morning, then the next night they'd dress up and sip champagne at thousand-dollar-a-plate fundraisers. Richard was so impressive: briefing Ted Kennedy's advance men, talking to Mayor Daley and Gary Hart on the phone. Lindsay had an office of her own. On a big map she charted the progress —precinct by precinct—of voter registration.

Richard usually walked her home to the apartment she shared with Nick, a drama major who'd dropped a lot of acid and claimed to be inventing The Theater of Orgone Paranoia. Sometimes Richard silently embraced Lindsay outside her door before she let herself in with her key. One night he held her by the shoulders and said, "I think we're falling in love." It sounded as if he'd spent some time reasoning this out.

"It's not something you're supposed to think about, dummy." The next day, she moved in with Richard, leaving behind a screwball lover with shoulder-length hair, a leather vest with fringe, and her diaphragm.

Over late breakfasts that October, they watched the leaves fall in Lincoln Park. At work they exchanged long, yearning glances across rooms crowded with dispirited Democrats. At the mimeograph machine, their fingers secretly entwined. Richard's response to McGovern's defeat in November was to enroll in law school at Loyola. "Maybe I'll run for office myself," he declared. At Christmas, Lindsay discovered that she was pregnant.

"That's wonderful!" he exclaimed, giving her a cautious hug.

"Is it?" she asked, feeling mostly terrified.

In late January they were married in Waukegan. Richard's father took him aside. "In a year or two," he said, "you pick out a nice house. Winnetka, maybe. And I'll help you with the down payment. What do you say, champ?"

Lindsay's mother flew up from North Carolina for the wedding. She wore a white suit and false eyelashes. Her prim, apparently aristocratic bearing impressed everyone. To one of the guests she confided, "Well, her father might have approved. But he was a wild irresponsible fellow. Isn't this punch awful?"

In July of 1973, when Alex was born, Richard dropped out of law school after less than a year of courses. Lindsay considered enrolling herself. "It's my turn to try," she wanted to tell him. But who would take care of the baby? For Richard, there followed a series of patronage jobs arranged by the Cook County Democratic machine. But some obscure political intrigue left him unemployed just

before Carter's nomination in 1976. That fall he was reduced to selling aluminum siding at home shows. He
often worked nights, traveling to Wisconsin and Indiana.
One week, Lindsay spent evenings packing old baby
clothes into cartons for storage. She carried them up to
the attic in the house they rented in Hyde Park. When
she was done, she looked at the row of cardboard boxes
and burst into tears. They contained, she realized, three
years of her life.

Richard turned out to be terrific at selling aluminum
siding. One night in Milwaukee, the sincerity of his pitch
particularly impressed a fat bald man with a Boston accent.
"My name's Kelly," he said, fingering the brochures and
stinking of whiskey. The guy reminded Richard of Mayor
Daley, and the two hit it off immediately. Robert Kelly
turned out to be the president of Alumico, the parent corporation. Richard hadn't even known that the company
had an office outside of Chicago. The phone call from Boston came the next week. Kelly offered him an executive job
at twice his present salary. Richard talked it over with his
father. "They're handing you the ball," Lloyd Smith told
his son. "You know what to do with it."

In November they moved to Massachusetts, bought a
house in Heathersford, a second car, and an upright Stein-
way for Lindsay. She felt as if the hard part of her life were
now over. Here was a nice neighborhood, the schools were
good, and Alex had tested into kindergarten a year early.
The only thing that made Lindsay pause, as the family took
this new step in the world, was a certain look that came
over Richard. It was fierce and self-righteous. Sometimes
she felt it aimed at her like a weapon.

Now she looks at her own eyes in the mirror. The haircutter, Manni, works the blow-dryer in quick, hot whisks.
She decides she ought to buy some new shades of eye
shadow, mauves and earth colors. She thinks again of the
stranger with the beard. All she has is a vision of his face

after it was over. She sees his eyes suspended in space before her own. Was it courage she saw there? Or simply raw terror like her own?

Manni turns off the blow-dryer. He's brushed the sides back into the kind of ducktail she's seen on thirteen-year-olds. "So you know what she did?" he asks.

"Who?"

"Pauline. She shot Ken in the face. It was just a twenty-two but it went through one eye into the brain. Of course, she'd never held a gun before. Ken was just doing one of his hilarious numbers—handing her the gun, I mean. So they called Robert down from the hospital. He's a physician, after all. And the coroner is taking his word for it that the whole thing was an accident."

"I see," nods Lindsay, trying to look attentive. "How much?" she asks.

"Shampoo, cut, and style? Thirty-five."

She frowns at the expense.

Manni gestures at the empty line of chairs ready for blast-off. "Overhead," he shrugs.

Standing up, she declines to look at the damp clumps beneath her shoes. She must fumble in her purse, push aside Garth's car keys, and count out the bills. But it's a blur. Because now she finds herself out in the corridor again. Where it happened. Between the two stone benches, a woman has parked an umbrella stroller that cradles a sleeping infant. Lindsay has an urge to kneel again on the spot. But the impulse vanishes when she passes a hand over the back of her neck—where her hair used to be. She decides she can buy a scarf at Woolworth's. With dark glasses perhaps she'll look like Garbo instead of what's-her-name, on *Laverne & Shirley*. It wouldn't be so bad if she looked like someone in a movie. But nobody remembers the old movies that Lindsay likes. An image from a French film sticks in her mind. Why has she suddenly lost her hold on names? *If only she'd asked his name.* Now she's got it. Jean Seberg. And Belmondo. But the name of the movie? Lindsay hurries off to buy a scarf. And a long-sleeved top with horizontal stripes.

At the hospital, things have gotten serious for Garth. They've examined his knee, X-rayed it, and now a young doctor—the guy can't be over thirty—is telling him he's torn the cartilage in the joint. They want to operate immediately.

"Operate?" says Garth. "Listen, I can probably bang it back into place if you just give me a minute."

"Mind if I watch?"

Garth is in no mood for sarcasm. He wants help. And genuine help, now that he thinks about it, would consist of someone who can make all this go away. Jesus, he thinks. People die during operations.

"Look, Mr. Willkie"— Garth has scrawled a pseudonym on the liability waiver they made him sign—"it's a pretty trivial surgical procedure."

"Oh? Trivial to *you* maybe." Garth notices, with grim satisfaction, that the doctor—in spite of his youth—is bald. He looks like the dome-headed before-picture in a toupee ad. Garth, at age thirty-nine, still has his hair.

Ten minutes later they've got him undressed upstairs. A nurse is shaving his leg—all the way up to his crotch.

"Is that really necessary?" he demands.

"Bacteria," she mumbles, deep into her art.

Another young doctor comes in. This one looks like Chevy Chase. "Hey, how you doing?" he says. "I'm Dr. Goodman. Anesthesiologist." In a lower tone he adds, "You can call me the White Shadow."

Garth watches the nurse gather up her electric barber clippers and Gillette Trac-II razor. When she's gone he says, "I've never had an operation before."

The White Shadow gives him a sly look. "No sweat," he says. "We'll do a spinal. So the lower extremities will be pretty well knocked out. But from the waist up, you've got your choice. Depending on what I shoot into the I.V. you'll feel real good. I got Luminal, Amytal, Seconal, and Brevital. I got Demerol and Dilaudid, morph and coke, STP, THC, a couple of soluble benzodiazepines and methaqualones—whatever you want. Hey, how about ketamine hydrochloride? No one's tried it yet here. They used it a lot in Vietnam. It's like LSD, right? Very weird. It moves your eyeballs down to about an inch from the incision so you see everything. Colorful, you know? And you feel all the cutting, too. Except that it's like music. Chinese music, I think the guy said."

"You're kidding," Garth says, meaning this entire conversation.

"These days," says Dr. Goodman thoughtfully, "who knows if they're kidding or not. Actually, I think he said Balinese music."

The mall custodian is wringing out a chamois cloth as he answers Lindsay's question. "Sure, I seen him," says the man. "A guy with a beard? He charged in here just as I was unlocking the doors. His car is still out there." He waves the damp chamois toward the parking lot. "Are you supposed to meet him?"

Lindsay thinks this over. Were they supposed to meet? It sounds spooky. She finally shakes her head, thanks the custodian, and pushes out into the wind. In her hand she feels the warm brass of a stranger's car keys. Garth's Plymouth, with its big fifties tail fins, is easy to spot. A boy she dated one summer in high school drove the same model. Boldly she opens the door and slides in behind the wheel. Old memories wash in. She and that boy used to make out in the front seat for hours. It always ended after he convinced her to give him a hand job using suntan lotion. "Cripes," he used to say. "Haven't I told you to warm it up first on your hand?" She wonders if she had a special knack as a teenager for getting mixed up with jerks.

Lindsay can't find the shift level, but spots a set of push buttons clustered on the far left of the dashboard. The phrase "Touch-a-matic Transmission" comes back to her from about the fifth grade. After her father died, she was the tomboy in Miss Northfelt's class. The boys studied all the new car models. On the playground they stood in groups and talked about rockets, Project Vanguard, and Sputnik. Tommy Michaelson once let her in his garage to watch them mix rocket fuel. They recruited her to buy potassium nitrate at the drug store. You had to lie and say your mother needed it for canning. When she came back, they snatched the chemical and locked her out of the garage. It was the first time she was consciously aware of having been used. Later, she followed them to the gravel pit. Hidden by trees, she watched the launch from a distance. The thing—a tube of rolled-up newspaper, tinfoil, and masking tape—actually went a hundred feet up in the air. She was thrilled to think she played some part in the project. But the boys never acknowledged her help. Tommy Michaelson, she's heard, now teaches physics at MIT.

Lindsay starts the car, pushes D for "Drive," and rolls out of the parking lot. Her plan is to deliver the Plymouth and its keys to the county hospital. Then she'll take a cab back to the mall. Successfully completing this errand of mercy may save the morning from utter disaster. Perhaps there's poetry in it.

The interior of the old Plymouth, she notices, is immaculate. For a moment, in her sunglasses and scarf, she has the eerie sense of flying a bright chrome vehicle into an imagined future. My God, she thinks, the 1980s! By then, everyone knew, the countryside would be laced by monorails. In cities, between spires and glittering arches, the air would be thick with private helicopters. Clothing, you'd wear once, then throw away. And here, unexpectedly, she's arrived to see it all. But the future's taste has surprised everyone by turning back to the past. McDonald's, Arthur Treacher's, and the Bonanza Steak House are all trying to look cute and colonial—their bricks, so multicolored and banged up that they must have been salvaged from the eighteenth century. The only futuristic thing in sight is the big red K-Mart sign. And beyond that an arrow marks a left turn to the county hospital. Lindsay hasn't a clue to where she's really headed.

Garth is talking a mile a minute as a faceless orderly wheels him down a corridor. Before they injected him with the pre-medication, Garth was uptight. He'd pictured some butcher in a mask opening up his knee like you'd pry the leg off a turkey, probing with the tip of the knife until the round white joint pops into view. But now he feels terrific. As the ceiling light fixtures flash by overhead, he's yakking about Secret Art, Reflexive Sculpture, and Mannikin Aesthetics.

In the operating room, the surgeon says, "Hey, Goodman, shut this guy up."

Garth stops talking. The air in the room feels like ice. "I'm cold," he says. Magically, something warm pumps through his veins. He welcomes it surging up hot from his chest. The warmth is delicious, like an extra quilt tucked in around his chin. It's a glow you could drown in, he thinks, as his head goes under into dark heat.

Meanwhile, in the lobby, a woman at Information directs Lindsay to the emergency room. The heels of her Bally boots click down the gleaming corridor and onto rubber mats where doors whoosh open without a touch. At the admitting desk, she gets in line behind old people making arrangements for out-patient care. Others sit on a row of bright orange chairs, chins pressed into their palms. Some look like they've been waiting all night.

Through dark glasses, Lindsay observes a young doctor conferring with a family. The woman and her sons, she gathers, have brought in the father with swollen legs. The doctor is explaining what the X rays might show and what drugs they'll employ to reduce the fluid. "If he does have clots, the treatment is the same anyway. But the bad news is that the medication is difficult to control. The active agent—what thins the blood—is the same thing they put in rat poison. You can buy it in the hardware store. In the case of rats, they get an overdose, then they bang around and die from internal hemorrhaging. So the danger would be if your husband fell off a ladder or something. Or there might be a weak spot in the body. Frankly, he has a potentially life-threatening—"

"Next?" says the clerk at the desk.

Lindsay steps forward. "I'm looking for a man with a beard," she declares.

The clerk, a plump woman with teased hair going dark at the roots, stares at her. She's taking in Lindsay's tailored coat, her silk blouse, and the gold earrings. Still wearing her sunglasses and scarf, Lindsay looks like someone masquerading as Jackie Onassis.

"His name?"

"I don't know. They must have brought him by ambulance. An hour ago."

"I just came on duty. I'll have to check. Will you take a seat, please?"

It's a depressing place, but not as bad as she feared. Once, in Chicago, Richard cut his finger slicing cabbage and decided he ought to have stitches. Lindsay waited for hours in a real emergency room. They brought in one bloody stretcher after another—victims of gunshot wounds, auto wrecks, street brawls—lining them up in the corridor like delayed flights at the end of a runway. In this modest suburban hospital, disease and suffering seem less dramatic. Nurses wander past, killing time.

"Miss?" says a voice from the desk.

Lindsay puts down the three-year-old copy of *Time*. The clerk tells her to go up to the fifth floor and ask for Mr. Willkie. Upstairs, a blond nurse says, "Yeah. Wendell Willkie. Is he famous or something?"

"I just want to leave these keys," explains Lindsay. "And write a note."

"Oh, it won't be long. He's in Recovery. Wait in the lounge."

Lindsay sighs. If this keeps up they'll have to treat her for tedium. Her stomach growls. It's way past noon. In the lounge, four nurses are eating bag lunches and watching a soap opera about a hospital. On the screen, the doctors get the nurses in their offices and embrace them. Lindsay eases down onto a plastic couch. Eventually the blond nurse comes and leads her to Room 516. She leaves Lindsay standing in an open doorway.

The room has two beds in it. Lindsay's heart pounds. There's no way out of this now. Against the far wall, a portly man with a mustache sits up in bed reading *Sports Illustrated*. They've pulled the curtains shut around the other bed. She parts them and looks in.

Garth lies under a sheet and a thin white blanket. His eyes are closed, and his head is twisted unnaturally to one side. The pillow cradles his sagging cheek.

"Mr. Willkie?" says Lindsay.

No response.

She sits down in a chair feeling relieved, curious, and oddly, a little triumphant. Men always have the advantage of the *Look*. They can stare you down. They take you in, voracious, gazing at your hair, your makeup, the lines on your face, while you're all a-flutter, searching the floor, his necktie, the shoulder of someone nearby—anywhere but into the force of probing eyes. So, in a way, it's Lindsay's chance now.

She studies Garth's hair and lined brow, his eyelids, creased even in sleep. She guesses how long ago he trimmed his mustache, observes the pattern of pores on his nose. She notes the firmness of his lower lip, chapped and flaked from the wind. His beard looks thick, and she wonders how scratchy it might feel against her face. She's aware of hair on his neck and chest, of his oddly slender arms and shoulders beneath the blanket, of his long outstretched legs—one bundled stiff, strapped in an unseen device.

The moment is becoming intimate. Exploring the body of this stranger draws her in, over the edge of the bed. Such a kind and gentle face, she thinks. Who is he? A professor or a telephone lineman? A veterinarian? Dare she touch him? The curtains wall them off from the world. His breath quietly comes and goes. Lindsay thinks of her son, Alex, newborn—such a helpless creature in slumber. Something in her breast goes out to this stranger. She feels a warm mildness—a melting.

Garth is in a dark place, straining upward to light. His limbs feel thick. With an effort that seems heroic, he opens his eyes.

Lindsay, trembling at her impulse, has placed her fingers flat against his cheek. Slowly his eyes open. Then his head turns to her hand, like an infant seeking the nipple. She feels his mouth—hot against her bare palm—and she doesn't draw back.

"Wendell?" she asks.

Garth, through his thick grogginess, experiences a moment of panic. He has no idea *who* he is, let alone *where*. He knew a guy once, an Action Painter, who had a breakdown. In the hospital they gave him shock treatments. It took him days to recognize his wife, his friends, his daughter. After a while, he caught on and greeted perfect strangers with enthusiastic familiarity. This smoothed things out for everyone.

Garth, too, has only the bare facts to go on. He's a man in pain, awakening in a hospital bed. And here's this woman. How deep and moist her eyes are. Such a fine mouth. *It must be his wife,* he decides. How long has he lived with this elegant stranger? Do we have children? he wants to ask.

His tongue wets his lips. "Would—" It hurts to talk. But he wants to do the proper thing. "Would you kiss me?" he whispers dryly.

The words hang in the air. Lindsay's heart pounds again. The blood thuds in her temples, in her cheeks, her throat, as she leans closer to his good-looking face. For the time being, a smile is all she gives him.

This scene coincides with a fantasy Lindsay put together in junior high school. The daydream included a bed and the prohibition: *No Touching Allowed.* Given those two ground rules, the question was how intimate you could get with a handsome man, wounded perhaps, dragged in from the mud of a battlefield—but now clean and pitifully immobile under the white sheets.

Their eyes lock. A heavy current really does pass between them. She feels it hum in her breast. His eyes are so steady, so guileless. And she gazes into them as if gauging the depth of a chasm before leaping. Abruptly she sits back to avoid tumbling over the brink. But it's too late. Lindsay reels in the vertigo of a long, helpless fall.

"I brought your keys," she whispers to break the silence, the force of her fall. She fishes in her purse and places the car keys on the bedside table. He's still gazing at her. At this instant she longs to press her mouth against his. But think of the risk. They're alone, walled off. No one would tell, would they? She wets her lips and and leans toward him—

A sharp, metallic "*SCHREEE!*" rips through the silence. "Oh!" she cries.

Someone has pulled back the curtains. It's the nurse. Behind her stands a man in a blue blazer, glaring down sternly. Her heart pounds now with fright.

Garth's eyes fall shut.

"Who are you?" demands the man in the blue blazer.

Lindsay sits there, feeling trapped. Once, when she was a girl, her father caught her snooping in his dresser. It's that same old sense of being caught—just on the verge of a guilty discovery—that assaults her. She can't bear to look up. But she does. The man looks angry, but he has a weak chin. Something tells her not to be afraid.

"You'd better tell me your name," says the man, but the authority in his voice is leaking away.

"Me?" she says, getting up and brushing past him. Reaching the door, she wonders how long this steadiness in her legs will hold out.

The man is on her heels. "There's no Willkie listed in the phone book," he says. "You must tell me who this man is. And your name, too!" His voice has pitched itself into desperation.

"Lynn," she tosses back at him. "Loretta Lynn."

He pursues her to the elevators. "Do you know who I am, Mrs. Lynn? I'm Wenolds, the Assistant Dwekter!"

Now she understands her edge. An elevator arrives, and she edges in.

Reynolds squeezes in beside her. He won't shut up. "Fwad!" he whispers harshly. "He's attempting to de-fwad the hospital!" The other passengers in the elevator glue their eyes on the numbers that blink the descending floors. "You're his wife, aren't you? Another quiminal!"

This is so ludicrous that she wants to laugh in his face. But she feels glances of disapproval now from the other passengers. They're not on her side. At the ground floor, she gets out and strides through the lobby. There's no need, she decides, to speak to this fool, to even pay him the courtesy of a glance. She can walk out of here and leave it all behind her. There's even a taxi waiting outside at the curb.

Behind her a voice calls out, "You can't get away with this! I'll twack you down!"

Lindsay climbs into the taxi and slams the door. An elderly woman sits in the driver's seat. She looks like a spinster, except that she's wearing a leather flight jacket. "Where to, sister?" snarls the driver out of the side of her mouth.

"How about the mall?" Lindsay suggests.

"Gotcha," nods the driver and squeals the taxi away from the scene of the crime.

At home she finds her husband sprawled on the living room couch with a drink in his hand. "You're back?" she says.

He looks at her. "What the hell did you do to your hair?"

"It'll grow out. You look tired."

"I'm bushed. At least it was warm in Houston. The grass was green."

"Oh?" She stares at Richard's face, experiencing the odd sense that now *he* is the stranger. Someone not entirely welcome in her household. Cigarette ashes powder the coffee table where he's missed the ashtray. She sits down beside him.

"How'd your day go? Write any poems?"

"Sort of." She realizes that she's been through a lot this morning. Richard's questions snag at her like hooks. She needs to keep some of this to herself. "I found out about poison," she says absently.

"Poison?"

"Rat poison. I'd never really thought about it—how poison works. It keeps the blood from clotting. The rats bang around in their holes and bruise themselves scuttling through walls. Then they bleed to death."

Richard makes a show of considering this. Lindsay often comes out with weird information that he can't follow. "Hey," he says. "Get me another drink, will you?"

"Sure." She gets up. "Look. It's the school bus." Out the front window the sun is low over the houses across the way. Lindsay observes its pale light streaming in on the rug, glowing warm on the walnut arm of a favorite chair. If only their house faced east, she thinks. Then, of course, it would be morning, not late afternoon.

6

THE NEXT DAY is Saturday. Lindsay sleeps until ten and sprawls for a time across the whole bed. Finally she hears Richard coming upstairs. He's brought her coffee.

"Hi," he says, cheerful and solicitous.

She sits up, fluffs the pillows, and takes the warm mug. "It's a little weak," she says after taking a sip.

He puts his hands in his pockets and looks out the window. It wasn't the right thing to say. They tried to make love last night. In his own way, Richard was very insistent. After all, he'd been gone for a week. But there was something unnatural in his eagerness, in the brusque frenzy of his thighs pulsing into her. It was a little exciting at first —until she felt the tension in his back and shoulders, felt him straining for something out of reach. "It's no good," he said. "You're tired," she said. He rolled off her, and she knew that talk would only turn into an argument. In ten minutes he was asleep. So Lindsay lay in the dark, still a little aroused, and thought about the man in the hospital. Perhaps they'd meet again, on the street, and he'd take her arm before he even said, "Hello." She pressed her palm to her mouth, the hand he'd kissed in his delirium, and she thought of all the other places where their paths might cross: in a supermarket or a discount store, at a band concert or an intersection in another city. She strolled, in her mind, from one scene to the next, as if passing through a series of stage sets, or the model rooms they set up in department stores to display furniture. In each new setting, she and a bearded stranger exchange a word or two ("Hello," "Well well," "It's you?"), and he leads her away —offstage—she dare not imagine where.

Lindsay feels the mug of coffee warm in her hands.

"I thought I'd take Alex to McDonald's," Richard is saying.

She glances at the clock. "It's a little early, isn't it?"

"Not for breakfast."

"You didn't give Alex any breakfast yet?"

"That's what I'm trying to do," he says, exasperated.

She sighs and sets the coffee down on the empty side of the bed.

"I can't find Alex's ski mask. We're going to walk."

"Tie a scarf over his face."

"He said you know where it is. The ski mask I bought him."

Lindsay slides under the covers. There's no easy way to explain her distaste for the mask Richard brought home. "Keep looking for it," she lies. In fact, she threw it out in last week's garbage.

"Maybe we'll drive over," he says from the door.

She just wants him to leave. Alone, perhaps she can recall a dream she's had. *A man with a bloodied head.* That's all she remembers.

Richard's voice comes from the stairs. "I forgot to tell you. My parents called. They're coming to visit. Easter, I think."

"Oh, God," she says aloud. Lindsay doesn't enjoy her in-laws. Richard's mother sends them a lot of junk. Telephone memo pads shaped like American eagles, coffee table cigarette lighters in the shape of giant strawberries, and an endless supply of clever devices that hold pencils, hang potholders, or dispense tape—all of them designed to light up, cling magnetically to the refrigerator, or mount somewhere handy with Velcro strips. Richard won't let her throw this stuff out. So she's made a terrible compromise. They keep his mother's gifts in a carton, wrapped in tissue paper, like Christmas tree ornaments. Once, maybe twice, a year these props come out to clutter her end tables and bookshelves. How, she wonders, do you put a stop to such well-intentioned deceit?

She rolls over in bed and pulls the quilt over one shoulder. The bloodied figure in the dream, she now remembers, was on a stage. Fascinated, she watched him from the audience, her hands folded in her lap. But the actor had singled her out from all the others. He was pleading. She wanted to help, but if she raised her hands from this sticky pool in her lap—even to applaud—she knew they would drip red and hot and wet.

Lindsay grips the quilt, feeling something wet in the bed. It seeps along the small of her back and buttock. "Oh, shit," she says, throwing off the covers. The mug of coffee has spilled on the sheets. She scrambles out to strip them off. The mattress pad is soaked, her nightgown is stained. Here she'd been half-pleased with herself for avoiding an argument with Richard. "Ha," she says aloud. Arguments. Isn't that what Saturday mornings are for?

Downstairs, Lindsay stuffs the stained sheets into the washer. There's a window over the dryer. Their yard runs back to a line of trees where a neighbor's property begins. These open spaces, the wide yards, the expanse of cold air beyond the window pane—these, she decides, are what define the suburbs. In the city—where there might be a restaurant on the corner—life is dense. You risk intrusion there, assault, encounters that might end in—

She doesn't like this train of associations. Surely it's the quiet in the house she wants to get hold of. The surface of apparent boredom you can learn to penetrate in order to reach the underlying stillness, the deeper serenity of the place. Nothing is supposed to happen in the suburbs. That's the point, isn't it?

Death and sexuality. Lindsay fears they surface from some abnormality in her family genes. She gets this idea from the stories her uncle tells about their ancestors. Uncle Alfred is fifty-eight, lives outside Los Angeles, wears a top hat, and designs stained-glass windows for churches, synagogues, and government buildings. "I've never lowered myself," he declares, "to making a goddamn Tiffany lamp. Ha!" Lindsay hasn't seen her father's brother since 1976, when he came east to watch the tall ships sail into New York harbor. That July, she recalls, he'd grown a beard and had a black eye.

"What's the story about your black eye?" she'd asked.

"Alas," he sighed. "Another erotic catastrophe. They run in our family blood, you know."

"I don't believe it," she said.

"Well, what about your great-grandfather?"

"What about him?"

"My God," he said, easing himself into an armchair. "I've never told you the story of Ernest Kleist? He was the Canadian with the frigid wife."

In Alfred's version of the story, Ernest and his wife went to spend a weekend at Niagara Falls in 1900. It was late winter. They joined a party of young people from the hotel who ventured out, in high spirits, to cross over the mass of ice at the foot of the falls. Halfway to the American side, the ice began heaving. The others rushed back the way they'd come. Ernest insisted on going ahead, certain it was the safer route. The white mass lurched. Cracks appeared, as if the terrain were rearranging itself beneath their feet. Soon their path was blocked by open water. They turned back and ran. After a hundred yards, his wife fell to her knees, exhausted. "Get up!" he cried. "We're almost there!"

She gasped, "I can't go on. Let us die here!"

He stared down at her. For a moment her wild eyes transfixed him. Far away, voices shouted. Suddenly another man had appeared and was gripping her under the arms. She went limp. Ernest and the man dragged her fifty yards, across slick mounds of white, until they were within ten feet of shore. There was only a slushy pool to cross now. The man sloshed through it, showing them it would hold their weight. Ernest felt his wife's hands tighten, clawlike, on his arm. "I can't!" she cried. The man crossed back to help, but then rushed to the aid of someone else thrashing in the water where great chunks were breaking loose to drift with the current.

Ernest stared at the shore five paces away. His wife was on her knees again, sobbing. He stated, "I will walk over. You follow." When he looked down, her eyes seized him again in their wild spell. Her hair had come loose and fallen in writhing tangles about her shoulders. The sight of her —face flushed, bosom heaving—again transfixed him.

On shore, people shouted and gestured to him. Some clambered over the rocks to keep pace, for now the ice floe on which he stood—his wife's arms clasped about his knees —was in motion, pulling away, drifting with the current.

Coming to Niagara Falls had been his wife's idea. Perhaps she thought there was magic in the place. Perhaps here among the gaiety of this honeymoon resort, there might be some hope left. For they were childless, and her crime—as she saw it—was worse than barrenness. Here, perhaps, she might discover the secret of opening herself in love, of tolerating the terrible press of her husband's body upon her, the rough intrusion (in the dark—always in the dark) of some reptilian beast worming in between her thighs. During seven years of marriage, she had never learned how to submit to this horror. So they remained a childless couple, innocent, a little formal with each other —especially in private.

During the last year in Toronto, Ernest had been twice to a brothel. Each time he'd suffered anguished guilt for months afterward. But he'd also developed a taste for plump, ruddy girls. Like that chambermaid here at their hotel. He'd caught the girl's eye the very day they arrived. And this morning she had teasingly led Ernest into a room where linen was stacked in soft, white piles—where a kiss had led to an embrace, where she'd lifted her skirts and drawn him down upon her, until suddenly he found himself awash in her hair, pumping her full of himself.

Ernest winced at the memory and knelt down next to his wife. This was absurd. They were being carried off downstream! He saw that people looked down at them from the ledges above. There were hundreds watching. Surely a boat would soon put out from shore to save them. He scanned the steep gorge the river had cut through the rock to Lake Ontario. Had they put all the boats away for the winter?

Up ahead, a railway bridge spanned the river. Upon it he could see activity. Men were making their way to the center, the place under which they would soon pass. They were lowering a rope. "Thank God!" he exclaimed and clasped his wife to his breast. "There's no hope," she murmured, and then whispered those awful words: "Let us die together!"

The current swept them onward. He felt her cheek, fever-hot, against his own. Her arms entwined about his neck. Their lips found each other's. Never had she yielded so in his arms.

The rope dangled up ahead. He caught the end. It felt stiff and icy in his fumbling hands. Overhead, men's voices shouted down advice. He was to pass the rope about her waist. Why did she press against him so—just now? He glanced at her face. It was there again, that look. He felt her breath coming hot in his face. Who was this wild creature looking out from behind his wife's eyes? What utter yearning answered his own there! He didn't feel the rope slip from his hands. He knew only the dizzying descent into her, as the gray current carried them on to the whirlpool. Breathless, they embraced. Their kisses grew frenzied, greedy. Around they went in a wide arc. Slowly the vortex drew them toward its terrible center. They must have known it was the mystery of themselves they circled. It was the thing neither had dared to admit: that once aroused their hunger for each other would be insatiable. An endless longing. It wanted eternity. It wanted the Deep.

Lindsay heard this story sitting on the living room rug. Dusk was falling. Her uncle sat, indistinct and silent, in the big chair against the front windows.

"You mean," Lindsay finally asked, "they died?"

"Absolutely. Over fifteen hundred people watched, horrified, as Ernest and his wife finally went under."

"How do you know these details?" she asked skeptically.

"It's on microfilm. Front page of *The New York Times.*"

Lindsay stared out the window at a bank of clouds moving across the overcast sky. She got up and turned on the floor lamp. "I thought this story was about my great-grandfather."

"It is," smiled Uncle Alfred.

"But if they were childless, and they died—"

"Ah," he announced. "You forgot about Lucy."

"Who's Lucy?"

"Among the crowd," Alfred explained, "the crowd that watched Ernest and his wife go under, was Lucy Wyatt, the chambermaid at the hotel. Two months later she would admit that she carried, in her womb, the seed of a man now drowned. In Buffalo, New York, nine months later, she gave birth to a son, Jason Wyatt—and you know the rest. Though I doubt you remember your grandfather."

Lindsay knew that Jason Wyatt had married Laura Bennett, daughter of a well-to-do farm implement distributor. Alfred was their firstborn. Her father was second. But it was true. In place of any memories of her grandfather, she had only a vague image of someone pointing out a big house with a mansard roof in upstate New York.

"So Lucy, the chambermaid, was your grandmother?"

"Ah," said her uncle. "A curious story there." He glanced at her slyly.

"I don't want to hear any more stories."

Alfred waved away her misgivings and explained that Lucy's parents had been American, having emigrated to Hamilton, Ontario, from Sherburne, New York, in 1883, the year Lucy was born. Lawrence Wyatt, a gangling, red-haired sheet music salesman with a fine tenor voice, was nine years younger than his wife, Ellen. Before their marriage, she'd taught grammar school. In fact, Ellen, fresh from the state teachers' college, had been Lawrence's sixth-grade teacher. She may have fallen in love with him, a skinny eleven-year-old, at first sight. But thank God, everyone later agreed, she muffled her secret for ten years, acquiring over that decade the reputation of a somewhat shrewish premature spinster: a social role which many people judged entirely appropriate for a woman into whose hands they placed impressionable Christian youngsters.

When Lawrence turned twenty-one, Ellen allowed her passion to break loose. She began trailing him down streets, over back fences, and eventually from one town to another. This public courtship of the young man, and his finger-shaking rebuffs of her advances, went on—tediously, it seemed to the town gossips—all through the 1870s. By June of 1882, she was dog-faced and forty, he was a confirmed bachelor, and both were on a morning train—she, as usual, in the seat directly behind him—heading up the Chenango Valley to Utica. Outside Sangerfield, masked men boarded the train—probably members of the Nine-Mile Swamp Gang, known in the area for petty theft and incompetent horse thievery. One of the passengers discharged a muzzle-loading pistol into the floor and frightened the fellows off. But the lead slug, ricocheting off a steel plate, struck Lawrence, then passed through to hit Ellen behind him.

At the next stop, in Waterville, the two victims were hurried to the office of a Dr. Briggs, who found a clean puncture wound in Ellen's lower abdomen. He removed the lead ball through her vagina, having found it lodged against the cervix. Lawrence's wound was a nasty business. The shot had hit him in the groin, glancing off the pelvic bone after tearing away his right testicle. Ellen's abdominal wound healed nicely. But after a month, Lawrence's other testicle became infected and had to be surgically removed. By that time, needless to say, Ellen discovered that she was pregnant. In a sense, she had been inseminated by a muzzle-loading pistol.

Lawrence, having experienced none of the pleasures of conceiving a child, and having only the hardships of rearing one to look forward to, gallantly proposed marriage. Ellen refused. Poor Lawrence pleaded with her. "Who'd want you?" she said. Back in Sherburne, he limped after her with flowers and Swiss chocolates. He sang serenades beneath her window. Passing the saloon, he endured hoots and whistles that ridiculed not only his own condition but Ellen's as well. In September, the schoolteacher, thinking she'd taught everyone a lesson, finally relented because she'd learned—at last—how it felt to be the object of a genuine courtship. After a hasty wedding, the couple packed up and moved to Canada.

Uncle Alfred took a deep breath and held both arms dramatically aloft. "All this they endured," he sighed, "so that their daughter, Lucy the chambermaid, could—on a single occasion, after making love to a billiards hustler in Buffalo, New York—claim to be the natural daughter of a virgin and a eunuch!"

Lindsay stared at her uncle. "That's ridiculous," she said.

"That's the truth," he replied.

She shook her head. How much of Alfred's stories could you believe? "Okay," she said. "Will you tell me one more thing?"

"Ask away."

"How'd you get that black eye?"

"Oh, this?" he said, touching the mauve and yellow flesh on his cheekbone. "I was in a bar in Santa Monica. Some dame hit me with her purse. But I ended up taking her home. Her boyfriend—a potter or something—was out of town." Uncle Alfred brandished his walking stick. "It's preposterous. At my age. The ordeals one must endure—just to get laid. You know what she had in that purse? Clay. She'd packed that goddamn purse full of clay."

Thinking of her uncle's theatrics, of Lucy the chambermaid, and of ice floes on the Niagara River, Lindsay finds herself sitting on the floral love seat in the den. From the kitchen comes the sound of the washer, spinning out of the first rinse cycle. Outside on the deck, a ceramic wind chime tinkles in the cold morning air. The stillness in the house has become an emptiness. A craving.

The phone on the end table rings. Lifting the receiver, she thinks of a man in a blue blazer who has threatened to twack her down.

"Hello, Lindsay? It's your pastor calling!"

Rev. Rudy O. Ekdahl from the Good Shepherd Church always announces himself like this. Sometimes he calls himself "Yours Truly"—like a 1950s disc jockey. For six months he's been doing the "Word for Tomorrow" on a local UHF TV station. That means he's got five minutes before they play "The Star-Spangled Banner" and the screen goes blank. This taste of show business may have gone to his head.

Pastor Ekdahl is calling to remind her that they've canceled Sunday's Communion service. She was scheduled to play the organ.

"I know," she says. "We decided last month. We're going biweekly. Until Sexagesima Sunday."

"When's that?"

"Washington's Birthday."

"Really? They never told me that at the seminary."

"I think we've been through this before." Lindsay is getting impatient. You'd think a clergyman would know how they calculate the church year. "Remember our talk about the first full moon in March?"

"It's coming back to me. But why did we cancel Communion?"

"Something about wine," she reminds him.

"Wine?"

"You said, as near as I can recall, that there was no sense in wasting a half bottle of good wine every week."

"I said that? By the way, how much do we pay you?"

"Sixteen-fifty."

"Sixteen . . . point . . . fifty." It sounds like he's jotting this down on a pad where this month's budget won't balance. "What about tomorrow?" he asks.

"No play—no pay. I assume." Lindsay says this a little derisively. Instead of all this talk about saving wine, Ekdahl could have been more frank about cutting back her salary.

"Thank heavens!" Over the phone comes the sound of a pencil thrown down on a desk—sign of figures finally adding up. "Listen," he says. "I'm grateful for this sacrifice— oh, call it a contribution—that you're making. To the Church. And your music, of course. Glorious hymns of adoration! And praise. But actually, what I called about— Is there something on your mind? What I mean to say is, what's eating you housewives?"

Lindsay is aware of holding the telephone receiver away from her ear. She's thinking that the end table needs a good waxing.

"How about this?" Ekdahl is saying. *Words for the Morning!* What do you think?"

"It's catchy."

"Yes! I thought so too. Do you get it?"

"Not exactly."

"My new show! A morning TV show. I'm being expanded to fifteen minutes."

"That's great."

"It's a wonderful chance for me to do the Lord's work."

"Great."

"So I'll need your help, of course."

"Of course."

"Just for some initial ideas. I need to determine what— in a general way—is on the mind of, ah—morning viewers."

Lindsay has to think. "You mean housewives?"

"That's it! Oh, I don't mean to bother you with all this just now. But think about it. We'll get together. Maybe next week?"

"I'll think about it."

"Good. I'll remember you. In my prayers. That's a fair exchange, isn't it? Have to go now. 'Bye!"

She hangs up and thinks about "getting together" with Pastor Ekdahl. It wouldn't be so bad if he really asked her out to lunch. But inviting himself over ("Oh, how about your place, at noon?") is more his style. Good grief. What's on the minds of housewives? She smiles, imagining the look on his face. "Actually, Pastor, we think a lot about sucking men's cocks."

Hush, says her conscience. *That's a lie.*

"No, it's a joke," Lindsay says aloud, and reaches for the phone book.

Only one "Willkie" is listed: "Mabel S." It must be true. The man with the beard gave them a phony name. Next she looks up the number of the county hospital, dials it, and asks for Room 516—an easy number to remember. In the Lutheran hymnal, number 516 is "Faith of Our Fathers."

"Hello?" a man's voice answers, a little hoarse. *It's him.*

"Hello." What else to say? *My God, what are you doing?* Her conscience isn't accustomed to impulsive gestures like this sudden dialing of the telephone. Now Lindsay's pulse goes up—out of control.

"Una?" says Garth.

Something pierces Lindsay. She almost gives a bodily groan. Of course, there'd be another woman. He's probably married.

"Who is this?" demands the voice.

"I called about the keys," stammers Lindsay. "Did you find your keys?"

"Keys?"

"To your car."

"Oh, sure. They're right here. Somebody dropped them off yesterday. I think I was asleep."

This disappoints her. He doesn't remember. And here she had nearly kissed him. It's just as well. What a ridiculous scene that had been.

"Wait a minute," says Garth. "It's *you.* Isn't it?"

Lindsay's heart races again. "Yes," she murmurs. Saying this feels like a terrible surrender of identity, like disrobing in front of a stranger.

"Hey," he says gently. "Don't hang up."

In fact, she's reaching for the button that will break the connection.

"I'm grateful," says Garth. "That you came."

Lindsay is too frightened to talk. He seems to sense this.

And that, in turn, terrifies her even more. That *he knows.*

There's a long silence. Lindsay presses the phone to her ear. Neither says a word. Oddly, this feels just fine—to sit there, knowing he's content not to say anything either. Gradually the silence grows dense and presses in hot, like the breath of a lover. An entire lush minute goes by. Who would have guessed such intimacy was possible over the telephone?

"This is incredible," he finally says. "I bet you do this with all the boys."

Lindsay gives a little laugh. "How *are* you?"

"I want to see you."

She sighs heavily, hearing her breath roar into the phone. "How can I find you?"

"You can't," she says.

"Do you go often to that mall?"

"No," she lies.

He seems to consider this. *"Meet me,"* he whispers. It's like his lips are brushing her ear and his face is in her hair.

"Oh," she says. "We mustn't!" And then she watches as her two hands gently lower the receiver to its place on the phone. She could be setting some sacred object on an altar.

You dumb cluck! says her conscience.

"Oh, shut up," she declares, defiantly.

Lindsay is getting out of the shower when Richard and Alex come back. It's an odd time to take a shower, early afternoon on a wintry Saturday. She had some idea of cleansing herself, of washing her mind clear of everything except her poetry.

Richard pokes his head in the bathroom door. "We're back," he says. "Safe and sound."

Behind him, Alex is saying, "I bet they took that guy to the hospital."

Richard steps in and closes the door.

"Hospital?" asks Lindsay. "What's he talking about?"

"We saw an accident. Nothing serious." Richard leans against the door, looking at her.

She clutches a blue towel against her breasts. For a moment she'd felt a spasm of guilt. "Don't you dare touch me," she states. "Your hands must be ice cold." But something urges her to him. She rests her cheek against the shoulder of his wool shirt. She got it on sale at Sears. "You smell like outdoors," she says, pressing against him.

"That's me. The old Eagle Scout."

She pushes away. "I think your pecker is getting stiff."

"It is."

"Some Boy Scout you are."

"It's part of my oath: Obedient, Cheerful, Thrifty, Brave, Clean, Erect, and Reverent."

She opens the door and pushes him out. "Later, big boy," she says.

The mirror has a wet haze on it. She wipes it off with the towel and looks at herself. Her left breast is a little smaller than the right one. But it's hard to tell. She likes the color of her hair better when it's wet. Auburn, she calls it. And the new haircut looks okay. In fact, that guy Manni was a terrific haircutter. As good as anyone in Boston. Everything, she concludes, is okay. Except for this odd spot at the edge of one nipple. A tiny thing.

Cancer, says her conscience.

"Oh, hush," she says. Her fingertips explore a minute thickening in the skin. Just a clogged pore. It's a tiny outward route that's blocked. One more avenue—leading out of herself—that's closed down.

7

Sunday at the hospital, the pain in Garth's leg awakens him at 4 A.M. A nightlight glows on the wall above his head. The patient in the other bed is snoring. In place of his knee, Garth feels only the pain of seared flesh, as if they've cut him with knives heated red hot.

Garth knows his car sits out in the parking lot. An escape ought to be easy. Sitting up, he draws back the flannel sheet and stares at his leg. Velcro straps lace it stiff into a fabric brace. Easing toward the edge of the bed, he feels himself go dizzy. He'll never make it alone. But he reaches the phone and dials a number. His friend Wally, who works nights, answers immediately.

"Where are you, Garth? I've tried to call you."

"I'm in a hospital. I need help."

"Okay. Which hospital?"

"I don't know. This is Room 516. Somewhere in the suburbs."

"I know the place." There's a pause. "Hey, are you okay?"

"I can't explain. Someone's coming. Just get me out of here."

Wally Czyzycki is a little guy with thick glasses who drives a forklift at the brewery. His ears stick out so prominently that, in his presence, some people lower their voices. He and his big wife, Helen, live in an apartment above Woolworth's, down the block from Garth's loft. They're in

their fifties and childless. Helen makes a fuss denying that
Garth brings out her maternal instincts.

Garth hangs up the phone. The snoring from the other
bed has stopped. But now the old guy down the hall has
started up. Garth has only heard his voice—a thin, plain-
tive call. It's partly a plea for help and partly a judgment
on his own condition: *Not good.* The voice repeats these two
words over and over: *Not good.* Now footsteps come down
the corridor from the nurses' station. "Oh, God," says a
woman's voice. "Call an orderly, will you, Jean? He's shit
all over the bed again." The old guy calls out, "Not good!"

"Jesus Christ," says the man in the other bed. "You
awake over there?"

"No," says Garth glumly.

The man chuckles. His name is Frank Pezzulo, and he
teaches algebra and coaches football at a local high school.
There's a chance that the surgery on his spine hasn't come
out the way the doctors predicted. On and off during the
night they've both been awake and have talked—mostly
about next weekend's Super Bowl game. It sounds like
Pezzulo is in a lot of pain.

"You change your mind about Oakland yet?" asks Garth.

"Those bums? Plunkett'll be sacked a dozen times."

In the darkness both are silent as a commotion sounds
from the hallway.

"What's that guy in for?" asks Garth.

"I hear it's a broken collar bone. But he's pretty old. Out
of it, you know."

This floor is an orthopedic ward. Garth decides there are
worse places to be in a hospital. Probably no one has died
in this bed.

"I'll say one thing," yawns Pezzulo. "The old guy has got
singleness of purpose. Not much mental toughness. But he
keeps at it." Garth knows this isn't meant to be funny. It's
the way coaches talk.

In high school, when Garth was on the track team, the
coach seemed to be teaching more than a body of knowl-

edge. He had a mission, a set of values to pass on. A way. During the late fifties, girls learned about dedication and perseverance in home economics as they sifted flour and threaded sewing machines. Later, in art school, Garth dated a girl who was ahead of her time, a female jock. She was just getting into metal sculpture. At her prep school in Connecticut there'd been talk of grooming her for the Olympic downhill slalom.

"Mental toughness," she told Garth. "That's what it takes to be an artist."

"I don't know if you're right about that," he said.

"But don't you see?" she insisted. "Artists have to give up a lot. You agree on the price you have to pay. Then, if you've got that toughness, you can forget the price and ignore the hurt. You learn to live with the small hurts."

Garth has decided that he's not a jock. He's a chicken. And the pain in his leg is awful. Worse, he can't even ignore the pain in the people around him. He prays to Wally and whispers, *Get me out of here.* The room is silent. Pezzulo must have dozed off. From down the hall comes one last drugged outcry: *Not good.*

At eight in the morning, as an aide clears away Garth's breakfast tray, a character in a white lab coat breezes in, pushing a wheelchair. He's wearing a green surgical mask. Into it he's tried to stuff a bushy gray beard. The mask puffs out like a big-cheeked pillow. At his Adam's apple, tangled gray fuzz straggles loose in vaguely obscene strands. He parks the wheelchair at the end of Garth's bed and strides over to peer at Pezzulo.

"Zo!" he announces, his voice muffled by the mask. "No apparent distress here?" He's untangling a stethoscope pulled from a lab coat pocket.

A nurse looks in the door and says, "Dr. Grinstein?"

The guy whirls around. "No no no!" he says, exasperated at the interruption. "Voczkowski! Say it like this: *Vozh-.*" He steps toward the door. "Purse your lips first. Good! Now slowly. *Vozh-kuff-ski.*"

The nurse dutifully repeats the name. At the same time she's staring at the spattered stains on his lab coat. They have the look of dried blood. Maybe he's a pathologist up from the morgue to see what a live patient looks like. Suddenly the eyes above the mask turn mean, and he advances on the nurse, swinging his stethoscope. She takes a step back.

"Who ordered a lumbar puncture and brain scan on this patient?" he demands, jiggling his stethoscope at arm's length like a serpent.

"Well, Dr. Blunt, I suppose. But I don't recall that he ordered any—"

"I'm making Dr. Blunt's rounds today, thank you." He strangles the rubber instrument in the air between them. "Chart, chart. Bring me his chart! And"—the green mask casts a mad glance in Garth's direction—"bring me this fellow's, too. For him I want a complete gastrointestinal workup. Upper G.I. series, liver scan, sigmoidoscopy, and a barium enema."

The nurse looks bewildered, shakes her head, and walks out.

"Okey-dokey! You're next," he tells Garth. "Let's get you into this wheelchair, and we'll take you down for some tests."

"That beard looks ridiculous," says Garth.

"Let's go. Nothing like starting the morning with a barium enema!"

Garth eases himself from the bed into the wheelchair. "Where'd you get the stethoscope?" he asks.

"They handed them out in medical school."

"You never told me you went to medical school."

"I dropped out and got married," says Wally, stripping off a pillow case. He fills it with stuff from the drawer beside the bed: loose change, Garth's wallet and car keys. In the closet he finds Garth's clothes and boots. He jams everything in the pillow case and flings the bundle onto his patient's lap.

"I don't think this is going to work." Garth is eyeing his

friend's stained lab coat. It's the one Wally puts on when
Helen serves spaghetti. Wally eats spaghetti with chop-
sticks—one in each hand, like he's playing the drums.

"What's going on?" asks Pezzulo from the other bed.

"I'm running out on you," says Garth.

"Well, good luck," says the coach. "You know what
Vince Lombardi used to tell his offensive backfield?"

"Something about nice guys finishing last?"

"Naw. 'Run to daylight.' "

Garth thinks that this is odd advice to give someone
sitting in a wheelchair. But now he sees that Pezzulo is
older than he'd figured. Close, maybe, to retirement. "I'll
remember that," says Garth. Then Wally wheels him out
the door.

Halfway to the elevator, they see a man in a blue blazer
charging down the corridor from the nurses' station.
"Hold it!" he cries. "What's going on here?"

"Blood urea nitrogen!" barks Wally. "Pulmonary infarc-
tion! Bacterial endocarditis! Who are you?" Wally juts up
his puffy masked chin.

"Weynolds. Administwation."

"What are you doing here on Sunday? Blastomycosis!
Did you wash your hands? Why are you wearing shoes
with buckles?" Wally's questions have backed the guy up
against the wall.

Garth thinks the jig is up. You can *see* the wires from
Wally's phony beard hooked over his prominent ears. But
just now Wally rips off the surgical mask, and the beard—
stuck to it—comes loose, too. He hands the matted mess to
Reynolds, who holds it, cupped in one hand, like a man
staring at a bird's nest.

"You mean Atlanta didn't call you?" demands Wally. He
seizes the administrator's elbow and steers him a few paces
down the corridor. Reynolds looks worried as he nods to
Wally's rapid questions.

Garth is left alone. To his left, the door of another
room stands open. Inside, chrome and whiteness glare
harshly in the light of a winter morning. Under a thin

blanket, two feet stick up. Garth watches them strain forward and tremble. They must be connected to some higher agony out of sight beyond the edge of the doorway. Then he hears it—uttered with something like precision. "Not good."

Garth realizes now what terrifies him about this place: the grim bonds of loyalty that the patients—victims all of them—weave about one another. It happens in the night, he decides. Fine filaments snake out and entwine along the corridors, until they're all braided into the same network of shared agony. Suffering together. *Patience.* He wheels himself through the doorway and up to the edge of the bed. The old man's left arm is raised stiff and bent in a white cast. It looks like he's fending off an assault. Gaunt, with a beak-like nose, he stares at Garth over this barrier like some angular, defeathered bird. "Not good," he croaks. The voice seems to come out from the gray hollows about his eyes. They dart from Garth's face to the table next to the bed. A Bible lies open. Garth sees a passage marked in shaky ballpoint. He reads it aloud:

Save me, O God; for the waters are come into my soul.
I sink in deep mire, where there is no standing: I am
come into deep waters, where the floods overflow me.
I am weary of my crying: my throat is dried: mine eyes
fail while I wait for my God.

Garth doesn't look up right away. He's waiting to hear the voice croak its two words. But there's only the sound of the old man's breath evenly coming and going. When he finally looks, Garth sees an alert old fellow staring ahead at the white wall in a composure of perfect blankness. The depressing Bible passage has apparently given him the consolation he needed. Just now, Garth prefers not to probe this mystery. Instead he wheels his chair around and out the door.

Down the corridor, Wally is shaking hands with Reynolds. A nurse looks on and hands Wally a file folder. Then

Garth's friend comes trotting down the corridor. "Hold on!" he calls. "We'll have you out to the airport in no time. There's a helicopter waiting!"

At the elevator, another nurse is holding the doors for them. They descend to the basement, where Wally races the wheelchair in skidding turns past the laundry, down a corridor where the pipes overhead are color-coded, through the kitchen, where young black women wipe the sweat out of their eyes with their aprons, and out to a loading dock. Wally's pickup truck sits backed in with the tailgate down. Garth finds himself rumbled aboard and parked, facing the truck's dirty back window. The race through the basement has jolted Garth's knee into burning pain. Now an icy wind whips at his pajama sleeves. Wally is shoving concrete blocks against the chair's wheels. Then he throws up the tailgate, climbs in behind the wheel, and guns the engine. As the truck screeches through the parking lot, Garth catches a glimpse of his old car, windows frosted over—probably on the inside. He hugs his bundle for warmth, as Wally speeds three blocks west, past Burger King, and careens into the empty parking lot of a K mart where there's another loading dock.

"Chilly, huh?" says Wally as he climbs out and zippers up his heavy woolen jacket. Garth shivers in the cold. "Okay," he says. "What did you tell them?"

Wally kicks free the concrete blocks and pulls the wheelchair onto the dock. "Can you stand up?"

Garth hands the bundle to Wally and tests the icy concrete with his one bare foot. On the other, his good leg, they've put a tight, elastic support stocking. He's able to get up and balance on it.

Wally scratches his head. "I think we need a forklift."

"Maybe we better go back. It was nice and warm in that bed."

"How about if I pull the truck alongside?"

"Okay. But hurry up. I'm freezing and my knee hurts. What about this wheelchair?"

"I don't want it. It's stolen property now."

Garth makes a face. Here he is, standing on one leg, his pajama bottoms starting to slip off, and it's starting to snow. "Take me back," says Garth. "The wheelchair, too. I'll apologize. I'll explain that it was a joke."

"They don't want you back."

"Yes, they do. I'm a sick person. I belong in a hospital."

Wally is fumbling inside the pillow case. "You want your coat?"

"What do you think?"

Wally is staring at him. "I created a new disease."

"I'm getting pneumonia. Wally, the coat's right on top!"

"You're so sick they never want to see you again."

"Coat! COAT!" yells Garth. His teeth are chattering.

Wally finally holds up Garth's greatcoat so he can slip his arms in. The weight of the garment nearly makes him keel over. Garth puts a hand on Wally's shoulder to steady himself. "Take me back," he says.

"They don't want anybody with Legionnaires' Disease II. It attacks the body's immune system. Like cancer. Except—get this—it's contagious."

"And they believed you?"

"Sure. That guy, Reynolds. He's afraid of the effect publicity might have on out-patient profit ratios. That's why I'm flying you to the Centers for Disease Control in Atlanta."

"That's ridiculous."

"Why else would a specialist like me show up in a fake beard? To keep this out of the media. Reynolds was real grateful."

"He must be an idiot."

"You look cold." Wally seems to have just noticed. "We're going to my place."

"How come?"

"Hey, did you hear about Iran? They're going to let the hostages go."

"We saw it on TV," says Garth, searching Wally's face.

"What's wrong with my place? Was there a fire or something?"

Wally jumps off the loading dock and shuts the tailgate. "I stopped by yesterday. Una was there."

"Oh?" Garth steadies himself on the arm of the wheelchair. He spent a long time last night trying not to think of Una. All the images that came to mind pictured her in the arms of her new boyfriend.

"There was someone with her," Wally is saying. "They weren't in bed or anything."

"Well, what the hell were they doing?"

"I don't know. Sitting around. I heard the washing machine going."

"My washing machine!" yells Garth. "You mean, she's washing *his* underwear in *my* washing machine?"

"Maybe it was her own underwear," suggests Wally.

"Come on. Let's get over there. We'll check out the lint filter."

"Barge right in?"

Garth looks indignant. "You think they're still there?"

"Could be. And, you know, Sunday morning? Probably still in the sack—"

"Don't say any more."

"I mean, it's kind of exciting to make it in a strange bed, right?"

"Would you cut it out!"

Wally finally opens the door of his truck. He pauses, as one more thought seems to occur to him. But he shakes it off, gets in, and drives away. Garth slumps down in the wheelchair and rubs the one stockinged foot he's been standing on. Wally is one of the most absentminded persons that Garth has ever met. He also has a photographic memory. In a normal person, the two traits wouldn't make a good match.

The truck finally stops at the exit. Now, the backup lights come on. Garth sighs. Wally backs up all the way across the empty parking lot. When the Arabs run out of oil, thinks Garth, they'll have to decide what to do with all these flat spaces on the landscape. Snowflakes come down, lightly. Garth watches the wind swirl into small eddies. Having submitted to the cold, he only now feels how deeply it has penetrated.

"Let cold go through,"

he says, having composed a new, crystalline work of art.

8

THE MAN WHO calls himself Toby Morton stops the Blazer
next to a steel shed, out of the wind that gusts across this
deserted railroad yard. He grips the steering wheel and
glances at a single gray glove flopped on the dashboard. Its
mate—canvas stitched to a leather palm—is lost.

Toby decides he lost the glove in Lindsay's house. Fumbled it out of a pocket in the dark as he prowled the living
room opening drawers, sorting through old receipts and
photos. Dropped it, perhaps, stepping up on her kitchen
stool to flash a light on the shelf where she stacks boxes of
Kleenex and the waffle iron. There are a dozen places
where he might have missed the sound of the glove's fall:
on the stairs, in her closet, the kid's room—

He shakes out his sleeping bag, looks under the front
seats, and probes the space between wheelwells, canvas
sacks, and green metal boxes. He has to be sure. So he
spreads out a tarp on the asphalt and he begins unloading
the Blazer. What he brings on these trips to northern Massachusetts depends upon calculating certain risks. Given a
presidential inauguration and uncertainty in Iran, this is a
bad time. He's brought food (most of it freeze-dried), ammunition for two rifles, three handguns, and the M-16. He's
brought first-aid supplies and the telescope; rope, rawhide,
and snowshoes; several ten-gallon containers for fuel and
water. A decontamination suit. A Geiger counter.

On his knees he sweeps out the back of the vehicle before
loading it again. The glove is lost. Tomorrow he'll risk

retracing his steps to her house. But she mustn't see his face, so he can't knock on the door. There's no way to reassure her, to give her some sign that he's at hand, ready, and watching.

Overhead, stars wink on as he drives up the ridge to where he's made camp at the quarry. From up here he can see the frozen river winding past the creep of traffic on the Interstate. Over a ridge where the river loops north, a dull glow indicates downtown Heathersford: a cramped region of vacant brick mills and boarded-up storefronts where cars park diagonally on Main Street, and old men shuffle past a theater that shows X-rated films. To the west, past the receding glitter of Old Country Road and the shopping mall's bright parking lot, stretches the grid of suburban streetlights where—through powerful magnification—he can bring into wavering focus the lighted window of her bedroom.

After coming home from church on Sunday, Richard seems restless. He paces the house. "It's this extra weight I'm carrying around," he explains. "Christmas, New Year's —God, Thanksgiving. It's all right here." He pats the paunch of his belly. "I'm going to go lift some weights. Maybe take a swim."

Since October, Richard has made monthly payments for a family membership in the Fit 'n' Trim Health Spa. Lindsay has driven past the place, a concrete hulk that doesn't look big enough to contain all the interior shots from the TV commercial: squash courts, European-style tanning units, women in bikinis, and muscular men climbing out of a steamy pool. She can't bear the thought of entering a group shower with strange women, of scum around the drain, of the screech lockers make when you lift up the metal handle.

Alone in the kitchen, Lindsay considers clearing out the maple base unit whose bookcase top has filled up with china, glassware, and stacked-up napkins. The woman at Ethan Allen seemed amused when Lindsay declared that she wanted a bookcase in her kitchen. The woman pointed at the floor plan and insisted that the piece belonged in the den.

"Well," said Lindsay, genuinely curious, "where do *you* put all that stuff people send you?"

"For one thing," the woman replied, "I keep crystal behind glass—under lock and key—in the dining room."

Lindsay's dining room isn't fancy enough for Ethan Allen's Georgian Court Collection. To begin with, the room was badly designed. The whole house, in fact, is peculiar. The real estate agent had called it "a charming ranch-colonial." This meant it had white clapboards and two stories, but was built on a concrete slab with an attached garage. There are long, useless hallways, rooms with no windows, and cabinets mounted so high she requires a stepladder to reach them. In the living room, a huge bay window looks west. Richard, examining loose putty, claims that someone eventually is going to fall through this fragile expanse of glass and wood. But Lindsay loves the airy space and leaves it largely open—except for two wing-back chairs that face the blue Chesterfield couch across a coffee table. Lately the walls—with their botanical prints framed in hard chrome—have seemed a little stark.

Just now, Alex is in the den, playing by himself on the rug. He's humming to himself. It sounds like a hymn. Lindsay looks in the door and sees an assortment of Matchbox cars and Star Wars figures.

"Want to do some number work?" she asks.

"No way, Mom."

"Your teacher sent home that workbook. Maybe after supper. Okay?" Lindsay folds her arms—the house is chilly —and decides to do a load of laundry. Alex is a puzzle. He's falling behind in third-grade science and math, and he seems a bit lethargic. Lindsay has caught him lately sitting motionless in a chair staring at something—usually his hand.

Alex has stumbled onto certain feelings, states of consciousness. Last summer, spinning around with two other kids on the lawn until they all sprawled into dizzy collapse, Alex looked up at the blue dome of the sky, gripped sod wheeling furiously beneath him, and seemed to discover an opening, a fissure in his field of vision that edged apart— a little left of center.

"Do you see it?" he asked his friends. "There's a door." This struck the others as a hilarious joke. They giggled and rolled on the grass. Alex understood that he was exploring regions he would have to keep to himself.

Last fall, Lisa Manguso, a fifth-grader, taught him how to hyperventilate. She'd learned it from some girls in junior high school. "Grownups do it," she claimed. "It's like falling in love." Alex had blacked out in Lisa's garage and gotten a bump on the head. Lisa's explanation reminded him of the time he'd seen his mother naked, walking flushed and breathless to the shower after wrestling with his father in bed. Usually they wrestled at night. Once he'd glanced into the bedroom and caught an eyeful of his father's nakedness coming at him. Then the door was slammed in his face.

So Alex has made a detour around the mysteries of heavy breathing and Lisa Manguso's garage. Lately he's been experimenting with eyeball rolling. Last week he asked Lindsay to try it. "Make your eyes go around like this," he said.

She rolled her eyes. "It makes me dizzy," she said.

"Did you notice anything?" His mother was giving him that look. Like she was going to feel his forehead. "Everything goes around," he tried to explain. "But it goes around twice."

"What?"

"Dum-dum," he said. "Once for each eye. Right?"

Lindsay had looked at her son blankly, then walked away.

At grade school, where he spends a lot of time staring at the clock, they don't teach him what he wants to know. Now and then hints occur at church, especially upstairs, where you're supposed to sit quietly in the long pews. But except for Christmas and Easter, the kids have to stay down in the basement, where they pull out curtain-walls, giant accordions that make wheezing rooms for Sunday school. Children aren't allowed in church, Alex has decided, because *they don't know how to sit still.* And this is the key to everything.

In the den now, Alex sits still on his knees. Around him, on the beige nylon rug, a line of small vehicles stretches out —as if seen from a distant height. He feels huge, like stone. Monumental. Slowly he moves an orange Dukes of Hazzard sedan toward one leg of the couch. He's hidden something under there in the dark place. Alex loves to create mysteries. It's not time yet to tug the thing out of the dark.

This morning on the way to church, Alex sat in the back seat of the station wagon and sat still. With cold thumbs he rubbed the small envelope containing his twenty-five-cent Sunday School offering, until—miraculously—a coin-sized halo appeared around a phantom George Washington.

In the church basement, Big Mrs. Nelson handed out the pamphlets with the pictures they would color: men with beards in long robes who always wore sandals. It was hard to color on the shiny paper. Mrs. Nelson, jiggling her big chin, read the story aloud. Alex folded his hands and listened. If you sit still long enough, he decided, you become invisible. Like a ghost. The Holy Ghost.

Mrs. Nelson put down the pamphlet and reached for her black Bible. "Let's hear the King James version," she said.

But when they saw him walking upon the sea, they supposed it had been a *spirit*, and cried out. For they all saw him, and were troubled. And immediately he talked with them, and saith unto them, Be of good cheer. It is I. Be not afraid.

The other kids wanted to know if Jesus really walked on the water. Billy Jameson said, "He walked on the rocks!" and everyone giggled. Mrs. Nelson said, "It means something else. It's a parable. For instance, feeding the five thousand. Some may have brought food with them. They all shared what they had, and there was enough for everyone. What filled them was not loaves and fishes. They were full of generosity."

Alex hadn't said anything. He was thinking about walking on water. In winter, you could cross over on the ice. But in Bible stories it was never cold. That's why they wore sandals all the time.

Coming home from church, Alex sat in the back seat and watched the pavement going by fast and gray. In the empty parking lot of the K-Mart he saw a pickup truck.

"Look, Dad," he said. "He's driving backwards."

His father glanced over but didn't seem interested. Lindsay said, "Maybe it's a student driver." Then his parents went back to their argument.

"You'd think you could remember something so simple," said his father.

"The warranty has run out. It's not like missing a deadline."

"Don't give me excuses. Just get it done."

"Maybe I could do it myself."

"Change the oil yourself?" scoffed Richard. "Don't kid me."

Change the oil into what? wondered Alex. The pickup truck was backing toward the K-Mart loading dock. There, a bearded biblical figure sat hunched in the cold. Alex felt a visionary thrill. He wore no shoes or boots, and his legs looked ghostly white.

Now Alex sits on the rug in the den and draws a furrow through the carpet. He whispers, "This is *the dead line.*" Then he reaches into the dark place under the couch. "Come out," he says, and tugs the gray glove into view.

Lindsay, watching from the doorway, thinks:

MY SON, AT PLAY, IN LIGHT
She adores the age he's at,
with its mysteries and silences,
odd objects hid in small recesses

(she finds them when she's vacuuming),
as if he knows he'll search them out—
decades later, recalling cellars and attics—
looking for the lost child in himself.

"What have you got?" she asks softly.

Alex fumbles something between his legs, startled by her voice.

She walks in and looks down. "Let me see," she smiles.

He looks up, accusing her with his small eyes.

A shudder goes through Lindsay as she recalls, for an instant, the time in Chicago when she snatched a small screwdriver out of the toddler's hands as he sat, still in diapers, probing at an electrical outlet. In the laundry room, she's filled a shoebox with junk from his pockets: rusted nuts and bolts, stones, bits of string tied to dull metal objects. And she knows there's a level of fear below her mild curiosity as she unloads the lumpy pockets of his blue jeans—knows that one day she'll find something truly forbidden: a sharp knife, a cigarette, dope, a condom, something.

Alex holds out the glove for inspection.

Lindsay sighs. "I told you. Don't bring home stuff that's dirty."

He looks down at the rug. "I didn't bring it home," he finally says.

She senses that he wants to tell her something. "Oh?" she asks.

"It was here this morning."

"Where?"

"On the stairs. The ghost left it."

"Alex!" Her voice suddenly frays with alarm. "What are you talking about?"

"I think he left it for me. Last night. I kept very still, so he couldn't see me. I suppose it was a spirit. 'Be of good cheer,' he saith unto me. 'It is I. Be not afraid.'"

Lindsay, open-mouthed, stares at her son. He looks pleased at his recitation. But her mind is racing. Richard has gloves, but none like this one. It's in her hands now, heavy. She turns it over in wonder, noting grease on the palm and the place at the thumb's web where someone has repaired the leather with a row of small precise stitches.

"Alex, tell me the truth." She's trembling, on the verge of tears. "You found this in the house? And there was someone here—a ghost—in the night?"

"Yup."

"Oh!" she cries, kneeling and clasping her son in her arms. She feels the frailness of his small limbs, feels a strand of his hair curling moist against her wet, shut eyes.

Monday at the office, Richard and his secretary catch up on the backlog of mail that piled up while he was in Houston. Kate, a hefty divorced woman with two kids, knows shorthand. The two of them go through a hundred letters in an hour—Kate making quick notations in their margins, as Richard channels them through a grid of corridors in his mind that lead to files, phone calls, and form-letter replies.

With Kate back at her desk, Richard sits alone and looks out the door. Across the outer office, if he leans a little to the left, he can catch a glimpse of Gina folding up a long printout in the computer room.

Gina brought him his coffee this morning. Today she's wearing a raspberry blouse—a loose, silky affair, open deep from the throat—that announces she isn't wearing a bra.

As Gina set down Richard's coffee, she gave him one of her languid, pouting looks. "Is that okay?" she asked. "Just a little cream. Right?"

Richard looked into his mug. "Fine," he said, wondering whether he'd heard sarcasm in her breathy voice. He gave her a quick smile anyway. "You know just how I like it."

"I probably do," she said with a smirk and walked out.

Richard has fantasies about Gina. But face to face, he doesn't know what to make of her. She's a bright local girl in her mid-twenties who's learned computer programming at a community college. He gathers that she lives alone. In his imagination, she leads the life of a swinging single on weekends. These brief exchanges between them—over coffee, in the Xerox room—madden Richard. She knows how to tease, inflame, and intimidate him all at once. It's her voice—a low, gusty murmur—that does it.

Now Richard sits at his desk and decides that he knows how to handle Gina. He rings her extension and says he'd like a word with her.

When she appears, he says, "Close the door," and gets up from his desk.

She clicks it shut and leans there, palms pressed flat against the dark wood. With her shoulders squared and thrust back, her blouse opens even more.

Richard puts his hands in his pockets and faces her. "There are some things I think we ought to straighten out," he declares.

She takes a step toward him. "How about your tie?" she says, crossing the distance between them. Her long fingers tug his necktie into line. Her face is inches away. She's wearing lots of eyeliner and mascara. Her eyes—liquid, steady, and deep—lock onto his own. This is not what he had in mind, he tells himself. Her lips are so wetly made up that it looks as if they'd smear across her face in greasy skidmarks if he dared to crush them with his own.

Suddenly she's in his arms. His mouth gropes wet and greedy on her neck, delirious in the musk of her perfume. One of his hands moves inside her blouse and cups a pendulous breast.

She gives a husky laugh. "I ought to report you."

Richard stops. That's what he's forgotten. He told Lindsay he'd call the police this morning to report the glove that Alex found. As he gathers himself to stand straight before Gina, he has the sense of giving a smart salute.

"Hey," he says casually. "How about lunch?"

Gina wets her lips. "Okay. Thursday? We'll drive over to my place." She makes a smooching kiss at him, then clicks open the door and whirls out.

Richard goes to his desk. He feels like his knees might buckle. The whole thing took less than a minute. She's so *easy*, he thinks to himself. A new world seems to open before him, a new kind of life.

Alone at home, Lindsay is watching TV. She's tuned in to see what's happening in Iran. But all she's found is the usual morning garbage. Now Donahue, with his hand-mike, is stirring up the studio audience. Lindsay turns the channel past *A.M. Aerobics,* past Big Bird, to the dour face of a woman in a housedress. She's describing her out-of-the-body experience. "And the next thing I knew—Praise the Lord!—my body drew me back in. Just like a big vacuum cleaner. The flesh sucked me home."

She clicks off the set and goes down the hall to the living room, wondering what to do with her empty morning. What she needs is a project, a hobby. It's terrible to think that's what her poetry has become—worth about as much as needlepoint sewn from a kit. She ought to read a book —become an authority on something.

Lindsay strolls through the dining room, retying the belt on her velour robe. She's decided on a safe subject. Kohlrabi. She'll become an authority on kohlrabi, the weirdest vegetable she knows: *The Kohlrabi Cookbook. The Kohlrabi Diet.* Lindsay pictures herself on a TV talk show discussing her next book: *The Kohlrabi Assassination Conspiracy.* After that, *Kohlrabi UFOs.*

She finds herself in the kitchen, admitting that she's not an authority on anything. Her notebook lies open on the table. She sits and stares at her sleeve, at the narrow blue veins in her wrist. Here's something she knows about. Seizing her BIC pen, she feels it coming. A new poem. Writing it out frightens her:

> *If they cut off*
> *Everyone's right hand*
> *And then the militia arrived*
> *To liberate the prisoners*
> *And later you were called*
> *To pick through a bin*

Of amputated limbs
Would you recognize your own—
When you found it?

It's not like any other poem she's written. She closes the notebook firmly. Outside, at the bird feeder, a fat chickadee fluffs himself in the cold air.

It's 2 A.M. and Garth is awake on a lumpy davenport at Wally's. He writhes on his back, fighting off the glare from a streetlight. There are no shades on these big, second-story windows. The blinding light comes at him, diffused by frost, through a forest of floor lamps. Garth twists, wrestling with three heavy quilts. The pain in his knee is nothing compared to the ache in his back. Wally must have upholstered this davenport with scrap metal.

"Psst." It's Wally, looking in on him. "How you doing?" he whispers.

"Terrible. This sofa is torture."

Wally walks in and squats down. "Roll over," he says. "I think I left something under this cushion." He pulls out a large, gray brick.

Garth stares at the thing—granite glinting in the streetlight's glare. "What's that, a joke?"

Wally silently turns the brick over in his hands.

"I don't need any bricks in my bed," says Garth.

"This," explains Wally, "is a famous brick. In 1886 somebody threw this brick during the Haymarket Riot."

Garth gets up on one elbow. "How do you know?"

"That's what the guy said who sold it to me."

"How much did he want for it?"

"Forty-five dollars."

Garth flops down on his back. "You paid forty-five dollars for a brick?"

"Nope. I got it for seven dollars and thirty-nine cents."

"You drive a hard bargain," sighs Garth.

"I sure do." Wally is squinting at the glare coming in the windows. "Doesn't that light bother you?"

Garth holds back the impulse to yell again. He's thought of fifty ways to seal off those windows so he can go to sleep.

Wally stands up. He reaches for a gray metal box on the wall and pulls down a big switch. Outside, the streetlight sputters, goes dim—then out.

"Gee, thanks," says Garth. "How did you do that?"

"I had to rent a jackhammer and tear up the sidewalk," says Wally.

At 2 A.M. Lindsay is awake. She goes downstairs to the living room, turns on all the lights, and gets out the vacuum cleaner. She brushes the carpet pile forward and back— making overlaid swaths like linked *W*s. But it looks too tidy. So she steps out of her slippers and shuffles around in her bare feet to disguise the vacuum's tracks.

She's working off the depression brought on by reading the newspaper. Past the front-page stories about wildcat strikes in Poland and President Carter's efforts to ransom the fifty-two American hostages, things look even worse. Richard (*Have Gun Will Travel*) Boone has died. Throat cancer. Also Marguerite Oswald—mother of Lee Harvey. Cancer. Mary Tyler Moore is divorcing Grant Tinker after eighteen years of marriage. In Mae West's will, the muscle-man—her faithful companion for twenty-five years—isn't mentioned.

Outside Lindsay's front window, a streetlight gleams an odd shade of violet on the flat snow. Alex has tied a yellow ribbon to the birch tree. It hangs there motionless in the cold air. What an odd homecoming anthem America has picked, she thinks. The song doesn't say what the ex-con did time for. Assault? Armed robbery? She unplugs the vacuum. Giving the cord a yank, she watches as it winds itself eagerly into the base of the machine.

Tuesday, Lindsay watches CBS coverage of Ronald Reagan's inauguration. Walter Cronkite says, "The motorcade is now leaving the White House, and Jimmy Carter has apparently been denied his chance to announce the hostages' release during his term in office." The anchorman sounds bitter. He's going to retire, and this may be the last big story he covers. Perhaps that's why he's allowed to express his indignation so openly on the air: "Iran seems to dangle this in front of us," fumes Cronkite. "It's the most uncivilized—"

Lindsay's doorbell rings. She gets up, but pauses to watch a shot of Reagan and dignitaries in a reception room of the Capitol. In a corner, a television is tuned in. Watching it, Reagan gestures. He sees himself gesturing at a TV.

Lindsay goes to the front door. Two police officers stand on her front steps. She recalls leaving the drapes open last night as she pranced about with the vacuum cleaner hose. Then she decides that someone has twacked her down.

Opening the storm door a crack, she stammers, "Yes?"

"Mrs. Smith? We're here about an intruder. Something about a glove?"

"Oh, thank goodness!" gasps Lindsay. Richard must have called the police.

The older man takes off his hat when he steps inside. "I'm Sergeant Kowolski, ma'am. This is Patrolman Angini." The younger cop decides to take his hat off, too. His dark eyes catch at Lindsay's for a second. She looks away and heads for the den, where the TV is still on. They follow her, and the three of them stand looking at the screen. A young marine is singing "America the Beautiful."

"Any word about the hostages?" asks Kowolski.

"They're on a plane waiting to take off," explains Lindsay.

"Waiting?"

"Until Reagan's sworn in. So Carter won't get the credit."

"The bastards," says Angini.

They listen to the song. The TV cameras are picking out isolated faces in the crowd. In some people's eyes, tears glisten. The old songs can do that to you. Lindsay feels the sting of moistness welling up in her eyes. The hostages are coming home. "America, America! God shed his grace on thee—" She sees that Kowolski is holding his hat over his heart. It's what her father used to do at parades whenever the flag passed by.

They stand facing the TV until the song ends. We should all hug or something, thinks Lindsay. She needs a tissue.

"Look at that," says Angini. His finger traces a thin line across the screen. It cuts through the microphones clustered on the podium.

"Bullet-proof glass," nods his partner.

"I bet they're ready for anything."

"Probably."

"Check out that guy." The TV shows a young man in a suit.

"Secret Service," comments Kowolski.

"Look at his eyes," says Angini. "My brother saw guys like that in Vietnam. He's on speed—that's what he is. Makes you like a computer. A killer-computer."

Kowolski faces Lindsay. "There are a few routine questions."

"Sure," she says, and leads them upstairs. On the landing she points at the rug. "It was found here," she says. "Early yesterday morning."

"Anything missing from the house? Silver, jewelry, cash?"

She shakes her head.

"How about signs of forced entry? Marks around the doors, windows?"

"My husband didn't find anything like that."

"I'll take a look," says Angini and goes downstairs.

Kowolski glances into the bedroom. "So. Your husband finds a man's glove outside your bedroom door?"

"No. My son found it. I questioned him pretty thoroughly."

"Any odd phone calls recently?"

Lindsay thinks for a moment. Sometimes she answers the phone but the line goes dead. They're just wrong numbers. "No calls," she says. "Would you like to see the glove?" She walks into the bedroom and retrieves it from the dresser.

Kowolski examines the grease on the palm, the stitching on the mended place, and the crook of the index finger. "Somebody clever and careful," he says. "This, by itself, doesn't tell us much." He pauses, then asks, "Have you been seeing anyone, Mrs. Smith?" Kowolski stares at her coldly.

Lindsay flushes. "No," she declares and crosses her arms. She thought this man was on her side.

"Sometimes women," he says, "home alone all day—they do something they're ashamed of. Then some little thing turns up. Like they needed an excuse to make a confession."

Lindsay is glaring at him.

Kowolski finally looks away. "Okay. Can you think of anyone—a neighbor maybe, or some friend of your husband's—who's shown an unusual interest in you?"

She goes through a series of faces: the guy at the bank, the dishwasher repairman, the man in the hospital with the beard. It's quite a list.

Kowolski is staring at her. "Nothing unusual," she says, wondering if this is a lie. Who knows what's usual anymore? What are normal people's lives like?

Kowolski hands her the glove and puts on his hat. "Okay," he says. "I'm sorry. It's my job."

What an inhuman job, she thinks, giving him a quick, polite smile.

Downstairs, they find Angini coming in from the deck through the sliding glass doors. "Is this always unlocked?" he asks.

Lindsay frowns. "I don't know."

"Keep it locked, will you? We'll be keeping an eye on the place for a week or two." The patrolman looks at Kowolski, who nods. The older man is jotting down something in a notebook.

"Here's Nancy Reagan on the inaugural platform," says Cronkite's voice.

"We'd better watch," says Lindsay and shows the men into the den.

Mark Hatfield is announcing the national hymn: "Faith of Our Fathers."

Lindsay says, "I didn't know we had a national hymn."

"Me neither," says Angini.

After the oath of office, the Third Infantry Regiment fires a salute with artillery pieces. The camera catches Reagan looking startled at the first cannon's report. During his speech, the annoying sound of jet aircraft roars in the background. Lindsay wonders if a pilot would bank his 747 over the Capitol to give his passengers a look at the ceremony. Surely, today, they're keeping the airspace clear over Washington. Except for military planes—the Air Force riding shotgun over the new president. But what if a fighter pilot goes berserk and aims his surface-to-air missiles at the inaugural platform? Good grief. What's brought on thoughts like these? She glances at the two men sitting on her floral love seat. They both wear cartridge belts and handguns. After being interrogated, she feels tense, worried, and wishes the inaugural ceremony were over. On the TV, a man unbuttons his jacket, as if he's ready to reach for a shoulder holster. It strikes her that Washington must hire people to have thoughts like hers. Professional paranoids whose job it is to anticipate craziness in public places.

At last the speech is over. She sees Kowolski and Angini to the door. A mirror hangs in the front hall. Seeing herself in it shocks her. The house looked okay, but what did those cops make of these awful jeans—holes in the knees—and this old sweatshirt with the paint spots? They probably saw a woman with no self-respect and dirty underwear. She runs her fingers through her hair. It's been three days since she took a shower. She feels unclean. Staring at her hand, she searches for a visible sign of filth.

Gina's Thursday luncheon date with Richard turns out, in a way, to be disappointing. She'd imagined they'd go straight to her place. Even before they were through the door, clothes would fly off. He'd pull her down naked in the middle of her white shag rug. And she, straddling his massive executive thighs, would open herself to his thick, rising manhood.

Instead, Richard takes her to the small tavern downtown, where they order lasagna and drink beer out of heavy cold mugs. He's very polite, gives her advice about income tax deductions, and talks about playing golf. Gina understands that he belongs to a country club. Wouldn't that be something. She thinks about making an entrance. She and Richard pause in the doorway of a crowded ballroom, as hundreds of affluent, country-club eyes fasten upon her.

Thursday he's on the road again, heading up Interstate 89 where it cuts through New Hampshire granite. The highway leans into the hills. Off to the left, a lake nestles in a valley of pine and birch. It's nice country, he thinks. But there are too many roads. If Boston was hit, they'd surge up here like blood spurting from an artery. It might take a day for prevailing winds to bring in fallout from the strikes against Ottawa and Montreal. The smart ones would find a cave. A handful might be ready, like he is.

His own place in the Adirondacks is dug into the side of a hill. Big windows stretch open to the east, under a long porch. In summer, through dark screens, he has a nice view of the lake and the mountains. Winters, insulated panels shut out the cold. From down on the lake, even an expert might not pick out this long slit in the hill, this half-closed eye squinting into the dawn. The front roof supports tons of rock, dirt, and saplings. Knock out four timbers—and it all comes down. You're sealed off—safe—even from an artillery or mortar attack.

In six hours he'll reach Willardsville. He stores the Blazer there. Then it's another hour by snowmobile across the big lake and up the frozen river to a trail. In summer, the only easy way in is by canoe, and there are two long portages. It feels good to be heading home. The trip back is linked in his mind with strain easing in the joints. He's called Noland to verify his hunch that international tensions have backed off from a confrontation. Noland may consist of three or four men—with connections to the CIA and NSA. The phone number supplies coded information, mostly about what stages of alert certain air bases have gone through during the last twenty-four hours. It's a subscription service—like cable TV. He mails them cash every month. They send back a new access code. Usually the information only confirms what he puts together himself from newspapers and the shortwave broadcasts. Given the hostages' return, the presidential inauguration, and something going on in Poland, the last ten days were mildly perilous. Sometimes he just has feelings and intuitions to go on. He feels a tightening in the chest, as if he's attuned to subtle constrictions in the earth's mantle, a global wince before an expected blow. Whenever it happens, he makes the long drive—almost to Boston—to be near Lindsay. Before everything disappears, there'll be time, he's sure, to get her out.

Lindsay is sitting motionless in front of the TV. On the screen there's lots of movement—especially during the commercials. Meat cutters and produce managers march up and down the aisles of supermarkets. Shapely legs in panty hose kick out the doors of taxicabs. At fast-food restaurants, whole crowds of exuberant suburbanites sing and dance on tabletops. Finally *The Price Is Right* comes on. She's watching because her neighbor, Debbie, is in L.A. and wrote ahead for tickets. Lindsay searches the studio audience for her friend's face. The women are going crazy. As the camera pans over them, they wave their arms and jump up and down. She's not sure she can bear to watch.

Something makes her get up and click off the TV. Lindsay feels drawn out of the den. She hasn't left a kettle boiling on the stove. The mail hasn't arrived. But there's something in this house that wants her attention. She goes upstairs and looks at the clothes in her closet. Passing Alex's room, she surveys his bunkbed, his toys, his Star

Wars poster. Down in the kitchen, her fingertips brush idly along gleaming Formica, chrome, durable white plastic. She makes a tour through the dining room—past the downstairs bathroom with its clean toilet bowl. The thing drawing her on will appear, she's certain, in plain view, and it will be as familiar as her own right hand.

In the living room she stops and takes it all in. The end tables and lamps from Jordan Marsh, the big couch, and her antiques: a Shaker chair from the little shop on Newbury Street, others from trips on which the camping gear in the back of the station wagon was squeezed aside to make room for bureaus, china, rockers, and chests. She finds herself staring at the teak wall system they bought in Cambridge. It holds their old college paperbacks, the stereo and records (Bach and Vivaldi mixed up with Creedence Clearwater and Joni Mitchell), old photos of Richard at fundraisers with Mayor Daley and Ted Kennedy. And then she begins to feel it, coming up like a lump in her throat. It thickens into something hard like grief. She can't keep it down. Suddenly she bursts into tears. Sobbing, she stands there straight. Her hands make tight little fists at her sides. It's not, after all, the peril of the world that makes her weep. Not fears of craziness, assassinations, air disasters, armed men, or intruders in her bedroom. These have just softened her up, sensitized her to something else, something obvious. "Oh, God," she cries. It's her past, her youth—the promise of it—that she mourns. Here she's lived all these years and come to this. *Stuff*. A husband, a kid, two cars, a mortgage, and cable TV. It's worse than being cheated. Far back, someone must have lied to her about the world. "This is it?" she asks aloud, shaking her fist at the walls that lock her in safe—one more object displaying good taste. "THIS IS IT?" she shouts. There's a lamp within reach. Her favorite. A delicate Chinese ginger jar, hand-painted, with a linen shade. She seizes it and hurls it against the fireplace. The pieces splay out in a sharp pattern, like an iridescent blossom opening, whose petals—touching air—instantly fossilize and shower down in fragments of dust and dry bone.

9

On GROUNDHOG DAY 1981, things begin to stir, and Lindsay has the first of what she'll call "spells." Just now, for example, she's standing in the laundry room in her old flannel nightgown. The ceiling bulb has burned out. Dim light comes in through a north window. But she's just had a glimpse of herself, as if from the outside. This will be the first sign of a spell coming on—a sense of her identity split into two parts: one experiencing, the other observing.

What she sees is a pale, listless woman distracted by glinting chrome and glossy enamel. Something stirs within her. To her left a door opens into the dark garage. She finds herself crossing oil-stained concrete in her slippers, edging past her Volkswagen, and stooping to grip the icy handles of the garage doors. With a grunt, she heaves them overhead. Her arms are flung aloft.

Whiteness blinds her. The wind whips about her thighs and ankles. The sleeves of her nightgown slip down bare skin. At the age of five or six, little Lindsay ventured out the front door on a wintry morning in bathrobe and slippers. But this time no scolding voice calls her back into the warm household. The past has no access to the state she's in. For one thing, the cold hurts too much. But her eyes have adjusted to the light. And here comes the last stage of the spell: everything sharpens up. Clarity takes over.

> *Bare trees jut across fast clouds. Across the street,*
> *roof lines slant up and meet at sharp angles.*

Till now she hasn't seen the desperation
In the colors of her neighbors' window trim:
bright green, persimmon, teal blue. And now,

big and brown, here comes the UPS van.
The driver (paunchy gift bearer) slows down
to stare at this weird robed figure, airy
arms aloft, hailing him a double hello.

Sitting up ahead of all those parcels,
angular jumble of string and tape,
he grins and gives a wave of the palm
to this strange dame. His day is made.

Lindsay, a-tingle from the cold, clutches her nightgown closed at the neck and regally makes her way back inside. She's discovered one way out of the burrow of herself. In the kitchen, she seizes her pen. She'll address a big carton to a faraway place (New Zealand, she thinks), tape it shut from the inside, and huddle there as burly men heft the weight of her passage. But for now, she writes it all down —on brown wrapping paper.

Wednesday night, when Richard comes home late, he finds Lindsay in the den leafing through an old *Family Circle* magazine. He explains about the building-supply dealers in Maine who want commissions on the orders that bypass his salesmen. "You know what Karasian says? 'Tough shit for them.' So I'm the one who has to get on the phone to all these people and work out a compromise."
Lindsay is looking at him blankly. "You poor dear," she says. "You could have called to say you'd miss dinner."
"Aw, Linz," he says, touching her hair lightly with his fingers.
"Mmm, you smell good."
"Oh?" He sniffs the back of his hand. "Some damn pink soap in the office washroom. Any dinner left?"

"In the refrigerator." She notices, as he walks out, how rumpled his suit is.

Richard has, in fact, been at the office—briefly. He stopped off to wash his hands with pink soap in the women's washroom. He'd just come from making love to Gina—more or less successfully—on her white shag rug. Driving to the office, the smell of vaginal funk had been so strong on his hands that he wondered if he'd have to scrub the steering wheel.

Alone now in the kitchen, gobbling the cool white meat of chicken breasts, he can still smell Gina's odor. It makes him think of ocean air, of his semen dribbled like icing on her thighs, of faraway sardines.

> *"Yum yum,*
> *I'm a bum,"*

he says, having just composed his first poem.

By the end of the week, Lindsay's neighbor, Debbie, is back from Los Angeles. As a contestant on *The Price Is Right*, she won a microwave oven. She already has a microwave, so they gave her a check for $402—her winning bid.

"Well," asks Lindsay, "what are you going to spend your money on?"

They're sitting in Debbie's knotty-pine kitchen, where the Formica countertops are tartan plaid. Debbie is wearing gaucho pants and what she calls her Errol Flynn buccaneer shirt. A cascade of ruffles pours down its open neck. She's already stained a cuff with egg yolk.

"Maybe a suit," says Debbie, getting up to peer at the thin stream dribbling out of Mr. Coffee.

"How about something in the nonclothes department?" offers Lindsay. She knows that Debbie's husband, Stan, who programs computers, had to build two extra closets on the back of their house last summer. In one he put shelves, just to hold shoes. Debbie owns eighty-five pairs of shoes.

"Hey, you mean, like"— Debbie whirls her fist around in a tight little cheerleader's circle—"a night with a gigolo?"

"Four hundred dollars," says Lindsay. "They cost that much?"

"That's what I've heard. Does this coffee look okay to you? Some women in L.A. pay a thousand bucks a night." She snaps her fingers. "Just like that."

"Now that," says Lindsay, "must be a *very* homely woman.

"Or," says Debbie, "a *very* big cock."

Lindsay laughs, though she's embarrassed. She doesn't know what to call a penis in conversation. "What do gigolos do, anyway?"

"I think they do a lot of hand work. You know, ointments, vibrators."

"Phooey," says Lindsay. "It sounds like a gynecologist out of control."

"Yikes!" shrieks Debbie. "Cold stirrups and hot hands!" She bring over the coffeepot. "Hey, do I look like I've got the bloats?"

"Your period?"

"Not yet."

"When's it due?"

"Last week."

Lindsay reaches for the cream. "You've never been very regular." She watches her friend sit down and light a long Benson & Hedges from a pack on the table. When Debbie drags on the cigarette, puckered wrinkles appear about her mouth. Leaning her own cheek onto a palm, Lindsay is conscious that her own face—except for those little lines around the eyes—is in pretty good shape. It's marriage, she decides. It keeps you sealed in—it's hermetic—it shuts out time.

Debbie turns her head to one side and scratches the crown of her head with one long fingernail. Her dark brown hair would have gray in it if she didn't color it. "I'm not too worried," she says. "I went back on the pill before we left. A couple days—maybe—I forgot."

Lindsay sips her coffee, waiting. On a postcard last week, Debbie had written:

> Having a fabulous time! The sun is out! A guy wearing cowboy boots is taking me for a drive in his Porsche!
> Love, Debs!

"I could take another trip," muses Debbie. "Maybe New York?"

Lindsay says, "Now, about that guy with the Porsche—"

Debbie puts on her slow, sly grin. It wrinkles her nose girlishly, making you forget how much time she must have spent this morning putting on her makeup. "Oh, him?" she says, as if this weren't the cue she's been waiting for. "Well," she drawls, crossing her legs tight and tapping her cigarette in the ashtray, "he was waiting around by the elevators after they gave me the check. He tells me, you know, how terrific I was on camera. And didn't I need a ride back to my hotel?"

"So, who was this guy?"

"Look, we're on a floor with executive offices. I figure he's a producer or something. Anyone dressed that casually —jeans, you know? and snakeskin boots?—he's got to be someone important."

"Okay. So he drives you to your hotel."

"Yeah. In the Porsche. A white Porsche convertible. But I make him wait in the lobby for about an hour. I've been hopping around like a bunny all morning See, before the show, these guys do a warmup. They get the whole audience leaping around and screaming. It's a riot. So I need a shower."

"Where's Stan all this time?"

"He's at conferences all day. I've got the whole afternoon to fool around." Debbie grinds out her cigarette with a smile. "All afternoon."

Lindsay shakes her head in mock dismay. "I think you're terrible. Just terrible. How many times did you see this man?"

"Just that one day."

"What'd you do?"

"Had a few drinks in the bar. Then we drove up the coast. Pacific Palisades, I think. His place was up in this canyon. We went to his place."

"A nice place?"

"What do you think? So anyway, driving up this canyon, I'm a little dizzy. No lunch and three whiskey sours, right? Every time he shifts gears he works his hand up and down my leg. I thought I'd die laughing. And once we get there, we're kissing each other like crazy. Right in the parking lot."

"Parking lot?" asks Lindsay. She's pictured a Spanish-style mansion.

"Yeah. There are lots of cars around. It's sort of a condominium."

"Oh."

"So the first thing he does inside—this is in the kitchen —he unhooks my bra and slobbers all over my boobs!"

"Slobbers?"

"Sure. It's pretty exciting. So in the living room, we clear away some stuff. And he's really mauling my clothes off, you know?"

"Wait a minute. Clear away what stuff?"

"Oh, kids' toys and stuff. Some laundry. And his wife's typewriter. See, we're going to do it on the couch. So we've got to clear off the couch."

Lindsay frowns and rubs her forehead. "What's the story with his wife?"

"She's off at some library doing research. Writing a dissertation. Something about 'Women in the Nineteenth Century.' "

"And the kids?"

Debbie is staring into her coffee cup. "Day-care," she

says blankly. Evidently her adventure isn't coming out the way she planned to tell it. "But hey," she says, brightening up and reaching for another cigarette, "you won't believe what we did in the bathroom."

Lindsay, looking at the egg yolk on Debbie's sleeve, is beginning to get the mild sense again of seeing herself from a distance. What is she doing in this garish kitchen, feigning interest in this sordid anecdote? "Let's get this straight," she says, almost sternly. "This guy wasn't any producer, was he?"

"What difference does it make?" shrugs Debbie. "He did work in production. Technical stuff, you know?"

"Come on. Give me a clear picture. What kind of technical stuff?"

"Okay. So he worked with lights. He was an electrician. But he was good. We did it three times."

"You mean, did it on top of the dirty laundry and the wife's dissertation?"

"I said we cleared that junk away." There's a quaver now in Debbie's voice. "Why are you giving me such a hard time?"

"How could an electrician afford a Porsche?"

"He couldn't. That's the funny part. They were going to repossess it the next day. To tell you the truth, the guy was kind of a jerk. You know what I had to do on the way back to the hotel?"

"Was it obscene?"

"Sort of. I had to buy him a tank of gas." There are tears now welling up in Debbie's eyes. "I bought the jerk a full tank of gas!" She puts her hands across her eyes. "Oh, Jesus," she sobs. "I hope my goddamn period comes tomorrow."

Lindsay gets up to give Debbie a hug. But her friend is hunched over the table, weeping. So she ruffles her hair and rubs the back of her neck. "Hey, Debs? It's okay. Think about the money you won. Think about what you can buy."

"A suit," sniffs Debbie. "I want a suit like yours."

Debbie has drooled into her coffee cup. Lindsay stares at the froth of saliva as it circles the rim, then catches and climbs eagerly up the china to cling there. The spell has arrived, and she finds herself humming:

> Oh froth of sorrow given
> In cups of mercy blest,
> Wine of the body shriven
> For us in glory dressed.
>
> > *Amen.*

A week later, Lindsay drives to the shopping mall to buy Richard a milk chocolate heart for Valentine's Day. What she sees at the fountain near Florsheim's makes her skid to a halt. It's Garth. He sits, leaning on a cane, his bearded chin resting on folded hands.

Lindsay darts into Radio Shack. She doesn't think he's seen her. But his presence brings back last night's dream: a long cheek-pressing embrace—like a motionless dance. And now here he is—waiting. Has he come to the mall, she wonders, hoping for a glimpse of her?

In the back of Radio Shack, which looks deserted, she tries to catch her breath. When she runs her shaking fingers over the keyboard of a home computer, a tall salesman appears. "Yes," he says. "That's the TRS-80. And it's on sale!"

She stares straight ahead at his polka-dot necktie. "Golf balls," she says.

The tall man looks down at his tie. "How about that?" he says, as if he's never noticed the detail before in the pattern of dots.

Lindsay slides past him and walks to the entrance. She stops there to fiddle with her purse and peek around the corner. He's still there. The salesman is watching her. She can't stand in the doorway, but there's no way out.

She strides back in and says, breathless, "Now, about that computer sale—"

The salesman grins. "Who can resist a sale, right?"

Lindsay is trying to decide how long she'll have to hide in here. It could take hours. "You'd better show me"—she gestures vaguely toward an entire wall of sound systems— "oh, everything."

The salesman nods thoughtfully. "You're in the market, then, for a stereo?"

"No," she says, shutting her eyes and thinking of him— sitting out there with his cane, crippled. Waiting. "I mean —yes." Her excited confusion has turned into a light-headed giddiness. "You can never tell," she says gaily, "when you'll just want—to write out a check!" She scribbles her signature in the air with a flourish.

This impresses the salesman, who already has figured his percentage on a thousand-dollar sale. But a disappointed look appears on his face as she edges toward the door. Then she's back again.

The salesman doesn't let her get away this time. He leads her to one of the shelves and begins explaining watts per channel and frequency responses. Lindsay doesn't seem to be paying attention. She's fishing in her purse for a disguise. A way to sneak out.

"Now this model," says the salesman, clicking on a switch, "has L.E.D.-V.U. meters." He points to a row of glowing bars leaping from left to right in time with Dolly Parton singing "Nine to Five."

Lindsay has put on her dark glasses. She squints through them at the receiver's flashing display.

The salesman looks alarmed. "Is it *that* bright?" he asks. Working under these fluorescent lights has been giving him headaches lately. He blinks his eyes in panic. She's vanished. No, here she comes back from the door again.

Lindsay has just seen Garth limp away. Her plan now is to follow him. If he goes to his car, she'll tail him. Then she might find out who he is—where he lives. But she's too polite to simply walk out on this salesman after taking up so much of his time. "I want to buy something," she declares. "Fast."

"How about a nice videocassette recorder," he instantly suggests. "Nine hundred forty-nine dollars!"

Lindsay steps toward the cash register. "What I really came for was something chocolate," she calls back.

"Did you say 'chocolate'?" he asks, hurrying around the counter. These stereos blaring all day—maybe his hearing is going along with his vision. Lindsay is staring straight ahead through her dark glasses. It suddenly hits him. *She's blind.* The woman must think that she's next door at Fanny Farmer Chocolates.

Near the cash register there's a display of assorted batteries. Lindsay snatches a card with a little metal button sealed in a plastic window. For Valentine's Day, she'll get Richard a new battery for his digital watch.

The salesman lets out a cry at the blind woman's selection. "No, no. Don't eat! They're not candy!" He stretches across the counter and knocks the purchase from her grasp.

She looks now at this maniac, as if seeing him clearly for the first time. "You are very rude!" she says and stalks out.

The salesman lies prone on the counter with one fist clenched. Then he opens his fingers and stares at his empty hand, searching—it seems—for that vanished thousand-dollar sale.

Outside there's no sign of Garth at the fountain. Lindsay paces down a concourse that leads to one of the parking lots. He couldn't have limped this far so fast. She turns back and traces another route, all the way to Sears, Roebuck. The next half-hour she crisscrosses the mall, conspicuously pausing to scan the interiors of shops, peering out glass doors at the exits, searching the parking lots for a sign of a limping, bearded man. Eventually, as she's plodding past the little kiosk that sells fat pretzels, a man's voice says, "Busy day for you, huh?"

Lindsay glances back at a young man wiping down a counter. He gives her an amused nod. Goodness, she thinks, realizing she's passed this spot five or six times.

You're making a spectacle of yourself, says her conscience. This thought drives her out to her car and pursues her all the way home. Even sitting for a moment behind the wheel in the garage, she feels her face burn with shame.

If Lindsay had looked in the rearview mirror on the way home, she might have seen, following at a discreet distance, the chrome grille of a 1957 Plymouth Belvedere. Now, as she pulls down the overhead garage doors, she fails to glance up as this same vehicle glides down her street. It slows nearly to a stop in front of her house. Then it speeds off, its big tail fins thrust up in jaunty triumph.

Saturday is Valentine's Day. Richard gives Lindsay a bottle of Ralph Lauren perfume. She apologizes for not buying him a present. "I was so busy," she murmurs guiltily and resolves never again to shop at the mall. In Richard's face she sees a look of utter agony. How disappointed he looks.

But he looks troubled because he's bought Lindsay Gina's brand of perfume. Gina pronounces it "Rolf La Wren." In the back of his mind was the half-baked idea that he might make better love to Lindsay if only some subtle reminder of Gina's voluptuous flesh hung in the dark air of his own bedroom. This hanky-panky with a girl from the office actually amounts to a program of self-improvement. It will make him more manly and—in the end—a better husband.

Actually Lindsay doesn't think a whole lot of Richard's present. She's just relieved that he didn't buy her another kitchen gadget. Last year it was an electric can opener. The year before, a potato masher with a rosewood handle. He seems to have inherited his mother's talent for picking out gifts.

Perfume marks an improvement. But perfume is a touchy subject with Lindsay. For years she's exclusively worn the old Guerlain scent, Mitsouko. It's hard to find these days. She bought her first bottle on a trip to New

York in 1968 while still a junior in college. A striking, dark woman behind a counter at Saks sold it to her. The woman had enormous gold earrings. She told Lindsay that it was a Druid formula based on an oak-moss fixative. The Phoenicians, she claimed, brought its secret west, by way of Cyprus, to ancient Britain. Lindsay went back the next day to purchase a second bottle of the woody fragrance. But the woman was gone. A clerk at the next counter told her to inquire with the house detective, a suave-looking gentleman standing near the elevators. He told her that the dark woman wearing gold earrings was probably a Gypsy shoplifter impersonating one of their sales staff. They'd been after her all week.

"She was a terrific saleswoman," said Lindsay.

"What'd she sell you?"

Lindsay pulled the bottle of perfume from her Fred Braun purse.

The man looked at it. "Well, you'd better go pay for this."

"I did pay for it." She snatched back the bottle.

"You didn't pay Saks."

"But I've got the receipt."

"The money didn't go in the cash register."

"That's *your* problem, isn't it?"

"Okay," he said, scrutinizing Lindsay's pierced ears. "But I'll have to ask you to leave the store."

"Sure," she said, flashed him the peace sign, and walked out, thrilled at having purchased a Druid secret from a mysterious Gypsy.

Saturday afternoon, Richard drops by the Health Spa, where he's stashed Gina's Valentine's present in his locker. It's a classy-looking electric knife sharpener he spotted in the hardware store. Climbing the stairs to her downtown apartment, he thinks how surprised she'll be at this unexpected visit. But he's startled when a young guy with long hair opens the door.

"Yeah?" says the guy. He's wearing jeans and a black T-shirt that reads:

DAVE'S AUTO BODY
YOU BEND 'EM.
WE MEND 'EM.

"Who is it?" comes Gina's voice from the next room. Then she comes into view, wearing a bathrobe and rubbing her thick wet hair with a towel.

Richard feels stunned, like someone has just knocked the wind out of him.

"Oh!" cries Gina. "Hi, Richard!" She looks like she's thinking fast. "This is, ah—Dave. Dave, meet Richard."

A thick hand, with grime under the nails, grips Richard's briefly. He decides that the guy must begin each day lifting engine blocks.

"Uh—" says Richard. In Gina's soft eyes he's seen a look of something like anguished embarrassment. His gaze drops to the floor. Dave's feet are bare. Richard imagines he sees muscles rippling in the guy's toes.

"Hey, is that for me?" Gina has spotted the gift-wrapped box.

"Oh—" he says, and hands it over. "It's for you." He has finally managed to put a whole sentence together. He mumbles an apology and plunges down the stairs. He's vaguely conscious of a frenzied drive to the Health Spa, of frigid wind in the parking lot, and cold tile beneath his feet as he hangs up his clothes. In the bright, dry heat of the sauna he comes to. Sweat drips off his nose onto the towel in his lap. How could Gina have betrayed him so cruelly? Now, more than ever, he yearns to press her in his arms. "Oh, God," he sobs, having discovered the brutal power of love.

Since the day that Garth's girlfriend, Una, dropped by to use his washing machine, she hasn't been back to the loft.

But late on Valentine's Day, she comes up his stairs, lugging a suitcase.

"Hi. I'm back!" she calls out.

Garth is in a far corner, rummaging in a carton for his old binoculars. He's spent the last week sitting in the shopping mall, waiting for Lindsay to show up. Now that he's found her, even discovered where she lives, the next step will be to watch at a distance, just for a glimpse of her again.

"Well?" says Una. "Aren't you glad to see me?"

The loft is dark—except a row of spotlights glare down from the high ceiling. They throw circles of light on the bare plank floor. Una approaches through these sudden alternations of brightness and dark shadow, and she hurries the last few steps to throw her arms about his neck. She smells the same—always that hint of turpentine in her hair. Her haunches and pelvis press into his groin. It's like sliding into the familiar seat of his old car.

"Mmm," she says. "You feel the same."

It's true—this cluster of old sensations that the body remembers. Bone and tendon shift into place. Una's cheek settles into the hollow of his shoulder. His palms find their old fit at the small of her back.

"Wait a minute," says Garth, easing out of their embrace. "There's something I have to tell you before there's a chance to fib about it." He takes a breath. "There's another woman in my life."

"No kidding. Who is she?"

A worried look comes into Garth's face. He's forced to admit that he doesn't know Lindsay's name. "I don't know who she is," he says.

"What do you mean, you 'don't know who she is'?"

Garth shrugs. "That's just it. I don't know." He makes an impatient gesture. "I've only seen her two or three times."

"You mean, you've fucked her two or three times?"

"Of course not," he says. "I said *seen*. You know, looky-looky?" He points at his eyeballs.

Una frowns skeptically at him.

"Hey," says Garth, offering more evidence. "We talked on the phone once."

"Oh, yeah? What'd you talk about?"

"Nothing," says Garth, recalling his silent conversation with Lindsay. "We hardly said a word."

"Great," nods Una. "A blank in bed and a terrific conversationalist. She doesn't sound like much of a threat."

Garth kicks at the floor with his boot. "It's occurred to me that this whole thing amounts to an irrational obsession. I might be going nuts."

"Listen," she says. "You were already nuts when I met you."

"I was?"

"How come you had a boner?"

"With her?"

"No. A minute ago. We were hugging. And you got a boner."

"Reflex action." Garth brushes her suggestion away. "Doesn't mean a thing."

"Come on." Una runs her nails through his beard and curls one finger into the whorl of his ear. "You're glad to see me, aren't you?"

He shuts his eyes to avoid facing it. He grimaces in thought, then nods three times—quick. This obsession with tracking down a suburban stranger—hasn't it merely been a way for him to deny the ache of Una's absence?

She's put her arms around his neck again. He feels her tongue lolling behind his ear. "I love you," she whispers.

Garth still has his eyes closed. "I'm a little uncertain lately—about love in general. This is a strange phase. I don't even know about art anymore."

"Maybe it's your chart. Your progressed ascendant. A new sign."

He opens his eyes. It's that same old astrological crap. Isn't that why she walked out on him? "How come you're back?" he asks.

"Oh, once Jupiter turned retrograde it was all over. Just

add one Italian chick with big tits and you'll get the picture. You should have called me. I'd have come back sooner."

"How the hell could I call you?" says Garth and walks away. "I don't know who that guy is."

"Dave? He runs the auto body shop—north of here on route seventeen."

"You mean, all this time you were shacked up only four miles away?"

"I stopped by a couple of times to see you."

"Yeah. To do your laundry with some scumbag rising."

"Sagittarius rising."

"Whatever."

Una folds her arms and watches Garth pace. "You're limping."

"I had an operation."

"No kidding?"

"It's a long story."

"Tell me. I'm not going anywhere."

"I noticed you brought your suitcase," he says.

"I'll sleep on the couch."

"Fine."

"You look sort of horny to me."

"What do you think?"

"Oh, Garth. I wouldn't do *that* again." Una is talking about hygiene. The last time she moved out she brought home a case of the clap.

"Maybe you should see a doctor. A complete physical exam. I'm thinking of your overall health. How's your hip?"

"Fine. Venus is transiting my sixth house. My health is great."

"Una," says Garth. "Transits of Venus are no substitute for the American Medical Association and the invention of penicillin."

"Since when are you so big on doctors?"

"I'm not."

"You had an operation."

"That's different."

"Come on, Garth. Astrology is the only thing I'm good at."

"You could be good at a lot of things."

Una is silent for a moment. This is the old argument. Next, she knows, they'll begin accusing each other of squandering their talent—their lives. Each one has blamed the other for the waste. It can get pretty dirty. "You know what the word is," she finally says, "about President Reagan?"

"What about Reagan?"

"He's going to be shot."

"Don't joke about stuff like that."

"No, there's a curse on the White House. A Saturn-Jupiter conjunction."

Garth sighs. For a moment he thought Una had changed the subject.

"It occurred at New Year's," she's saying. "And it's coming up again in March. Every time those two planets come together, the president dies in office. But all the other conjunctions were in Capricorn, an earth sign." Una's eyes have taken on the fixed expression that says she's just veered deep into the spell of her art. On her fingers she counts off the seven doomed presidents. "Harrison, Lincoln, Garfield, McKinley, Harding, Roosevelt, Kennedy. This time Jupiter and Saturn are in an air sign, Libra. I get this picture of lungs. Air, right? Maybe Reagan will catch pneumonia." Una looks up to see if Garth is listening.

He's yawning. "Tell me tomorrow. Let's go to bed."

"Together?"

Garth feels something stir within him. A sheepish smile creases his face.

"Oh, baby!" says Una in her Big Bopper voice. "You *know* what I like!"

10

Lindsay knows that something is wrong with her husband. He works late, mopes about, doesn't sleep well, and pours himself stiff drinks after supper. The women's magazines are full of articles like "The Stress of Achievement" and "Is Your Husband the Heart-Attack Type?" But late in February she stumbles onto the real problem: *Richard is in love.* She blunders her way into this discovery the weekend that she's ill. Having called in sick to Pastor Ekdahl, Lindsay spends the weekend in bed.

Alex carries trays up the stairs. Lindsay sips chicken noodle soup, weak tea, and ginger ale. She nibbles toast, saltines, a graham cracker. Mostly she lies on her back and stares at the faint cracks in the ceiling. Looking at the wallpaper—a tight colonial print—makes her dizzy. Putting anything in her stomach, she decides, is a mistake. She draws up her knees when the cramps begin— gurgling constrictions that knot up, then uncoil and slither a few inches across the top of her abdomen. When she can't stand it anymore, she staggers into the bathroom and sits, humiliated, trying not to faint. After flushing the toilet, she squirts blue bowl cleaner into the toilet.

When Richard looks in the door, she's running the brush around the rim. "Are you okay?" he asks.

"Go away," she says. Back in bed, she burrows under the covers.

Richard sits on the edge of the bed. "Feel better now?"

"No," she says. She'll get through this—or get it through her—without any help. "I think I'd better sleep now." This is a way of telling him to leave her alone. "Wait," she says, as he's getting up. "What day is today?"

"Sunday." He pushes a button on his watch. "The twenty-second."

"Oh. Washington's Birthday."

"No, Linz. That was last Monday." He gives her a smile, then goes out.

"Dumb," she says to the door. What has the government done, moving these holidays around? February 22 was also her father's birthday. Her poor dead daddy.

Last year wasn't she also sick in February? She ought to keep a journal. Then, looking back, events would fall into patterns. You could tell if you were making progress, could touch the long-range pulse of your own life. But Lindsay already knows the dreary up-and-down beat of her days: "Up," she decides, is when you go to the supermarket with a fanned-out assortment of discount coupons, and you find all the products actually in stock on the shelves. "Down" means you stop by the drugstore to pick up Kodacolor prints, and two or three turn out over-exposed. If such minute changes in pressure can lift or dash your spirits, then someone—to begin with—must have filled out your days with pretty airy stuff.

Part of Lindsay's problem consists of not having any real friends in Heathersford. The couples who come over for dinner arrive like two-person career teams. They barge in all charged up for competitive talk and witty put-downs. The other night, Linda Harrison and Bernice Karasian (the boss's wife) took a hard line discussing Julia Child and Craig Claiborne. They exchanged odd looks when Lindsay declared that she was working on steaming the perfect hot dog bun.

Lindsay lies in bed and stares at the cracks in the ceiling. Maybe her problem is being too timid. In Uncle Alfred's stories, her ancestors always took passionate risks and made grand gestures. You'd think these things would run in her blood. Her own father, during World War II, worked for Army Intelligence. And on her mother's side, Wilbur Aldington, who owned a drugstore, took a famous risk. When the local physician brought home the town's first automobile, Wilbur became so indignant that he challenged the vehicle to a race. Over four miles of Ohio dirt roads, he won —riding a bicycle.

She turns over in bed and shifts her fevered cheek to a cool place on the pillow. She looks pathetic, huddled under the quilt. The eye of her other self has drifted ceilingward to look down upon her. It's the sign of another spell coming on. How weird, she thinks. Then it gets bad; the spell erupts like a wave of nausea. "Oh no," she groans. *Not this.* She shuts her eyes and in the blackness sees: *her father's old De Soto snaking up a mountain road, as the wind drives the rain in sheets. Over a rise, he guns it down the next slope, jamming the brakes too late when the headlights beam out insanely into mere space. A bridge has washed out in the storm. During that long fall, does he have time to calculate whether the impact will shred his body through jagged windshield glass, or mangle it into the upholstered ceiling? But instead he's heaving and thrashing out a window into the current—even stumbling through brush and woods to a farmhouse and dry clothing.*

Lindsay opens her eyes in terror. She's dreamed snatches of this scene since childhood. But she's never dared to wish it consciously, or imagine it in such detail. It's the old fantasy: her poor daddy has survived. And there's some good reason why he never came home again. She's never dared to imagine that part either. It was forbidden, she knew, to even ask.

"Your father ran off and was punished." Her mother put it that bluntly.

"But why did he leave? And where was he going?" little Lindsay inquired.

"Hush," said her mother.

But surely, she now decides, her father had a destination. One urgent enough, at that washed-out bridge, to vault him across an abyss. Lindsay has a vision of him on the road again at dawn, hitchhiking under the fast clouds of clearing skies, heading east.

If, instead of reaching for her notebook on the night stand, Lindsay hitched herself up on one elbow and looked out the window, she'd see the top of Garth's Plymouth parked down the block. A plume of exhaust steams from the tailpipe. He's got to keep the heater running. It's not a very inconspicuous way to keep a house under surveillance. And now he has to go to the bathroom. Leg stiffly tapping the gas, he pulls away from the curb.

Downtown, Garth parks his car in the big garage next to Sylvia's Red & White Taxi Corporation (which is a blue Chevy) and goes up the back stairs behind Woolworth's. One flight up at the pool hall, there's no sign of Harold, who's in charge of Garth's physical therapy. Harold Matlow used to be a trainer with the New York Jets. He's the one who removed the stitches left from Garth's knee surgery. Under Harold's care, Garth is building strength back into the joint.

Up another flight, Garth finds Wally and Helen sitting at the kitchen table, playing cards. After Wally calculated how much time the two of them spend sitting around in each room, he moved upholstered armchairs into the kitchen. Visitors shown into the living room—usually Mormons or Jehovah's Witnesses—have to sit on straight ladder-back chairs that really torture the butt.

"Hi," says Garth. "Can I use your bathroom?"

"Sure," says Wally, easing a card down on the table.

Wally's dog, Uncle Fred, comes over and sniffs Garth's leg. Her tail wags when she recognizes him. Mostly blind and deaf, she noses her way around the apartment by touch, smell, and vibration.

Helen taps her foot and says, "Come over here, Uncle

Fred." The dog obediently goes back to her place under the table.

"What's the game?" asks Garth. It occurs to him that most people don't play cards at eleven o'clock on Sunday morning.

"War," says Helen, peeling off a card from the deck in her hand.

"War?" says Garth. "I played that when I was a kid."

"You ought to try it again," says Wally, setting down the nine of diamonds.

Garth wants to ask Wally for advice about the unsuccessful stakeout of Lindsay's house. Ever since Garth confessed this yearning curiosity about a suburban housewife, Wally has taken a theoretical interest in the case. For example, when Garth could barely walk after his operation, Wally volunteered to track Lindsay down. He made cryptic phone calls to the hospital and drove out to the mall to question custodians and the security staff. He established that a small woman had been seen in both locations. One person compared her to Audrey Hepburn, another said she looked "kind of mousy—forgettable." No one knew who she was. Wally did manage, however, to trace Mr. Manard. The shopping mall had filed a report about his collapse with their insurance company. One day Wally drove out to the senior citizen high-rise and talked with the old guy in his cluttered apartment. They hit it off right away. Wally came back all excited.

"You mean you found her?" Garth had said.

"Naw. Maynard doesn't know who she was. But you ought to see this guy's collection. And his retrieval system. Get this: he files things by shape. I can't tell if it's primitive or incredibly sophisticated. I think he's on to something. For example, he files his insurance policy under 'rounded things,' because, he says, 'It's sad.' Think about that one, huh?"

Garth has come in to watch the card game. He wants to get his friend's attention so they can talk confidentially in the next room. Wally and Helen don't seem to be making much progress at War, which they play at a snail's pace.

"As I recall," Garth says, "you're supposed to play this game faster. We used to really slam the cards down on the table."

Helen's bright eyes drift up and settle on Garth's face. Then her attention returns to the card she's turning over. She lifts it through the air in slow motion, letting it settle silently on the table. It's the Jack of Clubs. "See how lost he looks," remarks Helen wistfully. "He faces to the left, like the spades. But in all the court, only the Jack of Clubs is clean-shaven."

Garth leans over for a look. "I never noticed," he says, rubbing his beard and feeling the eyes of the older couple fixed upon him. Every now and then, Garth has the sense that these two are trying to teach him something.

"How's your lady friend?" asks Helen.

Garth is staring at the Jack of Clubs. "Una?" he says.

"No. That housewife you're after."

Garth growls and glares at Wally. "You told," he accuses him.

"She asked," replies Wally.

"But this is touchy business. She's got a kid, a husband. I don't want this to get around."

"What are you so worried about?" asks Wally.

"I'm worried about me. That's what. I don't want to be accused of interfering in someone's private life."

Wally shrugs. "The government does it all the time."

"Well, they shouldn't. Listen, she's scared now. At the mall, when she spotted me? You should've seen her duck out of sight."

"I thought she walked all over the place, trying to find you."

"That came later. And you know what? It made me *very* uncomfortable. Like something criminal was going on."

"Well, cut it out if it makes you feel so bad."

"I can't. But I want to sleep." Garth yawns for emphasis. "Thinking about her, I can't sleep."

"You do look tired," Helen says. "But I think it's marvelous. Have you found out her name yet?"

Garth shakes his head. "You think knowing her name might help me sleep?"

"Why don't you look in her mailbox?" suggests Helen.

Garth looks shocked at the idea. "You mean—go right up to the front door?" He's scared even to look over the dashboard at Lindsay's house. The idea of approaching on foot is out of the question.

"The mailbox," says Helen. "That's how you find out her name."

"Oh, no." Garth is backed against a counter. "That's against the law."

"All's fair," smiles Helen, "in love and war." She glances at Wally. He's turning over another card. "Oh, goody," she says, seeing another Jack appear. "Now we have to do it face down, right?"

"Where are you going?" Una looks up from where she's sitting on the floor, working thinner into a stiff brush with her long, nimble fingers.

Garth has come back to the loft for his long underwear and a second sweater. He's going to try the stakeout without running the car's heater. "Oh"—he throws out a random gesture—"I'm going out."

"You just came in."

He nods, mulling this over. "Right," he says finally.

"I know where you're going."

He grimaces. He's never been dishonest with Una before.

"What does she look like? This woman you're after."

He clenches his fists. "Listen," he says. "I'm trying to cultivate a private little obsession here. And now suddenly everybody is horning in on it. Well, I'm sick of it!" He stamps his foot. *"Uff da,"* he grunts, and clutches his knee in pain.

"It serves you right," says Una. "Hey, pick up a loaf of bread on the way home, will you?"

Garth spends the rest of Sunday afternoon on the street where she lives. Scrunched down in the front seat, he tries to calm his nervous excitement. Every now and then he edges up with his binoculars to scan the windows, check out the location of the mailbox, and—for variety—look at a faded yellow ribbon hanging from the birch tree. After an hour, her kid comes out all bundled up. He tramps around in the snow, then goes back inside. He looks like a nice kid. Thinking this, Garth shivers—a childless man out in the cold.

Two or three times a week since Valentine's Day, he's waited here—without much luck—to catch a brief glimpse of her. Today he misses the weekday routine and bustle on this street: the yellow school bus stopping at the corner, the men brushing snow off their cars before taking off; the working wives who later ease their second cars down the sloping driveways. Garth misses the mailman and the guy from Sears; he misses the diaper service, and lanky Mr. Electrolux.

Two hours pass before he examines the pickup truck ahead of him with any care. It was parked at the curb when he arrived. Through his binoculars he inspects the pin-striping on the tailgate—a good job, done by hand. Angled into the truck bed rests the chrome bumper of some dismantled vehicle. Through the cab's rear window, he examines the fuzzy dice dangling from the rearview mirror. And in the mirror— "Jesus," mutters Garth. It's a human ear. Strands of long hair are tucked behind it. Now it moves. It's not a body, then, but someone asleep, hunched down in the front seat.

As Garth watches, the back of someone's head appears, and stiff fingers flex toward the windshield. The truck's engine starts abruptly. When the cloud of exhaust clears, the driver is pulling away. But he's rolled down the window and leans out to glare back in the direction of Lindsay's house.

Wha? thinks Garth. It's getting dark. The light in an upstairs bedroom goes on briefly, then out again. The family keeps to the back of the house, or else hangs out in some room that doesn't face the street. Garth doesn't recall that romance involved all this tedious sitting around. Time to head home, he decides, turning the key in the ignition. A slow wheezing groan comes from the starter motor: "Come on," he coaxes, rocking forward against the wheel to give the old girl the idea. He can't walk home in this cold. Finally the big engine catches, and Garth chugs back downtown.

Dave has sat in his pickup truck outside Richard's house once before—the night he tailed him home from Gina's apartment. All he wants to do is have a little talk. But this waiting makes him pissed off. And when Dave gets angry he also gets sleepy. Actually Dave is a reasonable fellow. At his body shop, for example, he's fair and meticulous about his work. Nevertheless, he's aware that something in his manner intimidates people. It's a useful trait to have for anyone running a small business. At bars, however, Dave has to be cautious. Occasionally a drunk, responding to some aggressive cue, will try to pick a fight with him.

Having seen Richard, Dave recognizes the type. These guys bring their wives' cars in with crumpled rear fenders and make a big deal about getting a written estimate. Then they drive off looking shrewd. Eventually they come back acting like old pals. They've found out that their dealer wants to rip them off for a few hundred dollars. So they stand around trying to make knowledgeable remarks—like, "Say, isn't that a ball-peen hammer?" If you're patient and a little forceful with them, these guys are not hard to handle. But Dave isn't sure what's going on between Richard and Gina. That's why they should have a talk. Just to straighten out the territory.

Gina claims it's office politics. "How do you think you get raises and stuff?" she asked the other night. They were in her bed watching the news, waiting for Johnny Carson to come on. "If men in the office take you out to lunch, it means they notice you. Like you're a good worker or something."

Dave hitched a pillow up behind his naked back. "Bullshit," he replied. "They're trying to get laid."

"Maybe," conceded Gina. "But you keep that—you know?—sort of far off."

He reached under the sheets, where he gave his testicles a vigorous scratching. "What is he, married?

"Yeah."

"You got to watch out for those married guys. Maybe I'd better have a talk with him."

"Oh, please don't. Please?"

"I don't know," sighed Dave. "Tell him not to come over here anymore."

"Hush," said Gina, fastening her eyes on the TV.

"And now," Ed McMahon was exclaiming, "he-e-ere's Johnny!"

Lindsay is awake in the dark. Her fever has broken, and she wants to take a shower. She rolls over in bed and turns on the lamp. It's not quite ten o'clock. She decides to call her mother in North Carolina and lifts the receiver off the phone. Richard's voice is on the line. He's downstairs, probably straightening out whatever tangle has sent him into a glum depression all week. Now a woman's voice is talking. Lindsay looks at the receiver that she's holding at arm's length. In Boston, one of the new vice presidents in Richard's company is a woman. Lindsay's arm trembles. It's from the fever, she tells herself, as she places the receiver on the pillow beside her ear. Her fingers don't actually touch the device, so it's not really eavesdropping.

"—you can understand that, can't you?" the woman is saying.

"In a general way, yes," answers Richard.

"I mean, from their point of view, if I didn't have a boyfriend to talk about, who knows what they'd think."

"You mean, you girls talk about this sort of thing?"

"Richard, what do you think coffee breaks are for?"

"Well, what do you tell them? For example, about Dave."

"Oh, I hint at things. I have a pretty good imagination. You know what they call him now?" She laughs into the phone. "The Hunk. Isn't that great?"

Richard is silent for a moment. "None of this sounds right to me," he says. "I don't know if you're doing the right thing."

"Aw, Richard."

"I'd better hang up now. Tomorrow, then?"

"Sure. 'Bye."

Lindsay hears the connection break. When she hears Richard clumping up the stairs, she hangs up the phone.

"You awake?" he asks.

Lindsay feels very much awake. Her eyes dart across the ceiling. A terrible clarity is coming on. "Who is she?" she demands flatly.

"Who?"

She sits up in bed and glares at him. "Goddammit! I'm not a complete idiot, you asshole!"

Richard is staring, not at her but at the extension phone next to the bed. He's thought about this moment. But now that it's arrived, he refuses to face it. "You were listening!" he says accusingly. Oh God, he pleads, this isn't happening.

"Don't pull that self-righteous tone on me," she says.

"Aw, Linz. Don't get all upset."

"Ha. So now I'm upset? Just tell me, okay? Who is she?"

"I can explain."

"Oh, sure. And who's this boyfriend of hers? This Dave?"

Richard unbuttons his shirt, calculating how much Lindsay has heard. "I'll make it simple."

"Oh, simple—so I can follow it? You asshole."

"Would you shut up and listen?"

Lindsay looks at his stern face. "I'm listening." It comes out sounding like an apology.

"Look," he says, counting now on a story falling into place as he tells it. "There's this young woman at the office. Gina Baghetti. She does the payroll for us. Runs the computer." He throws his shirt in the closet. "She turns out a lot of figures that are important to my work. I was talking to her."

"That was no business conversation!" declares Lindsay. Some advantage she had a moment ago is slipping away.

"Actually it was."

"You're a jerk."

"Let me explain, will you? See, lately Gina hasn't been very sharp. Distracted, you know? Making little mistakes." Richard realizes that he's really describing himself over the past month. "So I finally asked her what the problem was. And she starts crying. Right in my office." Partly, this is true. Gina did burst into tears last Monday when Richard accused her of lying to him. She begged him to believe that Dave was "just a friend." When she began sobbing, he couldn't stand it. He took her in his arms and kissed her wet face all over until his cheeks were smudged with mascara.

"Gina has this problem with men," Richard is saying. He plunges ahead. "Some kind of sexual problem. I don't know if it's a recent thing or not."

"This sounds like bullshit," remarks Lindsay.

"No, listen. See, her boyfriend, Dave, is not very understanding. He's giving her a hard time." Actually it is Richard, outraged at Dave's regular visits to Gina's apartment, who is giving her a hard time. But Gina claims that seeing Dave once in a while is the perfect cover for their own covert meetings. Now Richard feels a portion of his jealousy dissolve as he realizes that Gina may be right. On the phone, Lindsay evidently heard Gina refer to a boyfriend.

"So now there's pressure at the office. From the other

girls. And Gina has begun telling them fibs. She's ashamed, don't you see? About this problem."

Lindsay clasps the blanket about her knees. "You're telling me she's frigid?"

Richard sighs, knowing how preposterous his story has become. A boyfriend *plus* frigid. "I guess that's the word," he says, unbuckling his belt.

"She's the dark-haired one, isn't she?" At Christmas, Lindsay briefly dropped in at the office party. "The stacked one? Kind of a floozy?"

"Yeah. That's Gina."

"So where do you fit into all this?" The rage she felt a moment ago is rising again. Something's fishy. "Oh, I get it. You're the tender, understanding type who's going to help a poor girl. Help her cuddle up next to your cock. What a shit you are."

"Aw, Linz." Richard has a pitiful look on his face.

"How long has this therapy been going on?"

"There's nothing going on." He wonders how so much truth could mingle with these lies. Therapy, for example. Gina is the one who's been helping Richard with his intimate problem. She has this trick of squeezing the tip of his penis, tight with her fingers, when he says he's going to come. "I read it in a book," she said. "Are you sure it doesn't hurt?" In her hands over the past month, he's made some progress. But then there's Dave. Richard imagines that auto mechanics can bang away at it for hours without letting go.

Lindsay has lain back on the pillow again, wondering if a woman who gives off such shrill erotic signals could be frigid.

Richard has put on his robe. He's not coming to bed.

"How come you're involved in all this?"

He looks at her. "If something interferes with work at the office, then it's my business."

"Since when are you an authority on women's problems?"

He shakes his head—in dismay, apparently at Lindsay's

obtuseness. "I'm not giving her advice. But I think it did help to get it off her chest. Now she knows that someone understands. I'm doing what I can to ease up on her work load." Richard stands there. "That's the whole story," he says.

"Why don't you tell her to seek professional help?"

"Good," he nods. "That's a good idea."

Lindsay smiles gruesomely. "Maybe you should start reading Ann Landers."

"Oh?" He seems to give this suggestion some thought as he walks to the door. "I'm going to watch the news. Want to come down?"

Lindsay waves him away. She feels weak again. Alone, she tries to decide if she's just suffered a victory or a defeat. The clock says it's too late to call her mother. She turns off the light and lies there in the dark. Eventually Richard comes upstairs and gets into bed. She feigns sleep. Back to back, they both lie there in silence. Time passes. They wait for their dreams to sweep them under.

11

MARCH 9—THREE WEEKS before John W. Hinckley, Jr., will attempt to assassinate President Ronald Reagan—is a gray Monday. It's also Lindsay's birthday. As she leans out the front door to take in the afternoon mail, a car sits at the curb down the street. But she pays no attention to it.

In the living room, she sorts through the mail addressed to her. The long envelopes contain cute contemporary cards from Natalie (her old college roommate, now in law school, who has moved in with a waste-management consultant), and from Debbie, whose greeting pictures the soles of feet sticking up at the edge of a bed: "If you're feeling *laid up* on your birthday"—inside, another pair of feet, pointing down, have joined the first pair—"hope you get *knocked up*, too!" There's also a small card with a Japanese print from her uncle. He threatens to fly east sometime in the spring or summer for a visit.

The large square envelope is from her mother. The two of them don't really keep in touch. Harriet Wyatt, now sixty, still plays golf. Her father was a musician who led a small string orchestra that played at the Vanderbilt estate in North Carolina. After the crash in 1929, he moved his family north to Toledo, where he took a job as a conductor on a trolley line. Harriet grew up thinking she was a disinherited southern lady. Now, among other hobbies, she paints her own birthday cards. This year's greeting bears an original watercolor: a floral painted in lurid hues of turquoise, violet, and chartreuse. Inside is a verse:

Here's wishing you another year
Of joyous nights and days,
And blessings from the Lord above
In—oh!—so many ways!

Happy Birthday!—HAW

The final initials stand for Harriet Aldington Wyatt, and they signify that she is the author of the poem. Uncle Alfred claims that "HAW" unwittingly stands for any sane person's response to his sister-in-law's poetry.

Beside the cards, junk mail, and bills, there's a short envelope addressed in a hand she doesn't recognize—though it could be her mother's scrawl after she's put away a pitcher of martinis. Inside is an old snapshot. Lindsay stares at it a long time. In black and white, it pictures herself at about the age of nine. Wearing a print sundress, she stands barefoot in a shallow stream bed, looking up brightly at the camera, which is focused from higher ground. Behind her, wet rocks blur into dappled shade. The back of the photo is blank. She looks again at the envelope. The postmark is smudged off the top edge. It's evidently an afterthought of her mother's. But what a wonderful birthday present.

She goes to the drawer where she keeps old photos and letters in a thick black album, one of the few heirlooms that her family has passed on. The pages of the big book fall open at a picture of her father. There's little Lindsay, wearing pedal-pushers and sitting next to a skinny boy on a dock. It was the summer they rented a cabin at a lake. Her father kneels behind them, looking handsome and tan and flashing his smile at the camera. There's no sign of depression in his face. It couldn't have been suicide.

She hears Alex come in the front door and kick his boots into the closet. He pads into the living room. "Hi, Mom," he says, then stops and stares at what she's holding.

"Have you ever seen this?" she asks.

"That's the Black Book," he says.

"It's an *album*." She lets the book fall open in a creak of old leather.

"Hey, neat," he says, seeing how the photos have been slid in from the edge to appear in cut-out windows.

"Look. Here's your mother when she was a little girl. And this is my father. We were at a lake."

Alex's hand reaches out. "Can I touch it?"

"Sure."

"It's hot," he says, and draws his fingers away.

She looks at him. "I bet the other kids think you're weird."

"This is the Black Book," he whispers. "Turn the page."

The next photo pictures a big box wagon drawn by two horses. A man leans against one of the big spoked wheels. Alex leans close to examine the scene. Lettered on the wagon are the words:

—WILSON WYATT—
NEW PROCESS DAGUERREOTYPY

Lindsay explains that one of her relatives was a photographer. "He needed this big wagon to carry his cameras."

Alex is still nosed-in close to the photo. "Look at his eyes," he whispers.

"What?" She watches her son cautiously draw back from the page.

Something queasy turns in her stomach. She tells herself it's just lingering nausea from her recent illness. But what's this heat—or chill—she feels? A fluttering glow comes off the page. Minute eyes from the past lock onto hers. And then the edges of her living room begin to white out. Everything disappears.

Lindsay finds herself holding the heavy photo album in her hands. Alex is reaching across to turn the page. "And who's this person?" he asks.

She looks at her son. "Did something just happen?" she asks.

"I don't know," he shrugs.

She snaps the book shut. "We'll look at this another day."

"Where do you keep it?"

"In here." Lindsay pulls out the drawer in the coffee table. The drawer is the same place she's hidden the gray glove that Alex found. It lies palm-up, empty fingers slightly curled.

Alex watches her stare at it. Her pale face tells him that his mother is not well. What can he say that will help?

"Hey. There's the glove I found outside in the snow."

"No." She shakes her head. "Upstairs. You found it outside your room."

"Um," says Alex, about to tell a fib. "I think I found it outside."

"Alex!" she exclaims, glaring at the boy. "We had to call the police about that business!"

"The police?" His eyes grow wide at the news.

Lindsay feels a heaviness lifted from her breast. She's drawn to the big living room window, where she's kept the drapes shut for a month. She yanks light into the room. Thank God, nobody's watching her. Looking back at her son, she says, "Come here, you rascal!"

Gathered into her arms, Alex feels the weight of what he's done settle like a heavy cloak upon his shoulders. Through frosted panes of glass, he can make out, down the block, a plume of white exhaust from Garth's car. The vapor drifts up and across the branches of a distant black tree.

The next day, Lindsay pulls the front drapes shut again. Through the rest of March, past Hinckley's attempt to kill Ronald Reagan, she'll fail to push away the gnawing suspicion that someone is out there, watching her. And she won't crack the pages of the black album—whose windows open inward and back on time—until April. The black volume contains, among other things, her wedding pictures. Lindsay cringes when faced with her own photo image. Her face often bears the anxious look of someone laughing off an assault.

The single picture she's saved of her father suggests that a reservoir of easy confidence lies untapped, somewhere in the family blood. Listening to Uncle Alfred's stories about her Wyatt relatives, she's felt clues thrown out about the missing half of her origins. Alfred's words shoot jolts of recognition through her, as if he's telling the story of her secret self. Richard can't stand these long-winded narrations. "Why doesn't he get to to the point?" he complains.

Since Lindsay intercepted the phone conversation between her husband and his girlfriend, Richard has been paying for his erotic indiscretions. He and Gina have agreed, in her words, to "play it cool for a while." This means that he spends fewer evenings either "working late at the office" or claiming to work out at the Health Spa. Instead he hangs around the house in a secret panic over what Gina might be up to with Auto-Body Dave. Slouched in front of the TV, Richard sips bourbon on the rocks until his eyes won't focus. Things appear washed out and colorless. Lindsay grows irritated when he adjusts the picture on the TV. He makes the flesh tones bright orange. Every night he wakes up at 3 A.M. Weekends are the worst—especially Saturday nights. Claiming to go out for cigarettes, he races all the way downtown to drive past her apartment, to note which of her windows are lighted. His car radio is tuned to a country-western station that plays songs of love and betrayal. Now he understands all the lyrics. They speak, with twangy poignancy, to the grimy ache and too-solid pulse of his melting heart.

In the Xerox room, he and Gina manage to have quick, whispered conversations. She looks at him with doe-eyed innocence and confesses how terribly she misses him. "I'm leading the life of a nun," she declares. Richard wants to believe this. But observing her joking around with the other women in the office, or flirting with salesmen passing through, he watches for minute lapses of enthusiasm that might betray an inner agony to match his own. "Oh, I think about you all the time," she assures him in that breathy murmur of hers. At such moments he strains against the impulse to crush her in his arms, to possess her by force of will.

Gina has given him a color photograph of herself taken last summer. Lounging beside a pool at some resort, she looks very tan, and her bikini reveals as much flesh as a commercial photo lab will legally develop. He's hidden the photo in the medicine cabinet behind a row of bottles. Mornings, he takes out her image and fastens it to the mirror while shaving. Next to her dark limbs, his own lathered face looks clownish and absurd.

Late in March, he can't stand it anymore. On a Saturday evening, he drives downtown and marches up the stairs to her place prepared to face the truth. He'll burst in the door —break it down if necessary—to catch them in the act: Gina and Dave, naked on the couch, nude in the bathroom, or hurriedly putting on the clothes they've flung on the kitchen floor. But when Gina answers his knock, she's alone, wearing jeans and a T-shirt, munching on a red apple. "You're very naughty to come here," she scolds him, then lets him into the apartment. They sit on the couch and kiss like they used to. Her breasts are massive in his hands. He buries his face between the words "Ft. Lauderdale '79" emblazoned on her bosom. He's out of control. One slow press of her hand at his zippered crotch is all it takes. He lets out a long, spent moan. Eyes shut tight, he feels a stale taste in his mouth. This isn't how he's imagined their reunion. Gina gets up and looks around for where she set down her apple. Her apartment is a mess. The white shag rug looks gray. An ironing board has been set up to sort bills on. The room is strewn with clutter: newspapers, crumpled panty hose, tissues, cups and saucers.

Richard looks down at the wet stain on the thigh of his polyester slacks. It looks like he's spit on himself. He stands up and says, "I've got to go."

Gina comes over, swallowing the bite she's chewing, and puts her arms around his neck. "I think you should stay," she says, wetting her lips. There's a flake of apple skin wedged between her front teeth. "I mean, we've only just started." She presses herself against him, and he works his mouth on her neck. It tastes of sweat. Giving her a quick kiss on the mouth, he walks to the door. "I'll see you," he says, smiling as he leaves.

Outside, things look exposed. Headlights glare on jagged mounds of ice. Across the street, they've put a new front on the tavern—barnboards weathered to silver gray. A streetlight angles the edges of these planks into hard vertical lines. His eyes focus on the sharp clarity of this pattern. He gets in his car, ignoring the pickup truck that pulls in at the curb behind him. Richard drives off, marveling at his new visual powers, the cutting precision of his eyes.

Just past noon on Monday morning (about the time Hinckley, in his Washington hotel room, writes a note to Jodie Foster), Pastor Ekdahl drops over unannounced to Lindsay's house. With an inordinate amount of hand-fluttering regrets, he agrees to stay for tuna fish salad on toast. "Mix in a little mustard and sweet relish with the mayonnaise," he suggests from his chair at the kitchen table.

"Anything you say," says Lindsay, slamming two slices of Pepperidge Farm into the toaster. She feels a little unwashed. Richard took her out last night to a new Chinese restaurant. Since answering the door, she's been trying to catch a glimpse of herself in something chrome to see if last night's makeup is still clinging to the right places on her face. Actually, there's not much reason to look terrific for Pastor Ekdahl, who is a balding, nearsighted man in his forties with slightly bucked teeth.

The pastor isn't familiar with the subtleties of women's makeup. To his eyes, Lindsay's leftover blusher looks like classic high cheekbones. Her violet eye shadow strikes him as part of the haunting mystery of her gaze. Never has a woman's face looked so radiant when he's made a pastoral call. Even her gliding movements about the kitchen from countertop to refrigerator charm him with their delicate authority, their womanly vibrancy. Lately he's been moving fast himself, naming two new head ushers, leading an extra Bible study class for Lent, and making extra trips to the TV station—the police have stopped him twice for speeding.

Lindsay is squatting down to peer into a lower shelf of the refrigerator. The posture tugs her sweater up to reveal six inches of naked back and the waistband of her underwear. Lilac panties, thinks the pastor. His own wife, Jean, sticks pretty much to white.

"So you'll have to be at the TV station before six A.M.?" asks Lindsay.

"Thank God, no." The expression is mildly profane. But Ekdahl finds himself in a devil-may-care, rakish mood. After his recent tour of the TV studio, he's been picturing himself as a member of a media team, a group of confident technicians united by the lingo of their craft. "We'll V.T. the show in the afternoon," he says. "Then after the fellows in the cutting room have done their thing—as it were— we'll punch it up and run it. At six A.M."

Lindsay's not really listening. She stands up. "Sorry. I can't see that bottle of Chablis."

"Oh"—he flutters his hands—"it was just a thought. Wine with lunch. Now and then one has to—take a risk. Don't you think?"

"I guess so," sighs Lindsay as she sits down. "Oops, sorry." Her knee has bumped his under the table.

The physical contact makes the pastor's eyebrows go up as he's taking a bite of his sandwich.

"Is it okay?"

"Mmm," he says, his mouth full.

She tries a bite. "Not bad. This must be Jean's secret: a little mustard and relish in the mayonnaise?" Lindsay smiles at him, trying to be polite. She fears that Ekdahl has really dropped over to make another adjustment in her schedule as assistant organist. Yesterday only six people showed up for Communion.

"No, the mustard is *my* secret." Beneath the table, Ekdahl moves his knee an inch to the left, where it encounters the leg of the table. He mistakes this resisting press for Lindsay's knee. So intensely does forbidden excitement seize him that he wolfs an enormous bite out of his sandwich.

She glances at him. He's chewing hard and fast. "You certainly like that, don't you." She means the tuna fish sandwich.

He stammers and presses harder against the table leg. He never knew that establishing intimate contact with a woman would be so easy.

Lindsay can't help smiling at him. She's heard that the pastor's wife is a lousy cook, but this voracious tribute to her skill as a sandwich-maker is ridiculous. "You're a hungry man," she laughs.

He beams at her madly, thinking how cloistered a life he's led within the ministry. "Yes," he nods eagerly. "I hunger for—" A sudden pang of guilt wrenches his knee away from the sinful reassurance that the table leg has been giving him. He spins in his chair toward the wall. "This is all so sudden, don't you see?"

Lindsay frowns at his abrupt change in mood. "Maybe you eat too fast?" she suggests.

Now he leaps to his feet. "There's something—something I must put in your hands." He hurries out to the living room. While he's gone, Lindsay sniffs at her sandwich. Has she poisoned the man? Here he is back again, hunching himself into the arms of his overcoat—chin down to hold his muffler in place—while fiddling with the snaps on his briefcase. He eventually pulls out an eight-by-ten glossy photo and hands it to her. "For you," he whispers intensely. His expression alternates between goony good humor and pained indigestion—as if demonic and angelic enzymes are doing battle in his stomach.

It's a photo of himself in clerical collar. His hair recedes from the gleaming forehead that so many focus on during his sermons. But the photo has been printed so that his torso tilts in at an angle from one corner. He seems to hover over a microphone (a late-fifties model, perforated metal,

about the size of an up-ended brick) with the call letters
WBVD mounted on top.

"Edgar Lundquist printed these up for me." Ekdahl
points at his photo image. "Oh, Edgar's retired now, of
course. But he used to do all the big disc jockeys. In Boston."

"Is this the station?" Lindsay indicates the call letters.

"No-no-no. He inserted those. In the darkroom. A nice
touch, no?"

Lindsay hopes that someone isn't playing a joke on poor
Pastor Ekdahl. At heart he's such an innocent soul. She
follows him to the front door, where she gives his hand a
gentle squeeze on the way out. "Take care," she tells him.

Back in the kitchen, she dumps her sandwich in the
garbage. At least her organist's job—if she can decipher
Ekdahl's state of mind—has not been scrapped. She glances
at the photo on the table. Ekdahl's smile looks winning—
in a nerdy sort of way. But his ambition to rebuild a small
congregation into some grand instrument of the Lord's
will seems to be driving the man to collapse. From her
vantage point behind the organ, Lindsay has watched the
pastor perform the Communion service, his trayful of glass
wine thimbles rattling in a nervous palsy. Viewing church
services from the side, as if from the wings of a theatrical
performance, has conditioned Lindsay's feeling not only
about Rev. Ekdahl, but about church rituals in general. A
wide-eyed and eager part of her wants to believe in the old
Christian myths. But sitting half-offstage, managing certain musical effects, has driven her into skepticism and
doubt. Years ago, the sight of a tiny flame burning steadily
on the altar could plunge Lindsay into genuine religious
awe.

Garth still doesn't know Lindsay's name. During the
month of March, he's spent only two or three days sitting
down the block from her house. She doesn't seem to go out
much. Once he followed her to the supermarket, where he
wheeled an empty cart up and down the aisles, thrilled at

the distant sight of her pausing before Imperial margarine, Empress tuna, and Ritz crackers. Another time, after she drove off somewhere in her VW, he spotted the mailman coming down the block. With her gone and letters about to arrive, the moment of discovery seemed imminent. But it took half an hour for the mailman to work his way first down her side of the block and then out of sight up the other. Garth was a nervous wreck by the time he approached the house. The mailbox was jammed. After sifting through the stuff—catalogues, flyers, and promotional samples—he wanted to holler. Every item was addressed to either "Postal Patron" or "Occupant."

He's spent the weekend going through the telephone book, reading addresses. At hand he keeps a map he's made of her street with neat little boxes for each house. Having reached the letter *P,* he's filled in the names of forty-seven of her neighbors for two blocks in either direction. The thought has occurred to him that he should have begun with "Zynowski, Roman," and worked backwards through the alphabet. But with his luck, Lindsay's name would then turn out to be "Mrs. Ansel Aaronson."

Una comes in with a bag of groceries. "Still at it, huh?"

"That's right," he says, trying to focus his attention on the small print.

"Have you heard the news?"

"Please don't bother me just now."

"Okay," she nods. "Say, I notice that you've been reading the phone book."

"Oh—it's art. I'm doing a piece on names in space."

"I think it's been done. Sol LeWitt or Robert Barry, I think."

"Well, I'm doing it again. Names are potent objects."

"I forgot to buy milk."

"Haven't you heard of those aborigines who won't let anyone take their photograph? They're afraid someone might capture a piece of their soul. Names are like that."

"I see. Mind if I turn on the TV?"

"What's on?"

"The news. Somebody shot Reagan."
"You're kidding. Who?"
"I don't know. They haven't released his name yet."

Tuesday, at the quarry that overlooks Heathersford, dawn eases up dull gray. Toby has the Quasar telescope focused on Lindsay's street. Freezing rain on the roads from New York made this a slow trip. But the line of clouds marking the front is passing well to the north—probably over Manchester, New Hampshire. For Toby, dressed in wool pants and a wool shirt—because cotton, if it gets wet, has no warmth to it—this will be a balmy day. He wonders if Lindsay liked the photo of herself that he sent.

Yesterday, within two hours of hearing on the radio that the president had been shot, he'd reached Old Forge, New York. The town was full of snowmobiles. In a bar he watched TV coverage of the assassination attempt. The men scrambling for the pavement outside the Washington Hilton looked scared. He knew what they were thinking. The Secret Service agent in charge, telling everyone to get down, looked scared. But he, at least, had that Uzi poised upward in one hand as he pounded in a clip with the heel of the other, knowing he could spray thirty rounds in any of the next three seconds. And already the agent was probably soaring in the thin clarity of an adrenaline high. Dan Rather looked scared. Alexander Haig, at the news conference, was falling apart. And he claimed to be in charge of the country. Haig would be the one who gave the order for the military alert. A frightened secretary of state was a very bad sign. Near Rome, New York, that afternoon, the B-52s thundered up from Griffiss Air Force Base. Near Cracow, Poland, Soviet troops were poised for an invasion. And in the confusion outside the hotel in Washington, only one person looked like he wasn't pissing in his pants. A TV cameraman. Those guys were idiots. Maybe seeing it all through the lens made them think they weren't really there. Someone ought to kick them in the balls so they'd wake up.

The sun comes up now through clouds. News on the VHF radio says Reagan is okay. A rib stopped the bullet, and they've reinflated his left lung. Three other victims weren't so lucky. The would-be assassin, another nut, is obviously not an agent of the KGB. Global pressures ease back a notch.

Toby turns his attention to Lindsay's street. By noon it's clear that two—maybe three—men are watching her house from parked vehicles. If he had a sense of humor, this accumulation of doubles to his own watchful presence would strike him as funny. He starts the Blazer and heads down the muddy dirt road for a closer look. By the time he reaches her house, the vintage Plymouth has vanished. But the Ford Fairmont is still there. The vehicle bears a bumper sticker: AMERICAN LUTHERAN JAMBOREE, AUGUST 9TH TO 11TH. A nervous balding guy in a clerical collar peers over the wheel at Lindsay's house. Farther up the block in a GMC pickup truck, a long-haired guy squints back at her front door.

Toby cruises slowly past the parked vehicles. One glimpse of both men tells him all he needs to know. Getting rid of them presents a purely technical problem. He's not consciously aware of anger or jealousy clicking his plan into place. In case he has to get at Lindsay—to get her out, safe—he doesn't want any clutter in the way. He'll brush these two other men away, like dirt on a clean map.

Pastor Ekdahl has been wrestling with dark angels. Now he's reduced to this, hoping for a glimpse of Lindsay as she cracks open the front door to reach into her mailbox. Perhaps he misread the signs she gave him. In matters of lust, the pastor is a novice. As a divinity student, he heard the rumors about clergymen who led double lives. Men of national prominence. Their names household words. A signed photograph of one hangs on the wall of his study. Huge audiences fill football stadiums to hear their sermons. On the road, women knock on the

doors of their hotel rooms. The most attractive are singled out to travel among their entourages, like Magda-
lenes to wandering Christs.

Monday night, Ekdahl pored over the Scriptures, especially Paul's cryptic references to "things sensual and car-
nal." He went over the mystical marriage of Christ and the
Church in the Book of Revelation. At dawn, he admitted
that his old assumptions about the nature of Christianity
had never gone very deep, and now they feel rigid and dry,
like a plaster mask ready to crack and fall away. His wife,
Jean—alarmed and confused by his sleeplessness and blas-
phemous talk about "the resurrection of the body into the
flesh"—left after breakfast for a long visit to her mother's
house in Baltimore. "Don't you see?" he tried to explain as
she packed her suitcase. "The Bible is an utterly subversive
document!"

Now he clenches his fists on the steering wheel and wonders what rough and beastly form of worship slouches him
down in the seat. He broods upon the vast abyss of doubt
within himself. That last squeeze that Lindsay gave his
hand at the door—what a terrific laying-on of hands was in
that gesture. What sweet balm the body offers to help all
sin-sick souls.

Tuesday night, Dave is pissed off. And now he's cold
from squatting under Richard's kitchen window in the
dark. The double game Gina is playing has driven him to
this. Richard was at her apartment again Saturday night.
Dave wonders if Richard knows some secret way to turn
her on. Tonight Dave has brought a tire iron along. He
hefts it in his cold hand. Jeez, you could hurt a guy if you
hit him with one of these things. Eventually Richard will
come down to the kitchen again. The glass doors on the
deck are unlocked. Dave plans to step in dramatically—out
of the dark—for a little chat. Man to man.

Suddenly he's wrenched up and choked back hard. An
arm like steel cuts off his wind. Pain sears his throat as he's

lifted off his feet and the air is gone. He can't breathe. Oh, God, he thinks, feeling the spasms that pain and terror have triggered in his arms, the involuntary kicks of his legs that threaten to snap his spine. He'd scream, but his tongue is forced out like raw meat. Whoever has seized him from behind tightens his stranglehold enough to bulge out Dave's eyeballs, then slacks off and allows his feet to touch the ground.

"Make a sound and your windpipe breaks," says a voice in his ear.

Dave gasps for air. His body shakes in convulsions as hot urine streams down his thighs. In his right field of vision, a stubby automatic weapon appears. The winter moon gleams on black metal. The gun is thrust, hard, up one of his nostrils.

"God, no. Please!"

His assailant makes every move with unforgiving, precise brutality. "Listen," hisses the voice. "Stay away from this house. Consider moving to another state."

The arm releases him. Dave falls to his knees, then collapses, gasping for air. Blinding pain hits again—in his left buttock. He's aware of being hurled forward, of his face grinding into a crust of snow and frozen mud. He lies there twitching in panic. It's an agony to heave his breath, but the pain assures him that, at least, he's alive. Minutes pass. There's no sound. Inside the house, footsteps sound. The kitchen light goes off. Dave gets to his knees and makes out a puddle of bloody vomit on the moonlit ground before him. There's no one in sight. He limps back to his truck, his ass so bruised from a single kick—hard metal toe in that boot—that he'll bear its mark for as long as the nightmares last, well into spring. By that time, Dave will have moved to Florida.

Wednesday morning, Pastor Ekdahl backs his Fairmont out of the garage and heads over to Lindsay's street. When he arrives, he sees a bearded fellow on her front steps put-

ting something in her mailbox. The man dashes to his
waiting vehicle and drives away.

"Who is that man?"

"I don't know," says the pastor, shaking his head. Then
he freezes, realizing that the question has come from the
back seat.

"Don't turn around," says the voice.

Ekdahl's eyes dart toward the rearview mirror. It's been
ripped away.

"What's your business here?"

"Oh, I've— The organ—" Ekdahl is frightened into silence. He heaves for air. Is this a police interrogation? Has
he broken some parking law? And when did this fellow get
into his car?

"Why are you watching Lindsay's house?" the voice demands.

The pastor trembles at the question and contorts his
face in shame. This voice knows his secret sin. Or is it a
voice? Ekdahl's mind veers sideways, like a plane bank-
ing into a turn. He's heard of people who suffer from
auditory hallucinations. Schizophrenics. They wander
the streets fending off accusing voices. He shuts his eyes
and clasps his hands in fervent prayer. "Dear Lord," he
whispers. "Lead me not into madness, and deliver me
from lust."

"Yes, *lust,*" echoes the voice.

"I confess it!" At these words a cool hand settles on the
pastor's forehead. Desperate and disoriented, he decides
that he is being touched by a miraculous event. "Oh," he
groans thankfully, "the balm of healing." He feels the hand
slide down over his shut eyes, as if anointing him with
soothing oil. It stops at his chin, then makes a few passes
over his white clerical collar. To his right, he keeps a Bible
on the passenger seat. He hears the volume being flipped
open. There's the sound of pages tearing. Ekdahl opens his
eyes in time to see a black, satanic hand move back out of
sight. It has ripped out a good portion of First Corinthians.

Fear grips him again. A fiend is wiping his filth on the Word of God!

"Stay away from this house," says the voice. "You're here on the Devil's business. Why don't you try attending to the meek and the poor in spirit?" The back door clicks open as the pastor stares ahead in holy terror. The missing rearview mirror is flipped onto the front seat, and footsteps walk away out of hearing. Ekdahl fumbles for the mirror and lets out a cry when he sees his image in the glass. It's the worst thing he can imagine. How will he even drive home? *His face is black!* Someone has smeared black grease all over his face!

Garth didn't need anyone to tell him that he should stay away from Lindsay's house. He's come to understand the real meaning of the phrase "invasion of privacy." It's not a mere intrusion. It amounts to an actual assault. Tuesday night he stayed up composing a letter to her. It went through a lot of drafts, all of which he threw away. Words were never his great strength. But at dawn he was inspired to conceive a minimal statement. The message he eventually settled upon went into an envelope marked "Occupant." After all that time going through the phone book, his eye must have skipped over her address hidden among a long list of Smiths. This morning he put the envelope in her mailbox. But he's not going back again. There's nothing to do now but sit by the phone and wait.

Wednesday is April Fool's Day. As Lindsay takes in the mail, she stands for a moment and looks down the empty street in front of her house. The lawns stretch flat and vacant in front of her house, lot after lot. There's no one in sight, no movement, no life. But President Reagan is alive—that's something. Her hands feel sticky as she sorts through the junk mail and bills. She's been trying to cure her depression by doing manual labor, stripping the paint off an old bureau. One long envelope is addressed by hand to "Occupant." There's no stamp.

What she finds inside takes her breath away. It's a little picture.

"*It's him,*" she whispers aloud. Underneath is a phone number. That's the whole message. She ought to be alarmed that he's discovered where she lives, but a smile tugs at her lips as she stares at the slip of paper in her hand. How long has she dreamt of this face? Seventy-five days. She blushes to herself. All this time Lindsay has secretly been counting the days.

Inside, she gets out the black photo album. It opens to the snapshot of herself—a girl at play in water and light. She glances at Garth's sketch, then presses the two images face to face and shuts the thick pages upon them. "Occupant," she laughs. "That's good." She doesn't quite get it. But now that she thinks a moment, his version of her life sounds like the whole story.

12

IN HIS LOFT, Garth sits and stares at the telephone. It hangs
high over the kitchen table, a vintage pay phone, the model
Western Electric produced in the thirties. An earpiece dangles on one side from a two-pronged hook. You talk into a
nozzle that swivels up and down. At one time, there must
have been a high platform in this corner of the loft—perhaps for whoever supervised a roomful of women bent over
sewing machines. At any rate, there must have been a platform, because Garth's phone is way up there—eight feet off
the floor. He ignored the thing for a whole year after he
moved in. Finally he hauled over a stepladder, climbed up,
and plugged in a nickel. The coin dinged a bell and fell out
the bottom. But a dial tone hummed in his ear. New England Telephone has evidently forgotten that it's connected to their wires.

When Una moved in, she made calls to Madrid, London,
and Nice.

"I wish you wouldn't do that," he told her.

"You're afraid I'm going to wear out this nickel?"

"Illegal stuff makes me nervous."

"Come on. Ma Bell is the cheater. Even the government
is suing her."

These days, if the phone rings, someone has to climb up
on the kitchen table to answer it. This presents a problem
if people are over for dinner. "Here, hold this," says Garth,
handing his plate to a guest. Everyone looks around, trying
to figure out where the sound of the ringing is coming

from. The next thing they see are his socks, standing between his wineglass and salad fork. "Hello?"

Now Garth sits on one of his three couches, staring up at the phone. It doesn't ring. Actually they're not couches. They're the seats out of old cars—covered with large throws. He gets a beer out of one of the miniature refrigerators and puts his feet up on the coffee table, an old manhole cover polished to dull umber. The table's two inches high. Those seats really sink you down there.

Garth has six second-hand refrigerators scattered around his place—each about the size of an oven. Two more sit stacked up in what most people would call the kitchen. Garth's loft is one enormous room: thirty-six feet by sixty-five. It's like living in a gymnasium—full of little refrigerators. Actually, the first thing you see when you come in is Garth's weather balloon. He ordered it by mail, army surplus, when he realized that he finally had room for one. Inflated, it goes all the way from the floor to the ceiling. Twelve feet in diameter. Army green.

The green matches a Rauschenberg print that Una finally convinced him to hang on the wall. "Aw, jeez," he said. He objected on principle to the notion that art was something you hang up in a frame. Garth still keeps his collection of prints stacked on a deep shelf. He slides one out now and sits down with it in his lap, like he's reading a book. But the phone doesn't ring.

At the body shop, Dave stands back from the fender he's sanding. There's one high spot that keeps breaking through the layers of body putty and primer, a bright gleam of bare metal he should have tapped flat with a hammer. But if Dave gives it a rap now, he knows he'll create tiny lines of fault for the rust to follow. He's worked on this fender for two days. It should have taken four hours. His helper, Tiny —a gorilla of a man with a kid in the hospital—has taken the week off. The unfinished jobs are piling up in the lot outside: cars with crumpled front ends, bruised fenders, and gashes slashed across door panels. The tools in Dave's hands have grown heavy, and he wields them with irritable clumsiness. Sounds startle him from behind: birds at the window, the phone jangling, the air compressor cycling on, a 10mm socket inexplicably rolling off the bench and clanging into an upturned hubcap.

Outside a car pulls in. The sound of tires mashing cold gravel grates on his ears. The last thing he needs now is an interruption.

"Where the hell have you been?" It's Gina's voice, edged into the shrillness he associates with fat Italian women shrieking at unemployed husbands. She's standing there in a bright yellow and red ski jacket, fists on her plump hips. "And how come you're not answering the phone?"

Dave rubs his eyes. He feels a tightening coming up from his intestines—two fists squeezing until they force up a small mass of nausea. "Go away," he says, trying to concentrate. The disk sander. It's under the car.

"Dave?" she says, her anger turning to worry. "What's the matter?"

His eyes pass over tools and rags heaped on the bench.

"You're sick," she says. "Oh, Davie. Hunkie." Gina touches his shoulder, wanting to take him in her arms, but she knows his hands will leave grease on her clothing. "Let's go upstairs. You should be in bed."

Dave lives above his shop in a room strewn with dirty clothes. The air always smells of sweat, paint fumes, and engine oil. Spending weekends at Gina's has opened a vista beckoning him into another kind of life: hot showers and clean sheets, a case of beer in the refrigerator, and extra pillows on the bed.

But seeing Gina will get him beat up again, he thinks. His neck is bruised and it hurts to swallow. Most of his strength goes into blocking out the memory of being seized by the throat and flung about like a dead rat. Dave knows who beat him up and why. True, the voice didn't mention Gina's name. But why else would someone tell him to leave town? Dave has considered calling the police about the incident. But he's too scared. The authorities ought to be

aware that a psychopath is living unnoticed in the suburbs.
"He's a killer," says Dave aloud.

"What are you talking about?"

Dave looks at Gina's face, at the smooth blush of her
cheek and her vulnerable wide eyes. The thought of a fist
marring her features makes him shudder. "Oh, Gina," he
implores her. "Stay away from him!"

"Who?"

"That married guy. *Richard.* Stay away!" He cups her
face in his grimy hands. Until now, he's thought only of
himself. "Quit your job." he says. "Don't go back to work
today. You could get a good job in Boston. You could come
with me!" Dave pauses, having admitted to himself that
he's leaving town. He'll sell his business, auction off his
tools. That's why the work is piling up outside. He's
through with mangled car bodies, fumes in the air, flakes
of rusty metal falling into his eyes from the work overhead.
This place is burying him alive.

Gina pushes away his dirty hands. "What are you talking
about?"

Dave slumps. "Something happened," he finally says. "I
went to that guy's house. I've been a couple of times—on
the chance that I'd see him. It was dark, see? And cold. He
must have come out another door." Dave is taking deep
breaths. He fears to put the rest into words.

"You're making this up. A fight with Richard? Come
on."

A week ago Dave might have yelled at her, squeezed her
wrist to make her listen. But now he cringes at the thought
of even raising his voice. He's felt the same reluctance
today swinging a hammer at dented metal. He's had
enough of loud blows and voices cutting like shears. One
last time he tries to say it. He may never see Gina again.
"The guy is fucked up. Don't set him off."

Gina watches Dave pace in a circle. He's limping. And
what's wrong with his neck? "Hey, Davie," she says. "I
gotta go. You look sort of sick. I bet you'll feel better tonight. Call me. Huh, sweetie?"

Dave doesn't hear her leave. He's brushing aside junk on the bench, looking for the phone book. "A realtor," he says aloud. "That's who you call if you want to sell a business. A realtor."

At her kitchen table, Lindsay turns over the last page of Zs in the phone book. She's gone through the whole thing reading phone numbers, looking for Garth's. The number he jotted down below his self-portrait ends in "9968." She thought it might be easy to spot his listing, to discover his name and address. But the search has dragged on for three days. She's scanned down hundreds of pages, pausing at those that end in "8." Every page or so she's turns up a "68." And every seven or eight pages, a "968." Gradually, however, the task has became an ordeal. Her eyes ache. Now, finally, on the last page—having held out for the slim chance that a romantic affair is simmering between herself and "Roman Zynowski"—she allows her eyes to drift up the whole naked page. She searches for a single number that ends "99—."

"Wait a minute," she says, flipping back a few pages. Nobody's phone number seems to end with "99—". It takes her thirty seconds to establish this fact. She slams the phone book down bitterly. "April Fool's!" she calls out. The guy has given her a phony number.

Lindsay marches out to the den and picks up the phone. All week long these four digits have floated before her eyes like mystic ciphers, promising some terrific revelation. She's handled the slip of paper with shaky reverence. And now it's turned into a cruel joke. He could have signed his name—for Pete's sake.

She dials the number roughly, knowing she'll reach dumb buzzing blankness, or a machine telling her that the number "cannot be completed as dialed." But it's ringing.

"Hello?" says a woman's voice.

Lindsay stands there, suddenly frozen numb. "Who's this?" she croaks.

"What?" says the voice.

Lindsay wants to hang up. But a queasy mixture of spite, curiosity, and confusion works her mouth into the words: "What's your name?" The question comes out sounding pleasantly dippy.

"I beg your pardon?"

Lindsay's heart is racing. Her next statement comes out with ding-a-ling cheeriness: "You've just won a subscription. To ten magazines! Now if you'll tell me your name and address—"

There's a silence on the line. "Listen, honey," says Una. "Telephone soliciting is the pits. Take my advice. Go back to school and learn to type. It'll do you good to get out of the house. 'Bye and good luck." And the line clunks dead.

Lindsay stares at the receiver. "Oh, God," sighs Lindsay. *He's married.* That explains something, doesn't it? The ritual reluctance of his pursuit. His desire and curiosity must be bound up—just like her own—with old loyalties and pledges of fidelity. This thought, far from calming Lindsay's heaving breast, strikes a tremor. She's felt it before, this resonant hum in her heart—like a string set in motion by another tuned to the same pitch. It scares her to think that Garth might turn out—in some uncanny way—to be her exact counterpart. This possibility—that someone out there might be her mirror image, might answer, part for part, to the uncompleted portions of herself—makes Lindsay catch her breath.

She finally hangs up the phone. The woman is probably a brash know-it-all, overweight, a terrific cook, and chock full of self-righteous confidence in her own opinions. The kind of bustling, big-breasted woman who takes over the microphone at PTA meetings. Lindsay goes up the stairs, imagining her rival's wardrobe: full of peasant skirts, muu-muus to disguise midriff bulge, and blousy shirts worn outside polyester slacks. Most likely she batiks shirt fabric herself at the kitchen table, dyes it in an old laundry tub, and wrings it out with rough hands, nails chewed to the quick.

Lindsay has reached the bathroom. She needs an emery

board. There's a pack of them on the top shelf of the medicine cabinet. She fumbles behind a row of old pill bottles. But instead of emery boards Lindsay finds Richard's secret picture of Gina. She recognizes the face immediately. "Ha!" she snorts, having penetrated one of her husband's secrets. "Big tits," she says aloud. "So that's the name of the game."

Garth watches Una climb down off the kitchen table. She's not wearing any clothes. "Who was that?" he asks, as she comes back to bed.

"Somebody selling magazines." Una looks down at him flat on his back, the sheet pulled up to his chin. Something pokes up in the middle, making a tent of the sheet. "I think you've got a condition," she says.

Garth tried to sleep late this morning. When he woke up he had an enormous erection, and Una was sucking his cock. By such small gestures she's been doing what she can to win him back from the obsessive fantasy he's been pursuing. At night she lights incense and massages his feet with almond oil, pinching the toes to stimulate the meridian that she claims runs up along the spine. Yesterday she asked him, for the first time in years, to take a shower with her. She soaped him up stiff, then asked him to kneel for his shampoo. The warm water coursed down his back so luxuriantly, as she worked herbal suds into his hair and beard, that he found his tongue lapping the inside of her thighs, his lathered head writhing in slow dips and weaves through her pubic hair until she murmured, "Oh—oh—oh—"

Now Garth watches her slip into her robe, a Japanese kimono—white blossoms on a purple ground—whose long sleeves are lined with red silk. "I thought you were coming back to bed," he says. The tent pole under the sheet is noticeably sagging—to the left.

"I'm hungry," she says, tying the sash. "I bought Canadian bacon."

Garth's taste buds make a joyous little squirt. "You better quit being so sweet," he says, eyeing the floral geometry of the kimono stretched across her ass. The leaves among the blossoms, he notices, are touched with silver. Now she disappears behind Garth's weather balloon.

Inhaling the smell of bacon frying, he stretches out across the whole bed and sighs, contented but sleepy. The days are growing longer now, and the air has been mild enough to melt the ice that sealed the big windows stuck, entombed him here all winter. Mornings, sparrows on the ledge have been making a real racket. Yesterday Garth saw a robin. It's April and they're back. Birds, he yawns. What a strange species. Slipping into the hazy state between sleep and waking, he seems to recall that one of his crazy Swedish ancestors studied birds. Surely he didn't dream this fact. Someone has passed down this story about his relative, his crazy kin.

Six generations back, Olaf Erikson came over from the old country to study American birds in the 1830s. At that time Andrew Jackson (a morose man with tuberculosis) was the president, and the first American locomotive had just been put into hazardous service.

On the voyage to America, Olaf tried out his English on the other passengers without much success. A year earlier, he had sent away to Edinburgh, Scotland, for a mail-order course *(English as It Speaks in the New World)* designed by a Professor Raj Satjit Nanda. Soon Olaf mastered the slangy exclamations ("Heigh ho!" "Pish!" "Tra-la-la!") by which this trickster from Bombay plunged the student, neck or nothing, into his imaginary version of the American tongue. As his ship sailed into New York harbor, Olaf leaned at the rail, feeling himself in a high mettle, eager to trade drolleries with genuine native speakers. A Danish fellow edged up to the rail beside him. "A lovely sight, wouldn't you say?" said the Dane, whose stiff British version of English seemed to lack the colorful exclamations that Olaf had mastered in fifty-two weekly lessons.

"Ja, süre," said Olaf. "It fills the eye like a lakh of rüpees!"

"I suppose," said his fellow traveler, "in a manner of speaking—"

"Lack-a-daisy!" broke in Olaf. "She's a humdinger!"

The Dane gave him an odd look and walked away shaking his head in dismay. Olaf understood that the churl hadn't followed this waggish banter.

In Manhattan, he fell in with a group of artists, landscape painters who sketched their way up and down the Hudson River Valley. They introduced him to Victor Audubon, a young man about to leave for England to arrange for the publication of his father's book, *The Birds of America*. Seeing the enormous and meticulous drawings was a terrible blow to the Swedish ornithologist.

"*Uff da,*" he sighed. His grand work had already been completed by someone else. They were sitting in a tavern near Gramercy Park, where he'd rented a room. The laughter of the barmaids sounded shrill and harsh in his ears. And something in these detailed illustrations spread out before him—the younger Audubon pointed out which ones he'd helped collect and mount—disturbed him. Why, these were drawings of stuffed, dead birds!

Olaf rose to his feet. "Carpet knights and mashers!" he declared, making a bitter gesture toward his artist acquaintances. "If I glout about here, I'll soon be out at the elbows!"

"Glout about?" said Victor.

"Ja," nodded Olaf, and clenched his fist. "Now I'm in a fine pickle. The elephant of fate has let fly a güd one!"

Victor, alarmed at the Swedish scholar's wild swings in mood, suggested that he might profit from spending some time among speakers of his own language. At Victor's direction, then, Olaf ferried over the East River that afternoon and hiked south. At Breuklyn Heights he failed to find the promised Scandinavian settlement. But he did wander up a broad cow pasture where, through the pines, he had a fine view of Governor's Island with its lush stands of oak, hickory, and chestnut. Overhead, a small voice chirped, *"Fitz! fitz! fitz! Wee sir-wee, sir-wits, wits!"* It was a ruddy little song sparrow (order Passeres—perching birds—of the family *Fringillidae*), its breast spotted with streaks of sepia over white underparts. Olaf smiled at the greeting.

"Sir wits-wits!" insisted the bird.

Olaf playfully called out the reply of the sparrow's European cousin: *"Rup-it, rup-it, rup-it spits wig a gee!"*

The bird hopped about in evident excitement. *"Spee-ge, wee-ge-dee!"* it twittered, as if greeting a long-lost relative.

"Güd Gott!" gasped Olaf, as the realization dawned on him. He knew bird talk. The North American continent, which that morning had slammed a door in his face, now rolled open as a vast arena of untranscribed *sound. "Tra-la-la-la! Wee sir wits-wits!"* he cried. And with that salutation to the class *Aves*, Olaf began his American odyssey.

Circling up through Vlachte-bosch in Breuklyn, he crossed over again to Manhattan Island and headed north through Haerlem, past the farmland settled by Jonas Bronck, whose numerous descendants had prospered and spread the family name all over the landscape: Bronck's Livery Stable, Bronck's Inn, Bronck's Beanery, etc. In the trees overhead, the percussive call of *"Chick-a-dee-dee-dee!"* heralded Olaf's northward progress like an advance guard of fife and drum. Hot afternoons, the same bird's mystic call (*"Phoe-bee!"*: two pure tones stepping from *re* to *do*) held him steady on his course. And at twilight, the evening song of the robin—in *Allegro agitato*—promised him sweet dreams: *"Cheer-up! cheerily, cheerily, cheer-up!"*

Olaf crossed over the Hudson at Dobbs Ferry and plodded on to scale the heights of Fort Putnam. In the distance the majestic river bent around a lofty promontory. And below on the plain of West Point, the tents of the encamped cadets spread out like a brigade of sandpipers. Here among the maples and gray birch, Olaf first deciphered the reedy contralto of the yellow-throated vireo: *"See me! I'm here, where are you?"* and the *presto* call (in F sharp) of the chestnut-sided warbler: *"I wish, I wish, I wish —to see Miss Beecher!"* Here also, Olaf encountered more artists. They sat on campstools overlooking the Hudson (painting outdoors), experimenting with this new medium called "watercolor." As he peered over one painter's shoulder, the true nature of Olaf's grand work—his vocation, his *calling*—finally took shape in his mind. What these colors daubed on paper lacked was a kind of soundtrack. And he, working not in pigment but in the language of birds, could supply it. Olaf felt a vast thrill in his breast as a panorama of cries and twitters beckoned him into hazy, unlimited space.

He turned west and climbed over Bear Mountain. There, in a broad valley—about the spot where Highway 17 now intersects the New York Thruway—he made his solitary camp. He sat with his notebooks and made cryptic jottings —casually at first, then more frantically—as networks of cries and whistles wove in densely about him. Close at hand a raucous *"Caw! caw! caw!"* cut through the more distant pastels of *"Bob-olink, spink-a-wink, link-a-jink!"* and *"P-s-s-s-t, zee-zee-zee!"* To one side sounded a bright *"Per-chip-y-cher- pee!"* From the other came the meadowlark's oriental song: *"Kong-quer-ree, Oolong tea!"* while overhead a black-throated warbler sang, *" 'Tis, 'tis, 'tis sweet here!"*

Olaf spun around when, from a thicket behind him, a wood thrush burst out, *"Tra-la-la-z-z-z!"* Olaf leaned left on his campstool to catch the quick *"Wee-zee-up!"* of a flycatcher. Olaf leaned right, drawn by the low *"Yank- yank"* of a nuthatch. Without warning, a chorus of wheezy whistles overhead flung his gaze upward, and a long trill rang in his ears as he tumbled over backwards, hit the soft earth, but held onto his notebook and pencil to keep scribbling notations. A rich warble swooped over him low—a purple finch arriving in flight! Now chirps and cries pressed in from all sides. *"Keep back!"* warned the scarlet tanager. But the twittering *crescendo* would not be stilled. *"Per-chik-o-ree! Caw caw! Drink your tea! Buzzz! Link-a-jink!"*

Then it died down. *"Che-bunk! Pip pip!"* A long pause. *"Ps-s-s-t."* Silence. *"Peep!"*

Olaf would spend the next three years recording such moments. He let his blond beard grow, exchanged his tattered clothing for buckskin, and camped far into the Adirondacks, where he traded bird lore with the Onondaga tribe. Having mastered the patterns by which one species of bird replies to another (how a single cheep passed on through a stand of pines can swell like a tide of gossip, or how one stern squawk can silence a flock of scolding grackles), he began experimenting with the effects of his own whistling calls. Olaf discovered that he could call together varieties that usually shunned one another, that he could raise and lower their volumes and pitch at will, that he could—in a word—shape the flux of nature to suit his fancy. With this discovery, he advanced from mere notetaker to conductor—nay, composer—of vast works for woodland clearings. Perplexed birds found themselves lined up on branches side by side, twittering in strange minor keys. Their little throats, the instruments of Olaf's art, grew hoarse from cheeping in rhythms that anticipated Bartók and Stravinsky. Olaf's scores were now massive. He carried a big basket of them, Indian style, on his back. A single piece might go on for a hundred pages and take months to transcribe. Far from the sight—or ears—of other men, he had created symphonic orchestrations that called for acres of virtuoso songsters supported by choruses of thousands.

In late 1835 he decided it was time to reenter the human world. He boarded a sloop at Albany for the two-day voyage down the Hudson. The other passengers found him a curious spectacle. Moss in his beard, a bright quickness in his beady gaze, he seemed startled by loud noises and confused by the sounds of human speech. The sight of the wind filling the sails like big wings evoked from him an excited flurry of whistles and chirps. But gradually he turned his attention to the others on board, formed intelligible syllables, and greeted them with exuberant chatter. *"Heigh ho! Wits-a-wee! 'Tis a mild monkey-wind. Ja, süre. Per-cheep!"*

At the newly formed New York University, a group of frock-coated professors didn't know what to make of Olaf. They gathered in a drawing room where he displayed his manuscripts, strutted about in buckskin, and filled the silence with woodsy chatter and piercing cries. One by one they tiptoed out the door as Olaf, lost in his art, whistled himself into the *scherzo* movement of the Onondaga Symphony. Outside, the window ledges were packed dense with pigeons, sparrows, and wrens. From the trees in Washington Square, they'd picked up the faint sounds of his performance, and now they jostled one another aside to peer in curiously through the glass at this figure puffing his cheeks in an empty room.

Rumors of a lunatic backwoodsman reached Columbia University before Olaf did. The police they called in to block the door at the Department of Natural Philosophy were jovial young fellows. Admiring his buckskin outfit, they mistook Olaf for one of the new breed that the lower classes had begun to idealize in Jacksonian America, rough men who swarmed across the mountains and down the great rivers, wrestling the wilderness into submission, grinning the bark off trees, and corrupting the language with words like *bulldoze, scoot,* and *kick the bucket, with* vulgar coinages like *round-up, square meal,* and *ker-plunk.*

Ouch! said Olaf as two beak-nosed constables seized his arms. It was the cry of the black skimmer, a red-nosed bird he'd observed flying low over the surface of the Hudson.

"Ouch?" repeated the police. They decided his cry was new backwoods slang, and they eagerly added the birdcall to their vocabulary. Did he really know men who chewed tobacco without spitting? they asked. Men who tossed down whiskey and rattlesnakes—just for breakfast? "Bet you were sired by a hurricane," joked one amiably. "And your mama was the smallpox!" added another. "Ouch!"

cried the third. They were trying to impress Olaf. And they had no intention of jailing him. They were giving him a police escort to the offices of an impresario who booked novelty acts into New York City music halls.

For the next month, Olaf endured the hoots of drunken ruffians who booed him off the stages of saloons. He began sleeping in Gramercy Park, an unhealthy place, due to the dampness. (Some still called it "Crummashie," after the Dutch, *krum marisje:* "little crooked marsh.") And the neighborhood was in transition. Lots were up for sale. His old lodging house had been condemned. Some developer had seen a chance to make a buck. There was no sign of his old artist acquaintances. In their place, all manner of lewdness and whoredom now flourished in the area. Gamesters and strumpets prowled the streets where Olaf shuffled along, coughing up phlegm.

In December, he put down all his money booking return passage to Stockholm. He spent his last night in America shivering for warmth in an empty stable. To save himself from frostbite, he lit a small fire using the only fuel at hand: some pages torn from his ornithological symphonies. By morning he'd burned them all and made his way empty-handed down to the docks. A few sparks from his fire were lofted by the wind and caught beneath the shingles of an adjacent house. About the time that Olaf's ship weighed anchor, the house was ablaze. Soon the fire raged out of control.

By evening, from where Olaf leaned on a ship's rail far out in the Atlantic, the western sky glowed dull orange long after sunset. Gulls hung motionless on outspread wings and cocked an accusing eye at him. The Great Fire of 1835 eventually consumed six hundred buildings—New York City at that time being built largely of wood. Thus, death and destruction became the Erikson family's first gift to the New World. The second was the exclamation *ouch!,* whose slang popularity spread from New York municipal employees—by way of firefighters drawn from as far away as Philadelphia—to all classes of American society. The origin of the cry (originally a meaningless squawk, for a time the final note of the Loon Lake Concerto for Junco and Adirondack Chorus) has puzzled grammarians ever since. Olaf Erikson died of pneumonia in the asylum for the insane at Södertalje in 1837.

Una circles around the weather balloon and finds Garth asleep. She shakes his shoulder, then watches the muscles rearrange themselves behind his face as he comes up from sleep in stages, like a diver decompressing. Every morning he comes up from a dark place, putting levels between him and it. What good is all his goofy cheerfulness, if below it a reservoir of suffering lies bottled up?

Abruptly his eyes open and he sits up. "Just resting my eyes," he says. "What's on the schedule today?"

Una takes a sip of coffee. "I might go out. I'll need your car."

"Okay. What about me?" He watches her hold her coffee mug in two hands. "Oh, oh," he says, and flops down on his back. "I know that look. You think I should look for a job today, right?"

"I didn't say that."

"Ah, but you were thinking it. That's what you get for being mixed up with"—Garth leaps up and stands naked in the middle of the bed—"Lieutenant Onan of the Thought Police!" He makes several brisk salutes with alternate hands.

She stares at his cock dangling before her eyes. "I think we should make a baby," she announces.

Garth gets down off the bed and looks for his underwear.

"I'm almost thirty," she insists.

He has to sit on the edge of the bed to put on his jeans. The knee is not yet very stable.

"Why won't you talk about this? You like kids. What's wrong with babies?"

Garth is staring past his weather balloon toward the kitchen table. "You know?" he muses. "I'm thinking about moving that telephone."

"Great. It's only taken you about seven years to figure that out. I'm tired of standing on the table to talk."

"I think I'll move it up higher. Right onto the ceiling. See?—we'll put up scaffolding with a mattress on the top. Then when you stretch out on your back, the mouthpiece will hang down to your mouth. Isn't that better than standing on the table?"

Later that morning there are two phone calls. The first is from New York. Una learns that her Aunt Ava has had a stroke. "I'd better fly down to the city," she tells Garth. "You remember Aunt Ava. The one who lives in Gramercy Park?"

"I thought she lived on the Upper East Side."

"That's in the summertime."

"Oh, I remember. She's the one who goes south for the winter. All the way to Twenty-first Street."

After Una goes out, the phone rings again. Garth climbs up on the table and answers it. There's no reply. It sounds like the receiver at the other end is being muffled by a palm. Finally a quavering voice says, "Hello?"

It's Lindsay. She's been pacing the house for an hour, in a state. The full significance of Gina's photo, hidden in the medicine cabinet, has finally sunk in. "Oh, the lying bastard!" she's repeated to herself, walking from room to room, imagining Richard together with that cheap hussy. But there's an odd sense of relief bound up with Lindsay's discovery. The pain, cutting into her, has sheared through certain threads that have been holding her back, restraining her on the edge of a brink. She tried to call Debbie, just to talk, but no one answered. She's thought of going out and running up a big bill on the VISA card. Possibilities seemed to open up. There was no reason not to call this odd phone number a second time. The impulse gathered behind it all her accumulated bitterness and longing. But the sound of Garth's voice has made her balk and muffle the phone. Now she's sunk mute onto the love seat in the den, cradling the receiver against her ear.

Garth hears Lindsay trying to catch her breath. He knows it's her. Three days have passed since he slipped his phone number into her mailbox. Now that she's finally called, he feels weak in the knees. "Just a minute," he says to the silent phone. He climbs down and hurries past his weather balloon all the way to Una's easel for a stool. As he carries it back, a jubilant mood puckers his lips into a jazzy whistle. He hoists the stool and himself onto the table.

"Okay," he says, perched in front of the phone. "As you were saying?"

"George Shearing," says Lindsay. "I heard you whistling."

"Ah," says Garth. "But can you—Name That Tune?"

" 'Lullaby of Birdland.' "

"Good. Now can you find words to—"

"Reveal?"

"What a feeling!"

"We should be singing this," says Lindsay.

There's a silence. They've both become a little self-conscious.

"How are you?" Garth finally asks.

"A little depressed."

"Really? I'm sorry. But I'm glad you called."

"Was that your wife I talked to?"

"When?"

"Earlier. A woman answered."

Garth thinks for a second. "Wait a minute," he laughs. "Are you selling magazine subscriptions?"

"Yup."

"That's pretty strange." It strikes him now that Lindsay is jealous of Una, and that this call might have taken a lot of courage to make. "Hey," he says. "Ask me something. Anything."

"Okay," sighs Lindsay. "What's going on?"

"*Uff da.*" What a question. Garth scratches his beard. "I don't know."

"I do."

These words set Garth's heart pounding. He has the

sense that all the confused feelings within him are about to
be sorted out and given a name. It's something he's not
been able to accomplish on his own.

"In that case," he says, "I know too." He listens for a
response. The silence grows a little dense. She's still there.
Garth is aware of the hairs standing out on his arm. "I'm
getting goose bumps," he says.

"Me too," laughs Lindsay.

"Hey," he says after a moment. "I want to tell you something."

"Are you sure?"

Garth blinks and stares at the wall. It this the reason the
two of them have been proceeding by such minute degrees?
It's only taken about three months to introduce themselves.
Each of them wants to be *sure*. But at some point, one of
them will have to make a blind move.

"Listen," he declares. "My name is *Garth*. Garth Erikson.
I live downtown above the Broadway Shoe Repair. I don't
do much of anything—except think about you all the time.
You're very special. You're extraordinary. And I want—"
He hears the dial tone. "*Uff da,*" he says. She's hung up.

13

LINDSAY IS waltzing around the living room, hugging a couch cushion for a partner. She felt this way in the seventh grade after Tommy Thompson kissed her behind the bowling alley. Her reaction then had been to run, to flee with her prize, seeking a private nook (behind Wilson's garage) where no one could observe her fling out her arms in whirling ecstasy. Hearing Garth pronounce his name has triggered the same influx of sweetness. It was too much. She didn't exactly hang up on him. Her hand joyfully thrust away the phone.

But now something intrudes to darken her bright mood: a quick vision of Richard and Gina. "Oh, God," she says, slumping to the couch. She expects the salt of tears to blind her. She even squints her eyes to make them come—but they don't. When a woman discovers that her husband is betraying her, a terrible storm is supposed to break. She sits and tries to feel bitter. She waits for deep hurt to erupt into hysterics. But nothing happens. Wouldn't one of her ancestors, given a similar situation, have done something dramatic: busted a mirror, shot her horse, or leapt screaming from a cliff?

In Lindsay's throat there's the hint of gagging. But it's a pleasant click, back at the roof of her mouth: "Guh—" Then she feels the breath mount up and splay out between her tongue and teeth: "—thh." Her mouth is saying his name: "Garth." She pronounces it aloud, letting the breathy "ahhr" hum in her breast. The sound drives away all other thoughts. There's magic in it—as if a secret chamber is about to open.

When Alex comes home from school at three o'clock, Lindsay has showered and blown her hair dry. Since January, her severe haircut has grown out to shaggy, Christopher-Robin length. Planning an outing, she's put on a new shimmery bra, makeup, and perfume. And she's spent an hour trying on different outfits. Finally she's settled on a silk blouse—a geometric print in dull sienna and beige—and a wrap-around denim skirt.

Alex finds her sitting on the couch, tugging on high boots with crepe heels. "Where are you going?" he asks.

Lindsay holds the cuff of her blouse against the boot's brown leather. She makes a face at the mismatch. "Is it warm out?" she asks.

"It's neat out. There's a big puddle down at the corner where the bus stops. And water's running out from under the old ice. Underneath it's hollow. On top it's hard with lots of sand and stuff. Under the ice there are secret rivers. You know what I mean?"

Lindsay gets up. She hasn't been out all day. Alex is describing the first real spring thaw. Most of the snow on the lawn is gone. "If I go out for an hour, can you play by yourself?"

"Outside?"

"Better stay inside. You'd get wet playing in the water."

"Oh-kay," he agrees. "Okay."

As Lindsay backs her Rabbit out of the garage into bright sun, she admits to herself that she's never actually gone all the way into old downtown Heathersford. From the Interstate you see a line of abandoned mills. Once she ventured as far as the main post office. Near the railroad yards, a jumble of frame houses strung wash out into fenced backyards. There seemed no reason to look further.

Lindsay takes the exit at the lumberyard, passes warehouses, a truck depot for Interstate Fruit, and so many kids on the street, shrieking home from school, that this could be a town wholly populated by children. Some stoop to poke in the gutter and run with the lightfootedness that comes the day you finally put off the weight of winter snowshoes.

Now the buildings are mostly brick. Lindsay follows Main Street as it turns right and widens up enough for diagonal parking. She pulls in where a storefront's windows have been boarded up. Old election posters say RYAN FOR SHERIFF. A coarse man wearing a railroad cap stares at her and blankly puffs on a pipe. Above an open doorway, a sign reads CROSSROADS MISSION. A man with a white beard appears in the doorway. He pauses at the threshold chewing on a knuckle, then turns around and goes back in, stops, comes back again—balking at the expanse of the wide street. Up the block a hunched figure in a stocking cap sits on a stoop holding a bottle wrapped tightly in a brown bag.

She can't bear to get out of the car. She backs out and drives slowly up the street, passing the Lone Star Lunch and the Thrift Shop, Mary's Boutique ("25% Off All Uniforms"), and Hal's Groceries. There's no traffic, but there are people on the street, mostly standing around: a woman with her neck wrapped in two thick mufflers, another wearing a pink headscarf, and a man in an overcoat vigorously swinging his arms and talking to himself. Lindsay parks across from a dingy Woolworth's. She gets out and hurries past the El Lago movie theater, where a double feature is showing: *Bottoms Up* and *Girls at Camp*. A one-armed man passes her, his empty sleeve stuffed into the pocket of his coat. Up ahead, a sign hangs out: THE BLACK FOREST INN. It must be the tavern where Richard claims they serve good lasagna. Across the street a faded sign catches her eye: BROADWAY SHOE REPAIR. The second-story windows are bricked up. Her eyes fasten on the top floor: hanging plants, Levolor blinds, and spotlights hung from a white ceiling. Having dared to penetrate the downtown's derelict landscape this far, she's expected the worst: torn shades pulled over grimy windows. But Garth's loft looks classy enough to be an architect's office.

She can't stand here in the street gawking, so she edges

into the doorway of the tavern, takes a breath, and pushes inside. A bald bartender and two thick-waisted men stare at her. The air in the place smells stale—like her living room the morning after a party. Straight ahead there's a pool table, to the left another room with empty booths, and to the right a counter along the window with stools. Lindsay wants to back out the way she came, but the stools by the window draw her in. She hoists herself up on one and opens her purse. Closed shutters cross her line of vision just below eye level. Perfect, she thinks, casting an eye up at Garth's windows.

"Can I get you something, ma'am?" It's the bartender.

"Sure. White wine?"

He nods and reaches under the bar.

Lindsay has discovered a single dollar bill in her wallet. She stares ahead out the window. She ought to have asked the price. The bartender brings the wine over and sets it down on a paper napkin. "That's a dollar," he says, and takes the bill. He stands for a moment, looking out the window beside her. "Nice day, huh?"

"Peachy," says Lindsay.

"Right," he nods, and goes back behind the bar. The men resume their discussion of the Boston Celtics.

It is a nice day, she decides. The sun goes in and out behind puffy clouds. The light comes up fast, warming the old brick across the street. With this shuttered glass barrier between herself and the outside, the people passing on the street now look less eccentric. A man walks along swinging his briefcase, a carpenter carries tools in a long wooden tray, and a mother pushes a stroller. On this side, two yellow hardhats pass by. The door opens and the two construction workers come in and take seats at the bar. No one pays any attention to Lindsay.

Casually she's been examining the windows of Garth's loft. Up there she's seen the top of someone's head. The sight made her pulse quicken. In her purse, she's brought along a pair of opera glasses in a zippered gray case. But it's silly to think she can take them out here. And the excitement she feels is absurd. Still, she's a little proud of having managed this adventure so shrewdly. Lindsay has seen women in bars sitting by themselves. Some even bring books to read. What she's doing is not that unusual.

Abruptly she gasps. *It's him.* Garth has come to the window. He stands and looks down into the street, first one way, then the other. She covers her forehead with a palm and looks down at the counter where streaks of a rag have left a filmy arc on the varnish. He's looking for her. She's certain of this. Her heart races as she waits for him to glance down at her. Should she wave? He'd rush down flights of stairs and she'd run out the door to meet him.

Now the window where he stood is vacant. From her right comes the sound of the tavern door opening and shutting. Another regular, she thinks. But something tells her that a man has stopped to look in her direction. Oh, God, she thinks. What if it's someone who knows her? A neighbor. A friend of Richard's.

"Well, hello," says a man's voice. "What a nice surprise."

She swivels to see who has discovered her in this awful place. Lindsay finds herself looking into the clean-shaven, athletic features of a familiar face. He's wearing jeans and a tan down vest like a workman, but he could be an actor dressed for the part. As he approaches, she recognizes the top-stitching on his shirt as Calvin Klein. A memory comes to her of a young Steve McQueen sucking on a length of plastic tubing. It's the guy who came to fix her dishwasher. The one she knelt beside and nearly— Her cheeks flush hot again at the memory.

"Come on. You remember me?" he smiles, leaning one elbow on the window counter and folding his hands. She stares at his laced fingers. The nails are clean. "You're Mrs."—he squints at the ceiling—"Smith."

Lindsay wants to shush him. But at least it's not someone who really knows her. At the same time, this interruption has her miffed. Behind her, a woman's laugh sounds, and balls click on the pool table. More people are filtering in.

He looks amused at her silence. "I'm Gray," he says.

"Grayson Chandler." His fingers unlace and a hand offers itself. It closes on hers a little tentatively.

"I'm Lindsay," she replies, and adds a smile. He's still holding her hand. "Of course I remember." She pulls free and looks at her empty wineglass.

"I'll buy you another. Unless you're expecting someone?"

She shakes her head.

"Fine," he says. "Don't go away."

This isn't what Lindsay expected. Another burst of laughter sounds from the bar. Across the street an attractive woman strides along swinging a suitcase. Her hair is long and thick, pulled back with combs, and she's wearing one of the new Perry Ellis sweaters—very expensive. Lindsay watches, fascinated, as she enters the doorway next to the Broadway Shoe Repair. Stairs go up behind the door.

Gray Chandler returns with a glass of wine and a mug of beer for himself. "So," he says, hitching his boots on a rung of the stool. "You come here often?"

"Not really. Thanks for the wine."

"Sure. What do you mean: 'not really'?"

"Oh, I'm just looking around."

He laughs. "Me, too," he says.

She feels his eyes examining her face. High across the way, a woman's head passes the length of Garth's windows. Lindsay lets out an involuntary sigh.

Gray looks out in the direction of her gaze. "It's a fine old building, isn't it? See how they arched the bricks to set back those windows?" Outside, late-afternoon shadows creep upwards. She steals another glance at Garth's windows. The pulse-quickening giddiness that she felt a few minutes ago has vanished. In its place a dull ache knots in her breast. Her eyes search for another glimpse of that striking woman up there with him. Was she the one on the phone? Garth's wife is a fashion model? At least he could have told her he was married. She feels tricked, betrayed. Another married man on the prowl.

"I like your earrings," remarks Gray.

"Oh?" Lindsay touches fingertips to the gold loops dangling near her cheek. Gray's eyes are pale blue. She risks a long glance into them.

"You look a little sad," he's saying. "But mysterious, you know? By the way, your hair looks terrific, short."

Lindsay knows she's being flattered. But just now, these attentive compliments feel pretty good. How touching that Gray actually remembers her longer hair. Across the way, she can see both of them now. Garth is talking to the woman as she moves in and out of sight.

Lindsay turns her attention to the man beside her. "You've been very sweet," she tells him. "But it's time for me to go."

He touches the back of her hand. "Don't go yet."

"No, really—"

"Well, at least finish your wine." His fingertips still rest on her hand.

Lindsay averts her eyes from his face. At his touch she's felt a tremor in the loins. Her conscience tells her not to drink more wine. Across the street, a blue taxi stops at the curb. Now Garth's door to the street opens. The striking woman emerges, followed by Garth lugging a suitcase. He puts it in the front seat of the taxi. Then the two face each other on the sidewalk. Lindsay's heart thumps fiercely. She looks down hard at her wineglass, then lifts it abruptly to her lips, gulping the whole thing down. It burns sweet in her throat. The man beside her looks amused. She tosses back her head and gives him a gay laugh.

"Did you know I'm a poet?" she boasts.

"That's wonderful," says Gray. "I should've known. You have the eyes of a poet. Such lustrous eyes."

The gulped wine gives Lindsay the courage to face the full intensity of his gaze. It's nearly enough to shut out what's happening across the street. Garth and his woman are sharing a long, curbside embrace.

Lindsay wants to cry. She's decided that the only reason Garth gave her his phone number is because his wife is leaving town for a few days. *What a rat.* First Richard, now him. "Please," she says to Gray. "Give me a hug, would you?"

At once his arms are around her. For an instant she fears the bar will grow silent to stare at them, but the hubbub ignores them. She grips the unfamiliar breadth of a stranger's shoulders, feeling a scratchy cheek brush her own. Tears burn her eyes. Over Gray's shoulder she can faintly make out her own reflected face in the glass. Framed by the line of her cheek and brow, a man and a woman across the street unlock their embrace. The scene blurs over in her wet eyes. She shuts them tight. When she opens them again, the taxi is pulling away, and Garth stands at the curb watching it go. Then he goes back inside.

Lindsay eases herself out of Gray's arms, having seen enough—actually, too much. "You're a good hugger," she sniffs, slipping the strap of her purse over one shoulder. With the napkin from under her wineglass, she dabs at her eyes.

"I'll walk you to your car." He sounds concerned, but also calm and steady.

The two of them go out. Halfway down the block, Gray puts an arm around Lindsay. She's grateful to have this strong man to lean against. At her car he asks if he can kiss her. The street seems deserted. She shakes her head dumbly.

"I'll call you," he says.

She shakes this off, too, and gets in. Driving away, she concentrates on steering a straight path over the patched asphalt. This main street seems to have narrowed. Brick walls tower up and tilt, threatening to collapse. She imagines the way ahead lined with people, a gauntlet of drunks and cripples—each of them bearing the sign of some maiming disfigurement. Pressing in from the curb as she passes, they jeer at her sluggish progress—out of their zone.

Garth had gone up a whole flight of stairs before he realized that Una had left with his car keys. Sylvia's taxi was blocks away. And the old car was out in the cold again.

This morning, Una had run it out of gas, abandoned it somewhere near the mall. She'd walked the rest of the way to her shopping trip and then hitchhiked home.

"Why didn't you call?" Garth had demanded when she finally showed up.

"I like to hitchhike," said Una, swinging her new suitcase onto the bed and snapping it open. The thing was half-full of new clothes.

"Oh, Jesus." He smacked his forehead. "You weren't shoplifting again?"

"No. I charged this stuff on Aunt Ava's American Express card."

"But she's the one who had the stroke."

"Right. She'd be miffed if I arrived at the hospital looking like a slob."

"How long have you had her credit card?"

"I thought you knew. She sends me a new one every year."

Una's finances are a mystery to Garth, who tells himself that he's supported the two of them for years working part-time jobs: teaching nursery school, instructing night drawing courses at the community college, and—for a whole year—working a paper route. The monthly rent on his loft is only eighty-five dollars. And he buys his clothes used at the Salvation Army thrift store down the street. The public library recognizes him as a regular, and he qualifies for food stamps. Garth's goal is life without labor.

Anyway, that's what he'd told himself as he watched Una carry an armload of garments from the closet to her suitcase. "What happened to your old suitcase?" he'd asked.

"I lost it."

"Really? And how about my car? You just abandoned it?"

"It's in the Dunkin' Donuts lot. Have you got any cash? Sylvia's driving me to the airport."

Garth handed her his last five dollars. "How long will you be gone?"

Una tossed four pairs of shoes into the suitcase. "A couple days."

He knew this might mean two weeks. "You're taking a lot of stuff."

"It depends on how sick my aunt is. And I might go out to East Hampton."

Una knew some of the people who hung around in the Larry Rivers crowd. He noticed that she'd purchased a new black dress. Perhaps she expected a funeral—or the reading of a will. Garth went and looked out the window. A dump truck loaded with sand rumbled up the street. Was it mere coincidence that Una was leaving on the very day that what's-her-name had finally called him? Una sensed things. She still hadn't explained her prediction about Reagan being shot in the lung. He wondered if she'd seen some fateful configuration in his astrological chart that didn't include her. Behind him, the suitcase was being snapped shut.

Una came over and hugged him from behind. "I'll send you some money."

"I'll be okay," he said. Down in the street, a taxi pulled in at the curb.

"We've got to hurry," she said, releasing him.

Garth lugged the suitcase down the stairs after Una and put it in the front seat. "How you doing, Sylvia?" he said.

"Cut the gab, buster," said the driver, who reminds everyone of their mother—until she opens her mouth. "I gotta get this fare to the airport. Pronto!"

Garth gave Una a long, intense hug. Then she got in, and he watched the taxi pull away. Then he went back inside.

Now Garth stands on the landing of the dusty stairwell. He's trying to decide whether to go straight to Wally's for his spare keys. Finally he trudges back down to the door and wrenches it open. A jolt goes through him as he glances across the street. Stepping out the tavern door, Lindsay doesn't see him. But Garth senses magic in the air. Una's gone, and here *she* is. He's about to wave his arms, when another figure appears. Some guy in a vest. Garth watches in disbelief as the stranger catches up with Lindsay and puts his arm around her slender shoulders. "What the hell?" Garth says aloud. It's not her husband.

He breaks into a trot on his side of the street. "Hey," he calls, not loud enough. She's already getting into her car. "Wait!" he yells. Garth is running now, thinking of all the days he spent parked down the street from her house feeling satisfied that she was safely buffered within its walls. A few seconds ago, with mere air between them as they both stepped out from facing doorways, the barriers were down—he could have closed the distance between them in an instant. But now he's missed his chance. He should have run sooner, yelled louder, seized her from behind. The VW turns the corner as he comes breathlessly to a halt next to the fellow wearing the vest.

The guy looks at Garth. "Guess you missed her. You a friend of Lindsay's?"

Garth's mouth drops open. He's just learned her name. "Lindsay?" He repeats it, lolling the sound of it around on his tongue. At the same time, Garth is thinking fast, calculating how to plunder more of this fool's precious knowledge. "Oh, sure. Lindsay and me. We go way back." Garth tosses this remark off casually with a big sweep of his arm. "Yes, sir," he beams. "Good old Lindsay!"

Chandler is eyeing Garth. "She was upset. Were you supposed to meet her?"

"Me?" shrugs Garth. "Oh, in a way. I suppose." He clasps his hands behind his back and studies the pavement. "Yes, sir. Good old Lindsay Woolsey. Related to the famous judge, right?"

Gray shakes his head. "No. Smith. Her name is *Smith.*"

"Oh, boy," laughs Garth and rubs his hands together. He's got what he wanted now, her whole name. "Lindsay Smith!" he repeats, a bit too loud.

"Wait a minute," says Gray suspiciously. "You don't know her, do you."

"Oh yes I do!"

"Christ, you don't know what you're talking about," sneers Chandler. "What are you, from the halfway house?"

"What's that supposed to mean?" Garth has sobered suddenly. He regards the people on this street as his neighbors.

"Forget it," says Chandler and walks off.

Garth watches him go, then races back to his place and flips through the telephone book. In the third column of Smiths—under "Richard R."—he spots her address, the listing he missed last week. He leaps onto the table and dials her number. She ought to be just getting home. Her kid answers.

"Is Lindsay there?" asks Garth.

"Nope. She went somewhere."

"Who's this?"

"Alex. I'm home alone."

Garth pauses. "Listen, Alex. The next time you're by yourself, and someone calls, don't tell them you're alone. Tell them your mom's busy. Okay?"

"Oh. I see. Sure. Who are you?"

Garth sighs. What do you tell a kid? "I'm a friend," he finally says.

"Are you the ghost?"

"I don't think so."

"Have you got a beard?"

Alex's questions are a little unnerving. "How did you know?"

"I've seen your picture," says Alex. "Mom keeps it in the photo album. Besides, I've seen you lots of times."

"Really?"

"In your car. The old fashioned one—with fins in the back."

"You notice a lot. Better not tell your mom about the car. Okay?"

"Sure. Should I tell her you called?"

Garth has decided that his intrusions into Lindsay's household have gone too far. "Better not," he tells her son.

"Well, maybe I'll call you sometime. Your number's in the album."

"Fine," says Garth. "We'll have a nice talk. Bye."

14

For LINDSAY, events will have to turn worse before they get better. Early Sunday morning at the Good Shepherd Church, she sits behind the oak console of the organ, leafing through the hymnal. The sanctuary is empty. She's come early to practice, since she hasn't played for two weeks. The empty expanse of the pews to the right distracts her. Somewhere a radiator wheezes as the heat comes on. If a man slipped in the door at the far end of the aisle and found her alone here, they could embrace under the lights hung from chains under the arching beams. She has lit the altar candles on either side of the cross. But ritual objects offer no absolution from these thoughts—sinful visions of reclining with a forbidden lover in one of the long, wooden pews.

Without turning on the console's switch, her fingers move soundlessly over the two keyboards. It's the action of the instrument that her stiff hands need to recall—the organist's clutch and creep from one note to the next. She strains to keep her mind on the silent music. The hymns themselves are easy to sight-read. Ekdahl picks them out, old favorites for the conservative regulars. He won't stand for any toccatas or fugues at this brief early Communion service. He once confided to Lindsay that the head organist's taste for Bach and Maurice Duruflé was hurting attendance figures at the main service.

With a dull bang, a distant door opens. Lindsay flinches

at the sound. At the back of the church, the head usher has arrived. She watches him set down a stack of programs and shuck one arm out of his overcoat. Lindsay half-expected to see Gray Chandler come striding down the aisle in his boots. He called her last night, just as he'd promised.

With Alex asleep, Richard had gone out, for cigarettes, he said. Lindsay went to bed early—it was just ten o'-clock—and twisted under the quilt, certain that her husband was out visiting Gina. Just as sleep began tugging her along a subterranean passage, the phone rang shrilly at her ear. She lunged for it. "Yes?" she said, hoping it was Garth.

"That was quick," said a man. "How are you feeling?"

She needed a moment to place Gray Chandler's voice. "Oh," she said, wondering whether she might require a bedside list of the men who would dial her number at this hour. "I'm okay. But you shouldn't have called."

"I was worried about you. Yesterday you seemed pretty depressed."

"No. I'm fine." Actually Lindsay had spent Saturday pushing back visions of Garth embracing that stunning woman beside a waiting taxi. At noon, taking a pee in the bathroom, she'd found herself hunched forward, weeping into her palms. "Oh, Garth," she had whispered. "You rat."

On the phone, the sound of Chandler's voice in her ear only made her think again of the tavern and the view she'd had out the plate-glass window. "Really," she said to the phone. "Forget about yesterday."

"I can't," declared Chandler. "I *must* see you again."

This theatrical line made her smile. She ought to have slammed down the phone, should have told this clown to get lost. Hadn't she learned about men yet? Instead she said, "Seeing you again would be impossible."

He laughed into the receiver. "You're funny."

"I'm not trying to be."

"What are you trying to be?"

She thought for a moment. "I'm trying," she said, "to be decent and sane." She'd never had to put it to herself quite this way.

"And it's not working out?"

"Usually it does."

"You told me you were a poet."

"Oh, that." Lindsay realized she hadn't opened her notebook for weeks. Neither had any spells come on lately. "I must have been bragging," she said. "I'm just a beginner."

"I'd like to see your work sometime. I know some poets."

"You do?" How many appliance repairmen knew poets?

"I could get advice for you. Who else has seen it?"

"Oh, nobody. I mean, it's private. No one knows I write."

"You told *me.*"

"Well—*you* don't count," laughed Lindsay.

"See? You *are* funny."

"Oh, goodness," she sighed. "We shouldn't be talking like this. It's not right."

"What's the difference? Remember, I don't count."

"I was just kidding about that."

"I'm not so sure," he said. "Maybe that's what you need. Somebody—oh, to talk to—who doesn't count. You know what I mean? Someone who won't complicate your life. Or be critical of what you say or feel."

"What is this, therapy?"

There was a silence. "Let me put it this way. I know how to keep my distance."

"Then why are you calling me?"

"I'm calling to ask how your dishwasher is working."

Lindsay puzzled over this remark. "My dishwasher? It's making a funny noise," she confessed. "When it shuts off. Kind of a thump."

"Maybe I should come over and take a look?"

"Oh no you don't!"

"Not tonight. Monday. How about ten in the morning?"

"Impossible."

"In the afternoon then?"

"Listen, Mr. Chandler. I can't see you again."

He seemed to think this over. "So," he said. "If I show up the day after tomorrow, you're going to slam the door in my face. Right?"

"Right."

"My feelings will be hurt."

"Too bad."

"Okay. Then they won't be hurt. I don't have any feelings."

"Oh, I see," said Lindsay. "That's how you keep your famous distance."

"In a way. You learn when feelings are appropriate. And when they get in the way."

"You sound like you've had lots of experience," said Lindsay.

"Enough to tell—in advance—how the two of us might get along."

"How's that?"

"Marvelously."

"I'm not interested in finding out."

"We'll see about that."

Before Lindsay could reply, he'd hung up on her.

A light on the organ glows red as Lindsay flips a switch. Somewhere—perhaps behind the big pipes stacked like ascending tubes over the pulpit—a machine readies a column of air that her hands will release into pure tones. She thinks of her doorbell chimes, four brass cylinders hung conspicuously in her front hall like trophies. If Gray Chandler presses her bell in the morning, will she hide in a closet? Under the bed? To her right, a middle-aged couple comes down the aisle—the first to arrive. It's time to start the Prelude.

By the time Lindsay finishes repeating "Beneath the Cross of Jesus" and "Dear Lord and Father of Mankind," the first six pews are full. Why the big turnout? she wonders. Six days have passed since the assassination attempt on Ronald Reagan. Do attacks on the president dredge up the need in people to commune?

The door behind the pulpit opens and Ekdahl emerges, dressed in a flowing white surplice. At least he's not late. But the pastor looks tired. His eyes stare ahead without seeing Lindsay as he makes his way to the chancel steps and welcomes the faithful to the Holy Sacrament which the Church has provided for those ready to confess.

Lindsay bows her head and tucks her feet back, clear of the big pedal keys. There's a run in her panty hose. Ekdahl's bright little prayers at this service usually take five or ten seconds.

Almighty God, unto whom all hearts are open, all desires known, and from whom no secrets are hid: cleanse our unclean thoughts.

Blot out our transgressions, wash us and we shall be whiter than snow.

Make us hear gladness and joy: that the bones which thou hast broken may rejoice.

Deliver this nation from blood guilt, so that our tongues shall sing aloud of thy righteousness, and worthily magnify thy holy name.

And assuredly wilt Thou visit the iniquities of the impenitent and unbelieving upon themselves if they turn not from their evil ways, ere the day of grace be ended. Amen.

Lindsay sits motionless. What has come over Ekdahl? His phrases have hooked at rough edges within her. *That his broken bones may rejoice?* She studies the pastor, who now juts his chin defiantly at his parishioners. He's not inviting them to commune, decides Lindsay. He's daring them.

Her hands move automatically to the keyboards. An introductory refrain swells massively into the silence:

Lindsay sings along as she plays:

> *Just as I am, without one plea,*
> *But that thy blood was shed for me,*
> *And that thou bidd'st me come to thee,*
> *O Lamb of God, I come, I come.*

She wonders if there is any theology behind such images. The Mighty Fortress of the church's founder, she recalls, seemed fashioned from sterner stuff: *Here I stand. Faith not works.* But all the lessons of Sunday School, then Confirmation, finally come down to something simple:

> *Little ones to Him belong,*
> *They are weak but He is strong.*

In other words, once things get bad enough, once the ground you stand upon begins to crumble and fall apart, you can save yourself with a leap of faith—a plunge into darkness where strong, fatherly arms will halt your descent.

> *Just as I am, though tossed about*
> *With many a conflict, many a doubt,*
> *Fightings and fears within, without,*
> *O Lamb of God, I come, I come.*

It's true, she thinks. Her fears are both within her and without—half-real and half-imagined. Mostly she's frightened by her own passionate urges, these visions of swooning into the arms of a handsome stranger, not caring who.

Ekdahl is standing in front of the altar, reading from the New Testament: "This cup is the new testament in my blood, which is shed for you. . . ." There's nothing sexy about the pastor. The set of his mouth looks flinty and unforgiving this morning. Now he gestures for the first pew to come forward and receive the sacrament. This is her signal to play again. She flips the stops for Vox Celeste and Stopped Flute, adding the Tremolo that Ekdahl expects in the background of his rite. The melody is her own choice —she ran across it last month, playing through the hymnal at home—a surprisingly lush tune in E flat:

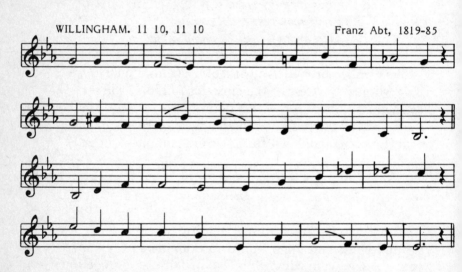

WILLINGHAM. 11 10, 11 10 — Franz Abt, 1819-85

Lindsay sways dreamily to the melody. She hasn't paid much attention to the words of this piece. Now the name "Harriet Beecher Stowe, 1812–96" catches her eye at the bottom of the page. The lyrics to most hymns were written by men. What sort of woman, she wonders, was the author of *Uncle Tom's Cabin?* The second time through, Lindsay whispers the words as she plays:

Still, still with thee, when purple morning breaketh,
When the bird waketh, and the shadows flee;
Fairer than morning, lovelier than daylight,
Dawns the sweet consciousness, I am with thee.

Good heavens, smiles Lindsay. What's this verse doing in
the Lutheran hymnal? There's a name for such poems, she
recalls. *Aubade.* Usually it's the man, awakening in the bed
of love, who greets the dawn. But how touching to see the
moment from a woman's point of view. Lindsay brushes
through cobwebs of nineteenth-century corniness to decide that only a deeply romantic soul, unashamed of the
sensuality both within and without her, could have set
down these lines:

Alone with thee, amid the mystic shadows,
The solemn hush of nature newly born;
Alone with thee in breathless adoration,
In the calm dew and freshness of the morn.

As, one by one, Ekdahl's petitioners rise stiffly from their
knees and return to their pews—wondering, probably,
how to pry loose the Communion wafers stuck to the roofs
of their mouths—Lindsay's mind has floated off, dreaming
of an airy bedroom at dawn. The breeze wafts gently
through floor-length, apricot curtains. Beneath sheets the
color of sugared peaches mulled in cream, the limbs of her
phantom lover lie entwined and bronze about her own. His
mouth awakens her with sweet kisses, and the light streams
in on their nakedness from a world transmuted by love:

So shall it be—at last!—in that bright morning
When the soul waketh and life's shadows flee;
O in that hour, fairer than daylight dawning,
Shall rise the glorious thought, I am with thee!

Lindsay finds herself all a-tingle at this fantasy. It's
put her in touch with what she thinks she hungers for.

Vaguely, she's aware of finishing the hymn. Ekdahl is standing before the altar pronouncing words she can't make out. Then her hands are playing again—an easy Mendelssohn piece. The service must be over. The people are filing out, taking away what they came for.

Lindsay is turning off the organ when Ekdahl approaches. He doesn't look particularly pleased at the large turnout. These people probably drank up a whole bottle of wine.

"Next week," he's saying, "I want to hold an extra Communion service. It's Palm Sunday."

"Fine," she nods, still suspended in breathless adoration of an imagined lover. She finds her coat and makes her way out into fresh morning air. Driving home, she's aware of a dewy wetness between her thighs, a softness about her mouth and face—as if this lovely daylight were caressing her flesh.

Monday morning, someone's forgotten to pull out the button on the alarm clock. Lindsay's household has overslept—and they run on a tight schedule. She stumbles down the stairs to fly about the kitchen, shaking orange juice and buttering toast as, above her, Richard and Alex scramble into their clothes. Richard takes his mug of coffee out to the garage, saying he'll drink it on the way to work. Alex dashes after the school bus waiting at the corner. Lindsay finds herself abandoned, staring at a frying pan of scrambled eggs. A wisp of smoke curls up from the toaster, where a crumb must be wedged against the wires. She pours herself coffee and sits in her usual chair at the kitchen table. Her place. She decides to go upstairs and take a shower. Then she puts on slacks and a lamb's-wool, cowlnecked sweater. Just to lounge around the house in.

By ten o'clock no one has rung the bell. She puts a load of laundry in the washer. Fiddling with the toaster, she presses a catch that springs the bottom open and showers her with crumbs. She changes into jeans and a long-sleeved shirt. By eleven the toaster is gleaming and she's scouring the sink with stainless steel cleanser. In the afternoon she washes the bathroom floors, scrubs the film off the shower curtain, makes a shopping list, and rearranges the spice cabinet. When Alex comes home from school, she starts browning a pot roast. Richard arrives on time—for a change. He fixes drinks for the two of them. Lindsay realizes she forgot to eat lunch. She drinks two glasses of wine with dinner and falls asleep watching *The MacNeil/Lehrer Report*. At 3 A.M. she's wide awake, wondering how she got upstairs, into her nightgown, and under the covers. She lies in the dark, waiting for the hours to pass. Thinking of Gray Chandler makes her excited and giddy. Thinking of Garth makes her rub her eyes in the dark, hug the pillow to her cheek, and murmur, "Oh, you rat. You rat."

By noon on Thursday, the house is gleaming. She's vacuumed, polished furniture and silver, even shined the chrome pipes under the sinks. The refrigerator has been cleaned out, also the medicine chest and the back closet. She's kept her mind on her work, scouring away every trace of her thoughts about being embraced by strange men. A bundle of dirty clothes lies heaped in the front hall. When the doorbell rings, she's putting on her boots for a trip to the dry cleaners. It must be the mailman—postage due again on Richard's Wall Street newsletter.

Heaving open the front door she catches her breath. Gray Chandler stands on her front steps, holding his toolbox in one hand.

He cracks open the storm door and smiles. "May I come in?"

Lindsay takes a step back. It must look like she's making way for him, because suddenly he's through the door. Without warning he kisses her on the cheek. It's a friendly peck, but it makes her pulse pound. She glares at him. But the play of his eyes over her face makes her look away. Fearing he might try something else, she backs out of the hallway and heads for the kitchen. "The dishwasher's in here," she says mindlessly, knowing he's obediently following. Past the den he's fallen behind.

"I'd forgotten what a lovely house you have," he re-marks, running a hand over the commode she uses as a miniature buffet. She refinished it herself. "Someone did a good job restoring this," he says. "It's perfect in here."

"You think so?" She's never thought of using the word *restoring*.

In the kitchen he bends and turns the knob on the dish-washer. After listening for a moment he turns it all the way to "Off" and straightens up. "There's a relay that clicks a little. But nothing wrong."

"Well, then—" she sighs.

He leans against the counter, his eyes drilling into her. "I think you're gorgeous," he says. "Especially in that sweater. It's a terrific color for you."

Lindsay tugs self-consciously at the cowl of her sweater, resisting the impulse to brush a hand over her abdomen. She recalls spattering crumbs on this sweater earlier in the week. The deep burnt sienna matches her boots pretty well. But she feels both pierced and hurt by his remarks. What right does he have to breeze in the door, flinging compliments about so casually, after ignoring her all week?

He's gazing about the kitchen, taking in the spotless floor, the clean countertops, the gleaming chrome. "You're very neat, aren't you?"

She's not sure how to take this. It makes her feel prim. Overly tidy.

Gray walks toward her now. "I see a lot of women's kitchens," he's saying, extending a hand. "And I want to congratulate you on yours."

Lindsay wonders what's going on. She watches her hand go out to meet his. At his touch her heart leaps. She looks up as he steps closer, looming toward her. Suddenly he's inches away, smiling down at her. His free hand brushes a wisp of hair back from her temple and then traces a line down along her jaw. The lightness of his touch makes her tingle. She's aware of her butt pressed to the edge of the table. There's no backing out of this. His hand tips up her chin, and she feels his breath on her face—his mouth is that close. For an agonizing moment she gazes into his pale blue eyes, as his fingertips explore the line of her lips. Her pulse thuds. Could she stop this now if she wanted to? His feathery touch is teasing a secret nerve, a hunger coming from her loins. "Mmm," she moans as he presses his mouth to hers. Lindsay lets her eyes flutter shut. In dizzying darkness, she throws her arms about his neck. She hangs onto him. Arched back luxuriantly in his embrace, she opens to the hot thrust of him, the tip of her tongue against his. But she's held her breath and has to smack free to pant for air. As she takes in the musky scent of his aftershave, he's kissing her ear, her hair, her neck, burrowing deep into the cowl of her sweater, sending a hot current through her. His hands move in circles on her back, then down to her ass, smoothing her hips along the outside seam of her slacks.

"Where were you all week?" she whispers.

"Shh," he says, nuzzling her hair and kissing behind her ear.

Lindsay squints an eye open. Over his shoulder the wall clock says one fifteen. Gray has slipped a hand up under her sweater to smooth her bare back. She pushes away. "I thought you were coming on Monday," she says.

He holds her at arm's length and gazes into her face. "Is that what I said?" He looks a little sheepish. "I had a lot of calls to make."

"Oh," she says, slipping free from his grasp. "Can I fix you a drink?" The excitement he's triggered within her subsides long enough for Lindsay to calculate the minutes ahead. The school bus will bring Alex home before three. Her conscience has been shocked into silence. Now, weakly, it tries to warn her. "You don't even know this man." But that's his appeal. He's just a pair of hands, a quick tongue, and a bulge in his— She forbids herself a glance at the crotch of his jeans. Instead she strains to picture the inside of the liquor cabinet.

"Scotch, bourbon, gin, vermouth—" She's counting them off on her fingers.

"Bourbon would be fine," he says. "Over some ice."

"But is there time? I mean, you probably have other calls to make." Lindsay has decided they'll have a chat on the couch in the living room. Then he'll have to leave.

"Oh, there's time." He flashes a broad grin.

She gets down two big glass tumblers, ice from the freezer, and goes into the dining room. There she sloshes in Richard's Jack Daniel's, wondering whether her trembling legs will collapse on the way to the next room. She pours in a lot, thinking that a full glass will keep his hands occupied. In the living room, Gray slips off his down vest, and they sit on the couch. Immediately he edges closer and kisses her cheek. He's able to accomplish this without spilling a drop.

Lindsay sits up and clears her throat. "Now, I don't understand," she says, "how you got into this business. Being a repairman, I mean." The front drapes are wide open. Outside the bare sidewalk settles into thin afternoon light. She feels secure in this room. The whole neighborhood has a view over her coffee table.

Gray clinks his glass against hers, and they both take a sip. Hers burns on the way down. She usually takes water in bourbon.

"Oh, my job?" he says, seeming to brush it away with a sweep of his hand. "It's research, actually. Before I start my apprenticeship."

Lindsay nods, but doesn't entirely follow this. She thinks of plumbers, masons, and electricians—the building trades. They have masters, journeymen, and apprentices. She thinks of the odd boys in high school who hung out in the metal shop, got into fights, and got girls pregnant.

"This position," he explains, "gives me a chance to see how people inhabit conventional space. Kitchens, for example. They haven't really changed much since the 1940s. But the patterns of people's lives have changed a lot."

Lindsay is conscious of how easily he's made himself comfortable on her couch—like one of Richard's friends over for dinner. And now he's talking less like a manual laborer and more like a sociologist. "But"—she frowns—"I didn't realize that appliance repairmen— I mean, you take a theoretical view of your work."

"Good grief," he laughs. "Quit calling me a 'repairman.' You make me feel like I'm the gamekeeper, and you've invited me in for tea at the manor house."

Lindsay blushes. Who is this guy, anyway? "You're somebody in disguise?"

"Ah," he smiles. "That's one way to put it." He stretches out his scuffed workboots. "Beneath this humble peasant garb beats a noble heart."

"I bet," she says.

"You don't think I look like a prince? You know, Harvard, class of '77?"

"Oh?" says Lindsay, mildly impressed. "But since then what?"

"Yale. The School of Architecture. And a couple of years in Italy."

"Really." She recalls now that architects serve apprenticeships.

"In the Boston area," he's saying, "the name 'Chandler' goes pretty far back. Colonial shipping, the clergy—all that."

"I see," nods Lindsay, sipping bourbon and gazing at his square jaw, at the lips that pressed her own. Her handyman has turned into an aristocrat. But determined to keep the upper hand during this chat, she asks, "How old are you?"

"Twenty-seven. How about you?"

Lindsay stares out the front window. Oh dear, she thinks. He's just a boy. Class of '77. She sips her drink and turns a coy smile on him. "Guess," she states.

"Twenty-nine," he replies confidently.

"Close," she says. He's only five years off. Lindsay is beginning to enjoy this. And she feels an advantage again, a sense of control. The bourbon has warmed and smoothed out her nervousness.

Gray sets his drink on the coffee table. "You were going to show me your poems," he says.

Lindsay leans her head back on the couch. "No," she declares with mock petulance. "Not today."

He grasps the hand she's let fall on the cushion between them. "Ah, but you must!" he insists.

"No, no!" she cries dramatically.

"Yes, yes!" Gray slips off the couch and kneels before her. His chest presses against her legs. She crosses them tighter at the ankle. "Yes," he murmurs, kissing the knuckles of her limp hand. Then he rests his head on her lap. She smiles to herself and runs her fingers through the hair of this amusing young man. It's probably time for him to leave. She's surprised to see that her glass contains only ice cubes. He sits back on his heels and takes the drink from her hand. A pleasant wave of warmth makes her sigh. Again he presses his face to her belly. This time she feels his chin moving across the hump of her groin. That ticklish itch stirs somewhere within as his hands stroke her thighs. The sight of his head trying to nuzzle in between her legs strikes her as ludicrous.

"What do you think you're doing?" she asks.

"I'm your home mechanic, examining a pivot bushing."

"That's a dumb joke." But Lindsay smiles at his touch and lets her eyes close. What a silly way to spend the afternoon, she thinks. Her eyes drift open as she feels one leg lifted at the heel. He's yanking off her boot. The slick glide of the other boot down her calf sends a delicious tremor up her leg. Then he stretches out beside her on the couch, and his arms encircle her. He's after that sensitive place on her neck, and his hands are busy along her hips, stroking and kneading her flesh in a luxuriant massage. It's driving her a little crazy. Lindsay stiffens when she feels the waist of her slacks get unbuttoned. Then his hand plunges all the way into her underpants, the coolness of his fingers touching her naked tenderness. She was spotting this morning. Her period is due tomorrow, and she aches a little. But he's very gentle, and she submits to the steady circling of his palm on her pubic bone, to his fingers—warming now, and wet—flicking in and out. In high school, this was called "heavy petting." How long has it been since she's felt the annoying stretch of a panty's elastic leg hole cutting a line into her groin?

He stops. Lindsay opens her eyes and watches him unzip her slacks and tug with two hands at her hips. "Come on, pull hard," she says.

With a grunt he yanks her slacks, panty hose, underpants all the way off. "You're going to tire me out," he says, unbuckling his jeans.

"I probably will," she says. Her taunt tells them both that she's going to allow this thing to happen.

Gray looms above her and lowers himself onto her. But he's not much of a kisser. Her mouth searches the rough stubble of his cheek, finds the lobe of an ear, and sucks. Her legs, bare now to the coolness of the house, rise to the warmth of him, the delicious friction of his hand moving along her thighs. She opens them wide, finally inviting the delirious stroke of his touch, the thick presence of him rubbing, probing the wetness out of her.

"Is that thing your finger?" she asks.

"No," he murmurs, gripping himself to rub the tip against her wet labia.

"What do you call it?" she whispers.

He hitches up on one elbow and smiles at her. "If I tell you, will you quit asking questions?"

"You're using it like a tool. I bet that's what you call it."

"As a matter of fact," he says, "I call it a strut. A tubular strut."

"That's pretty strange," laughs Lindsay. What he's doing feels wonderful.

Then he embraces her again, kissing her mouth, her cheek, her neck. "It's another dumb joke," he murmurs, his tongue at the whorl of her ear.

"No more jokes," she whispers, as her heart pounds. She decides that she could become fond of this young man.

Abruptly he stuffs it in. She gasps at his entry, then feels hot, gliding pleasure melt into softness. Oh, this is what she's wanted. But he's pumping in hard and fast, filling her again and again. "Slow down," she wants to tell him, but figures that he's over the edge, beyond reach. So she moans now and then for effect. Retreating into a nimble aloofness, she amuses herself by thinking that it's just another penis, right? Finally he pokes in deep and goes tense in spasms. So much for romance.

Gray lies heavily upon her, catching his breath. Abruptly he pulls out and stands up. Lindsay watches as he pushes the flaccid thing into his boxer shorts. It looks just like Richard's. Her concern now is whether they've left a stain on the couch.

"That was nice," he says, buckling his belt.

Thighs squeezed together to catch the dribble, Lindsay sits up. "Yes," she agrees. "Short and sweet." There's a round puddle, the size of a dime, on one cushion. It's pearly, streaked with blood.

Through the open front drapes, she watches her neighbor, Mrs. Clapp, walking her dog. The woman's gaze, like the dog's nose, is fastened to the pavement. Lindsay stoops to pick up her slacks, then takes duck steps to the downstairs bathroom. Passing through the dining room, she tries not to think of genital herpes. She doubts that, by some fluke of the moon, she'll become pregnant. But a damp depression is settling upon her spirits.

When she comes back, he's put on his vest and sits on the couch, leafing through a magazine. He hasn't made any more jokes, nor has he inquired—as he did last night on the phone—about how she's feeling. Now she wonders how many depressed women he's screwed in their tidy living rooms. The spot on the couch has been wiped away, smeared into the fabric. Something queasy turns over in her stomach. She ought to get a sponge.

"I have to go," he says, standing up and putting his arms around her.

"I wish I knew more about you," she says.

"Shh," he whispers into her hair. "You don't want to know about me."

"I don't?"

He shakes his head, pushes her off, and grins at her. "You're gorgeous."

"You already said that."

"Ah, but it's true." He heads for the door. There he gives her a quick, dry kiss. "I'll call you," he says. Then, toolbox in hand, he's gone.

In the shower, she puts her face up to the spray and tries not to feel dizzy. It's taken this long to realize that she's drunk. Something tightens within her. It's a menstrual cramp. The ache and the nausea in her belly double her over. She kneels in the tub as the water pounds on her back. Poking a finger into her mouth, she gags and heaves a stream of yellow vomit that spins around the drain hole.

It feels good to kneel. The posture reminds her of a time in high school. Her church group—both boys and girls—had played touch football. This was shortly after her First Communion. Lindsay caught a pass by mistake and ran with it. She scored a touchdown. Out of breath, she'd knelt on the grass, and all the kids came and patted her on the back. Later, she found out she'd run the wrong way, had scored for the opposing team. But kneeling there on the grass, she'd felt only exhausted pride in her feat. That's what the shower—beating in spatters on her spine—feels like: a thousand little hands patting her in mock admiration. "Way to go, Lindsay!" say the cleansing drops. "Way to go!"

15

LINDSAY AGONIZES over what she's done. But her guilt doesn't provoke remorse. Instead she prods and explores the shameful memory of what happened on her couch—as one presses at an aching tooth. She decides that she's testing the limits of her ability to suffer.

Perhaps Ekdahl has started it, this stretching of things to the breaking point. Perhaps the lines of fracture were already there, fissures in the crystal, cracks ready to split. For the pastor it came as a vision the night before taping his first TV show. Sleepless, he had arisen and gone down to the kitchen, where he drank an entire bottle of red wine. Then it appeared, first hovering out of the corner of his eye; next, pressed writhing against the white refrigerator. "Ah," he winced, seeing his Savior crucified, the bones shattered by blows, the joints pulled into horrid distortions, the flesh rent like the ragged edges of broken bread.

The next afternoon at the TV station, a lone cameraman trained his lens on the pastor, who sat stiffly in a wing-back chair. Once the videotape was rolling, Ekdahl looked immobile—nailed down. The cameraman yawned, took off his headset, and strolled out to join the director at the coffee machine in the corridor. At some point during their absence, Ekdahl departed from his prepared remarks to reenact for viewers his gruesome vision of a body contorted by pain. As he got up from his chair, his lapel-microphone yanked loose. An engineer in the booth waved both arms to signal his confusion. Out in the corridor, the studio door muffled the sound of a ghastly wail. The two at the coffee machine exchanged a glance, then broke into a run. Bursting into the studio, they saw maintenance men in blue wrestling someone to the floor of the set.

The station manager escorted Ekdahl to the parking lot. Informing the pastor that his TV show had been canceled, he tried to seem offhand. But the way he slammed the door of the clergyman's Ford Fairmont made it clear that the matter was not open for debate. Back in the studio, the crew gathered to rerun the tape. The last two and a half minutes looked pretty bad: a wildly contorted face had approached the camera lens as the soundtrack went dead, then anonymous men in blue uniforms pummeled someone thrashing below the bottom edge of the screen.

Twelve hours later, a college kid working the booth on the night shift (eager to fill the station's FCC quota of public service programming) found the tape lying around and played it by mistake. He'd just washed down 375 mgs of methaqualone (two sopes: one green, the other orange) with a Diet Coke, and he sat back to mellow-out on the warm and witty contortions of Pastor Ekdahl's face. When the tape went blank, the young engineer resourcefully filled in the last fifteen minutes with a video graphic, punched out from information taped to the cassette:

Faith in the Morning!
with
Rev. Rudy Ekdahl
The Good Shepherd Lutheran Church
Hillsdale Rd. (just off Commercial Drive)
Sunday Services at 8 & 10

At 3 A.M. no one from the FCC was watching. Neither was anyone from the station. The next day, the station manager erased the tape.

Early Palm Sunday morning, when Lindsay arrives to play for the eight o'clock Communion service, the parking lot is already full of vehicles: rusted hulks patched with masking tape, strange autos fabricated from plywood and corrugated cardboard, pickups with shotguns racked in the back windows. Inside, the church is nearly full. Here and there she spots a familiar face from the regular congregation. But most of these people are haggard strangers wearing old clothes and the look of gaunt desperation. They sure don't look like Lutherans. She has no way of knowing about Ekdahl's 3 A.M. broadcast, or what disinherited souls might have been awake—watching—at that hour, or through what channels the word spread of a clergyman who knew, who understood the agony of their condition.

As she stares out from behind the organ, the force of their accumulated bitterness washes over her in waves. She has tossed, sleepless, for three nights, battering herself against hard regret. Something's broken in her—her innocence, perhaps. Crossing her arms, she clasps herself tight, as if she fears to let the wreckage of herself float off with the soggy debris of these people's lives.

Something's wrong with the organ. The keys stick in pairs, as if someone has anointed it with maple syrup. It's impossible to hit the right notes without sending terrible throbs of dissonance into the sanctuary. There's no time to fix whatever is stuck—because here comes Ekdahl, out from behind the pulpit. My God, she thinks, look at his face. His expression goes through her—and out again.

Lindsay shuts her eyes and puts a hand to her forehead. It's feverish. A touch of the flu, she decides. Looking up, she imagines an acid flux streaming off the eager mob. To the other side, Ekdahl's face sags like molten metal as he heaves some ritual object overhead. She has no choice but to sit here and bear this crosscurrent of malign heat. Lindsay shudders, fearing that her thoughts are veering into a dangerous region. A sick insight comes to her about the nature of guilt. Once absolved, it has to drain off somewhere. The idea is insane, and she pushes the thought away. She knows that if you fear going crazy, you probably are. She refuses to believe that a dark current converges on her as she sits at the organ, denies that she's been chosen to take it in and channel it out—making herself its conduit, its hollow victim. Otherwise she's cracking up.

On Long Island—where Una paces the dunes of East Hampton—the sign of breakage, of crucifixion, appears merely in Una's crossed fingers as she hunches against the wind. Scud of gray clouds to the north promises merely a break in the weather. But it's a lucky break—for Garth and his art—that's brought her to this place, now that Aunt Ava is back on her feet. The doctors said she had suffered a tiny cerebral clot whose paralyzing symptoms disappeared after twenty-four hours.

Una leans into the wind and heads back to the cottage. A man waits in bed there, expecting to get screwed before catching the train back to the city. This one brought amyl nitrate in ampules that he breaks and inhales just before orgasm. Una doesn't like the smell—like rotten fruit. Two nights ago, a red-haired guy brought cocaine—which wasn't so bad, because they stayed up all night talking. Toward morning he got a nosebleed and left, upset, before she had a chance to show him Garth's work. Her old suitcase wasn't lost. She's brought it along full of old copies of *The New York Times*. She and Wally saved them. In the classified ads of each issue is one of Garth's minimal works of art. Una figures that they're now worth something, and Garth is due to be discovered.

The men who visit the cottage are art dealers and gallery owners, critics and collectors. Una's vulnerable hip has begun to ache from all this sex. But one lucky break is all Garth needs. She tells herself that she's racking her body for him—only for him.

Meanwhile, at the Good Shepherd Church, Lindsay cowers behind the organ. Ekdahl is lurching about waving a staple gun in his hand. His lips move wordlessly as he gestures in the general direction of the crowd. Their eyes are riveted on him, but they're an unruly group—like an

audience at a movie theater. A low murmuring undertone
swells from the sanctuary.

Lindsay hopes this scene is a nightmare. It's possible that
she's imagining at least half of it. Certainly the church isn't
quite so full as she first thought. And what's happened to
that staple gun? Did she imagine it too? Ekdahl clasps his
empty hands, measures his words, and falls back into the
familiar routine: "And Jesus took bread, and blessed, and
brake it, and gave it to them, and said, Take, eat: this is my
body. . . ."

Eventually he gives Lindsay a sign. It's time to play. Her
hands, as she places them on the sticky keys, seem to blur
before her eyes. She tells herself there is no crazy force
streaming through her. Such a thing—even the idea of such
a thing—would do some terrible damage to her interior.
What she feels, she decides, is simply her own hot blood
coursing through the veins of her body.

Downtown, two flights up from Woolworth's, something in the air breaks Helen's train of thought. She
freezes, confused, in the middle of her kitchen. A terrible
blank crosses her mind. When things white-out like this,
there's always the chance that she'll lose it—lose the whole
world.

When Helen was in her twenties, she slipped in the
bathtub and fractured her skull. She suffered no loss of
consciousness—that is, no immediate impairment of cerebral function—but did see stars. A week later she lost her
sense of smell and couldn't distinguish flavors. Alarmed,
she took a bus downtown to see her doctor. On the way she
saw that posted notices contained certain words ("Rear
Exit," for example) whose meaning she didn't recognize. In
the Medical Arts Building she found herself staring for a
long time at the elevator buttons. She couldn't decide what
these metal disks were for. Upstairs, a receptionist asked
her to fill in a form. Helen took the pen in her hand and
strained to lift it to the top of the page. Her arm wouldn't

budge. By the time a doctor examined her, she was unable to remember her own name. Immediately, they sent her down the street to the hospital for tests.

In a small room, a medical student wearing thick glasses took down her case history. The student seemed especially charmed by her inability to say the word "chair" when he indicated the one she was sitting on. "Oh, it'll come to me," she blushed. "It's right on the tip of my—" Her cheeks went a deeper shade of red. "Oh, dear. That thing in your mouth, you know?"

The young man patted her hand and explained that she was suffering from aphasia. Her inability to smell or taste things he called anosmia. When he wrote down the word "fled" and held it up, Helen insisted that such a word did not exist in the English language.

"You've got alexia, too!" he exclaimed. He seemed torn between exploring the theoretical oddity of her case and reaching out to administer reassuring caresses to her palm, her plump forearm, the creamy flesh that her sundress revealed.

Helen had decided that the medical student was cute. But when he offered her his pencil to test her writing skills, she drew back in fright. "What's that thing?" she demanded.

He held up the pencil. "You don't know what this is for?"

"It looks dangerous," she confessed.

"Can you make a fist?"

She strained her fingers, but then gave up the effort. "I know how to make a fist," she said, "but I can't make myself do it."

The student pushed his thick glasses up on his nose and announced that he was adding agnosia and ideomotor apraxia to the list of her ailments.

"What's wrong with me?" she pleaded.

"I'll try to explain," he said. "You see, links exist between things and words, between ideas and actions. For you, all the possible connections seem to be"—he bit his lip—"breaking down."

"You mean I've got brain damage?" said Helen. "Well, gee. What's the cure?"

He looked like he was about to weep for her ample, but now doomed, loveliness. "Helen, the medical profession possesses only the crudest of tools for intervening in the mind. And the long-term therapy for—"

"Just a minute!" she snapped. "No cure? You mean all you've got are fancy names for what's wrong with me?" She shook her fist at him. "Lexia-prexia to you, buster. You doctors are a bunch of fakes!"

The student looked down at his clipboard and mumbled something about being just a student.

Helen fumbled in her purse for a scrap of paper. "Let me borrow that thing," she said bitterly. "I guess I'd better write down this list of what's wrong with me." She scribbled a few notes, then paused thoughtfully with the eraser end of the pencil between her teeth. Suddenly she grimaced. "Aagghh! Ear wax! Is this your pencil?"

Helen stared into his astonished face. Her bosom made a quick gasp as a spark leapt the space between them. They both knew it now: her *sense of taste* had returned!

"Can you stand up?" he asked cautiously. She could. He gave her commands to test ideomotor kinetic response mechanisms: "Raise your left arm. Hop on one foot!" Helen hopped, waved her arms, and squealed with delight.

"Wrinkle your nose! Pat your head!" Tears of joy streamed down both their faces. "Pucker your—"

Suddenly Helen seized him in a hug that lifted him off his feet. Pressing all of her to him, he sensed a flickering aura circling about them. Bright flashes forced Helen's eyes shut as, somewhere within her skull, switches clicked back into place. "What's the word for this?" she asked in awe. "The word for what's happening?"

"It's *love!*" he cried.

Yelling "Follow me!" he yanked her out the door. Together they burst into an office down the hallway. The dean of the medical school looked up. His brightest second-year student flung a clipboard onto the desk.

"I quit," he declared. "You doctors are a bunch of fakes!" Then he and Helen stamped arm in arm out the door, down the hallway—in step—to the front entrance, and into bright sunlight. The name of the medical student, of course, was Wally Czyzycki. Two months later he and Helen got married.

Now, thirty years have passed. Helen still suffers brief episodes of "absent-mindedness." This Palm Sunday morning, something in the air swirls her cerebral fluids into confused eddies. A blank crosses her mind as she stares at the spatula in her hand.

"What's this thing?" she says aloud. She whacks it against the edge of the kitchen door, thinking it might be an around-the-corner fly swatter. Maybe it's a shoehorn—for someone with really flat feet? When Wally comes in, she's pressed the blade flat on the countertop, catapulting grapes ceilingward with the springy handle. At once he understands that she's lost something—the concept *spatula.*

"I think," he says, "I'll make some French toast. But I can't decide how I'm going to *flip them over* in the pan." Slyly he watches her reaction.

Helen gives him a perplexed look. "Why don't you use a—"

"Yes?" he coaxes gently.

"Oh, what's it called?" Helen irritably lobs another grape into the air. "You know, a—"

"Yes? Yes!"

"—a flerg!" she announces in triumph.

At the church, Ekdahl is administering the sacrament to those kneeling at the altar rail. The keys of the organ have loosened up. Lindsay no longer feels like she's playing the soundtrack for *The Phantom of the Opera.* The people get up and file back to their pews in an orderly manner. Everything looks normal—except that the pastor, a loaf of French bread wedged under his arm, is serving the wine out of a big Tupperware bowl.

Downstairs from Wally's at the Billiard Emporium, Harold Matlow opens a beer and racks the balls for another solitary game of pool. For him, this is a Sunday-morning ritual before he opens the doors at noon. The break offers him no clear shot—except a long cross-corner bank. Something already broke in Harold years ago when his wife died. But the strain that others feel this morning hits him, too. It comes up, as he paces the hard linoleum, to pound the bones in his legs.

Harold's tragedy occurred in 1958 on his honeymoon to Louisiana. Driving the old Studebaker north from New Orleans through a maze of bayous, he and his bride followed muddy back roads. At one point, he stopped the car when she spotted a cluster of brilliant blossoms growing near the roadside. Holding her skirt, she waded into silent, brackish water. She stretched out in one last reach, then slipped and plunged in. Abruptly she stood up, sputtering a stream of water from her mouth, holding an enormous flower aloft in the hot, steamy air.

An hour later, they found the main highway and a motel. Stripping off her wet garments, they were horrified to discover half a dozen black leeches stuck to her abdomen and thighs. The slimy things fell off writhing when Harold patted them with salt.

They followed the Mississippi north. At Vicksburg, his wife complained of difficulty swallowing. In St. Louis she coughed up blood in a ladies' room, but didn't tell Harold until they crossed over from Missouri into Iowa. In Davenport, she woke in the middle of the night gagging, wheezing for air. He rushed her to an emergency room, where they put her in a curtained-off area and paged the respiratory therapist. Nothing seemed to happen for twenty minutes. When Harold looked in, there was blood at her mouth, her face was blue, and she wasn't moving.

The death certificate said that she'd died of an obstructed epiglottis due to internal hirudiniasis. When the pathologist began to explain what he'd found during the autopsy, Harold nearly struck him in the jaw to make him shut up. His wife had evidently ingested small leeches. Attaching themselves to the mucosa of her trachea and esophagus, they had swelled, engorged with her blood, to strangle her finally from within.

Now Harold circles the pool table and sets down his beer next to the corner pocket. He drinks cold beer in the morning to wash down the pretzels he eats for breakfast. He's forgotten where he acquired this massive need for salt in his diet. He likes hard, dry things. The notion of eating anything dark and soft revolts him. The sight of raw liver, foods without texture—even the deeper shades of Jello— sends him into a panic. Ah, but a nice crisp pretzel. And the quick crack of balls on the hard, green felt. He even likes this sharp ache coming up from his legs. He smiles grimly, imagining the bones in his shins. They are dry and hard, brittle, and starkly white.

The Communion service is over. The faithful have shoved out the back door. Lindsay hears them in the parking lot, gunning the engines of their derelict vehicles. Switching off the organ, she wonders if she was the only one who found the service unusual. Did only she feel assaulted by its symbols—as if the point of the ceremony were not to face one toward regeneration, but perversely to head one toward—what is the word?—a breakdown?

16

AT HOME, Lindsay finds Alex in the den watching TV. He's just switched from a religious program to coverage of the first Space Shuttle launching. "We have solid rocket ignition," says the voice of the countdown. She stands and watches, transfixed by bright orange flame and billowing smoke.

"Is this it?" she asks her son.

"Naw, they keep replaying the liftoff. It went up just after you left."

"It looks so big. Heavy."

"Four and a half thousand pounds," he replies, a little bored.

"You mean *million* pounds. That's a couple thousand *tons*, right?" She imagines a mountain pushed up by energy that it has stored away for centuries. "Wasn't there trouble on Friday?" she says, "The backup computer out of sync?"

"They must have fixed it."

She's thinking that the *Columbia* looks like a phallus, a display of national power and ingenuity especially suited to the imaginations of boys. Alex is gripping his bare feet, matching the soles together like hands in prayer. "Dad's upstairs getting dressed for church," he says.

"How come you're still in your pajamas?"

"He says I can stay home."

Lindsay shakes her head. "No siree, young man. You march right up there."

"Aw gee, Mom."

Upstairs, Richard has put on the suit that Lindsay detests, a rust-brown and green plaid that makes him look like a used-car salesman. He glances at her and says, "You look exhausted."

"At least put on a different necktie," she suggests, sitting down heavily on the unmade bed. "I told Alex to get dressed for Sunday School."

Richard whips the tie out of his collar. "I understood that he wanted to stay home to see the Space Shuttle."

"The shuttle is up already." She kicks off her shoes, then adds, "It spurted right out of sight."

He can see her in the mirror as he puts on another necktie. "You okay?"

"Sure," she says, stretching out on the bed. "But don't ask me to go back to that church. Something weird is happening to Ekdahl."

"Weird?" He stands at the bedroom door and slips on his jacket.

"Maybe it was my imagination," she says, throwing an arm across her eyes.

"Well, take it easy, okay? See you later."

She lies there, listening to her husband going down the stairs. Eventually, she hears them start her VW and back out the driveway. Then she gets up and takes off her clothes, leaving them in a heap on the floor. A dull-red spot stares up at her from a mini-pad stuck in her underpants. The mirror on the closet door reflects her whole pale figure. She approaches, wondering at this image, watching her hands explore the flesh—as if they were searching for a secret bruise, a rent torn in the skin at one of those places you can never see directly.

Richard heads Lindsay's car west and swings up a ramp onto the Interstate.

"This isn't the way to church," says Alex.

"I have to make a stop on the way. It won't take but a minute. Okay?"

Richard had this worked out. Lindsay would be tired as

usual after the early service. And if Alex stayed home, then by claiming to go to church he would have an hour to stop by Gina's apartment. Now, with his son along, he's improvising. Downtown, he parks in front of the tavern and tells Alex to wait in the car. Gina's place is just around the corner.

From the window of his loft, Garth stares down at Lindsay's red Rabbit parked diagonally in the street. During last month's vigil on her street, he memorized the license plate, that small dent in the back fender, and the patterns of road grime spotting the chrome bumper.

More than a week has passed since Garth learned Lindsay's name in front of the tavern. He's certain she came to see him that Friday. Realizing this has made him balk at making another move. The chance that he's tampering with a household, disrupting the psychic life of a kid—it all generates too much guilt. And guilt has driven him into respectability, all the way into a temporary job. With Una gone and no money in the bank, he called the school board, where he's registered as a substitute grade-school teacher. They put his name on their active list. Last week, he filled in two days for a suburban art teacher out with a broken ankle.

Garth goes down his stairwell and peers at Lindsay's car. From the back, with those high seats, it looks empty. He steps out, goes down the street, and crosses over to walk on the other side. "Oh, what a coincidence," he'll say. But passing the VW he suddenly quickens his pace. It's her son, alone in the car.

"Hi," calls the boy.

Garth slows down. He ought to keep going.

"Mr. Erikson," says Alex, rolling down the window.

Garth stops and glances back. "How'd you know my name?"

"You know me. I'm Alex. We talked on the phone. I saw you in the hall at school. Sydney said you were a substitute. In his art class."

"Ah—" Garth nods. "School." He puts his hands in his pockets. The street in either direction looks deserted. "Where's your mom?" he asks.

"She's at home. I'm with Dad. He has to see someone. It's business, I think. We're going to be late for church."

The last person Garth wants to run into is Lindsay's husband. "Well," he says. "Nice seeing you."

"Are you going to church? You're not dressed up."

Garth spreads opens his Salvation Army sportcoat like wings. He's slipped it on over a T-shirt. "You don't like this outfit?" he says.

"Sydney said you taught them how to tap and bang on things."

Garth is anxious to leave. But he's also curious about what children think of conceptual sculpture. "Did the kids like it?" he asks.

Alex leans his chin on the rolled-down window. "Okay, I guess. Sydney said it was stupid. But it was an art project, right?"

Garth nods and looks at the pavement.

"I like quiet better than banging." Alex is frowning slightly, thinking.

"Quiet?"

"You know, like sitting still? No sound."

What a strange, serious kid, thinks Garth. "Well, if the teacher tells you to tap on things until you find your own sound—the one that fits you—what would you do?"

Alex looks ahead out the windshield. "I'd get a big stick or a hammer. And then I'd find a statue— no, a cross. Like in church?"

"Wait a minute," says Garth. "If you banged a cross with a hammer, how would that sound quiet?"

"Oh, no one would dare bang a cross!" Alex's eyes look mischievous. "See?" he says. "*No sound.*"

Garth looks at the kid. Then together they burst into laughter. "That's good," sighs Garth. "You might grow up to be a first-class lunatic."

"I don't know what that means."

"It's a joke."

"Oh," says Alex. "Look, here comes my dad."

Garth cringes and glances at the big guy striding toward them in a plaid suit. What is he—trying to look like Johnny Carson? Garth steps back from the car, knowing that this scene doesn't look good: a bearded derelict—maybe a wino —getting chummy with a kid alone in a car.

"What's going on here?" says Richard. He's a little out of breath.

"This is Mr. Erikson, Dad. He's a teacher at my school."

Richard looks at Garth's clothing as if he's calculating how little they pay grade-school teachers. Then he introduces himself with a quick handshake but goes around to the driver's side of the car. "Sorry we have to run off," he says.

"Sure," says Garth. They exchange a look over the top of the car. "Good kid you got here."

"Oh?" Richard shakes his head in dismay at something. "Hey listen, we're late. Nice to meet you," he says, getting in.

Garth watches them back out and drive off. Jeez, he thinks. Now he knows the whole family.

Richard drops Alex off at the Sunday School entrance, then finds a place in the crowded parking lot. Inside, Nat Nelson, the head usher, waits in the narthex for latecomers.

"What's happening?" asks Richard.

"Beats me," whispers Nat. "I've run out of programs. I think there's a seat in the back row."

In the sanctuary, the unfamiliar sight of a full church— all those heads bowed in prayer—puts Richard on tiptoe as he steps through the back door. A woman in sunglasses, wearing a man's blue trenchcoat, slides over to make room for him on the aisle. Her right cheek and temple bear the bright raspberry stain of a birthmark.

He clasps his hands and takes a breath. Ekdahl is mumbling a prayer in the pulpit. Richard's mind still whirls from his tire-squealing drive from downtown.

At her apartment, Gina was expecting him. At work, he'd told her that they must talk, that he'd try to stop by Sunday morning. She answered his knock wearing a black satin gown, naked beneath it.

"I don't have much time," he'd said, standing firm in the doorway. "Maybe it's better this way."

"Don't be so dramatic, Richard. Come on in." She tugged him over the threshold and shut the door.

"Really. My son's in the car outside. There's just one thing—one last thing—that I want to make clear."

Gina seemed to prepare herself for a scolding. Lacing her fingers together, she looked down penitently at the floor.

"My silence these past two weeks"—he declared—"it hasn't been any kind of ploy. I've genuinely lost interest in you. Now then, you have your friend—what's-his-name—and I have my family."

"Dave." She supplied the name, tears welling up in her mascaraed eyes.

"Right," he nodded. "So, at the office, I hope we can manage—"

"Dave's gone," broke in Gina. "He left this morning with all his stuff."

Richard looked into her glistening eyes. "I'm sorry," he said. "But that doesn't concern me."

"Doesn't it?"

He looked away. She'd set out orange juice and rolls on her coffee table. The place looked like she'd spent a whole day cleaning it up for his visit. The white shag rug—where they'd first made love—was spotless and fluffed up.

"I'm sorry," he repeated and turned away to grasp the brass doorknob. Cheap metal, he thought to himself. Then he felt her arms encircle his waist from behind. He'd have to shove her back to get out the door.

"Oh," she sighed behind him. "Just let me touch you."

Through his suit, he felt her hands slipping toward the hollows of his groin. "Listen," he said, and spun around to face her.

She looked up at him, wetting her lips with a kind of

pout. Without any apparent effort, her gown fell open, parting on either side of her bare breasts. "Just let me touch you," she whispered, again.

"Listen—" he said mechanically and looked down, astounded by the sight of her deft fingers unfastening his belt and unzipping his trousers. "Oh, no—" he murmured weakly, as Gina sank to her knees. How had he become so stiff, so fast? She'd never offered to do this before. The room seemed to revolve. Gina had tapped into an adolescent fantasy—a gesture of womanly submission that Richard had dreamed up, thrashing himself astride toilets, alone in dark garages, off by himself in weedy lots.

Abruptly he pulled back and fastened his trousers. "I have to go," he said, clutching her to keep his balance.

"Hey, Richard?" Gina nuzzled against his chest. "I wouldn't dream of hurting you. Or your family. Don't you see? You need something extra in your life. Why not two women? You can handle it."

"You think so?" Light-headed, he strained to follow this logic.

"Uh-huh," she said, as if clinging to something heroic in him. Then, abruptly, she opened the door for him. "Now get out of here," she joked and pushed him, staggering, out into the hallway.

Richard now stares at his folded hands, the right thumb crossed over the left. Loud applause rings in his ears. He sits up and looks about at the congregation. Clapping in church?

In the pulpit, Ekdahl is waving his arms. "And if we lift up our eyes unto the hills, and ask 'From whence cometh our help?' there isn't any help. For the sun hath smited you by day! And the moon by night!"

The woman sitting next to Richard nods and audibly murmurs, "Yes." He notices that a man, sitting three pews ahead, is wearing a baseball cap and presses a transistor radio to his ear.

"I am reminded of the story," says Ekdahl, "of an old

race driver who pulled into the pit after only three laps. He took off his dirty goggles and climbed out of the car, saying that he couldn't go on. His career was over. An unfamiliar young man stepped forward from the crew and said that he could drive the car. The old man looked skeptical. The young man held out his hand for the key. The old driver handed it to him. Then the car roared off into the race, and the young man drove with genius, skill, and daring. The crowd had never seen such a performance, for this was the world's first exposure to the driving of Mario Andretti. Tears streamed down the cheeks of the old man as he watched his car cross the finish line in victory. 'Suppose,' said the old man, 'just suppose—I hadn't given him the key!' " Ekdahl pauses and scans the hushed crowd before him. "And who, I ask, has given *you* the key?"

Someone in the middle of the church starts clapping. Others join in, until the place rings again with applause. Richard looks around, perplexed. He leans over toward the woman and whispers, "I don't get it."

"Of course not," she says. "We don't have the key."

"We human beings," Ekdahl is saying, "are like electric batteries. And Jesus Christ is the great storehouse of energy and power in the universe. But no one charges up a battery unless it is run down. Drained. Powerless. For only the run down shall be charged up!" A burst of applause and cheers answers these words. "For oppression maketh a wise man," declares Ekdahl. "And a gift destroyeth the heart!"

As both Ekdahl and his audience grow increasingly demonstrative—and incoherent—Richard folds his hands and shuts his eyes. Something crazy is happening here. He tries to picture Gina as she knelt before him. To both left and right the congregation now rises to its feet and then sits back down. Across the aisle, a woman shakes her mop of hair in a frenzy. There's a mystery in this church that has shut him out. A hand touches his left arm. The woman beside him whispers, "Oh, dear friend, cast away all vain thoughts."

"In the mouth of the wicked, the serpent turns to ashes!"

Richard looks up, and for an instant the pastor's glasses seem to flash directly at him. "Jeez," he whispers. This is getting to him. He feels the expense of lustful thoughts draining away his spirit into waste. Yet about him the congregation has found the energy to clap and stamp their feet. Is he the only one without the key to unlock himself?

"The lips of the wicked will swallow up themselves!" shouts Ekdahl.

Richard shudders at these words. They seem unrelated to anything, yet he feels them go deep, as if probing for an opening.

"The keepers of the house shall tremble!"

Richard feels something within himself go rigid and brittle. What a relief it would be, he thinks. To be free of this love-sick agony. To feel lust crystallize and drop away—as if the flesh were turning to granules, to dry sand.

"The doors—!" shrieks Ekdahl.

Richard heaves himself up from the pew. Everyone else has leapt to their feet. He's got to get out of here. The rear door is just a pace away.

"—the doors shall be shut in the streets!" screams a mad voice.

Richard pushes through and nearly collapses into the arms of Nelson, the usher. From the sanctuary comes a ghastly wail and thunderous applause. As the two men look back, Ekdahl keels over backwards behind the pulpit. Strangers rush to his aid. They drag the pastor's limp body out a side door.

"We'd better call a doctor," says Nelson. "I'm supposed to be in charge."

Inside, the organist has begun a hymn, and the congregation sits down, giving one another nodding looks that say, "Now *that* was a good sermon."

Ten minutes later, Richard finds Alex in the crowd outside that watches Ekdahl wheeled out of the church on a stretcher and into a waiting ambulance.

"Did you see the blood around his mouth?" asks Alex.
"We'd better go home."
"Somebody said he bit his tongue off."
Back home, Richard finds Lindsay sprawled naked on the bed. As he hangs up his suit in the closet, she opens her eyes and stares at him.
"How was church?" she asks.
He rubs his fingers back through his hair. "It was very strange," he says. "Ekdahl passed out during his sermon. I think he had some kind of fit."
Lindsay pulls the sheet over herself and gets up on one elbow. "And you?" she asks. "How did it affect you?"
Richard shrugs. Should he tell her? His memory of what happened in church threatens to bust him open, to strip all his secrets naked before Lindsay's eyes. For example, what Gina did to him before the service, and the mingled guilt and pride of adultery, and now this sense that something at root is crumbling within him. He surprises himself by saying, "I think I nearly had a religious experience."
From the bed, Lindsay regards him curiously. "Did it have anything to do with sex?" she asks.
"In a way."
"Are you getting much these days?"
Richard stares at her. "Not really." They haven't made love for weeks. Is it possible that his wife is having an affair, too? "How about you?" he asks.
She slides down under the sheet. "Nope," she sighs. "I've given it up."

Alone in the house Monday morning, Lindsay takes a shower, then puts on jeans, a T-shirt—no bra—and a sweater. At the sink in the kitchen, she yawns and begins scouring the cast-iron frying pan that she let soak overnight, risking rust to loosen burnt crud.
Richard's parents called last night. They're coming for the weekend, flying out from Illinois on Friday.
"Good grief—Good Friday," sighed Lindsay. She and

WATCHMAN TELL US OF THE NIGHT

Richard were in the den watching *60 Minutes*. "They'll want to attend an Easter service, right?"

"I hadn't thought of that," said Richard. "Maybe we could go to the Methodist church?"

"It was that bad, huh?"

Richard shook his head. "I don't know where all those people came from. I don't think Ekdahl will be back in the pulpit very soon."

Lindsay examined the face of Mike Wallace. "The synod will probably send out a substitute," she said. "Like they did when Ekdahl caught the chicken pox. Some guy from the seminary. Well, at least the house is clean."

Now Lindsay finds herself staring at the heavy pan in her hands. The floors, the closets, and the toilet bowls are all ready for inspection by Richard's mother. Lindsay plans to lounge around this week. She figures Gray Chandler will ring her bell in a day or two. He'll try to embrace her at the front door. And she'll say, "Not today, Gray. Sorry." But already his arms are locked about her, and she feels his kisses grow more frenzied on her face, on her neck, on her naked shoulders—

She grips the soap pad in her fist. All night she's pushed away such thoughts. As she lay in the dark bedroom, her conscience screeched itself hoarse to keep her from falling into erotic dreams. But part of her, she admits, wants to do it again—with a stranger.

Lindsay strives to make herself blank, to stretch a sheet of vacancy over the place in her mind where these lurid scenes pop into view. The mental effort this act requires is now beginning to take its toll. She hasn't slept since Thursday. In her weary hands the heavy, black pan clunks against the walls of her sink. She fears she might doze off, relax her guard, and allow some erotic scene—awful in its vividness—to appear.

The pan is clean. She'll have to season it again, having scoured away the oil. But the tan grime of the soap pad has lodged at her cuticles. She squirts white dish detergent across the back of her hand. It runs, viscous and pearly, into the valleys between her knuckles. She smoothes the lotion into her palms, growing dreamy as the lather swells thick and soft. She glances about her orderly kitchen—canisters of flour and sugar on the countertop, wooden spoons and wire whisks at hand, in their assigned places. But she knows Chandler is coming. She knows she'll let him in.

17

At DAYBREAK, Gina's friend Dave crosses the Massachusetts line into Rhode Island. Past Provincetown he feels more certain that no one is pursuing him, driving him out. On the map, crossing over to Long Island by boat looks like the shortest way south to New Jersey and beyond, the quickest way to break all ties with life in New England. Driving a rented truck that bears what's left of his possessions, he waits at the ferry in Bridgeport, Connecticut.

Ahead in the long line of cars, a motorcyclist—bearing both skull and crossbones and Nazi swastikas on the back of his leather jacket—heaves one leg over the saddle of his vehicle. Dave's hot hands grip and release the unfamiliar steering wheel. His bones ache from his beating. He's not going to be anyone's victim. He's getting out.

Meanwhile, back in Heathersford, Sylvia's taxi has broken down on the Crosstown highway. The sixty-five-year-old spinster raps a bony knuckle on the dashboard. "Oh, you nasty thing," she says to the car.

Sylvia's speech patterns depend on what outfit she's wearing. For example, she owns a red wig that she wears with sunglasses. When she drives around chewing bubble gum (now that they sell a brand that doesn't stick to dentures) this getup—combined with the stress of engine trouble—brings out the French accent of her girlhood: "Jheez! C'est la tzurd time zis muntz. Whatta hunka

jhunk!" But most days, zipped into her cracked leather
flight jacket, she'd snarl, "Piss on it!" and "You stubborn
bitch!"

Today, at the senior citizen co-op, she'll be picking up a
bunch of old biddies for their Monday luncheon at the
Holiday Inn. They turn into stingy tippers if Sylvia's wearing what they consider inappropriate dress. So this morning she's wearing old-lady lavender and lace. Her polyester
blouse is pinned at the neck with a brooch. Over it she
wears a knit suit whose lapels she's edged with tiny embroi-
dered forget-me-nots.

"Fucking carburetor," she mutters, getting out of her old
Chevy. Then she pauses to adjust her lavender hat and
adds, "Mercy sakes!" After throwing open the hood, she
stares for a moment at the silent engine, as if sizing up an
opponent. Then, with a few expert twists, she loosens the
wing-nut on the air cleaner.

When Alex gets home from school, he finds a note from
his mother taped to the refrigerator:

I went to the store. I will be right home.

Mom

Alex wanders into living room. He knows that when he's
alone in the house, there's always some mystery that deserves poking into. From the drawer in the coffee table, he
gets out his mother's photo album. Garth's drawing of
himself is still in there. Alex flips through the heavy pages,
feeling them riffle past his thumb. Midway through the
volume, a variation in the color of one page flashes past. He
flips back and finds it, a yellowed window where the paper
feels different, less creamy to the touch. He notices, too,
that the slit has been glued shut.

He gets a table knife from the kitchen and pries into the
paper crack. Breaking and entering, he whispers to himself.
He's learned the phrase from watching *Hawaii Five-0*

reruns. Sure enough, there's a folded page inside. It's a letter, but the handwriting is hard to read:

29 Sept. 1945

Mon Cher John,

    A friend has given me your address in America. The end of this septembre is cold. Ordinarily the automne here is a charming season, just sad enough to be poetique.

    In my heart, I sense such splendeur, such a chaleur enorme (enormous heat?), at the thought of you.

    There is no news of my father. I think that he is disappeared—with all the others. Millions, they say.

    I have made the acquaintance of an american who could arrange passage to the U.S.A. Do you understand? It would be necessary for me to marry him.

    Time passes so slowly.

Je t'adore,
Michelle

Alex stares at the letter. It looks very old. At school, they're just beginning to learn cursive writing. A girl in his class is named Michelle.

Out in the garage a car door slams. Carefully he refolds the mysterious letter and slides it back into the album. When his mother comes in, Alex is sitting in the den, watching TV.

"Oh, hi," she says. "How was school?"

"Okay. Hey, I need to know something. What does 'Jetta door' mean?"

"It's part of a car, I guess. Is this a riddle?" she smiles. "A Volkswagen?"

"I don't think so. Let me write it for you."

"Okay. There's a pencil in the kitchen."

Alex makes a big production out of sitting down at the

kitchen table with a sheet of paper. Laboriously, from memory, he traces the phrase he has in mind. *Jet ador,* it comes out this time.

"Jet odor?" says Lindsay. "Hey, super. You're learning to write script."

Alex screws up his face at the page. "There was a little mark—you know. An aposterphee, here."

"And an 'e' on the end?"

"Yeah!"

"*Je t'adore,*" she pronounces the French. "Alex! Has some girl been writing you little notes in school?"

"Zhuh tah-doar," he repeats.

Lindsay is grinning. "Who wrote this to you?"

Alex fiddles with the pencil. "Michelle wrote it. What does it mean?"

"It means"—cries Lindsay—"that you have a girlfriend!" She's tickled and astonished at the thought. "Michelle is in your class, right? She must know French. It means 'I adore you—I love you.' "

"Oh."

"Well, I must say, you're taking all this pretty coolly."

"Uh-huh," he says and goes in the other room.

Lindsay carries in the rest of the groceries from the garage and puts them away. She's folding up the brown bags, wondering where Gray Chandler lives, when Alex appears again.

"What was Grandpa's name?" he asks.

"Lloyd," she says. "They're coming on Friday, you know. And on Sunday, you know what? The Easter Bunny comes."

"No. The other grandpa. The one who died."

"Oh. My father. His name was John. Why do you ask?"

"I was just wondering, that's all. You never talk about him much."

Lindsay sighs. "I don't remember him very well. There's not much to say. He was in the war. Then he and your grandma Harriet got married.

"Oh," says Alex, who may be on the verge of a break-through.

Harriet Aldington, Lindsay's mother, was engaged to John Wyatt before he left for Europe in 1943. In the early 1940s she was a coquette who drew after her a dozen young men in officers' uniforms. Well-to-do girlfriends saw that she got invitations to dances at the country clubs. She was cute and threw out daffy fibs about her family's background. Her fluttery imitation of a southern belle became quite a hit.

Harriet met Lindsay's father on the golf course. John Wyatt had taken up the game to accompany Heinz Jurkin, professor of physics at Carnegie Tech, who claimed he did his best theoretical work on the back nine of the Oakmont Country Club. Wyatt worked in the Dutchman's lab, and —like Harriet—had to fib now and then to keep up a pose. Officially his exemption from military service called him an "electrical engineer," but actually he tinkered with switches, chuckled at the old professor's jokes, and took notes when his mentor—spewing saliva as he talked—raved complex equations into the air. Because the content of these inspired fits would have been lost unless someone was at hand—even on the golf course—to jot them down, Wyatt thought of himself as a kind of portable blackboard. His was a genuine contribution to the war effort.

One breezy day in the summer of 1943, the professor and his lab assistant were thrown together with Harriet and a girlfriend on the first tee at Oakmont to make a foursome. Twice, Wyatt observed Harriet kick her ball out of the rough to improve her lie. In turn, she must have seen him descend into a hazard and simulate a brilliant shot by throwing up a handful of sand while he tossed his ball to within a foot of the cup.

Walking with him later, she said, "You cheat, don't you."

"So do you," he smiled.

By the end of August, they were lovers. They met fur-tively; she never introduced him to the country club crowd, and forbade him to visit her house—a modest bungalow located down from the wealthy heights of Mt. Oliver. But evenings—often outside under the stars, on the soft grass of putting greens—she opened beneath him like some exotic flower.

In September, word was passed from MIT to Prof. Jurkin about something called the ALSOS Project. As the Allies prepared to invade Normandy, Washington was concerned about Germany's nuclear research. They were assembling a team of technicians and scientists with the skills to track down Hitler's atom bomb. Some members of the ALSOS team would land on D-Day with the Allied troops. Jurkin submitted Wyatt's name for the project.

Harriet was delighted. "Oh, John. You're going off to war."

"It's not the Army," he said, and gripped her shoulders. "Listen, when this is over— When I come back—" He didn't know what to say next. "Let's get serious."

"Well—" drawled Harriet. "Just what is this new assignment?"

"I can't tell you. It's secret."

"Like your work at the university?" Her eyes lit up. "Honey, you're going to be a spy!" She flung her arms around his neck. "Of course I'll marry you!"

Wyatt arrived in London in January of 1944. There it became apparent to everyone that his background as a mere lab assistant didn't qualify him for crucial intelligence work. A group of them sat and sorted through captured documents, invoices, and factory records— searching for clues that would establish where the Germans' uranium was being refined and amassed. On D-Day they left him behind in London with the office staff. Through the summer of 1944, he packed soil and water samples that the ALSOS team sent back from the Continent for radioactive testing in Washington. Nights, trying to ignore the distant thud of buzz-bombs and, later, in September, the abrupt rumble of V-2 rockets falling out of London's sky, he spent nights writing long letters to Harriet, pleading with her not to let the boys at home kiss her.

In October, as the Allies pushed on toward the Rhine, ALSOS headquarters in Paris sent for Wyatt. When he arrived, the excitement of the city's liberation was over and Americans were commonplace. He hadn't heard a shot fired, or seen a single German.

He was assigned to an Army Intelligence unit directed by a Colonel McKenzie. He found his new superior in a cramped office talking into two telephones. From the next room came the sound of clattering typewriters. The colonel shot a glance at Wyatt and seized a random page from a pile on his desk. "Here," he said. "Find addresses for these names. You want a car? Hell, don't ask stupid questions. Legwork. That's the name of the game in this outfit. Got it? Legwork."

"But—" said Wyatt. Typed on the page was a message from the German theater of operations: *"Can anyone find Jules Michelet?"*

"Out!" yelled the colonel.

Wyatt got the impression that he was in the way. He folded the sheet and wandered down the corridor. At the next doorway, Wyatt found another civilian like himself. Feet propped up on a desk, the man was leafing through an old copy of *Signal,* the magazine put out by Goebbels. His name was Frank Richardson. In Chicago he'd been an accountant. A heart murmur, he explained, had kept him out of the service.

"Don't take this place too seriously," Richardson told him. "Did you hear them, down the hall, going after cases of wine? You know what the colonel thinks? He thinks uranium is some kind of fertilizer. In other words, Germany's atomic research is a plot to make French wine radioactive. Can you believe it?"

Wyatt traced the name he'd been given anyway. Six years earlier, a Jules Michelet had worked with Madame Joliot-Curie and her husband bombarding uranium to produce the first nuclear chain reaction. In 1940, he'd disappeared from the Rue d'Ulm laboratories shortly after the Germans rolled into Paris.

December 12, 1944, it rained in Paris. John Wyatt gripped the collar of his trenchcoat as he plodded past the Pantheon. Back here the streets had been too narrow for tanks. His eye singled out pockmarks on walls left by bullets—probably Resistance snipers. His destination was an address just off the Place Contrescarpe. He'd spent two weeks running false leads into dead ends. Now he had one chance left: locating some kid, the missing scientist's daughter.

Wyatt paused on the dark stairs of a dingy apartment house. "Ahh-jou!" he sneezed. What a terrible cold he'd caught. Everyone seemed to have it. Last week in a café, he'd enraged a Frenchman by saying *"Gesundheit."* Now he was conscious, though a bleary fever, of trying to make even his sneezes sound un-Germanic.

Up four more flights, he felt faint as he knocked on a door. Finally it opened. He felt a kind of thud in his chest. It was a woman—hard to tell her age. Twenty-one? Thirty-five? Wyatt stared into enormous long-lashed eyes. Dark circles under them gave the impression of exotic makeup. She wore a thick, ragged sweater and folded her arms against the cold. Was there no heat in the building? Her cheekbones were high and pale, her full lips a little cracked. Parisian women, after the Liberation, all had this gaunt look. Fashion models, thought Wyatt when he'd first seen them. Actually the look was a product of hard bicycle pedaling and wartime rations under the German occupation. The woman's hair was cut very short. He'd heard that in August, they'd shaved the heads of girls who had slept with German soldiers.

"Michelle Michelet?" he said weakly. This was no schoolgirl.

"Yes?"

"Thank goodness," he sighed. "You speak English."

"Ah. You are American. Come in and sit."

He stood delirious in the doorway and gawked.

"Come in, please." She smiled, then her expression changed. "But you are not well! Take off your wet coat. Quick!"

"Sure," nodded Wyatt, swaying on his feet. He looked once more into her eyes—then he tipped forward and fell flat on his face.

In early 1945, Harriet received a cryptic note from Paris:

I've been injured—broken my nose. All in the line of duty, of course. Ha ha!

Love, John

In January, Wyatt stopped writing to his fiancée because by that point he had moved into Michelle's one-room apartment with its view over the rooftops straggling down the Rue Mouffetard. She never went out. They spent a lot of time in bed, drinking wine and smoking American cigarettes.

Michelle had been the mistress of an SS officer connected with German Intelligence. During the occupation, Communist members of the French Resistance had arranged this liaison for her. She'd lived opulently in the 16th Arrondissement and transmitted certain facts, messages, and codes—in both directions. But by 1943, her French contacts had all been shot. Next her German lover was arrested when the July 20th plot against Hitler failed. After the Liberation, no one could prove whether she was a collaborator or an Allied spy. In August, a man confronted her as she was parking her bicycle. He called her a Nazi whore. A crowd gathered and roughed her up. They tore at her clothes, sheared off her hair, and kicked in the spokes of her bicycle. A young woman stepped out from a doorway and yanked her into the safety of a dress shop. This saved Michelle from even worse treatment. The next day, a colleague of her father's found her a room on the Left Bank. But he had little influence over the bitter internal struggles within the parti communiste. Now she feared the

Communist Party, the police, and pedestrians in the street. She was hiding out, she confessed—from everyone.

The day they first met, Wyatt had said he was a civilian —which was true. But he lied about his mission in Paris. He claimed he worked for Westinghouse Electric. Like the government, his company was looking for nuclear physicists.

Eventually, Michelle opened up about her father. She knew that he had discovered something terrible in his research at the Collège de France. The last time she'd seen him, he was getting into a German staff car. Her mother, at the time, was dying of cancer. She died a month later— of shame.

Hearing this story, Wyatt said, "That's terrible. Simply terrible."

"No. It was very heroic."

"I don't understand."

"But of course. He hated the Germans. A man with his knowledge—if only they trusted him—would be in a position, within Germany, to tamper with things, to make errors—"

"Sabotage?"

"It is possible?"

Wyatt looked out at the gray January sky and ran his hand across the blanket. "Do you think he is still alive?"

"He was alive in July."

Wyatt sat up in bed. "You've heard from him?" This was the whole point, he realized, of his ALSOS assignment. The official reason for his presence in this room, for the delirious hours he'd spent in this bed.

Michelle went to the closet and came back with a packet of letters printed on photographic paper—the German version of V-mail.

Wyatt seized them eagerly. Then he looked up at her. "May I look?"

She shrugged. Her expression was odd—a disappointed frown.

The mail had all passed through the Berlin censors. They'd cut away whole paragraphs. Michelle sat beside him and pointed out that even references to the local weather had been brushed over with black ink. "He writes me to say that he eats sometimes in a restaurant. The wine is too sweet. He sends me his love."

"What's this?" he asked, pointing to a half-obliterated word.

"I think it is 'dahlia.' A flower."

Wyatt peered at the word and said, "*Dahlem.* It's outside of Berlin. The Kaiser Wilhelm Institute. Szilard studied there."

Michelle merely shrugged. She seemed suddenly bored with their discovery. "I want to eat in a restaurant. Will you take me?"

The next day, wearing dark glasses and a headscarf, Michelle held his hand tightly as they circled down the stairs. Outside, temperatures were unexpectedly soaring into the fifties. She stood uncertainly in the outer doorway, testing the air, the light, the expanse of space. At last, she pushed off, he caught her in his arms, and then they were off. Wyatt broke into song. At the corner she caught her breath and laughed at how her legs trembled. The two strolled down the Rue Descartes, avoiding the crowded boulevards. Michelle's eyes seemed to devour the street, the pavement, the sky. At a brasserie, Wyatt made a phone call to Hank Richardson, who told him that the lab was finished with those letters. Back at the bar, Wyatt glanced about. The eyes of a dozen men were fastened upon Michelle. He took her in his arms. "*Je t'adore,*" she whispered.

They walked as far as the Seine. She pointed out the address on the Quai de Tournelles where she had grown up. Beside the river, they leaned on a wall and looked across at the buttresses of Notre-Dame. She took off her scarf and shook her hair free. "I think you would make a very bad spy."

Wyatt looked down at the river. A barge was passing under the bridge. "You think I'm a spy?"

"I think," she smiled, "that you have a very peculiar nose. It is still blue and black."

After this they went out evenings and walked the boulevards. Young people leapt up from café tables to embrace Michelle as an old friend—girls in short pleated skirts, young men in huge jackets and tight pants that she called "*zazou.*" Once, a corporal from McKenzie's unit hailed Wyatt—or was it Michelle he had hailed? Wyatt hurried her off into a crowd of pedestrians.

Her friends began dropping by the apartment. Wyatt spent whole afternoons sitting in his bathrobe while young men in zoot-suits paced about, making enormous gestures that made Michelle laugh.

One afternoon in early March, a sharp rap sounded at the door. Wyatt was sick of these intrusions. He got up and flung open the door. It was Richardson, who looked in, nodded to Michelle, and stepped back into the hallway.

"What are you doing here?" asked Wyatt.

"This arrived." Frank was holding a piece of German mail. It was addressed to Michelle. "Patton's troops intercepted it."

"How did you know I was here?" demanded Wyatt.

"Oh, McKenzie had a tail on you since the day you arrived."

"Had me followed? What did he think—I was working for the Germans?"

"No. Westinghouse. There are a lot of sides in this war."

When Richardson had gone, Wyatt went in and looked out the window. Suddenly everything was coming apart. He tossed the letter on the bed. "From your father," he said.

Michelle sat up and read it. She didn't ask how Wyatt's friend had come to deliver it.

"What does he say?"

"He's at a place called Haigerloch. But I think he may be ill."

His eyes took in the room where the two of them had

spent three months together. His face burned with shame.
Why hadn't he told her the truth?

Michelle was sitting on the edge of the bed. She let the
document flutter to the floor. "Well," she sighed. "Now it
has all come out."

He put on his coat. He wanted to hide his face.

"You're leaving, then?" she said.

"What else can I do?" Already he was dashing down the
stairs.

On April 22, acting on information from several sources
—including Michelle's letters—American troops would
parachute into the village of Haigerloch in the Swabian
Alps, blow up Germany's last site for refining uranium,
and round up its technicians and scientists. Michelle's father would not be among them.

Wyatt went back to the apartment a week later. It was
empty. No one in the building knew where she'd gone.
Over the next month, he thought he caught sight of her a
hundred times, on the street, in cafés, walking alone in the
parks. But it never turned out to be her.

Richardson tried to cheer him up. "You could never trust
that woman."

"You don't know anything about her."

"Well, we can't find her either."

"Why should you?"

Richardson was giving him an odd look. "You mean you
don't know? She was working for us."

"She was what?" said Wyatt.

"Sure. After you located her in December, we found her
file and I had a talk with her. She was a pro. She was
checking you out. For us."

"But"—Wyatt's thoughts were trying to reshuffle themselves—"the letters. You faked them. Just to test me?"

"No, the letters were real. You did a good job. Actually,
she was pretty broken up about stringing you along. I
talked with her last week—after you'd left. She thought
you'd figured it out. Yeah, she was pretty broken up."

"Then—she loves me!" Wyatt said aloud.

"I doubt it," said Richardson. "By the way, you've been ordered back to the States. You've got a few days to pack."

Wyatt spent three frantic days pacing streets, ducking in and out of shops, trying to locate her. At a café, he ran into one of those young men who wore zoot suits. In case Michelle showed up, he gave the fellow his address in Pittsburgh.

Wyatt was back home in time for the Fourth of July. Harriet greeted him coldly and showed him into the living room. They sat on the davenport.

"You're a beast," she said. "You had an affair, didn't you."

"It's all over now," he told her.

"How absolutely beastly. Who was she?"

"Actually, we never got to know each other very well. I want to forget the whole business. Will you give me a break?"

"You've broken something inside me," said Harriet bitterly.

He tipped her chin up with his hand and said he was sorry. Tears glistened in his eyes. "Help me," he whispered, embracing her tightly.

It's Thursday, and Sylvia has a call to pick up a party at the county airport. Her Chevy is humming along fine since she fixed the choke. And Sylvia loves to drive. As a girl in Paris during the German occupation, she dreamed of owning an automobile. There was no gasoline. Everyone rode bicycles. A good bike cost as much as a car. She saw a crowd destroy a bicycle once. It was after the liberation of Paris. The crowd was attacking a young woman. Sylvia, who had thought the violence would end when the Germans left, watched from the window of her dress shop. Finally she stepped out and pulled the young woman to safety. The crowd had sheared off her hair and nearly torn off her clothes. Someone from the university came and took the girl away the next day. She wonders what ever became of such women?

At the airport, a middle-aged couple waits at the curb. The man is wearing plaid pants, and the wife has slung canvas bags on each shoulder. They pile in and give Sylvia an address on Hillcrest. "We're just off the plane!" says the husband.

"Gotcha," nods Sylvia.

"How's the weather been in these parts?"

"Snappy."

"It was cold in Waukegan," puts in the wife. "It was simply raw."

"But it was a dry cold," adds her husband.

Sylvia glances at them in her rearview mirror. They're beaming at each other about something. "I bet you're here for the Easter holidays," she says, trying to match their enthusiasm.

The man wags a finger at Sylvia's back. "We're here to visit my son and his family. But we like to live dangerously."

"See? We're coming a day early!" exclaims the wife.

"Terrific," nods Sylvia.

"We think so," says the husband, cracking up.

"Yes siree," says Sylvia, as she pulls onto the Interstate. "I'm picturing it. Your daughter-in-law thinks you're arriving tomorrow. But you're showing up a day early. Well, I guess I'm not the first to break the news. You two live pretty dramatic lives."

18

"W E'RE ALL STANDING in the mud, but some of us are reaching for the stars."

"Did you just make that up?" asks Garth.

Wally is sitting at his desk, sorting through old index cards. "It's a famous quotation," he says.

Garth scratches his head and puts his feet up on the old couch. "Okay, I give up," he says.

"You want the answer?"

"Yup."

"Aw, make a stab at it."

Garth looks up at the ceiling and says, "Ralph Waldo Emerson."

Wally sneers at this. "That answer will get you two points."

"What do you mean, two points?"

"That's what I said. Two points."

"Out of how many?"

"How the hell should I know?"

Garth sits up. "Well, this is your test, isn't it?"

"Listen," says Wally, pushing up his thick glasses on his nose. "Did I ask you who said it?"

"You said it was a famous quotation."

"Well?"

"Well, what?" Garth is getting exasperated.

"I'll give you a hint. Mud."

Garth looks at his shoes. "Okay, I get it," he says, and leans back again. He laces his fingers behind his head and

233

stares upward for a moment. "The notion of mud," he begins, "as a way of describing the ground or basis of human nature—that is, the condition in which we find ourselves mired— How am I doing?"

"Better. You're up to twelve points already."

"Twelve! You mean ten isn't the top?"

"I didn't say there was a top."

Garth sits up and swings his legs to the floor. "This is a stupid test."

"I didn't claim it was a wonderful test."

"Well, it's stupid."

"What are you so upset about?"

"I'm not upset!"

"Yes, you are. You're upset about Una."

Garth sighs, folds his hands, and leans his elbows on his knees. Una hasn't called for nearly two weeks. The last he heard, her Aunt Ava was out of the hospital. "Too much time has passed since she left," he says.

"Time doesn't pass," says Wally, taking off his glasses. "That's an illusion."

Garth stares at his friend's thick glasses.

"The important thing"—Wally licks the lenses with his tongue, then wipes them on his shirt—"the thing about time, it seems to me, is this: *You always are where you are.*"

Garth looks at his friend. This could be a joke. You can never tell with Wally. So Garth mulls it over for a long time before looking up. "That quotation," he says. "About the mud and the stars. Who said it?"

"Ida Lupino."

"You're kidding."

"Nope."

Garth smacks his forehead and flops on his back. "Ida Lupino!" he yells at the ceiling.

Meanwhile, Lindsay sprawls face down—naked—across the bed. Behind her, Gray Chandler must be staring at her bare buttocks. "How you doing?" she asks.

"Better," he says. "This is okay."

She squints at a patchwork landscape that runs from a blur to a sheer drop before reaching her bedroom dresser. Things began badly this morning when Lindsay answered the door. In delight, she threw her arms around Chandler and kissed him on the mouth. But he drew back —almost alarmed.

"I knew you'd finally show up," she said, leading him into the living room. She tossed this at him over one shoulder—a one-sided shrug, cute, like Cheryl Tiegs. Then Lindsay's mind went blank. The lines she'd rehearsed for his arrival had slipped away. Sinking to the couch, she put her hands to her face.

"How are you?" he asked.

She opened her palms and gave him a tight smile. "I feel terrific," she said and patted the cushion beside her.

He stood there with his hands in his pockets. "Let's go somewhere else."

She recalled a stain on her couch. "Oh, this is the scene of the crime? And how come it's taken you so long to come back?"

He smiled. "What is this—an interrogation?"

She stood up and hugged him. "I want to do something naughty," she whispered. "Just once."

He chuckled and brushed his lips through her short hair. "Naughty gets you guilt," he said. "And guilt gets you caught. And—" He stopped.

She looked up at him. "And?"

"If you're doing something just to get caught—"

"Oh, I get it. I'm being adolescent."

"Hey," he said. "I'm not putting you down. I feel it, too. Guilt, I mean."

She was silent for a moment. "Well, I'm not used to it." She flopped her arms down. The drapes were half-closed. She stared out the window. "You're involved with someone else, aren't you?"

He stared at her.

"I think you live with someone," she was saying. "Otherwise—why any guilt?"

He was smiling now.

"You're *married*," Lindsay announced.

"Not quite. I have—a roommate."

"A lover, you mean." She felt pleased at having wrung this much from him.

"Okay," he nodded. "I'm cheating, too." He let that sink in. "Does that clear things up for you?"

"It's very"—she sensed herself stepping into an zone where the rules—if there were any—didn't tell you how to feel—"it's very flattering." Finding the word, she stared into his eyes. "What's she like?"

"Not more questions," he said, exasperated. "Come on, let's play in the bedroom. Okay?"

Halfway up the stairs, Gray had seized her from behind. She twisted back as he slid her skirt up to her hips. He was wearing a western shirt. She easily pulled the snaps open. Then she sat on the carpeted stairs as he yanked down her pantyhose. Lindsay wondered how this was going to work. Bump, bump, bump—down the stairs?

As Gray unzipped his jeans, a pained expression appeared on his face and he put a hand to his leg. "I've got a cramp," he said.

That was just the beginning. Upstairs on the bed, she massaged his calf. When they embraced, one of his shoulders seemed to go out of joint.

"I've been working out," he explained. "To get in shape."

"Whatever you're doing," she said, "I'd quit it. How about a drink?"

"It's ten in the morning."

"Well, I need a drink. Some wine and candlelight. That's what we need."

"It's been a long morning, actually. But okay. Let's try some wine."

Downstairs, a bottle of Chablis made them both a little silly. "Let's play chase," Lindsay suggested.

"I don't know that game," he drawled. "How about bondage? I know that one."

"Phooey," she said, and led him into the laundry room. "Help me get up here," she said, trying to hoist her naked butt onto the machine. "This is called, 'Load the washer.' See? This is where you put the fabric softener."

He looked irritated. "Aw, I'd have to stand on tiptoe to reach. Now listen," he declared. "The problem is this. You're displaying too much initiative. Could you act a little more passive? That's it. Great. Go a little limp. That turns me on."

That was half an hour ago. They drank another bottle of wine. Now she lies on the quilt and feels Gray passing his hands over her round butt, spreading her thighs apart. Something feels stiff back there.

"Are you going to stuff your strut now?" she asks. "Oof," she gasps to the quilt as his weight presses the wind out of her.

"Ah," he says, sliding his hand under her mashed muff.

"Quick, get it in," she says.

"Now touch the tips of your thumbs together," says Wally, "as if you're holding a slip of paper between them."

Garth is sitting cross-legged on a cushion, one open hand lying in the palm of the other. Wally still lounges at his desk, calling out directions.

"Keep your back straight. Your chin down. Good."

Garth opens his eyes and watches Wally get up. "Where are you going?"

"Out."

"You coming back?"

"In a while. Just sit and watch what happens. Just watch."

So Garth sits. It's hard to keep his back straight. His arms feel unsteady, and his heart pounds unnaturally. Wally didn't tell him what to think about, but Garth presumes that he's supposed to clear his mind. Or else focus on something. Everything is churning—a flood of things on his mind: Una, his heating bill, and Lindsay's red car. His legs ache and he finds that he's already slumped, has allowed his chin to unlock. An April breeze streams in an open window. Garth listens to the hiss of tires rolling on pavement. His thoughts have settled into waves. The frenzy is over, or else he's passed through into something else. How long has he been sitting? he wonders. This isn't working, he decides, straining to sit still. Then there's a pleasant numbness between his brows. A kind of blank that keeps arriving.

He concentrates on holding his hands in the position Wally described. "Like you're holding a precious ritual object," he'd said. Between the tips of Garth's thumbs, there's a peculiar sensation. A current flowing. And the blank numbness has spread—warm and calm across his whole face. Now here's something else arriving—up from below. Up the spine. No, up the stairs. A dream is coming up the stairs. Racing right up! Bursting in upon him!

"Hi," says Una's voice.

Garth, the hint of a smile on his face, doesn't open his eyes to this illusion. He mustn't let the ritual object fall from his hands.

"I've got good news," says Una. "You're going to have a show."

"A show?"

"Yeah. At the 112 Greene Street Gallery. And *Art International* wants to interview you."

Opening his eyes, Garth stares at her. She's wearing makeup and a two-piece silk dress—narrow, black and white vertical stripes—and red high heels. Her hair has been done, swept back over one ear, where something clunky—red plastic—dangles. The sight makes his hands fall apart in his lap.

"I don't want any show," he declares, straightening out his stiff legs.

"I knew you'd say that. That's why I went ahead and arranged it."

"Listen." Garth is on his feet now. In high heels, she

seems to look down at him. "I could have shows if I wanted. It's just that I've chosen not to."

She folds her arms. "Let's not go over that old bullshit. We've got something in the car for you to sign."

"We? Who's we?"

"Oh. I forgot to tell you. Norman flew up with me to Boston. You remember Norman?"

Garth looks dumbfounded. "Not that guy who pushes Gruder's work?" he says in disbelief. William Gruder had been in art school with Garth in the early sixties. They'd collaborated on a project in design class: some words simply listed on graph paper. Their instructor had given them a failing grade. Everyone thought the incident was hilarious. Three years later Gruder exhibited a similar work with the Fluxus group, and Hilton Kramer had praised the piece in the *Times*. Since then, Garth's former collaborator has gone from one success to another, cashing in on ideas that were supposed to insult the art market. Now Gruder lives on some big piece of property in Westchester. And he has an agent, Norman Steinbrunner, to handle his finances.

"Come on," says Una, and tugs Garth down the stairs.

Waiting at the curb is a black limousine. A driver opens the back door, and Una climbs in. It's like an office, thinks Garth. He's supposed to get in. This is unreal, a bad dream.

Norman is a fat, bald guy wearing his collar open over the lapels of a black-and-white-checked jacket. He and Una must look quite the pair, jetting around the countryside in their coordinated outfits. Garth climbs in and shakes a pudgy hand.

"Wonderful. Just wonderful," says Norman, as he strips a brown wrapper off a framed print. He holds it up for Garth to see. It's a page of newspaper want-ads, matted in levels of Plexiglas with a kind of lens embedded in the center, so that one entry springs out at you. The magnified notice says:

Consider whether the
space below is really
BLANK.

"Hey," says Garth. "Where'd you get this?"

Norman looks at Una, who just grins. He begins fiddling with temporary clips on the back of the frame.

Una is holding out a pen. She points to a lower corner inside the mat.

Garth stares at her red nail polish. "I never sign my work," he declares.

Norman chuckles. "It's no good unless it's signed."

"But—it can't be worth anything. It's not supposed to be worth anything. Do you know how many copies of this were printed?"

"About a million and a half," laughs Norman.

Garth is alert to a con here. Who saves old newspapers? Maybe only a handful of these pages have survived the years.

"Do it," urges Una. Her voice sounds like a recording.

The pen is in Garth's hand. Someone did a fancy job matting the thing. "It's against my principles," he states.

"I need the money," insists Una. "I've put a lot of my own into this deal."

Garth looks at her, wondering whether she's let this bald guy fuck her. The chauffeur slides open a little window and leers at him. Him, too? thinks Garth.

Una says, "You want to know what I've had to go through to arrange this deal for you?"

Garth understands that she's about to make him pay— for what, he's not certain. But over the years, living with her, certain debts have accumulated that now, apparently, are being called to account. The door of the limousine is still open. He could walk away from this. But instead, he grips the pen and signs his mark, an ampersand.

Norman peers at it. "What is he, illiterate?"

"That's his mark," Una assures him.

From a breast pocket, Norman takes out his checkbook. "A deal is a deal," he says, scribbling an amount.

Garth says, "I bet there are hundreds of these old newspapers still around."

"Maybe," replies Norman. "My men have located sixteen. That's from used magazine dealers on the East Coast. See, just like you, that's the first thing that hits me. How do you corner the market? But now—see? I got the only signed one. We can destroy the others, or dribble them out every few years. Somebody else comes up with one? So what? It makes publicity. Here's your check. Did I spell your name right?"

Garth is staring at the amount. It says *$11,000.00.*

Una pushes him out of the car and joins him on the curb. The limousine door slams and the vehicle squeals off in a rush.

"Now what?" he says. This can't really be happening.

Una grips his arm, and calculates. "First you kiss me," she says. "Then we go to New York. It'll be the fastest way to clear the check. I've opened an account at Chase. Gruder gave me the name of an attorney."

"Gruder!" cries Garth. "You've been seeing that asshole?"

"Take it easy. Gruder is about to publish an article in *ARTnews.* About his minimalist period. He mentions your name more than once. 'A real pioneer,' he calls you. 'An unrecognized genius.' Now a lot of people are trying to locate you. You're about to be discovered."

Garth slumps down to sit on the pavement. This is all wrong, a nightmare. Abruptly, Una's high heels stride off into hazy distance. As she walks away, he observes how their bright red fades to a distant mauve. And now an icy wind has come up. He slides his butt across broken glass to lean against a hard brick wall. He decides he's made a terrible mistake. Snow begins falling. Time passes. His hands are frigid, but out of desperation he forms Wally's mudra—palms flat, thumbs faintly touching—and closes his eyes. Finally everything is very still and calm— and he's not alone.

Garth opens his eyes. He watches Wally lift high-topped black sneakers to the top of his desk. What's going on here? The breeze coming in the window has the smell of spring in it—root growth, garbage, and dog-doo thawing in the sun. Better, someone is frying onions in real butter.

"Did you see Una?"

"A couple weeks ago," says Wally.

Garth frowns. "I suppose you haven't seen any black limousines lately?"

"Not many."

"Where am I?" asks Garth.

Wally shuffles one more index card. "You're right here. Same as always."

"It couldn't have been just a dream," Garth says, mostly to himself.

"You probably had some kind of vision. I noticed when I came back that you'd lost your posture and slumped into a worthless state. Close your mouth. You're gaping at me."

Garth swallows hard.

"Stretch your legs out," says Wally. "Don't get up too fast. Your feet might be asleep. Here's the last question on my test. What's Helen cooking for supper?"

Garth submits to the heady odor of mushrooms and garlic now joining the onions in butter. "Tuna delight?" he says.

Wally makes a check on one of his cards. "That answer," he says, "will get you seventy-three points."

"Is that good?"

"You pass. Get it? Time doesn't. You do."

Lindsay, crushed beneath Gray Chandler's weight, has finally figured out that he's masturbating between her legs. Well, okay, she thinks. Lindsay is open-minded. But she's not having fun, and she doesn't feel naughty. She's not sure what she feels. Sad, angry, and a little scared. Why does

everything turn out so crummy for her? Gray lunges now
and then, pressing her butt flat with his groin. Between
him and her quilt, she feels like the ham in a sandwich. This
adultery business isn't what it's cracked up to be.

"Ah—ah—" moans Gray.

Lindsay wishes the poor guy would hurry up. Now she
levers herself up, surprised at the strength in her arms.
What's that sound?

"Ugh," comes a grunt. Lindsay has just heaved her Don
Juan off the edge of the bed. "I had it," he says, from the
floor. "I just know I had it there."

"Did you hear something?" she asks. "Hush. Oh, God.
The doorbell."

"Forget it."

"But someone's at the door!"

"So what?"

Lindsay scampers into the bathroom, where a dormer
window looks out on the street. "Someone's come in a
taxi!" she cries. "Oh, God, get dressed. It must be Uncle
Alfred!"

Gray sighs. "Put on a robe," he advises Lindsay. "I'll be
in the bathroom."

As Lindsay rushes down the stairs, she seizes garments
that lie strewn on the steps. Gripping them to her bosom
in fright, she races into the living room. Her eyes spot two
wineglasses on the rug. She stoops to snatch them and
dashes into the kitchen. Now what? Her arms are full.
Someone is really leaning on that doorbell. She dumps her
bundle into the open dishwasher, heaves the machine door
shut, and trots to the front hall, where she catches sight of
her face in the mirror. An absolute mess. Opening the door,
she lets out a shriek.

"Hi!" they wave through the storm door, then bust in as
if the manager of the K-Mart has just unlocked for the
early-bird special.

"Boy, she's really surprised, isn't she?" says Lloyd.

But Florence doesn't pause to say hello. She's making a
beeline for the stairway. "Gotta take a wee!" she calls back.

"No!" cries Lindsay. "Use the downstairs bathroom!"

But now the doorbell rings again. Lloyd jabs a thumb back over his shoulder. "That'll be the driver with the bags," he says.

A cry sounds from the top of the stairs. "Linny! There's a man on the floor up here!"

Oh, God, thinks Lindsay. The last she saw, Gray was naked.

"A man upstairs?" calls Lloyd from the front hall.

"Oh," stammers Lindsay. "It must be the dishwasher repairman." It takes all her strength to climb up the steps.

Florence is standing in the hall with her legs crossed. "Ooo, hurry!" she says, watching her daughter-in-law grope upwards toward her.

Lindsay pushes open the bathroom door. Gray is fully clothed, but he's lying on his back, head behind the toilet. Has he passed out from exhaustion?

"Toilet's all fixed," he says, leaping up. There's a small screwdriver in his hand. "I always carry this with me." He gives Lindsay a patronizing look, as if this whole scene is something he's been through before.

She feels an instant of relief. Then the fright in her turns to rage at his glib tone. "You bum," she whispers. He pushes past her and clomps down the stairs in his boots. Lindsay pursues him. "Get out!" she hisses at him.

At the door, he acts smart, wetting his lips like they're going to kiss good-bye. Lloyd is out of sight. Suitcases have appeared in the front hall. She wants to slap him. But the starry-eyed dreamer in her wants to salvage this fantasy by melting in his arms. He's tipping her chin up to his mouth. Suddenly the door bangs into the side of his head.

"Coming through!" yells Sylvia and heaves an Adidas bag through the open doorway. Metal clanks as it lands on Gray's foot. Richard's father jogs in the morning, carrying fist-sized dumbbells. Gray's face goes pale at the pain.

"Hey" Sylvia scowls now at Lindsay. "Tell that wacko from Waukegan that I want my tip!"

"Lindsay, get in here!" calls a voice from the kitchen. It's

Lloyd. "I think I know what's wrong with your dish-washer." Behind her, the front door slams. Gray has left.

Lloyd comes in holding out her bra by the straps. Cra-dled in one cup is the globe of a wineglass. It swings there —a perfect fit.

"What's going on here?" says Lloyd sternly.

Oh, they've found her out, she thinks in panic, and looks to Sylvia for help. But the old woman only scowls at her. Wafting in from the front hall, a thin whiff of spring picks this moment to reach Lindsay's nostrils. High treetops must wave somewhere out of sight, budding boughs rock. A terrifying fatigue sets in. It tells her that she's climbed up to a forbidden and precarious height, and now she can't hold on. Something cracks. Everything is coming down, casting her to the muddy depths she deserves. She breaks into tears, then, in slow motion, she falls. Hitting the thick rug face-first, she sees stars.

19

AFTER LINDSAY passed out, the three senior citizens carried her up to bed. Actually Sylvia—who knows the fireman's carry—did all the work. Lloyd, imagining he was raising the flag at Iwo Jima, braced Sylvia from behind to prevent a backwards tumble down the stairs. Florence came last, hanging on to the back pockets of her husband.

"Aw, she's okay," observed the taxi driver, throwing a blanket over Lindsay. "Hey, I gotta beat it. I left my motor running."

"Leave her be," said Lloyd.

"Yes, let her motor rest," agreed Florence.

Now they've left Lindsay alone, and she opens her eyes. Something bad has happened and it hurts. As nervous breakdowns go, hers is not very serious. She couldn't ward off the desire and the threats that came at her from all directions. So she gave up. Instead of hospitalization, a good rest is all she needs. And she's got the gumption to make a fresh start. But the world, from her point of view, looks pretty hopeless—a bombed-out landscape where she's forced to clamber over piles of smoking, dusty debris, searching for something to salvage.

Eventually she comes upon the remains of her old conscience. Oddly, it's just an old rag doll. Where thread-like connections were wired into her brain, filaments have pulled apart into ragged shreds. All this time it was hiding —on her back like a monkey, or within a secret chamber in her skull. She's never had a good look at its face. Those hard button eyes must have glared at her a thousand times. My God, she thinks, it's got breasts. And it's not dead, it's moving, trying to reassemble its secret, wired interior. Suddenly the thing seizes her leg. She's so weak that it easily pulls her down. It wants to climb aboard again. It's going to plug back in.

Outside, rain beats against the bedroom window. Lindsay lies flat on her back and wonders where you trade in an old conscience for a new one. "It got squashed," she'll explain. "You're going to pay for this," says a voice. No, she's paid enough already. And she knows who's astride her back now, whispering duty and guilt in her ear. This time she refuses to join the old conspiracy against herself. She arches her neck until some neural fiber tied to the old rag doll stretches to the breaking point and snaps like an old rubber band. The relief is instantaneous—a cool rush of blank knowledge. Then a sharp regret forks its way through the darkness ("Shame on you!"), but an easy turn of her jaw snaps its brittle filament. So that's the trick, she decides with a grim smile. One after another, she breaks the threads that tie her to a dusty doll's world of obligations and dues. Although she may destroy the whole past in the process, it feels real good. But the interior of her conscience is immense, and she has shrunk to the dwarf of herself. Lindsay feels like someone clawing at the wiring of an old telephone exchange, intending to dismantle a ten-story edifice by hand.

Downstairs Alex is home from school. Grandma Florence hugs him and chatters away about how much he's grown, would he like cookies and milk, how wet his shoes are, should he change his socks.

"What's wrong?" says Alex. "If there's something wrong, you should say so."

"Wrong? Oh, where's my camera? We've missed a photo opportunity. Look at you—hair hanging down like a wet pup."

In her own way, Florence is an excellent barometer of

emotional tension. It's just that her dial is calibrated backwards. In the midst of fun and hilarity, she grows silent and morose. Yet Florence is the woman who takes surprise snapshots at funerals. From her, a burst of cheery talk indicates catastrophe in the household.

"Where's my mother?" persists Alex.

"Oh, her? She's resting. She must have been up all night, scrubbing this house!" Florence looks about in dizzy admiration. "Take a sniff. Pine-Sol!"

Alex tiptoes upstairs and into the bedroom. As he looks down at his mother, her face seems to change from one moment to the next. Her eyes keep darting to their aim, keep shooting the gulf, as if their new power might cease in an instant of repose. Finally they fasten on the bedroom alarm clock. She looks perplexed—then terrified.

"It's a clock," explains Alex, placing it in her hands.

She grips the thing, then viciously she hammers it against the quilt.

Alex stares at this exhibition. "Oh, dear," he says, frowning. If time itself is what she's trying to destroy, then he understands her rage. "Hey. Take it easy. I'll help." He takes the device, presses a catch, and the plastic front falls off. She snatches the clock back with a look of fiendish gratitude. The black hands are now accessible. Her fingers pick at the sharp points, but find that they're tough metal.

He wants to tell her there's an easier way to stop it. But the job is already done. Hands clawed away, the clock's empty face beams like a full moon. His mother looks up at him. Her blank expression comes alive. The worst, for her, is over. "Hi," she whispers.

"You can talk?" he says.

"How was school?"

"Okay."

"You'd better go down and spend some time with Grandma and Grandpa. I just need a rest."

The storm has passed. Garth and Wally climb down an embankment to the swollen stream that runs through

town behind the old mill buildings. The muddy current
rushes over rocks that, in summer, form a bed of round
boulders.

Wally lobs a rock into the river.

Garth stands with his hands in his pockets. He's been
trying to explain his vision to his friend. "I've had a
glimpse of my future," he says. "And I don't like what I
saw."

"Baloney," says Wally.

"No, really. I've seen into future time. Una is probably
on her way right now. In a black limousine. My whole life
is going to be changed."

Wally bends to select a flat rock from the gravel beneath
his shoes. He flings the stone out, where it skips seven or
eight times across swirling eddies.

"Nice toss," remarks Garth. "Are you listening? I said
my whole life is going to be changed. Big bucks are going
to shower down on me."

Wally heaves out a big rock. It plunks out of sight.

Garth looks at the current rushing past. Then he looks
at Wally. "Is that all you're going to say?"

Wally just stands there.

"Jeez," says Garth. "You're no help."

Wally hands him a flat rock. Garth checks it out, and
crooks it into his index finger. "Okay. Watch this." He
flings it sidearm and watches it skitter far over the water.
"Did you see that?"

On the narrow bank, Wally has stepped behind him.
Garth feels his friend's hands on his back, one on either
side of his spine. There's a slow shove. "Hey—" Already
he's in motion, head-first into the muddy current. Wally
has pushed him in! The icy water engulfs Garth. He goes
under into bright cold. Rocks bang his shins. He tries to
stand up, but the current sweeps him under again. The
cold makes him gasp, swallow water, and flail his arms.
This could drown him! His arms embrace a boulder and
he hangs on, frigid water rushing past his chin. He's
about a foot from shore. Dragging himself out, he sees his

friend climbing up the bank above him. Wally is not looking back.

Lindsay stays in bed Friday and all day Saturday. The household takes turns bringing up trays of food that she refuses even to look at.

Downstairs, they speculate about what's wrong with her. Richard suggests that it could be her period. Lloyd says it's the flu.

"Overwork," insists Florence, digging into a cardboard box. Richard has revealed the location of the carton where they store his mother's presents. She's got it out on the kitchen table and rustles through items wrapped in tissue paper. "Isn't this cute," she says, displaying the Piggy Beach Party salt-and-pepper set. "It's a good thing Lindsay put these away for safekeeping."

"Lindsay, overworked?" asks Richard.

"It's a mystery," says Alex.

"There's a hole in her head," says Lloyd. "The piggy in the green bikini."

"I don't think a doctor would help," muses Alex.

"That's a big hole," notes Richard. "There must be a cork. What, does the pepper come out her rear end?"

Florence hoots. "The hole is for toothpicks, dummy!"

"Honey, speaking of toothpicks—" winks Lloyd.

A smile spreads across Florence's face. "The Toothpick Caddy!" she exclaims.

Richard's parents have brought a whole shopping bag full of gifts with them—all useful items. In addition to the Toothpick Caddy, there's a Bathroom Tank-Top Organizer, Check Caddy, Coupon Tote with built-in digital clock, Cosmetic Caddy, Greeting Card Organizer, Tidy Tote, and Tote Caddy.

Richard stares at the cluttered table. Lindsay will die when she sees this stuff. But the Tidy Tote catches his eye. Gina has one of them in her bathroom—she keeps her makeup in the thing. He was in her bathroom last night, taking a pee after making love. It was nearly eight o'clock when he got home. The sight of his parents, washing dishes in the kitchen, mortified him. But his nervous apology about late work at the office apparently satisfied them. Still, fibbing to Lindsay was one thing—lying to his father was another. Now he stares at the Tidy Tote and decides that Gina and his mother would probably hit it right off.

Everyone has ignored Alex. He's examining the digital clock. Alternately the date and time pulse on and off. He doesn't see any way to stop it. With a sweep second hand, you have a kind of leverage in the mind. But the liquid-crystal pulse is inexorable, illusory, terrifying.

Easter Sunday dawns through a low haze in the eastern sky. Lindsay is out of bed at 6 A.M. Down in the kitchen, her hands automatically measure coffee into the percolator. Lloyd appears in his jogging outfit and gives her a hug. There are dark circles under her eyes. When he inquires about her condition, she puts a finger to her lips. Eventually the others straggle downstairs in bathrobes. No one asks why Lindsay spent two days and three nights in a dark bedroom. Alex, especially, puts on a show of indifference to his mother's condition and talks instead about how well he slept on the floor in a sleeping bag. He wonders if the others notice how hollow her voice sounds.

At breakfast, Lindsay makes a diplomatic speech after examining Florence and Lloyd's gifts. "You're both very generous," she says. "What I can't use, I'll send back with you. This Tank-Top Organizer, for example, would really go better in your bathroom, Florence. With your fish."

Richard glares at turquoise eggshells on his plate. To his ears, Lindsay's voice sounds coldly assertive. He braces himself for his mother's bitter reply to these insults.

"Oh, my Rattan Fish Family!" cries Richard's mother. "You have such a memory for details. Those critters really gave my bare walls new life!"

"Good. That's settled." Next Lindsay declares, "It's time to get ready for church." The kitchen is silent, as if there's something everyone knows that she doesn't.

Lloyd looks over the top of his glasses at her. "Richard told us," he says, "about your minister. Some kind of break-down? And a recent change in the character of the congre-gation."

"There are some lovely services on television," suggests Florence. "I like that optimistic fellow from California. The one with the glass church?"

"Nothing doing." Lindsay's arms are crossed defiantly. "I spoke with Jean Ekdahl on"—there's an instant's pause as Lindsay's mind leaps the chasm of two lost days —"Thursday morning. A young fellow is coming to give the sermon. And Robert—he's our head organist—has in-vited some musicians up from Boston."

"But—" sputters Florence. "I don't have a hat. I always wear a hat on Easter."

By 10 A.M. the day is turning perfect. High cirrus clouds feather an azure sky. Crocuses open along the walk up to the Good Shepherd Church. When the five of them arrive, the church looks less full than last week. Word must have passed among Ekdahl's new and ragged following that their leader won't be preaching today. The sanctuary has sprung alive with color: red tulips, lilies, and yellow jon-quils have been set out on either side of the altar. The big stained-glass window blazes with bright morning sun. And the older ladies in the congregation have arrayed them-selves in their most astonishing polyester hues—blueberry, fuchsia, raspberry, and lilac. But Lindsay feels shut out. Everything registers in her eyes as dull shades of gray.

The organist's friends from Boston turn out to be a brass quartet. They must be professionals—perhaps from the symphony. The Prelude (Elmore's "Fanfare for Easter") rings so gloriously through the narthex that it brings tears of joy to people's eyes. Lindsay stares blankly at instru-ments tipping up golden against a background of greenery and scarlet and white.

A tall young man—he must play basketball at the semi-nary—crosses the chancel wearing Ekdahl's white surplice.

It hangs way too short on the visiting minister. He hunches over the lectern and puts on round, wire-rimmed spectacles. After reading the scripture lesson (Mark 16: 1–14), he looks up and says, "The congregation will please rise for the Gradual Hymn, number ninety-nine." Even the old ladies get up eagerly for this one. They've been waiting all year to belt it out:

> *Christ the Lord is risen today!*
> *Ah-h-h-ha-le-lu-ia!*

Lindsay mouths the words in the hymnal. She holds the volume in fingers so dulled to sensation that she feels like she's wearing gloves. The big organ thunders triumphantly as this modest crowd, faces a-beam, rings out the alleluias. Lindsay's voice croaks a note here and there. The congregation is probably trying to impress the professional musicians present. These mostly old folks stretch flaccid vocal chords into harmonies, crescendos, and even—from somewhere in the back—a fine counterpoint. Between verses, the organ changes keys, up a half step, and quickens the tempo. The music pulls at Lindsay. She feels it dragging her up out of herself. Then the brass quartet joins in, so that the final notes, which seem to raise everyone on tiptoe, amount to an enraptured shout. Then everyone flops down out of breath, but refreshed, just tickled pink to be Protestants united in song. Everyone except Lindsay. It was Luther, she recalls, who started the tradition of congregational singing.

The sermon disappoints most people. The divinity student plods through a scholarly reading of Mark's Gospel, dwelling on the darkest hints about the historical Jesus and his execution on April 7 in the year 30.

"Now, Mark," declares the young man, "writing forty years later, mentions no stone rolled away from the tomb. Instead, we read that the three women 'trembled and were afraid.' In the text, only doubt is affirmed: 'they believed not,' 'neither believed,' 'they believed not!' The less accurate narratives of Luke and John, of course, were written much later, at the turn of the first century. So, there's no proof that Christ left the tomb, let alone rose—bodily—from the cold oblivion of death! Can you understand, dear friends, what a terrible burden our Christian faith really is?"

The silence in the sanctuary is broken here and there by the sounds of yawning. Lindsay finds herself staring at the flowers on either side of the altar. *Colors,* she whispers to herself.

"Please rise"—says the seminary student, rubbing his brow—"for the Hymn. Number—ah, 525?"

Everyone stands obediently. Lindsay watches the organist leafing through the hymnal—as if playing number 525 is news to him. The hymn is not familiar, and that means the congregation will stumble through it.

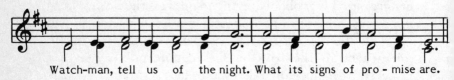

Watch-man, tell us of the night. What its signs of pro - mise are.

A few voices drone over the difficult intervals. Lindsay has found her voice, and she hits each note precisely, hoping those in the pew ahead of her are fast learners. Some man in the back sings louder now. And this gives her the confidence to sing out herself:

Trav-eler, o're yon moun-tain's height. See that glo - ry beam- ing star.

About here, she's aware of a passage opening into herself. The current of aspiring sound must require an access, a route upward and out. She especially will feel it making the repeated leap up from F sharp to D, and that interval will assure her that an airy height has been reached, a promontory scaled, from which the rest of the notes spread out like an ordered landscape. Her eyes are aware of bright blues and scarlet blazing from high stained glass. She gazes about in wonder—feeling both within and without herself—and decides that she's finally been admitted to the spaciousness of her own interior.

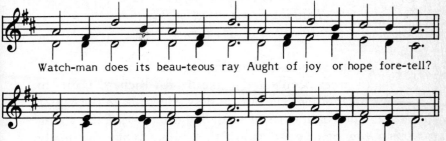

Watch-man does its beau-teous ray Aught of joy or hope fore-tell?

Trav - eler, yes: it brings the day. Prom-ised day of Is - ra - el.

During the second verse, a few others in the crowd have caught the melody. One row up, a black woman with gray hair sings. Across the aisle, a man in a business suit. Ahead of him, a long-haired kid. Piano or guitar players maybe. Veterans of choirs or barbershop quartets? These days, how many people can read music? Enough, she decides, and lets her clear soprano voice loft up to fiery stained glass. Still, she's conscious of that other voice from the back of the church. It seems to mount up with hers, to join her on this height that bright sun and azure sky have called her to ascend.

> *Watchman tell us of the night,*
> *For the morning seems to dawn.*
> *Traveler, darkness takes its flight,*
> *Doubt and terror are withdrawn.*

A chill strikes. This scene has happened before. The hymnal, formerly a dead thing in her hands, now feels like it's growing new leaves of paper along its spine. She's aware of her garments, of the minute rub and rustle of them against naked flesh. The light and color in this place have become nearly blinding. She feels the air drawn up from the deep, a windy gust in the breast, feels it coursing through all the singers—especially she and he—they're vessels of its spirit:

Watchman let thy wanderings cease;
Hie thee to thy quiet home.
Traveler, lo! the Prince of Peace,
Lo! the Son of God is come!

After the service, the student minister waits at the back door to greet people and shake hands. Richard wants to leave by another exit, but Lindsay edges out to the center aisle, where a line has formed. She wants to ask the young man how he came to choose that hymn. When she finally reaches the doorway, he looks embarrassed at her question, like she's putting him on.

"It was a goof," he says.

"What a glorious goof!" She smiles.

Outside, she pauses for a moment on the steps, shielding her eyes from bright sun. She's wearing an off-white, two-piece suit that she bought last fall. It's only polyester/rayon, but has the nubby texture of real silk. Across the street, forsythia blooms. On this side, the high branches of a maple look ruddy with sap, greening faintly in a haze of bud tips. Her eyes are hungry now for color. They follow black limbs down the tree's thick trunk. Clusters of people stand on the green turf chatting. Such a mild, mild wind, she thinks. Such a sweetness in the air.

Garth didn't know this was Lindsay's church. This morning, he simply felt the urge to see what some Lutherans were up to on Easter Sunday. So he put on the only necktie he owns (handpainted: a Hawaiian sunset with palm trees), brushed the lint off his Salvation Army Harris tweed, and made a pilgrimage out to the suburbs in the old Plymouth. The sermon was pretty interesting, he thought. But the straight-looking guy seated next to him in the back pew didn't share his interest. The man leaned forward on his knees and seemed to be practicing his grip on an invisible golf club.

Garth leaned over once and asked what iron he was using.

"Sand wedge," said the guy, in a daze.

Garth shook his head. "Nine—maybe an eight," he whispered.

"You think so?" He looked toward the figure in the pulpit, gauging the distance.

"All that rain Thursday? The greens are soft. It'll bite," said Garth.

"I hadn't thought of that."

Outside after the service, Garth notices this same golfer jawing with Lindsay's husband and a couple of other business types. Then she finally appears—stunning, in white, as in a recurring dream he's had. He considers hiding behind a tree, but leans against it instead. Maybe he'll blend into the bark. She stands there in the entrance to the church. His eyes fix on her, and everything else—these strangers dressed in bright colors, a dog barking down the block—blurs into silence. She finally looks in his direction and—oh, Jesus—comes straight down the steps in his direction. Alex tags along and then runs ahead across the spongy grass.

"Hello, Mr. Erikson!" calls Alex.

Garth puts up a hand in greeting, but he's looking past the kid at Lindsay. She looks older than he remembers.

She stops, leaving a good stretch of grass between them. "Hello," she finally says.

He doesn't know what to say. That he's surprised to see her? That he sure liked singing that hymn—the one that told him she was present in the same building? Or that he's been through a lot: sleepless nights, visions, an icy plunge into present time? There's no time to say it all. Alex has wandered off. Her husband is yards away. But in the face of the look she's giving him, he can't think of a reason to say anything. The clarity of her gaze cuts through him like a scythe.

She tips her face up to the light. "This sun is wonderful."

He wants to say what he feels. But in this public place, with people passing by on the sidewalk, what can he do? Holler? Fall on his knees before her loveliness? Finally he says, "I'm sorry."

She lets her eyes shut dreamily against the brightness.

Garth makes an impatient noise. "You're supposed to ask me what I'm sorry about."

She looks at him. "Oh, really? So you can say, 'Everything'? Like you're apologizing for the way the world is arranged?"

Uff da, he thinks. She's not going to stand for any bullshit.

"Just feel the sun," she says, basking in light.

He feels it warm on his back. "Wally says that the sun suppresses the night secretion of the hormone melatonin."

"Night secretion?" She glances at him and smiles.

Garth laughs. "It does sound like something you'd want to suppress."

"Hey, Grandpa. This is Mr. Erickson." It's Alex, approaching with a middle-aged man and woman. The old guy's shoes are really shined up.

Lindsay introduces Lloyd and Florence as Richard's parents.

"He's a teacher," announces Alex.

"Not the one who's been failing this boy in math and science?" puts in Florence sharply.

Garth scratches his beard. "Actually," he says, "I don't work."

Lloyd grunts sympathetically. "It's Reagan, Carter—the whole bunch. Thousands unemployed in Illinois."

Now Richard arrives. He says hello to Garth and the two shake hands. "Bill Spence over there—he says you're quite a golfer." The group now forms a circle on the grass.

Lindsay stands primly in her white suit, clutching her handbag, listening. It may seem a little odd to her that Alex and her husband know this bearded stranger better than she does.

Garth is explaining that he was a caddy for a couple of weeks as a teenager. "To be honest, I've never played. But I've always liked the scale of the game. The vast landscaping—like deer parks, or vistas out of Poussin and the French Renaissance. All that *space.*" Nervousness keeps Garth talking. He stretches out his arms in a gesture that displays the frayed cuffs of his jacket. "Picture the distances. And a ball—like *this!*" Everyone watches as his gesture suddenly collapses into a little circle made with thumb and forefinger. "The smallest ball in sports. Am I right?"

"Um—" says Richard. "Ping-Pong is smaller." Lindsay's husband must think he's just scored a point.

"Sure," says Garth. "Ping-Pong. With that cute little net. And table that fits down the basement. It cramps you up, like this." Garth ducks and makes a painful grimace. "Bumping your head on furnace pipes, right? That's what I mean about golf. The space!" He's getting carried away with his arm gestures again. "And light! Changes in weather. The texture of turf, sand, and water—" Abruptly his arms flop down to his sides. "But you know," he says, shaking a finger. "Fertilizer. You know how much fertilizer a golf course takes?"

There's a silence as everyone considers this.

"It always seemed to me," says Lloyd, "that golf was a scientific game."

"That's good," nods Garth, and they all fix their eyes on him again. "Sure. Mathematics! The angles of loft on the clubs. Tiny increments in the angles. They shape the trajectories—" He looks into space a moment, then yells, "Parabolas!" Everyone flinches at the word. Garth's stiff palm is arcing upwards. All heads turn, tracking this gesture into a long flight that seems to plop something onto the ground at their feet. They all find themselves staring down at the grass. "And then there's angular momentum," Garth is saying. They look up at him—to hear more. "Slice and hook, backspin, pitch and run!" he exclaims. "Yes. A scientific game. Mathematical, even."

"Exactly," declares Lloyd, with a shrewd look.

259

Richard puts his hands in his pockets impatiently. "Look, it's getting late," he says.

"Wait," says his father. "I'm thinking about Alex here." He tousles the boy's hair. "You know what he needs?"

"Golf?" says Richard.

"Hoo!" squeals Florence at her husband. "What you said last night, honey. Alex needs a tutor."

"A tooter?" says the boy.

Richard examines Garth, calculating.

"He needs a coach," says Lloyd. "Someone who knows how to explain things in an interesting way. Scientific things. Math. Angles and trajectories."

"Well—sure," nods Richard, finally catching on. "Maybe you can help us here," he tells Garth. "What's your schedule at the school?"

"Me?" Garth takes a step back and points a finger at his chest.

"Rich," says Florence like she's repeating the obvious to an inattentive child. "He's un-em-ployed."

Garth puts up his hands at them. "I can explain that," he declares. He's got a whole utopian theory about alienated labor.

"How about after school?" suggests Lloyd. "You could drop over to the house, oh—how about three times a week?"

"Wait a minute—" says Garth.

"A tutor," Richard repeats to himself, trying out the sound of the word. "Can we afford a tutor?" He looks at Lindsay.

"Forget about the cost," breaks in Lloyd, fishing out his wallet. He slaps it on his palm for emphasis. "My grandson is worth it. What are we talking here—five, six hours a week. Call it fifteen or twenty dollars. A round of golf these days must cost more than that."

"Wait a minute," says Garth.

"How about Monday, Wednesday, Friday?" asks Florence.

"Hold it," insists Garth. "You people are cooking up this deal without even asking me. Or Alex. Or her."

"It's a neat idea," says Alex.

Everyone looks at Lindsay. The bright spot of sun she was standing in has shifted. Now light and thin shadows play over her face as she looks into the distance.

"You heard him explain about that little ball," puts in Florence, on whom Garth has evidently made quiet an impression.

"Hush," says Lloyd. "Can't you see that she's making up her mind?"

"I think—" muses Lindsay, letting her eyes settle on Garth's face. "I think no harm would come of it." She takes a little breath of resolution. "We'll start on Wednesday. You know the address? Say, three o'clock?"

Garth's face has gone pale. Her clear gaze is piercing him. He wants to ask if she knows what she's getting them into. God, he thinks. Invited to her house. He drops his head in a show of humility. "Okay," he says.

20

Two shrill days pass before Lindsay's in-laws leave. Tuesday, Richard drives them to the airport on his way to work. Once the house is empty, Lindsay takes her coffee cup out on the deck. The sun is a dim glow somewhere to the east. Events have conspired to push her, far back again, into herself. And her sense of time is peculiar. Internal clocks wind down, start up, and whir unexpectedly. She leans over the railing and examines a perennial flower bed that runs along the base of the deck. Cleared now of winter's debris, the black soil has cracked, and tender shoots nose up searching warm light. But a night frost has made them stiffen and recoil, caused them to reconsider another spurt of growth.

Sunday after church, Richard and his father had done yard work. The lawn was strewn with fallen branches and soggy, matted leaves. They disagreed about inane details: the proper way to hold a rake, to load the wheelbarrow. At dinner, their arguments veered into politics. Lloyd was tired of seeing the ACLU go to court to get public Christmas trees torn down. He was fed up with liberals, weak judges, and government bureaucrats. His son sat and listened to this tirade in silence. "Carter gave away the Panama Canal," insisted Lloyd. "Then he betrayed Taiwan. Now the Reds run Nicaragua. And that's just the crust of the pie."

Richard stood up and threw down his napkin. "I'm going out," he said.

With their son gone, Lloyd and Florence unpacked old grudges and disappointments. Richard should have stayed in Illinois. He could have had a good job at Abbott Laboratories. Alex could have gone to a decent school. And Lindsay deserved a bigger house, a better TV, a microwave oven. These were visions of their life as grandparents they must have entertained when Richard was still in high school. He'd marry a local girl and settle down in Chicago's northern suburbs—a twenty-minute drive to Waukegan for Sunday dinner.

Out on the deck, Lindsay looks up from black soil to stare at a lilac bush. The leaves are thumb-sized. The distant maples are hazy green, wispy with pollen. Here in the Northeast, it takes weeks for the earth to green itself. Spring ought to come suddenly, the leaves full-blown and thick the morning after a thunderstorm. She leans her weight on the deck's railing, flesh of forearms pressed to warm wood. Overhead the sun has shifted way west. Suddenly Alex is back from school. Now it's sunset, and Richard is home. Dinner passes in a rush. Lindsay finds herself frozen in one posture for hours, leaning to stare down at stains in the kitchen sink, over toothpaste dribbled in the bathroom washbowl. The others are asleep. She stands stuck in the night and looks down at matted fibers in the carpet, cracks between planks of the hardwood floor, nail-heads raising tiny disks of paint along the baseboards.

Wednesday, no more leaning. She finds herself erect and in motion. She's on the go all morning, clattering from room to room, seeing the framed prints on walls slip past like stations at which her train isn't stopping. She hauls a basket of laundry to the washer, chugs the mail into the den from the front hall, and steams into the kitchen to turn off the teakettle. When the doorbell clangs, she feels like a conductor, swaying down an aisle to the front door, punching tickets and making change. In one motion, she swings the door open, sees the school bus pulling up—right on time—and gestures her son's tutor in across the threshold.

"Hello," he says, standing there, looking nervous in his

beard. Behind him, Alex lugs his backpack up the front walk.

"All aboard," says Lindsay, already rolling off to the kitchen. She reappears with a list she's made of weak spots in her son's school record. The page is sent sailing into Garth's fumbling hands. She backs into the den and indicates a place for him and Alex to sit. Then she steams off around a corner, accelerating toward the laundry room.

On Friday, Garth appears again just before the school bus arrives. For Lindsay, it's been a morning of pauses and stops. Things strike her that deserve writing down: motes drifting in shafts of light, the shape of veins running straight in celery stalks, veins branching in the leaves of potted plants, or wavering thin and violet at her wrist where the skin is nearly translucent. Her notebook bears a sweat stain from carrying it around all day. Throughout the house, she's left chairs pulled close to end tables, the TV, windowsills—any flat surface to write on when her pen has flown to the page. All her movement and flight from two days ago has compacted itself and drilled a channel down her arm to her fingertips, which are bruised and dented from a ballpoint pen.

She's carrying her notebook when she answers the door. Garth seems full of energy. Since his first day on the job as Alex's tutor didn't match his expectations, he's pumped himself up for this visit. Earlier, he'd imagined romantic interludes breaking up the kid's math lesson. He'd pictured himself alone with Lindsay—around a corner, out of sight —the two of them straining, heroically, to resist a passionate embrace. But good grief, she barely allowed him a glimpse of her. Today he's determined to keep pace with Lindsay's quick moves. Strutting in, Garth glimpses pictures on the walls. He spins to point out the school bus's arrival. He paces in a tight circle. This way, if Lindsay makes an abrupt takeoff, he'll get a fast start and be pointed —he hopes—in the direction of a successful pursuit. All he wants is to exchange a word or two. And to gaze, bewitched, into her eyes.

"What are you jumping around for?" she asks.

Garth jolts to a stop facing her, and stands tense—almost crouched—as if he's prepared to dive headlong across the room.

"Hold still," she says. Something about his face has caught her attention. She passes a slow hand across his eyes, shading them from the light.

Garth feels like an enormous but disciplined beast pushed into a cramped space. He feels gates close behind his lathered haunches. "Easy boy," he says, gathering the reins. "It won't be long now."

Lindsay is peering at his eyeball, examining the aperture that opens and closes down with the changing light. His pupil is dark, and in it she sees an image reflected— one ringed by the magic circle of the flecked and fibered iris.

"It bounces," she tells him. "If the change in light is abrupt enough, the little muscle in there tightens up so fast that it has to let go. Then it adjusts again. What's the word for that? I said 'bounce.' That's not right."

Garth gives her a quizzical look. "You said the same thing last month."

"I did?"

"Yup. Is there any coffee left in the pot?"

The two of them are sitting at Lindsay's kitchen table. Next to her coffee mug, her notebook lies spread open.

"How did we get in here?" she asks. "Weren't we just in the living room?"

"We always sit in here."

"We do?"

"Are you okay?" Garth touches her hand, then gently grips her wrist.

Lindsay gazes about in wonder at the kitchen cabinets, the spice rack on the wall, the chrome toaster on the countertop. There's something tentative about this man's touch. But he lounges comfortably in the other chair, laced boots thrust out on her linoleum.

"We were talking about the tomatoes, remember?" He

frowns at her and snaps his fingers in front of her eyes. "Peat moss? Lime? Hello?"

"What day is it?"

"Wednesday."

"Where's Alex?"

"He's watching *The Electric Company.*"

"And you're the tutor, right?"

"That's me. Listen, it's getting late," he says, standing up. "So anyway, if it doesn't rain on Friday, we'll fork that peat moss into the bed by your peonies. We might as well put out the tomatoes. Okay?"

Lindsay shuts her eyes, straining to make sense of this conversation. She never plants tomatoes before Memorial Day. "Wait," she says, growing worried now. "What month is it?"

"You're not kidding, are you? It's May. The twentieth, I think."

Lindsay shakes her head. "Impossible. It was just Easter."

Garth shrugs. "Time flies," he says, deciding not to make a big deal out of whatever fluke of memory she's suffered.

She knows that something went wrong with her brain. But this is hard to believe. April has passed—and most of May. All those days lost? "So," she sighs, "I missed Mother's Day."

"Nope. Richard took you out to dinner. Remember, you stood in line about an hour at the Holiday Inn?"

"I don't recall that. It's all a blank."

"It'll come back."

"But—" She looks sharply at this shaggy stranger in a blue workshirt. "You've been coming here, then—" She's thinking of the familiarity of his touch a moment ago. If a month has gone by, then exactly what, she wonders, has passed between them? There must be some dark reason to blank out an entire month, to wipe a dirty slate clean.

Garth scratches his beard. "Alex and I have been working—let's see—since the end of April. We've done the solar system and constellations. We've done binary numbers, some old-fashioned drills on the multiplication tables. Jeez, those calculators they let them use are poison. So anyway, now we're starting geology. You said you might come along Saturday. We're going rock hunting."

"I see," she nods. "But what about me? And you?"

"Us?" he says. "We've drunk a lot of coffee. And a couple times we sang hymns together at the piano. And I took you and Alex to my loft one day. You two met Wally and Helen and their dog. That's about it."

"Did I meet that woman you live with?" she asks.

"Una? She moved out on me. She lives in New York now with a guy named Gruder. Let's not go over that again."

Lindsay is staring at the two coffee mugs on the table. The clock on the stove says it's nearly five. "I don't know how to ask this," she says. "But—do you always stay this late?"

"*Uff da,*" he sighs, steps over, and crouches next to her chair. "You're really confused, aren't you?" He seizes her two hands and gazes into her face. "Listen, everything is okay. This is a routine we've fallen into. When I'm done with Alex, we have coffee and talk. You're a terrific talker. Lately I've been coming early. Helping you out with projects—you know, housecleaning, gardening? Trust me. It'll all come back."

She stares at his big hands. What she really wants to know involves feelings. And how she feels right now is—peculiar. This has happened before. In some other life, she has lived this moment. Last week, perhaps. Or ages ago. A pulse throbs in her fingers. She can't tell if it's his, or her own.

"Have the two of us"—Lindsay blushes to ask this—"have we *kissed* yet?"

Garth's mouth drops at this question. In Lindsay's house, he's been scrupulous about manners, keeping his distance, and attending conscientiously to the task of tutoring Alex. At school, the boy's teacher has been impressed. Richard gave Garth a raise last week, joking that he was working himself out of a job. How he feels about Lindsay has grown both more complex and more simple. For one thing, she no longer represents a dreamy ideal. He's lugged her dirty clothes. He's observed plaque on her teeth and dandruff dusting her shoulders. He knows that her hair, backlit with yellow afternoon light—as she sits, legs curled under her, in the red living room chair by the window—nearly moves him to tears of joy. He's heard all the stories about her family, childhood, and courtship. He's watched the tongue in her mouth form words. He's ached to take her in his arms. Last week, he touched her for the first time. Today for the second.

Now, gripping her hands, he can't tell whether her question is an invitation or an accusation. "No," he says. "I swear to God, we haven't kissed."

"Well," she pouts a little. "What's taken you so long?"

Garth restrains a groan. She's just transformed weeks of heroic self-restraint into cowardice. "Me? Taken me so long? What about you!"

"Well, you're the man," she replies, indignant.

"That's a pretty old-fashioned attitude," he says. They're still holding hands. Holding back. Holding on. "Well," he adds, "maybe we should try it?"

"A kiss?" To Lindsay, it seems she's waited ages for this moment—hundreds of pages if this were a book.

Garth nods. His eyes are locked onto hers. The sweat on their palms is like glue. They're so stuck now that anyone, coming upon them in the kitchen, would have to douse them with a pail of water to get them apart.

"Are you comfortable?" she asks. "I mean, on your knees?"

"I'm okay. Maybe you should tip your head a little to one side."

"How's this? Here, let me put a hand on your shoulder."

"Fine. Except I've got to lean on something." Garth rests one hand on the edge of the table.

She wets her lips. "Okay. I'm ready."

"I'm ready, too," he murmurs, his lips an inch from hers, her face a blur.

"Wait," she says.

Garth eases back.

"Do I know who you are?"

"I think so," he says, feeling drawn irresistibly to her mouth, and neither can stop it now. But the kitchen table, bearing Garth's weight, skids loudly across the gleaming linoleum. His momentum carries his mouth passed hers, but Lindsay swings herself aboard—as if hopping a freight —and clings to him in a descent that lands both on the floor. From there they roll over and over in a tight embrace until Garth's boots crash into the base of the refrigerator.

What they remember, however, is their lips brushing lightly, then pressing and melting into fluid. Lindsay felt herself soaring into airy darkness as she clutched this gentle stranger, and both of them thrilled to its dizzy power: a low rumble that quickened to a shriek, then a tumble into the unknown that jolted them hard, a jarring thump like abrupt pain, followed by swirling motion that pressed their bodies together in urgent, dizzy revolutions.

"Wow," says Garth, opening his eyes. "You really know how to kiss."

"Incredible," she whispers, staggering to her feet.

"What happened in here?" It's Alex, come to investigate a crash in the kitchen. He stands next to his mother and looks down at the man lying on the floor.

"Heh, heh, I fell," says Garth. "I don't think I've ever fallen so hard."

Lindsay is staring out the window. The trees are green and thick with leaves. Spring has suddenly arrived. The play of light in the boughs has music in it: endless leafy variations on the old tune. She decides this is finally the one about June coming and seeds busting out and the round moon rising up to roll through warm nights.

21

ON THE LAKES IN the western Adirondacks, the ice broke up
in April. Toby emerges from the woods and steps onto the
road. Overhead, a big KC-135 heads east to refuel a B-52
over the Atlantic. To the west—in the restricted air corridor that aviation maps list as R-5203—high vapor trails of
interceptors loop into the knots of mock dog fights.

Toby is thinking about dogs. Last month, some dogs
running a deer set off a fragmentation grenade he'd wired
in the woods back of his bunker. The charge didn't stop the
dog pack. Toby followed the tracks into a ravine. There he
found the doe in deep snow. When dogs run a deer into
exhaustion, they don't kill it. They gnaw at the hindquar-
ters and leave it—eyes wild and haunches torn open—in
order to come back and feed again.

Toby walks the muddy road as it winds past the lake's
vacation cottages. He thinks of wild dogs running in packs.
On winter nights they circle up to Beaver River and howl
at the chained German shepherds and spaniels, calling
them to the hunt. He's seen a half-breed pup from a golden
Lab's litter that had the nose and snout of an eastern coy-
ote. In the woods, a genetic experiment is under way—wild
blood mingling with disciplined intelligence. The dog species is preparing itself for survival.

The road turns to asphalt at the abandoned railway
depot. It's a mile west to Willardsville. Toby unlocks the
door where he stores his Blazer. He sees immediately that
someone has broken in and tried to lift the hood of the

vehicle. He's rigged several nasty devices to discourage vandals. The one they tripped probably broke a couple of fingers on some kid's right hand. The battery is still there, and the Blazer starts right up. In seven or eight hours he'll be in Boston to see a man about a case of 60mm mortar rounds.

The guy in Boston calls himself Parnell and runs guns to Northern Ireland. "Sure, I got mortar rounds," he said last month. They had met at the Boston Aquarium. Someone was in the tank feeding the sharks. "Sixty millimeters got fins on the back, right? Listen, I got armor-piercing shells, AK-47s, FN-MAGs. Whatever you want. I got a bazooka. You want a bazooka?"

Parnell tapped on the thick glass of the big tank. "What a dumb shark," he said. "A goddamn dreamy shark. I told you my grandfather was a poet? That was the trouble. I'm talking about 1916. Those guys were all goddamn dreamers and poets. They wrote plays, for Chrissake. So they get these second-hand rifles, see? Mausers. What a bunch of chumps. Listen, we ain't making that mistake again. I mean the IRA. Good guns and no goddamn poets. You understand what I'm saying?"

On the way to Boston, the Interstate passes within a mile of Lindsay's house. Toby is thinking about stopping on the way back. He's not certain anymore that Lindsay remembers him. They've got to talk and make plans. It's not enough that he's ready to get her out. She has to know for certain that he's at hand, close by, watching.

22

Aʟʟ ᴛʜʀᴏᴜɢʜ ᴛʜᴇ month of May, Richard has been in agony. He thinks he's in love with both Lindsay and Gina. Pulled in one direction or the other wouldn't be so bad. It's this tearing of himself apart that hurts. He gets up in the night and sits on the lowered lid of the toilet, face in his hands. He tries to think of his golf swing, the roar of a basketball crowd—anything except what one of his country-western songs calls "the hollow echo in his plundered heart."

He hasn't asked Gina to be his next wife, nor has either uttered the word *divorce* yet aloud. It's madness, a fantasy surging out of control. The other day he actually pledged to take Gina to a dinner dance at the country club in September. He wasn't too explicit about arrangements, but Gina is all a-whirl in a Cinderella dream. At the office, she recites the TV shows she sits home and watches. "I don't know what's come over me," she smiles. "A guy asked me out on a date and I said no to him. Isn't that weird?"

It's June and Lindsay is in love. Weekday mornings, Garth's old car appears regularly in her driveway. At the door, they meet in a rush, but always stop short of embracing until he's stepped inside. Then, in a confused mingling of eyelashes and sweet saliva, Lindsay feels the hairs of his mustache go up her nostrils.

Up and down the block, everyone speculates about the old Plymouth's appearance. The mailman raps the right tail-fin approvingly as he makes the turn up Lindsay's walk. The driver of the UPS van notes the vehicle and says a little prayer for Lee Iacocca and the Chrysler Corporation. Mrs. Clapp hasn't noticed the vehicle yet, although every morning at 11:15 she's watched her dog pee on its hubcaps. "Yup, that's the tutor's car," nods Phil, the retired carpenter who lives across the street from Lindsay's house. "A real scholar, he is."

Last week, Garth and Lindsay lay side by side on the living room rug. Five days had passed since their first kiss. From the FM radio came the voice of Robert J. Lurtsema, droning on about Chopin, George Sand, and the Third Ballade.

"So it's back now?" Garth asked. "Your memory."

"I've been thinking about it," said Lindsay "About blanking out all that time we spent together. I think I wanted you to be a stranger."

Garth got up on one elbow and looked at her. "A stranger? Maybe," he said. "Wally says that things disappear—go off and then on again—all the time. But nobody notices. Maybe, for you, everything got in phase. Some kind of gridlock in the circuits. It probably happens to a lot of people. But who's going to go around saying, 'Hey, did you notice everything disappeared yesterday?' "

She watched him, amused. His eyes drifted to the window, then back to her face. It was happening again. Another spell. Peculiar sensations had arrived lately to freeze both of them into silence. The first one must have struck them at the shopping mall, after the old man had been led away and they were left alone. Yesterday, two spells had arrived within hours of each other. And now, without warning, here it was happening again. Whatever random word or silent wish of the heart invoked the thing, they both felt its chilling power—like a draft blowing through massive doors cranked open by spirits. Maybe demons.

"We're thinking the same thing," she said, her voice almost cracking.

"I know."

"That we're strangers?"

"Hell, I'm thinking about everyone being strangers. Always."

She picked at the rug. "That's sad."

"In a way, it is."

"You mean the other would be worse? If you could yield yourself up?"

"It would be terrible," he said, touching her hair. "To get all the way through someone. To know everything."

"But this is terrible, too. It's—endless."

He nodded.

"Ah," she said. "Thank God."

He traced a finger along the line of her jaw. On the FM, Robert J. Lurtsema was describing the Chopin ballade as "a schoolgirl's delight, a coquettish toying with power that sports with graver and more passionate emotions."

"Should I turn this off?" he asked. The radio was within reach.

"No. Turn it up louder. I love this piece."

Garth turned up the volume, then leaned on his elbow as a piano began playing—tentatively—a mild inquiry whose answer it immediately supplied. Lindsay lay back on the rug and closed her eyes. The music urged Garth closer, drawing his mouth to hers. At the instant their lips touched, a high note startled them with its sharpness. Then the piano's texture went soft but mounted upwards.

"What elegant music," he whispered.

"Mmm, more," she said, pulling him by the beard. An urgency drew them higher in sparking leaps, and their mouths played the trills and arpeggios into an airy breathlessness until the heights fell away—ahh. A glittering descent.

"Whew," said Garth, sitting up to catch his breath. He'd never tried kissing to music before.

Lindsay lay on her back in a dream. "It's Paderewski," she said. As the Chopin piece circled back to its opening theme, she unfastened her jeans and slid them off with her underpants. Sitting up, she stripped off her top. The radio was still too soft. She turned it up, hoping to match the tingle shooting along her skin. When she stretched out again, Garth had slipped off his clothes, too.

"Try not to worship me," she smiled.

"You're asking a lot," he murmured, suspended over her.

Paderewski now touched the high-C octaves *(tink-pung)* that always made Lindsay think—though she tried to resist the thought—of rain dropping off wet leaves. Except this time she felt Garth's lips teasing her nipples erect, and the notes seemed to say *pink-tung, pink-tung, pink-tung.* And then it did get watery, but like waves lapping —a fillip and lilt of motion which their hands traced from armpit to navel, from yielding thighs to the hollow of collarbones. And when those high notes sounded again, it was his fingertip on her clit *(ting-ding, ting-ding, ting-ding),* and suddenly they were a-float in dizzy swirls and crescendos, limbs entwined like seaweed. Like an amiable aquatic beast, something nosed at an entrance *(pink-dink, pink-dink, pink-dink!)* and to this gentle knock, she opened wide—and so wet that waves seemed to wash in, and Chopin's fluid melody, streaming sweat, worked into a froth. A swift current caught them—raced them on through low rumbling turbulence and the high-flung spray of fountains, through key changes that swept them rushing up the keyboard, chords crashing *(fortissimo!)* like breakers on black rocks, sweeping them onward, out of themselves, to the brink—and beyond. Into pure sound—harmonies so sweet they pierced the ear. Into motion suspended—a weightless turning in misty air, as if caught in a high waterfall's lacy cascade. The first time, then, that Lindsay and Garth made love, all the neighbors heard the volume turned up, and it sounded like this:

Now they spend most mornings in bed. Then Lindsay fixes lunch. Garth cooked once—a complicated curry recipe that had him dashing off to the supermarket for fresh gingerroot and coriander, left her kitchen a mess, and wasn't ready to eat until Alex's school bus arrived. Afternoons they lounge around drinking coffee, talking, and leafing through the library books Garth consults for Alex's lessons: books about geography, anthropology, and marine biology—he looks for topics that can be scaled down to third-grade level.

"Listen to this," he says, reading from a book with big print. "In South America, the Indians do not attempt to walk the mountain ledges which their loaded llamas can

travel. Instead they follow safer paths, guiding their ani-
mals by flinging stones at them with slings."

"Great," says Lindsay from the stove. "You going to try
it?"

"Maybe. How long do you think the rawhide should be
on a sling?"

"What about the llama?"

"They could hit a target at 300 yards—those guys with
slings. You know, David and Goliath? Archers and sling-
ers. They had armies of them. Is that the word? In the
sixties a 'slinger' was a leaflet you handed out at a demon-
stration."

"You still didn't tell me where you're going to get a
llama."

"Oh, Wally knows a guy who's got a llama."

"He probably does. Here's lunch." She sets down a plate
bearing a hot dog.

"How did you know I liked hot dogs?"

"You're being polite."

"Perfect," he says, picking up the steamed bun. "This is
a *perfect* hot dog."

"If you like this junk, how come you're always talking
about French cuisine and Indonesian rice tables?"

"You started that. With that Julia Child talk."

"You ought to try my macaroni and cheese."

"I'm pretty fussy about that stuff. Out of the box?
Weirdly orange?"

"Of course."

"Now you're talking!"

"You want another one?" She holds a hot dog at groin
level and wags it.

"Shame on you. Am I that skinny? The poor thing looks
worn out."

"Are you?" she asks.

"A little. Maybe we're overdoing it."

She nods and looks down at the hot dog. "Do you say
penis?"

"I guess I say *cock.*"

"It sounds dirty."

"You get used to names if you use them often enough. *Dick, peter, dong, dink, weener, woobazz, prick, schlong—*"

"Woobazz?"

"I made that one up to fool you."

"Men have more names for themselves. *Cunt* sounds dirty. I wish it didn't."

"*Pussy* is nice. I like pussy."

Now the kitchen phone rings.

Garth leaps up, cups his hand to his mouth. "Call-for-Philip-Moe-Raze!"

"Hush," she scolds, and picks up the phone. "Hello?"

The line is silent. Lindsay frowns at the receiver.

"Wrong number, huh?" he asks.

"I guess so. It happens every month or so. Like someone checking in."

Garth steps over and gives her a nudge. "Hey. Let's go upstairs."

"Again?" She looks startled at the idea.

"Sure. I'll hum you my version of 'Donkey Serenade.'"

Sometimes when they make love, Lindsay herself hums, having felt a melody so fluid that it mounts and sluices out from the lake of herself. She exults in the gush and spill of it, until her coming is itself her yielding up, her welling out, her nameless surging song.

Garth reaches for a tissue beside the bed. He exhales a long sigh. "We should have a cigarette now," he says.

"There are some of Richard's downstairs if you really want one." She tucks her ear into the hollow of his armpit and lets one arm fall across his chest.

"You don't talk much about Richard."

"What's there to say?"

"Well, he is your husband."

"So that's what he's called."

Garth puts an arm behind his head. "What side of the bed is his?"

"This side."

"I think I know what's-her-name. His girlfriend."

"Gina."

"She's dark, about your size? A pretty woman, actually. She lives downtown in Harold's building."

"Harold?"

"He runs the pool hall downstairs from Wally's place. He owns an apartment building around the corner."

"What's it like, living downtown?"

"Don't you want to hear about Gina?"

She shakes her head, squinting her eyes at the hairs sprouting around his flat, male nipples.

"Oh, it's a neighborhood. Quiet at night, except for the pizza place down by the old railroad station. Teenagers, you know."

"I saw a lot of drunks down there. Weird types."

"Aw, you mean Bennie? Or maybe Ralph—he's pretty strange. Walks around swinging his arms? Guadalcanal did that to him. And there's Beatrice, wears a scarf and talks to herself. Everybody keeps an eye on them. It's not a bad setup. Unless the State Hospital discharges more and they all turn up here. Actually the Mission is in trouble, too. Reagan cut a government grant. I hear some church groups are getting together to bail it out. You know who's getting the money together? Your friend Ekdahl. They call him the Shepherd of the Streets."

"So that's what happened to him." Lindsay sits up and looks around for her underpants. "You know so much about the people where you live."

Garth shrugs. "It's a neighborhood. Nothing special."

"I don't even know the names of the people across the street."

Just now the phone beside the bed rings. Lindsay answers it but there's only silence at the other end. She sets down the receiver with a determined look. "You know what's for lunch tomorrow? My deluxe chicken nuggets."

When Garth makes love to Lindsay he often finds himself in another place, a landscape painter astonished by vistas. Sometimes he's in flight over lush valleys where palms line the canals and in the distance gray cliffs rise up to plateaus and the foothills of mountains. Entering her body, he plunges over the edge of green chasms where the sun filters through overhead mist and far-off streams cascade in glistening threads of silver. He clings to smooth rock and gazes across depths to lonely monasteries built atop pinnacles. He winds through the empty streets of whitewashed villages and mounts the terraced slopes where the wind moves in waves through barley and golden wheat. He wades through the grassy maze of salt marshes and skims over islands as the fog comes in.

"What do you think about?" asks Lindsay, propping a pillow behind her head. "I mean, when we do it."

"It's hard to put in words," says Garth. "I used to tramp around with an easel and watercolors painting landscapes. It's like that."

"Tramping around?"

"No, I mean mountains and trees. Sometimes water. It's hard to explain."

"I thought men went over baseball scores."

"Maybe some do. I wouldn't want to miss what's happening."

"But trees? Mountains? That's what's happening?"

He looks at her and says, "Well, jeez. It's all you. The depths, the lushness, the vast distances. It's *you.*"

With two weeks left in Alex's school year, Garth makes three discoveries. First, Alex resists thinking in arbitrary symbols. He wants the number seven, for example, to look bigger than six. Or thinks the word "long" ought to be a long word, stretching out across the page.

"They're just arbitrary marks," Garth tries to explain.

"Arbitrary?"

"That means somebody just made them up. Any old way."

"Who?"

"I don't know who. Some caveman maybe."

Alex thinks this over. "But some things look like what they mean. Like clocks. Time goes and the hands move the right distance."

"Sure. Analogue clocks, you mean. And graphs. Remember we drew some graphs? And maps, and—" Garth pauses. "You don't like—*digital* things. Especially number work. That's it!" He stands up and thrusts his fists to the ceiling.

"Digital," repeats Alex. "Like those dumb little clocks."

Garth's second discovery comes when they're leafing through an old *National Geographic*. Alex's hand shoots out as Garth turns a page. The boy smoothes out the photo of a stone Buddha.

"What is this?" Alex whispers.

"That's Buddha. You've never seen a Buddha?"

There's a silence as the boy's eyes rivet themselves to the figure. "What does Buddha do?" he finally asks.

Garth laughs. "Wally says that the Buddha sits quietly and does nothing."

Alex isn't amused. His small chest heaves. "I do that."

"Sit like that? You meditate? Who taught you?"

"Nobody. I figured it out."

"*Uff da,*" sighs Garth. "You've discovered meditation all by yourself? Next time you see Wally, ask him about this stuff." Garth laughs to himself. "You and Wally. Gosh, what a pair."

Garth pads back from Lindsay's bathroom. She sits on the edge of the bed, watching his penis dangle. She's pulled her bra around to the front to unhook it.

"So he doesn't like digital stuff," she's saying. "And all that sitting still that he does in some kind of meditation? What's the third thing? You said you discovered three things."

Garth lies down on the bed. "Alex has seen us," he says.

Lindsay gives him a puzzled look.

"It must have been last week. He said the bus brought him home early. Maybe the day it rained. There was a power failure at school. So he came upstairs and saw us. You know, in the act?"

"*Fucking?*" Her hands go to her cheeks. "Oh, God!"

"He said you were sitting on my lap—facing me—and *wiggling around.*"

"Oh, God," she repeats, horrified.

"So he went back outside. Over to some friend's house. Then he came back later, as if he'd just gotten off the bus. Get it? He didn't want to disturb us. Wasn't that thoughtful of him?"

"But—what should we do?"

"Don't worry about it. See, he thinks we were doing some kind of meditation. So he—get this." Garth shakes his head. "He gives me some *advice.*"

Lindsay struggles to look worried in the face of something amusing.

"Yeah. About—" Garth restrains a burst of laughter.

"Advice about what?" she giggles.

"About—how to *do it right!*" he explodes, then collapses, helpless.

"Do it right?" she shrieks and plunges to the pillow. She catches her breath. "Well," she cries, "what are we doing *wrong?*"

This crack sets off another gale of hilarity. Garth wipes tears from his eyes. "He told me you shouldn't—oh! This is the funniest part! He said, '*Don't wiggle*'!"

Lindsay hoots and rolls on her back. "Don't wiggle!" she cries.

Finally this storm of amusement passes. They lie side by side taking deep breaths. Garth is the first to say it. "Maybe he's right."

"Oh, don't start again," she giggles.

"I'm serious."

She sits up and looks at him. "You mean—" she starts to say, but something makes her hush. Over her flesh a sudden chill courses, like water streaming cold and fast. Their eyes are doing it again, entwining and locking. Garth sits up and discovers that his penis is engorged, enormous, and throbbing. A rush like a whirlwind roars at Lindsay's temples. She can't talk now. There's something they must do. They stare deep, wondering who has opened this door, this mystery, this windy rushing secret.

23

TOWARD THE middle of June, Richard begins to wonder whether or not his wife and his son's tutor are extending the limits of propriety beyond the boundaries of ordinary civil interchange. But the sentiments with which he has imbued Mr. Garth Erikson and Mrs. Lindsay Smith are so lofty and ennobling (entrusting to one the education of his heir, to the other the stewardship of his household) that their impertinences must advance far into nastiness and insolence before certain irregularities urge him to recognize the decomposition into which his domestic economy has fallen. Take, for example, his grocery bill. Lindsay is spending a fortune on chicken breasts, hamburgers, and hot dogs.

But having, during business hours, neither the leisure nor the inclination to pursue these suspicions, and furthermore having set aside his luncheon hour for the salutary pleasures to which a man of his stamp and sensual appetite feels entitled, he has engaged—by way of circuitous inquiry—another individual whose constitution and candid mind are better prepared than his own to confront the truth.

Richard has hired a private detective. Stanley Mankiewicz turned out to be a heavy-set man with hair slicked back, torpedo-fashion, like Spiro Agnew. He insisted they meet in the coffee shop at the Holiday Inn.

"So we got here a matrimonial incompatibility?"

"That's one way to put it," said Richard.

Mankiewicz settled back in the booth and darted an eye at the one customer seated at the counter. "Any kids involved?" he asked.

"I have a son."

"Okay." The heavy man took out a notepad and jotted something down. "So this is a child custody situation. You got a divorce lawyer yet?"

"Not yet," said Richard. He hadn't thought that far ahead. He merely wanted to know what Lindsay and Garth were up to. And he felt defensive about his curiosity, which seemed prurient, one step up from window-peeping. But now the seriousness of the situation struck him. Divorce was a possibility. And Alex. He couldn't give up his son. Especially if they determined that Lindsay was an unfit mother. Accordingly, he counted himself lucky to have engaged an experienced professional. This man was putting him in touch with motives that mattered. What father wouldn't do this for his son?

"Okay. So your wife is fooling around. Standard procedure in a case like this—I tail her, see? To where they're meeting. I know people who run the local hot-pillow motels. We enter the room, take a couple of flash pictures. That's it."

Richard rubbed his brow. This strategy suggested that the procedures of private investigators must not have changed much since the 1930s. Luckily, things were not so desperate as to require flash photos of the act itself. "Oh, they're meeting at my house," Richard explained.

"Oh, yeah? So you give me a key."

Richard sat up straight. "My house? I couldn't let you do that," he said. "What if nothing is going on?"

"Oh. I get it. We're at an earlier stage in the investigation. Lemme think." Mankiewicz took a sip of coffee. "Okay," he said. "We bug the place. And I'll put a tap on the phone."

"Is that legal?"

The heavy man lifted himself in his seat, checking to see that the next booth was still empty. "Listen," he said. The booth cushion wheezed as he lowered his weight upon it. "Between you and me—I just got some new equipment. I got the Dyna-Mike IC-18 and a couple X-3s. I got Super-Ear, model SB-5. In my van I got tape recorders. The whole schmeer. What do you say?"

"It sounds expensive."

Mankiewicz shrugged. "I get twenty an hour."

Richard gnawed on a knuckle. "Well, maybe a day or two. How would you install this equipment?"

"Easy. You get the family out of the house Saturday or Sunday. Fifteen, twenty minutes is all I need."

"I can't wait that long. My son's last day of school is this week. Could we do this right away? How about tonight?"

The man stared into his coffee cup. "Sure, if you clear the place out for an hour or two." He looked up slowly. "I get a hundred bucks up front."

Richard sighed and thought of his responsibility as a father. "Okay," he nodded, taking out his checkbook. "I'll take them out to dinner. Say, between six-thirty and eight?"

"They got a special here tonight." Mankiewicz nodded toward the dining room. "Two-fers, Surf 'n' Turf, and unlimited salad bar: nine ninety-five. Not bad, huh?"

By the weekend, Richard claims that he's taking Alex on a camping trip to New Hampshire. Saturday morning, the back of the station wagon is loaded with sleeping bags and fishing rods. With Alex in the front seat beside him, Richard cruises up Commercial Drive, looking for the address of Mankiewicz's office. There must be some mistake, he thinks, pulling in at a Sunoco station. The attendant jabs a thumb next door at a mobile home set on concrete blocks. Two signs hang in front of the structure, which is bright turquoise with lavender trim. One sign reads HILDA'S COIFFURES, the other STAN'S USED CARS. Richard parks the car, tells Alex to wait, and gets out.

Inside, a woman chewing gum and dangling a cigarette from her mouth looks at the business card Richard shows her. "Back there," she says, indicating a desk beyond a line of women sitting under hair dryers. Sure enough, there's Stan Mankiewicz, talking on the phone.

Richard makes his way past the whirring machines to the man's desk.

"You got a title?" the heavy man is yelling into the phone above the noise. "I can't buy it unless you got a title. Okay! So can you drive it or you want it towed over here? I see. Okay! Bye." He slams down the phone and looks at Richard. "Come on in back!" he shouts, getting up. "It's more quiet!"

"Now listen here, Mankiewicz—" begins Richard. He wants to question this fellow's credentials. This place can't possibly be his business office.

"Call me Stan!" shouts the big man and disappears behind what looks like a used shower curtain.

Behind the curtain is a flimsy door and beyond that a dark tangle of mops, rusty fenders, and three greasy engine blocks. Richard stumbles into an open area surrounded by stacked cardboard boxes. Stan has set up a temporary desk under a bare light bulb by balancing a piece of plywood on top of a carton that says "Modart Shampoo." He pulls up two folding chairs and they both sit down.

"Here's our data," says Stan, displaying a shoebox full of cassettes. Then he pulls out a tape recorder. Richard sees that it's the same plastic model he bought Alex for Christmas. Stan snaps in a cassette and punches the play button. Orchestra music blares from the tinny speaker, so he ejects the cassette and fishes in the shoebox for another. "Either we got some interference on the channel," explains Stan, "or these two lovebirds listen to a lot of classical music."

Next he holds up a cassette on whose label he's drawn a crude capital *T*. "This is my own code here. Telephone Tap." He looks at Richard to see if he's following this technical lingo, then flings the cassette back in the box. "Not much on that one. Do you know someone called 'Uncle Alfred'? He called to say he's arriving any day now."

"That's what he always says," sighs Richard.

"The other calls were wrong numbers. She says hello and the line goes dead. Once a guy says, 'Lindsay?' And she says, 'Yes?' And then he hangs up."

Richard frowns. "Maybe we better play it."

"Naw. You don't want to hear that. Here's the good one," he says, loading the machine and adjusting the volume.

Richard hears Lindsay's voice. "Tinfoil," she says. "I haven't heard that expression for years."

"I think Alcoa mounted a campaign against it," replies Garth's voice. Now the sound of a harpsichord fades in and blots out the next words. Abruptly the music dies away. "His Master's Voice?" Lindsay is saying. "Yeah," says Garth. "The guy claimed it was Caruso's dog." Then the harpsichord fades in again.

"What's going on?" asks Richard.

"I figure they're sitting in the living room. I got one device in there, another under the kitchen table, one under the bed, and another in the bathroom." Stan winks and adds, "It's in the toilet tank," as if to demonstrate that he's covered possibilities for infidelity that Richard might have overlooked.

"So you've got different tapes for each room?"

"No. They all transmit on the same frequency. The microphones are voice actuated. See, that way, they go upstairs, maybe into the kitchen—another unit takes over and puts it all on the same tape."

"I see," nods Richard. "But they're just talking. Look, I'm in a hurry."

"You want to hear the good stuff?" Stan consults his notepad and punches fast forward. "Get an earful of this," he says, hitting play.

"Oh!" says Lindsay. "I don't dare!"

"I'll help you. Put this in your hand. Now I'll guide your fingers."

"It makes me nervous. You want me to cut it off?"

"It's okay. Wait. The mattress is sagging."

288

Stan turns up the volume on the tape recorder.

"Isn't this illegal?" asks Lindsay.

"Of course not. Okay, now squeeze. I'll hold it."

"I've never done this before," she says.

"Ouch! Watch it."

"We did it!" she squeals.

Richard sighs, having understood what he's listening to. They're just playing around. Garth evidently has a pair of scissors, and he has just encouraged Lindsay to cut the tag off the mattress. Richard watches the detective he's hired fiddle nervously with the tone control of a toy tape recorder. Shaking his head in dismay, Richard checks his watch. Alex is waiting in the car.

"This is where it gets really weird," confides Stan.

"Ahh!" sighs Garth. "And that's just the beginning. Look here."

"Oh, no! Not the pillows?"

"Yes. The pillows!"

"Ohhh!" She lets out a long cry of apparent agony.

The blood is draining from poor Stan's face.

"You want to rest a minute?" asks Garth.

"No. This is fun. I want to do it by myself this time!"

"By yourself?"

"Sure. You can watch—"

Stan punches the stop button. "You heard enough?" His hands are trembling.

"You idiot," says Richard. "Do you know what you're listening to?"

"Yeah, I got an imagination."

Richard looks into the shoebox. "Have you listened to all these?"

"I've sampled here and there, made some notes. Understand, I got thirteen hours of tape.

"Didn't you monitor them in your van? While they were recording?"

"You mean sit there all day? Look, I gotta eat lunch, go to the bathroom. What do you expect?"

"What's on these other tapes?"

"Music—mostly."

"Music?"

Stan for the first time looks a bit sheepish. "Now and then you can catch a word or two. Like I said, there's some interference in the channel. See, right about that frequency, there's an FM station up in Concord."

"What do you mean, that frequency?"

"Well, the microphones broadcast over the FM radio. That's how I pick it up around the corner in my van."

Richard now raises his voice. "You mean, anybody could have picked up these conversations on the radio?"

"Not anybody. You gotta have the right frequency."

"But the whole neighborhood might have heard!"

"Aw, don't get all excited. It's over now. Look, I can tell you're not satisfied. Tell you what. You take the tapes and listen for yourself. I'll give you a discount on my fee."

Richard makes a disgusted face and gets to his feet.

"Just tell me one thing," says Stan. "You seemed to figure it out right away. Just what the hell were those two doing in the bedroom?"

Richard is torn between giving this sap a consoling pat on the arm and hitting him on the head with a carton of Modart shampoo. "They were cutting the tag off the mattress," he explains.

Stan gives him a blank look. "You're kidding. The tag that says 'Do not remove under penalty of law'?"

"Right."

"Gee," says Stan. "Isn't that illegal?"

Richard seizes the shoebox of cassettes and storms out, past the humming hair dryers and out to the car. He stands there for a moment in bright afternoon sunlight. He's told Lindsay they'll be back tomorrow night.

"Let's go, Dad," says Alex. "I'm tired of waiting."

Richard slides the shoebox under the front seat and gets in behind the wheel. Has Erikson already arrived to spend the weekend with Lindsay? He starts the car and waits for an opening in the traffic.

"You know what?" says Alex. "I left my compass at home."

Richard grips the wheel. Here's his chance to check up on things himself. "You want to swing back past the house? I could run in the house and get it."

"No, I'll go in," says Alex. "I know where I keep it."

Richard sighs, understanding the bind he's put himself in. They can't go back. Alex must be protected from barging in on a scene. "Sorry," he tells his son. "This will be a lesson for you. Next time you'll remember not to forget."

That night in the tent, the two of them lie in their sleeping bags, breathing air thick with insect repellent. The black flies have been vicious, especially along the shore, where they cast their lines and reeled in perch and brown trout too small, really, to keep. While canned beef stew was warming on the Coleman stove, Richard sat at the picnic table, scaling and gutting the little things. They'll fry them for breakfast.

Once Alex stops turning on his air mattress—his breath falling into the shallow and irregular whisper that frightened them so when he was an infant—Richard gets up and goes out to the car. By flashlight he arranges the tapes on the front seat and connects the ear plug to the recorder. He's brought a pint of Old Crow along and sips at it in the dark, punching fast forward, as the works of Debussy and Bartók, Haydn and Mahler, race by in fragments. During the last tape, he dozes off. A raucous blaring of brass and percussion jolts his eyes open. The voice of Robert J. Lurtsema tells him he's just been to "Putnam's Camp." Richard crawls back into the tent. Odd night sounds keep him awake. He wonders if Lindsay is alone in their bed. Or perhaps, at this instant, Erikson is tempting her to snip at the edges of this ragtag arrangement that Richard—in spite of all the deceit, the double-talk, and the silences—still insists on calling a marriage.

After breakfast in the morning, they take a hike. In the afternoon, the fish aren't biting. The line in Alex's reel snarls into one tangled backlash after another. Swatting at the flies, they decide they've had enough of the woods. Once the tent is folded and the gear packed back in the station wagon, Richard walks off by himself to smoke a cigarette and look at the lake. There's nothing sordid on the tapes. What he's heard of Lindsay's voice betrays merely a drift into youthful silliness. He tries to recall how long it's been since he's heard her burst into genuine laughter.

A sour knot turns over in his stomach and he feels a tight constriction in his throat. He tries to swallow it back, but the effort makes his eyes water. Richard's turn has come to let out a gasping sob. Tears mingled with insect repellent burn his eyes. The lake's far shore blurs into a smear of remorse. What a fool he's been. He assures himself that Lindsay, alone in the house with a bearded stranger, must have simply rediscovered her capacity for innocent fun. Is it too late to join her? he wonders, flicking his cigarette into the lake. He takes in a lungful of clean air and strides back to where Alex waits in the car. Overhead, the sun looks dazzling. The trees look green and brilliant and alive. In his pocket, his pint of bourbon sloshes nearly full. He'll save it for a jubilant toast to the Heathersford city limits. Home! he thinks. A fresh start, gaiety and renewal—they're only two hours away!

24

I'T'S SUNDAY afternoon, June 21. And they're in bed—have been since 9 A.M. The floor is littered with coffee cups, the Sunday *Times*, and saucers bearing the rinds of navel oranges. When Richard had gone off camping yesterday, Garth stayed away. He'd paced the floor, listening for knocks, waiting for signs. He'd have gone for a drive, but the car's battery was dead. His official duties as tutor had ended on Wednesday, Alex's last day of school before summer vacation.

On the phone, Garth and Lindsay tried to think of some other pretext for spending the summer together. "Maybe you need a handyman?" he'd suggested.

"A handy man?" she said. "How vain of you. Houseboy, maybe."

There came an odd silence, then a burst of laughter. "How can we joke at a time like this?" he asked. They didn't know the name of their situation. Lindsay claimed they could be together at a distance. Cheerfully they agreed that Richard's weekend camping trip would be a good test. No phone calls even. What an adventure, to turn being apart into a luxurious vastness.

This morning Garth decided he couldn't stand such rich intensities. He put on his necktie, made a cardboard sign that said "Going to Church," and hitchhiked out to Lindsay's house. At the front door, she looked haggard, equally done in by the thrill of distance. Her welcoming hug felt tight, almost desperate. Neither had slept. They went straight upstairs to bed.

Now they lounge, loins still locked, under the sheets. At the window, a mild breeze lifts the curtains. But they're both a little depressed, becalmed in the deadness of a Sunday afternoon in June.

"Are you thinking about those phone calls?" he asks.

"A little."

"Scare you? The last one where he said your name?"

"Sort of." Lindsay opens her eyes and looks at the ceiling. "Actually I was thinking about my father. They never found his body. Did I tell you that?"

"Don't think about it," he says.

"Maybe he's still alive."

"Don't even think about it."

"It's possible. He'd call. Just to check up on me. Don't you think?"

"No."

There's a silence. Finally she says, "You never told me about your brother."

"I didn't feel like it."

"You told me about your parents."

"That's different."

"And your brother?"

Garth's hand stirs on her round belly, then stays still. "My brother was autistic. He died in a fire. Ever since he was an infant, he'd been in this place. It was near Fort Snelling. God, he'd be thirty-seven years old now."

"You knew him?"

"I visited. Especially after my folks were killed. But eventually it seemed useless. He wouldn't look at you. And he didn't talk. He'd croak once in a while. You'd go to see him and he'd be looking out the window. Up at the trees and the sky. He didn't know anyone was in the room."

"Maybe he could tell."

"No, I don't think so. Once this specialist called me in

for a conference. I was in art school. This guy sits me down and says he's made some kind of breakthrough, he's figured out my brother's case. 'Your brother,' he says, 'thinks he's a refrigerator.' Then he stares at me, letting that sink in. So I nod and he goes on. 'A refrigerator—and the door is shut,' he says. So I nod and think that over. But I see where his analysis is headed. So I say, 'When the door is shut—the light goes out.' The guy looks dumbfounded because I took away his best line. But I don't shut up. 'At this point,' I say, 'there's no sense in prying open the door, is there? Because whatever was inside to begin with has turned to shit.' Then I stand up. 'Anyone could have figured that out, you asshole.' And I walked out."

Lindsay touches Garth's hand. "There was a fire?"

"Yeah. In 1968. I wonder if they hadn't written all the patients off by then. Some insurance angle, maybe. I don't know."

There's another long silence. Lindsay turns her head on the pillow. She can see the light from the window glistening in Garth's eyes. "Hey," she says. "Can you feel this?" One of her legs lies easily over his thigh.

"Oh, Jesus."

"Hold me tighter."

"Like this?"

She lets out a long breath. "When we die, then where shall we be?"

"Here," he says, as if he's thought it over.

"Here?"

"Uh-huh. Always."

Outside a sparrow chirps. Somewhere a church bell rings. A dog barks.

"Has someone come?" he asks.

She listens to a car door slam. "It's just the neighbors."

Garth presses the hollow of his eye to the curve of her shoulder. Their lazy moments together were never quite this solemn. "I wonder who we are?" he says.

"Us?"

"Everybody. The whole country. The world."

"Ah," she sighs dramatically. "We are the spawn of galaxies!"

"No, seriously."

Lindsay thinks for a moment. "We are the oppressed."

"You think so?"

"Uh-huh. But that's sad. Let's think of something funny."

"Okay. Wally told me—"

"I like Wally."

"—he said that when the railroads were first invented, people thought that over thirty-five miles an hour, the human body would explode."

She smiles. "That's pretty funny."

"Did I tell you about the time my mother hid my father's dentures?"

"What?" she giggles.

"So he couldn't leave the house," he laughs.

Lindsay chuckles.

"But listen—see, she was a Republican." This cracks Garth up. "And he was a Democrat!" He's getting out of control now.

"What so funny about that?" she squeals.

"HA!" he bursts out, squirming within her. "Oh!" he gasps. "She hid his dentures!" He can't get his breath. "—so he couldn't go register to *vote!*"

They both laugh, contorted, as if they're wracked by pain. Finally she wipes her eyes and says, "It's still stiff."

"Of course it is," he jokes. "What side do you think laughter is on?"

"Do you realize how many hours we've been doing this?"

"Well, it's Sunday, right? For us, this is church."

"Hey. Quiet a minute." She cocks an ear. "Did you hear a sound downstairs? I think there's someone here."

"Really?"

From the stairwell, a voice booms out, "LINDSAY! I LOVE YOU!"

"It's Richard!" she gasps. "What'll we do?"

"Pull up the sheet. I'll hide."

"That's ridiculous," she says.

Richard comes stomping up to sway in the bedroom doorway. "Oh!" he declares. "Here you are!"

"Have you been drinking? Where's Alex?"

"He's in the garage, unpacking the car." Richard's bleary eyes drift over to the shape hunched alongside Lindsay in bed. "What's that?" he asks.

"Were you driving like this?"

"Nope. I've been celebrating, sitting in my own driveway. I had to fortify myself. You see, I had entertained terrible suss"—he wets his lips—"suh-spi-shuns about you. But now I'm home." He makes a bow.

"Why don't you take a shower," she suggests.

"Excellent!" he says, then belches and swallows back something sour. "Oh hell, I'm really fucked up. Pardon me while I go puke." He lurches in the direction of the bathroom.

"See?" says Garth, peeking out from under the sheet.

"Shame on you," she says. "You could have at least slipped it out while he was talking."

"Are you mad?"

They hear the toilet flush.

"I'm scared to death," she says. "You know, he saw you right away."

"*Uff da.* I forgot about Alex. He must be downstairs." Garth slides off the bed and crawls around on the rug looking for his underwear. Near the doorway he runs into Richard's shoes, which—sure enough—are connected to his legs.

"Listen," says Richard, standing in the doorway. "We've got to talk."

Garth crouches, naked on the carpet, hoping he's invisible.

"What a fucking, shitty mess," declares Richard. "The adult thing to do is talk this out. Hey, where the hell do you think you're going?"

Garth is crawling into the closet, dragging his clothes

along the rug. He looks back at Richard. "Do you mind if I get dressed?"

"No, go ahead. Then we're going to talk."

In the bed, Lindsay has been hiding her face in her hands. She's not accustomed to this confusion of the serious with the ludicrous. Now she looks up. "Who's going to talk?" she asks.

"Him and me." Richard drags the back of his hand across his mouth. "We're going to finish this right. A little dignity!" he yells. "That's what we need around here!" Then he stands up straight, makes an about face, and goes downstairs.

Garth comes out of the closet, zipping up his jeans. "Is he okay?"

"He's upset."

"You know, he's right," says Garth. "About talking."

"What? Just the two of you? Man to man?"

"Don't be too hard on him. Come on. Get dressed and we'll go down."

When Alex comes in from the garage, he finds his father sitting on the living room couch. "The stuff's all back in the garage," he boasts.

"Come give me a hug," says Richard.

The boy's small arms wrap themselves around his father's big neck. "Are you sick?" asks Alex.

"Of course not."

"You, um—smell sick."

Lindsay and Garth come down the stairs, say hello to Alex, and shoo him into the den.

"Maybe you better go," Richard tells Garth. "Come back after dinner."

"He could stay for dinner," suggests Lindsay.

Richard glares at her. "Are you out of your mind?"

"I'll go," says Garth.

"What, walk?" says Lindsay. "Hitchhike?"

"I can call Wally for a ride."

"Let's not make this complicated," fumes Richard. "This is a simple, adult situation."

"My car is busted," says Garth.

"I don't want to hear about your car."

"I should fix dinner," says Lindsay. "What if he waits in the den?"

"Alex is in there."

"Fine. He can wait in the den with Alex."

Richard shakes his head. "That doesn't sound right to me."

"Of course it does. That's been their usual routine."

"Oh, sure!" Richard flings up his arms in exasperation. "Business as usual!"

"Take it easy," says Garth, looking into Richard's livid face. "I'm not leaving until you settle down." Then he walks out of the room. Behind him he hears Richard say, "But this is my house. Isn't this my house?"

Garth finds Alex sitting in the den. "How you doing?" he asks.

"I'm okay." Alex looks at his fingers.

Garth decides that it's not his job to explain what's happening in this house. The kid has probably figured it out anyway. "Well," he says, leafing through a stack of papers they keep on the end table. "Catch any fish?"

"Some little ones." He stretches out his feet and looks at his shoes. "I thought you weren't coming anymore. It's summer vacation."

"And it's Sunday, too. What'd we do last time?"

"We drew my heartbeat. Remember? You pulled the paper and I listened with that, um—stesscope. I drew the beats."

"Oh, yeah. We had to stop before getting to the best part. Want to finish it now? Let's count and measure the bumps in the line you drew!"

"Yeah, number work," sneers Alex. "Look what came in the mail." Alex pulls a children's magazine out from between the cushions of the couch.

"Didn't we read a story in there? Last month?"

"Look," says Alex, opening to a page he's marked. "There's more."

"Ah," says Garth. "Another installment. Do you know that word?"

Alex is flipping pages. From the kitchen comes the muffled blare of Richard's anger, then Lindsay's voice, sounding uncertain, perhaps contrite. Finally Alex points to the bottom of a page. Garth sees the words:

(to be continued)

He stares at the boy's hands. "So you think we should read this next installment?"

"I want to," says Alex.

"But you checked first, didn't you? To see that it would be continued. What if—instead—it said, 'The End'?"

Alex squirms on the couch. "I don't like things to end," he says.

Garth looks straight ahead at the wall. "I know what you mean," he says.

At dinnertime, Garth sits in the den by himself. From the kitchen comes the sound of silverware clinking on china. Lindsay finally appears.

"I used your phone," he says.

"Fine." She hands him a plate bearing two hamburgers and a mound of macaroni and cheese. "This was going to be lunch."

"The hamburgers look sort of squashed," remarks Garth.

"That's the way they're supposed to look," she says, and walks out. After eating, he slips out the front door and walks down the block, down leafy suburban streets lit by a bright evening sky.

When he comes back it's past nine and Lindsay has coaxed Alex into bed. The three of them take seats in the living room, Lindsay and her husband at opposite ends of the big couch. It's still light outside. Down the block, someone shuts off his lawn mower. Across the way, an old guy is taking down storm windows.

"So you two have had a chance to talk?" asks Garth. Lindsay won't look at him. He's never felt so uncertain about what the next moment will bring. He feels himself hung over a gorge, throwing lines out into the blackness, hoping one will catch and he can inch forward into the void.

"Yeah," says Richard, hunched, elbows on his knees. "My wife and I—" He closes his eyes to picture the way these words are supposed to come out. "We have decided that Alex is the first priority. He's the bottom line."

Garth looks at Lindsay, legs crossed at the ankle, lounging demurely within an enclosure she's thrown up around herself.

"Now, my son—" Richard says. "Thank God, we've got a handle on this."

These phrases leave Garth in the dark. Should everything have a handle?

Lindsay is only half-listening. She leans her chin on the heel of her hand. The plant drooping in the front window needs water, she thinks. In this light, its dark leaves weave themselves into the shaggy silhouette of the figure across from her in the wing-back chair, this man who's come into her life and touched her. How nice simply to sit in the same room together.

"—and I don't intend to tear apart my family," Richard is saying. "My house. The work I've put into this place." He looks about at the walls as if he's amazed they haven't collapsed upon him in a shower of dusty plaster.

Lindsay wonders what Richard is talking about. All these words clutching at "my house," "my wife," "my son"? She glances at Garth. He slumps, disheartened by the long speech. She lets out warm air from her lungs. Surely Garth feels the same thrumming in himself? This bond stretched over the gulf.

"Now, with labor unions," says Richard, "there's a cooling-off period. And especially with Lindsay here"—he throws a quick gesture at her—"you must know how sensitive she is. Impressionable. Why, the first guy to come along—she's likely to mistake a passing infatuation—mistake it for—oh, you know, a deeper, a more, ah—" Richard, at a loss for words, makes the gesture of drawing out an invisible mass from his chest. It could be pizza dough stuck to his belly.

Lindsay has closed her eyes and put her head back on the couch. Into the thick silence of the room she now says the words, "I love you."

Both men stare at her.

"You do?" says Garth, astonished to realize she means him. Neither he nor Lindsay has yet spoken the word *love* to each other. And here he thought this scene was going against him.

"Yeah, okay," scoffs Richard. "She told me the same thing in the kitchen. She claims that the two of you are in love. As far as that goes, I'm in love—whatever the word means. But that isn't the point, is it?"

Lindsay sits up. "Why isn't she here? She's a part of this, too."

"You mean Gina? Aw, come on," groans Richard.

"I'm serious."

"What, get her over here? Now?"

"Why not? Call her up. I dare you."

"We haven't got time for that. Isn't somebody picking up Erikson at ten?"

"You're a chicken," says Lindsay.

"Now don't start in on me, Linz." He actually makes a fist and shakes it at her. "Okay!" he declares, springing up. "I'm going to call her!" He glares at her, rigid, as if now the stakes have been raised and he expects her to back down. But she just stares back. So he heads for the den, fuming. They watch him veer out of sight and hear an angry kick aimed at a doorjamb.

Outside the sky darkens. Gray clouds, lowering from the west, creep over the roofs of ranch houses. The lavender and vermilion glow of color TVs flickers in windows across

the way. Lindsay sits silent in the dim light. Garth, too, is
motionless in his chair. Together they wait, scared, suspended—as night falls.

The doorbell rings. "Don't get up," says Garth, rising.
He angles a look out the front window. "It's probably
Wally."

There's a light switch in the front hall. Garth flicks it on
before opening the door. Outside stands a tall man with a
blond mustache. His long sandy hair is slicked back on both
sides from a hairline that recedes at the temples. A green
army jacket with buttoned pockets hangs from his broad
shoulders.

Garth cracks open the door. "Yes?"

"Is Lindsay home?" The voice comes up from a hollow
place.

"Is she expecting you?"

"Not exactly."

"What's your name?"

"Tell her it's Toby. Toby Morton."

Garth leaves the door ajar, but doesn't invite the man in.
In the living room, he finds Richard standing over Lindsay
with his hands on his hips saying, "—she's getting a ride
with someone." Impatiently, Richard flings up his arms in
the dim light. "Goddammit!" he shouts. "Doesn't anybody's car work around here?"

"Settle down," says Lindsay. "Turn on a lamp."

"Excuse me?" Garth cautiously interrupts.

His polite tone makes Richard cringe. A rasp snarls in his
throat, the frayed ends of his self-control. *"Ek-skewz me?
What is this crap!"* he yells, swatting at the shade of a floor
lamp. It tips from the blow. "I don't have to take this shit!"
He wheels back a fist like he's just begun to smash up the
place.

Garth lunges and catches the teetering floor lamp. Behind him he's aware of quick footsteps, a grunt, and Richard's incredulous cry of "What the fuck!" Someone tall has
entered the house. The figure grips Richard's wrist and
levers it downward with enormous strength. Garth clicks

on the lamp in his hands. The light bulbs glare in his eyes. The blond man is taking a step back toward the front door. Richard is grimacing in agony, rubbing his wrist. Lindsay sits rigid on the couch, staring at the stranger in the green army jacket. He looks like one of those drifters who run the rides at carnivals. The odor of wood smoke clings to his garments.

"Hey, do you know this guy?" Garth asks Lindsay. "Toby Morton. Did I get it right?" Garth looks back to see the tall stranger pointing a finger at Richard. Lindsay's husband looks suddenly small and badly frightened. He sinks down on the couch, breathing hard. Then the large man named Toby steps around the coffee table and squats down before Lindsay.

"Remember me?" he asks.

25

RIGID WITH FRIGHT, Lindsay stares at the acne scars on a terribly familiar face. The man's mustache is blond. Quickly she nods at his question, trying to be brave.

"How've you been?" he gently asks.

"Okay," she manages to say. But inwardly she's shrieking. *It's happening again.* In a minute, she thinks, two other men wearing ski masks will appear from the kitchen with guns. They will stare at her through those terrible round eyeholes. The pale-lashed eyes of this one are worse. They bore in, and they hurt.

"Did you guess it was me on the phone?"

Lindsay thinks now of all the times she's picked up the receiver only to hear the connection abruptly break off. "You called more than once?" she asks.

"Many times," says Toby. "For years."

"But why?"

"To hear you say 'hello.' "

"Oh?" Behind this squatting man, she's aware of Garth taking a single, slow-motion step. At some flicker in Lindsay's eyes, Toby swings about on one knee. His hands flash into stiff readiness—poised for a martial-arts attack.

Garth freezes in midstep. He's pointed toward the armchair, one tiptoeing foot poised on the rug. "Mind if I sit down?" he inquires.

"Go ahead," nods Toby, who now takes a cross-legged position on the floor to one side. From there he has a clear view of the three others, as if he intends to draw out a handgun and fire, in turn, into each of their faces. His posture is very erect, spine straight. His fingertips rest lightly on his thighs.

"So," drawls Garth in a familiar tone. "You two must be old friends?" The air in the room has grown thin with tension. Garth, desperately, is trying to inject a hint of normalcy. Richard sprawls limp on the couch. He looks terrified.

"Yes," says Toby, looking at Garth with new interest. "We go way back."

"There's nothing like seeing old friends," smiles Garth, slapping the arms of the chair. "Exactly—how far back?"

Toby looks to Lindsay for an answer.

"March 28, 1977," she recites. "It was a Monday."

Toby stares at her. "But—" For an instant his face loses its placid composure. "That afternoon," he says. "You were sitting here. On this couch. I thought—I was certain—that you recognized me."

"Recognized you? From where?" Lindsay's eyes go wide in bewilderment.

"Hey," he insists, and points to his chest. "I'm *Toby*." The name comes out oddly pronounced, like a childhood chant. He repeats it, earnestly. "*Toe-bee!*"

"Why, I know that name," she whispers. Her memory drags deep, snagging at the debris of the past. For a instant it catches something, but then the image of men wearing ski masks reappears. She's a hostage, but Richard doesn't work in a bank. She shakes away the memory and opens her eyes.

Toby is taking a deep breath. Now he actually smiles. "All this time," he says, "you didn't even remember."

"But those men," she says. "The masks. The guns."

"Guns?" asks Garth weakly, staring at Toby's bulging pockets.

Toby touches the back of his hand to his mustache. "I arranged it," he says. "Those other two? I met them in a bar. For a week, I had to put up with them, pretending to rehearse a job. Don't you see? Once I found you, I had to make an appearance. I couldn't just knock on the front door. Do you understand?

Lindsay shudders, and gives a quick nod. But she doesn't understand. What she realizes is that they're in the presence of a person who is not normal. Some chance encounter —maybe college, high school?—has driven this man to search her out and go to ludicrous extremes just to—what? Look in her face? Hear her voice on the phone? She wonders what comes next. She thinks of Alex, upstairs asleep.

Toby stands up.

"Time to hit the road?" asks Garth, looking at the back of his wrist. He doesn't wear a watch. So he peeks up his sleeve and, finding nothing, shrugs.

"Yes," says Richard, who has found his voice. "It's getting late."

Toby ignores the two men. He reaches directly for the drawer in the coffee table where Lindsay keeps her old photo album. Garth and Richard exchange a glance. Toby sets the big volume carefully on the coffee table. All his moves have the precision of ritual gestures. He sits and sorts through loose snapshots. Finally, he hands one to Lindsay.

Her thoughts are whirling from the album to the drawer. Through rooms and down hallways they fly, mounting the stairs, gliding through solid walls, and slipping though the brittle transparency of window glass. This stranger seems to know this house as if it's his own. She finds herself staring at a snapshot that trembles in her fingers. It's that picture of herself: a girl of maybe nine or ten standing barefoot in a stream bed.

"That's the one I sent you," explains Toby. "I've had it a long time."

Lindsay now recalls receiving an odd envelope about the time of her birthday in March. She thought her mother had sent it.

Toby is handing her another snapshot. "Look," he says.

It's the photo of Lindsay from the same summer. She's kneeling on a dock in front of her grinning father. Next to her is a sandy-haired kid in a dirty T-shirt. Behind them, a lake stretches out in a glittering network of sunny ripples. She looks again at the boy in the T-shirt. *"Toe-bee,"* she whispers.

Toby watches her reaction in fascination. He must have imagined this moment for years, playing it over in his mind, arranging the furniture, sorting the snapshots. "Now you remember," he says confidently. "See? There's the boat," he points. "The stream was down this way. Your family's cabin was up the shore, here. Ours was the next one. Remember?"

Lindsay looks at this sandy-haired man, close to forty now. "Oh, Toby. Of course I remember," she fibs. Tears well up in her eyes at the pity of it. And then a genuine memory does come back: the slap of water against a dock, a fishy smell in the air at twilight, and a woman's voice calling in her son: *Toe-bee, Toe-bee.* "How could I ever forget," she says.

"Boy," says Garth, rubbing his hands. "I really like old photo albums."

The front-hall chimes ring.

"That's the doorbell," explains Richard, rising slowly, uncertain whether he's permitted to get up. He goes out and they hear the front door open. Then, holding a Burberry trenchcoat, Gina appears, dressed in pleated slacks and a smart long-sleeved Oleg Cassini shirt. Her taste in clothes seems to have improved since the last time Lindsay met her. Probably Richard's influence.

"Hello," says Lindsay. "Won't you please come in and sit down?" She surprises herself with this cordiality. "You know Garth Erikson, I think? And this is Toby Morton. An old friend."

Toby nods from his cross-legged posture on the rug. Garth waves a neighborly hello to Gina. The room feels less ominous than it did a few minutes earlier.

"Come sit next to me." Lindsay pats the middle cushion of the couch.

Richard watches his mistress sit down next to his wife.

He wears the expression of a tourist gazing at some exotic monument that he thought he'd never travel far enough to see. Understanding that Toby has turned out to be merely a childhood friend of Lindsay's, Richard decides that it's time to return to the evening's script. "Say, Morton," he says, clasping hands behind his back. "Actually, we have a meeting scheduled here. I'm thinking that if you want to drop over for dinner tomorrow night, then you and Lindsay—"

"It's the ghost!"

Everyone looks at Alex, who is peering around a corner into the room. The boy walks straight at Toby, his mouth agape at the stranger's Buddha-like posture.

"Hi there, little cricket," says Toby.

The boy makes a circle about the seated stranger. Then he stands there, tugging at his pajamas. "What do you do with your hands?" Alex finally asks. "I mean—when you sit?"

"You make a mudra."

"Show me."

"Oh, there are different ways. Here's one." Toby holds up his left index finger and grasps it with his right hand. "This is the Fist of Knowledge," he says. "The five wisdoms embrace the wind of life. Do this, and you destroy ignorance."

"Oh," nods the boy. At his sides, his fingers curl, restless to try Toby's advice. "I found your glove," he says.

"So, you're the rascal," smiles Toby.

"What glove?" says Richard sternly. "Alex, I thought we were done with that talk about ghosts."

"Hush," says Lindsay.

"It's time to go back to bed, Alex," orders Richard. "A glove—" He chuckles to those seated in the room. "A few months ago," he explains, "we actually called the police because of this story Alex made up about a ghost who left behind a—" He stops and his face sags. It's taken Richard this long to figure out that Toby is the one who broke into their house, went through his wife's closets, and rummaged through drawers. A moment ago, someone spoke of guns. His wrist still throbs with pain from Toby's grip. Richard feels his legs going limp as he realizes he's just invited a maniac, a burglar—an armed robber—to dinner.

Alex is saying good-night to the guests. Obediently, he heads back to bed. But just now the doorbell rings. Alex scoots past Richard's legs, yelling, "I'll get it!" When he reappears, there's a dog sniffing the seat of his pajamas. "It's Wally and Helen," announces Alex.

Garth gets up from his chair and goes into the front hallway. "Can you wait a minute?" he tells Wally. "There's a very weird situation inside. We may need the police."

Wally has one foot through the door. "Okay, but Uncle Fred here—" Wally squints through his thick glasses, looking for the old dog. "Where did she go? Listen, can you get us a dish of water for the dog?"

Now Lindsay dashes into the hallway. "Come on in!" she says gaily, but her face is ashen, tense with worry. "Gee, it's nice to see you two again!"

"The pleasure," beams Helen, "is all—oh, what do you call it? *Us's!*" To Garth she confides, "You know who's out there waiting in his car? Harold."

"Well, get him in here!" says Garth. "The more people, the better."

"Yoo-hoo! Harold!" waves Helen from the doorway.

In the living room, Lindsay is making introductions. Richard shakes hands with Wally and says, "Nice to meet you. But actually—" Richard puts on a solemn face. "Actually, we have a meeting going on here. Now, just as soon as Toby leaves, we're going to have a very important talk." As he says this, Richard's head nods like one of those dog figurines people set in the back windows of sedans. "A talk is going to take place here," he nods. "An adult talk."

"Hey, everybody!" yells Garth from the doorway. "This is Harold!" Beside him, a beefy man holds up the can of beer that he's brought in with him.

Gina waves to her landlord. "I'll have a beer," she says. "Do you have any pretzels?" Harold asks Lindsay.

"Look in the kitchen," she says. "Oh, Helen. Will you do me a favor? There's a tray of hors d'oeuvres in the freezer covered with aluminum foil. Would you put it in the oven for me? Oh, about three twenty-five, I think."

"Wait a minute," says Richard, feeling the mood of things slipping out of his control. "This isn't a party. This is a talk. An adult talk."

Lindsay waves this aside. "Get some ice," she tells him. "And set out some glasses in the dining room."

Richard stands there and watches his wife sit down next to Garth on the couch. They're leafing through the photo album. He can't believe it. Wasn't it just this afternoon he caught them in bed together? This house ought to be quiet. For a while there, things were going just the way he'd pictured them in advance. His speech, for example. That went okay. After the formality of hearing all sides, he'd planned to allow his wife and Garth a few last minutes together—probably in the front hallway—to say their good-byes.

Bitterly Richard watches Toby join the two others on the couch. The three of them slide down to make room for Alex. Richard heads for the kitchen. He knows how to get rid of these people. He'll tell them he's sick. A sick person needs rest and quiet. Passing the den, he observes Wally tuning in the TV. A hand touches his arm. It's Gina. She tugs him into the dining room.

"This is really nice," she says putting her arms around him. "When you called, I thought maybe something heavy was coming down. But this is a party! Why don't you show me around? You know, like upstairs, the *bed*-room?"

Richard stares over her shoulder and sees their reflection in a dark window pane. "I hadn't planned on that," he says.

"Oh," she says. "I just called a guy I know at the liquor store. He's bringing over a couple cases of beer. Okay?"

The doorbell rings again. Richard winces at the sound and frees himself from Gina's arms. "It's the door," he explains, trudging off the way he just came. On the front steps is Stan Mankiewicz, the detective.

"What do *you* want?" demands Richard.

"What's this? Celebrating your divorce already? Look, I left some equipment here. My listening devices."

"Come back tomorrow." Richard closes the door but Stan shoves it in.

"All these people?—nobody will notice. I'll pick up the stuff and be gone."

"Tomorrow!" says Richard.

"Better do it now. You're still on the air."

"Broadcasting?"

Stan shrugs. "I picked up some talk, driving by in the van. Something about 'tearing your family apart'?"

Richard spots a figure pacing down the middle of the street. It's the accountant who lives up the block. He's carrying a portable FM radio and pauses now, steering the antenna toward Richard's house.

"Quick! Get in here and find those microphones!"

Stan assumes a crouched posture and edges in the door. Richard watches him prowl into the living room. Someone yells from the kitchen that the oven isn't working. Richard goes in and peers under the stove. The pilot light is on, but the oven won't heat up. He dusts off his hands and confesses that he can't fix it. Heading back to the living room, he finds himself following a dog. Near the den, he watches it bang into a wall. The dog backs off, makes a turn, and crashes into a table leg. I should have a dog, thinks Richard, reaching down and scratching the creature's head. "Good boy," he says. "You stick with me."

26

A BARE LIGHT bulb hangs from the ceiling of Lindsay's laundry room. In order to talk, away from the others, she has led Toby back to this harshly bright room where Garth is drawing out odd fragments of his story. "Now, let me get this straight," says Garth, leaning against the dryer. "You started with her old family name—you'd saved a business card or something that her father gave you at the lake. Is that right?"

Toby nods, betraying nothing with his blank composure.

"Okay," says Garth. "So you go to her father's insurance company in Pittsburgh. But this is, what—the late sixties?"

"It was the fall of 1971," says Toby. "I'd been—out of the country."

Garth understands this to mean that Toby was in Vietnam. The big blond man is touchy about certain subjects, and nervous in the presence of too many people. Garth is learning where he shouldn't pry too hard. "Right. So, of course, you find that her father has been dead for years. And Lindsay—"

"I was in graduate school in Illinois," Lindsay remarks. "Mom had sold the house in Pittsburgh and moved to North Carolina." She lays a hand on her washing machine. The surface is slick and sticky with a film of prewash spray.

"Yeah," says Toby, who appears to be loosening up. "In Pittsburgh, who remembers her father? They aren't very helpful at his old insurance office. A guy passing through the reception room thinks that John Wyatt died back in the

313

fifties. There's a young secretary. Those records were thrown out, she says. I tell her there must be somebody who worked here then. She points to a portrait on the wall. The founder's still around, she says. But he's half-dead, she says."

"So you've already called all the Wyatts listed in the phone book?" Garth finds himself fascinated by Toby's project. He's met plenty of men who talk of tracking down some old girlfriend—but no one crazy enough to actually try it.

"Sure," says Toby. "Ideally you'd start with old phone books, find a street address, and talk to neighbors. But the library, the phone company—they've thrown out the old directories. So I locate the old guy in the portrait. He's in a depressing place. A nursing home. Tubes up his nose. He can't talk.

"Okay," says Garth. "So all the leads, by way of Lindsay's father, turn into dead ends. Next, I'd check old newspaper files, wedding announcements, right?"

Lindsay hears the doorbell ringing at the front of the house. She leaves Garth and Toby to their discussion and makes her way to the front hall. Everyone is having a good time except Richard. She spots him sitting alone at the dining room table, pouring himself a drink. Wally's dog has curled up on top of his shoes. In the living room, a stout man she's never seen before is searching the underside of her coffee table.

On the front steps stands a crowd of angry neighbors. "Are you aware," says their leader, "that you're broadcasting your party all over the block?"

"We're missing a *Memory Hour* special," says Mrs. Clapp. "A whole hour of Russ Columbo recordings!"

"I don't know what you're talking about," says Lindsay.

The leader holds up his portable FM. "Listen to this."

Lindsay hears the sound of a toilet flushing. "It sounds familiar," she admits, steps into the living room, and yells, "Are we on the air?"

The stout man looks up from under the coffee table. "I've

misplaced two of these things." He holds out a small black box and introduces himself as a used car dealer. "We could locate them if we had a portable radio."

"Isn't that lucky?" she says, returning to the front door and inviting the radio owner inside. The whole troop of neighbors barge in after him. Mankiewicz leads the group in a crouched line through the household. Half a dozen slow down when they see liquor set out in the dining room. Richard waves his glass at the newcomers and says, "Sure, make yourselves at home. It's only my house."

Lindsay heads back to the laundry room. Passing the stairwell, she hears a shout and applause from the upstairs bathroom. In the kitchen, Harold is laying out slices of bread to mass-produce sandwiches for the guests. Helen is folding bananas into a bowl of something beige. Lindsay stops to sample the concoction. "Mmm," she says. "Peanut butter and what?"

"Oh, I forget the name," replies Helen. "You know, Rochester, Minnesota?"

Wally steps over, looks at his wife, and explains that Helen has lost a word. "She's trying to give us a clue."

"Rochester?" says Lindsay. "Rock? Chester? Worcestershire!"

"No." Helen shakes her head. "Two brothers." She strokes her chin like it sprouts a long beard.

"Brothers?" says Lindsay. "Beard? Smith Brothers."

Helen waves her hands. "Start over." She tugs an earlobe.

"Sounds like—" says Wally.

Helen seizes a bunch of bananas and slings them over her shoulder.

"Banana boat," suggests Harold.

Helen nods to encourage him.

"Gangplank?"

"She's loading bananas!" says Wally.

Helen cups a hand to her mouth.

"Top banana!"

"Banana song!" cries Lindsay.

"Harry Belafonte!"

"*Day-oh!*" sings Wally.

Helen tugs her ear furiously.

"Pay-oh?"

Helen squeezes her husband's lips.

"Pfay-oh? Mmm?"

"*Mayo-* nnaise!" cries Lindsay, and gives Helen a big hug. Gripping the plump woman's shoulders, she realizes what an odd day it's been with its mad swings between catastrophe and slapstick humor. No, not mad. It's familiar, she decides. Eventually America will choose a stand-up comedian for president: Johnny Carson's hand on the nuclear button. Lindsay looks at her new friends: Helen, Wally, and beefy silent Harold. She feels fatigue setting in at the muscles of her back. But her kitchen, with its bright light overhead, has always been a cheery place.

Back in the laundry room, the project of locating the former Miss Lindsay Wyatt has led to the West Coast. "So you get the Evanston address from whom?"

Lindsay pauses in the doorway at these words. To cross this threshold is to enter another zone. Good Lord. Toby was trying to locate her that long ago? She's not sure she wants to know about this extended invasion of her life. "Evanston?" she says aloud.

Toby is holding a can of beer. He runs a finger around the rim.

"This is an incredible story," says Garth. "He traveled all over the country."

Toby takes a sip of beer. "It's hard to get information over the phone."

"You found me in Evanston?" asks Lindsay.

"No. You'd moved away. I gave up for a couple years."

"Okay. Back up a minute," says Garth. "The high school reunion led you to Smith College?"

"No, her high school yearbook. It's funny. I didn't know her married name was 'Smith.' Neither did the college alumni office."

"I'm mixed up now," says Garth. "You attended a high school reunion?"

"I went to her *father's* high school reunion. Class of 1936. It was the fortieth."

"And someone there knew about Lindsay's marriage?"

"No. I met a woman who kept in touch with the older brother. Lindsay's uncle. So I drove back to Los Angeles." The sound of the doorbell breaks Lindsay's concentration. It has never occurred to her how difficult—how complicated—it might be to locate someone you knew years earlier. She feels a tense interest in Toby's bizarre story. But now she feels relief at the doorbell's distant summons and goes to answer it. Intruders have been mixed up in her mind with this inrush of others, people whose numbers promise safety. The living room, she notices, is full of people searching for something on their hands and knees. Mankiewicz is fumbling behind the bookcase. "I got it!" he says, and a cheer goes up. "Tune in the radio!"

In the front hall she encounters a young man carrying two cases of beer. "Bring it in here!" comes a cry from the living room. Lindsay closes the front door, which has been left ajar. But immediately the doorbell sounds again. When she sees who it is she slams the entrance shut. But he barges in anyway.

"You called," says Gray Chandler, carrying his toolbox. "I *knew* you would call!"

"Go away," she says.

"But there was a call—about an oven that doesn't work?"

"I never want to see you again."

"Listen. I know this sounds crazy," he says, pursuing her into the crowded living room. "But I can't stop thinking about you and I lie awake at night because you're the one I've been looking for all these years and I never thought I'd really find you!" He seizes her in his arms. "I adore you! Come with me! You're wonderful! You're real! You're—"

"—*too beautiful for words,*" sings Russ Columbo on the FM.

"Help!" says Lindsay, making a dash through the dining room.

Richard looks up drunk from his place at the table, then stares for a long time into space. He shakes off what he thinks is a hallucination and staggers into the den, where he finds Gina watching TV. Alex is curled up asleep on the rug. Richard's eyes won't focus. His son looks like twins. Wearily he sinks down beside Gina. "This is better," he belches. "A quiet evening at home." But the room revolves. Something odd is happening in this house. On the TV screen, people wear peculiar clothing. Pointing, he asks, "Who's that?"

"Dr. Spock," says Gina.

"The pediatrician?"

"No. The Vulcan."

"I see," he nods, as Gina cuddles up beside him. But he doesn't see. None of this corresponds to what he expected. And in that thought he seems to glimpse an important truth. "Nothing is what you expect—is it?" he says aloud.

"Hush," says Gina. "They're going to beam up."

Abruptly Alex sits up, looks about, then drops back to sleep. To this evening, there's no end in sight. And that's fine with him.

Meanwhile, in the laundry room, Gray Chandler lies on the floor holding a bloody nose. Toby stands over him and demands to know what he's doing here.

"He's here to fix the oven," explains Lindsay, staring at the bright redness seeping between Gray's fingers. Has it finally happened? she thinks.

"I'm here to see her," insists Chandler. "We're in love."

"Oh no you're not," says Garth.

"Oh yes we are." Chandler lets go of his nose and looks at the stain in the palm of his hand. He seems surprised at what he sees there. "I've come to take her away with me. Don't laugh. It's really how I feel. It's lucky my roommate moved out. Now she can come with me."

"That's ridiculous," says Garth. "There's plenty of room

at my place." Now he looks at Lindsay. "Hey, isn't this the guy who—" He scratches his beard, then throws both arms over the top of his head. Could it be? he thinks. Lindsay involved with another man? Years have passed since Garth has felt jealousy so intense as this. "Naw," he says, dragging his hands down over his eyes. He doesn't know what to do. Finally he peeks out between his fingers at her. "I thought—" he says. "I thought I was—" He takes a breath and yells, "—THE ONLY ONE!" Then he bangs the side of his head. "Why am I talking about myself? Hey, please. Come home with me, Lindsay. Tonight?"

"She can do what she wants," interrupts Toby.

Garth, who has seen what Toby's index finger did to Chandler's nose, puts up his hands and says, "Of course, you're perfectly right about that."

"But eventually," Toby goes on, "she's coming with me."

There's a stunned silence.

"I am?" Lindsay's voice falters. "Where?"

"New Zealand, probably. We'll talk it over."

"New Zealand?"

"It depends on the jet stream. There's a place on the west coast of South America. Another in Alaska. Places where we'll be safe." Toby's blithe expression suggests that this line of thought is so obvious that only a fool would have to spell it out.

"Safe from—" Lindsay coaxes the word out of him. It will explain a lot, she decides. It will tell her what has driven him over the years. It must be something terrifying.

"Safe from the fallout." Toby looks calm and surprisingly sane when he pronounces these words. He could be someone who has just stood up to voice his opinion at a PTA meeting. His manner nearly convinces Lindsay that maybe he's not dangerous after all.

"Come on," scoffs Garth. "Move out of the blast zone? If everyone thought that way, we'd be in trouble. Sure, everybody thinks about it now and then. But to really survive, hell—people have to get in touch with what's in them.

Ordinary people. There's life in everybody—there's energy." Garth looks embarrassed at having made a corny speech.

"Oh," says Toby, unperturbed. "I depend on death. You can count on that."

Lindsay's opinion of Toby flops about again. The man is absolutely insane. If it comes to physical violence, to a brawl in her laundry room, then Garth and Gray Chandler —who's finally getting to his feet—won't stand a chance against him. She shudders. Has anyone thought of calling the police yet? Oh, it's getting close now—the thing that's going to happen.

The three men stand at the corners of a triangle, and she boldly steps into its center, where the force of their desires converge. If there's going to be a victim tonight, she knows who it's going to be. *She is.* She holds herself erect, a little proud. Part of her mind looks on calmly at a distance. *You're ready,* it tells her. Past Gray, she can see Helen sliding a tray of hors d'oeuvres out of the oven. Wally must have fixed the stove. Where is Wally? Or Harold? She could trust them to help her. No, she has to do this herself.

She takes a step, and no one moves. Brushing past Chandler, she thinks she might have made it. Her shoes kick out in strides across the kitchen linoleum. No one can stop her now. She's getting out. Her eyes fasten on the carpet of the long hallway. A few more steps and she'll make it. But then she hits—head on. One last barrier to get past. She glimpsed his shoes first. Now she's collided with a big soft chest. Oh!" she cries, feeling large hands seize her in a suffocating embrace.

27

LINDSAY HOLDS ON, crushed by a massive and familiar hug. It's the old odor of him she remembers best.

"Hush," he says, smoothing her hair. "I rang and rang. Nobody answered."

"By now, the doorbell must be broken," she says, and pushes away. A long sigh comes out of her. "Well, how are you?"

"How am I? I'M EXTRAORDINARY!" bellows Uncle Alfred.

Lindsay's ears ring from this preposterous shout. Uncle Alfred claims his voice has the power to break wineglasses, drive out demons, and seal the mouths of politicians. He still looks like a short version of Orson Welles, his beard streaked with silver. Under his evening cape, he grips a gold-knobbed walking stick.

"Where's your top hat?" she asks.

"Ah ha!" he laughs. "I left it home. It made me look like an eccentric." A loud bump sounds from the front hallway. "That's my trunk," he explains. "The taxi driver is bringing it in. I hope you're expecting me. All these others—" He circles a finger about. "Is this party in my honor? Or have celestial forces gathered the cult of some other deity?"

"I'm sure you can transform it into your affair," she smiles. It's true. Uncle Alfred has magic in him. The house is coming alive. Ripples of laughter promise a glittering evening.

"There's a bottle of champagne in my trunk," he confides. "You know what I always say—"

"Never embark without extra champagne," she recites. "Ah!" He squeezes her in another hug. "Now then. I think you'd better introduce me to these people. And then—" He flings up his walking stick in a theatrical gesture. "And then I'll tell you a story!"

She looks at him suspiciously. "A new story?"

"Always a new story!" he cries. "About your great-great Aunt Myrtle. A remarkable woman. Walked across the continent barefoot. Bore seventeen children to four husbands, one of them a half-breed gunslinger."

"Better wait," says Lindsay. She glances around a corner into the den. Richard has passed out on the love seat, Alex is sprawled on the floor, and Gina is blinking in confusion. "I heard a yell," she says. On the TV, the usual plot unfolds: An automobile vaults over the camera through space. It lands in an explosion. Flaming bodies scramble out the doors waving their arms. When Lindsay introduces her uncle, Gina murmurs, "Pleased to meet you." Then her eyes close and she nods out.

"That's my husband's girlfriend," says Lindsay as she takes her uncle's arm.

"Of course," he coolly remarks. Living in southern California has accustomed him to such abrupt revelations. "One learns to ride these tides of marital turbulence," he says. Alfred takes pride in his metaphors.

Introductions in the living room are more complicated. First Uncle Alfred feels obliged to leap onto the coffee table and belt out a few upbeat bars of

Hi, neighbors! Hi, neighbors!
How d'ya do! And whahh d'ya say!

Everyone cheers. But it's clear to him that Lindsay's guests don't know one another very well. Alfred vaults over to the piano, plays a few chords, and chants over his shoulder:

Now this is a song that will introduce
One stranger while meeting another.
Just try it, the rhythm is easy to learn:
I'm Alfred, the uncle of Lindsay!

Actually, what the members of this group in the living room have in common is that they all just loved summer camp. Give them directions for a musical parlor game and they'll turn the challenge into old-time fun. The accountant slides onto the piano bench and takes over the keyboard. As Lindsay and her uncle leave the crowd behind, the room erupts into a rhythmic uproar of mutual introductions:

> *"So you're the one in the yellow house?"*
> *"Benson's the name of our paperboy!"*
> *"So that's her uncle. Then who's the guy—*
> *The little one wearing thick glasses?"*
>
> *"That's Wally," says Harold, who sits on the couch.*
> *A trio of neighbors cry, "Who are you?"*
> *"Aw, he bought the house that was up for sale."*
> *"Nope. I'm the landlord of Gina."*
>
> *"Who?"   "Who?"*

The question turns into a circle game. A chorus of voices rings it out. And from the piano the bass line plays: *"Dah-dump, da-dump, dump, dump—WHO?"*

With one ruckus already started, Uncle Alfred heads for the dining room in search of another chance to bring this party to life. Lindsay sees that Richard's chair and bottle of bourbon have been commandeered by Mankiewicz.

"You the wife, huh?" The stout man tugs at her arm as they try to pass.

"Ignore this fool," says Uncle Alfred. "He's not amusing."

"Ha, ha—I'm a bugger," says the stout man to their backs.

"He sells used cars," explains Lindsay.

"Ah, a soul doomed to perdition. May his genitals be reborn as a collapsed front suspension." Her uncle is steering her toward the kitchen.

"Let's go the other way. There's a guy back there who scares me."

"Nobody scares me." He points his walking stick out ahead like a saber. "Why, I fought duels with Douglas Fairbanks and Errol Flynn. Have I told you about my experiences as a Hollywood extra?"

In the kitchen, they find Chandler sitting on a chair as Wally examines his nose. When Garth comes over to be introduced, Uncle Alfred jabs his stick at him in menace.

"He's not the one I'm scared of," whispers Lindsay. She points instead at the laundry room.

"You ought to be terrified of this man!" insists her uncle, explaining that obviously Garth and Lindsay are in love. "And what," he bellows, "is more terrible than the power of love?" Alfred brandishes his stick at the kitchen cabinets, climbs onto a chair, and delivers a long soliloquy to the ceiling light fixture.

Everyone listens politely. Then Chandler pipes up, "She loves me, too."

"Would you cut it out," says Lindsay.

"It's not broken," remarks Wally, having completed his examination of Chandler's nose. "But you should have stitches."

Uncle Alfred climbs down and steps over for a look. "I saw a nostril torn like that in a barroom fight between a stevedore and a wild pig. This was in Bangkok in the late forties. I bet on the pig—and lost a hundred dollars. I take it you're the attending physician?" Alfred catches Wally's eye, then darts a glance at the laundry room door. "How serious is this case?" He points now through the wall to where Toby must be standing, perhaps listening.

Wally winks to show he understands they're not talking about Chandler's nose. "On the surface," he says, "it's odd but seemingly manageable."

"Ah, the surface," says Alfred. "But you foresee complications?"

Wally twirls a finger at his temple to indicate lunacy. "Deep complications," he says. "Potentially life-threatening." He puffs up his muscles like Charles Atlas, then cocks his thumb and points an imaginary gun.

Uncle Alfred looks about at those assembled. "An operation!" he declares. Wordlessly he steps over and takes Lindsay's cast-iron frying pan from the stove. He places it in Garth's hands and indicates a position to one side of the laundry room door. "Why rely on the incompetence of the medical profession in cases like this one?" Alfred unscrews the pepper shaker and hands it to Wally, who climbs onto the counter near the other side of the door. "We'll need to boil lots of hot water," Alfred says loudly, opening a drawer and hefting a carving knife. "And sheets. Start tearing up sheets." He puts back the knife and selects the long fork Richard uses for the barbecue. Flexing it like a rapier, he evidently decides the weapon is satisfactory. His walking stick is set aside, the fork concealed behind his back. "But without anesthesia," he goes on, "who will restrain the patient? Oh, I wish we had a strapping big fellow to hold down the patient!" Alfred faces the laundry room door and gives the ready sign to Garth and Wally.

Chandler, who may be in shock, has listened dumbly to this series of declarations. "Nobody's going to hold me down," he says to the linoleum.

"Yes, a strapping big fellow." repeats Alfred. "That's what we need."

Lindsay has watched the preparations of the men in silent horror. Surely her uncle can't be serious. She hopes Toby has slipped out through the garage by now. This comic assault on a psychopath is going to end badly. The room feels suddenly cold. Her uncle's hand, gripping its ridiculous weapon, trembles—as if he understands that his magic will prove useless against what's going to come through that door.

Chandler stands up. "Come on, Lindsay," he says. "Let's get out of here."

At these words, Toby appears. He looks huge—a bear in terrific motion—and already he's passed through a cloud of tossed pepper that mostly hits Garth in the face. The hand holding the frying pan is gripped and given a quick twist. A pop sounds—one of Garth's fingers breaking—then the heavy pan clunks harmlessly into a corner. Uncle Alfred is backing up before Toby's advance. "Oh, my God!" he cries. "Not you! This guy is dangerous!" The barbecue fork clatters to the floor.

Chandler picks this moment to leap at Toby. There's a confused tussle for an instant. Then Chandler is down. He scrambles at Toby's legs and gets kicked back. Blood streams from his mouth now as he rolls over and sways on his hands and knees. Toby strides out the door, heading for the front of the house. Chandler scrambles on the slick kitchen floor and races after him.

"Stop him!" cries Lindsay, who fears to see any more blood spattered in her house. Uncle Alfred and Wally dash out. Lindsay trots after them. Last of all staggers poor, pepper-sputtering Garth, cradling the fingers of his right hand.

Toby has jogged down the hall, where he finds his escape blocked by a pair of steamer trunks. Stepping over people crowding the living room floor, he finds himself in the center of a circle. Suburbanites pause in mid-clap, their group sing interrupted by shouts from the kitchen—and now this. On the couch, beefy Harold readies himself for a lunging tackle. Toby sees only one way out. Gripping the collar of his jacket, he hefts it over the crown of his head and makes a dive at Lindsay's big front window—head first. In a shower of splintering wood and glass fragments, his boots arc into the darkness of the front lawn. The neighbors flinch, then look around the circle at one another to see whether this performance deserves applause. Lindsay and the others arrive breathless from the kitchen. They stare at the shattered front window.

"I hope he got away," mutters Uncle Alfred.

A sharp rap sounds at the front door.

"Don't answer it!" coughs Garth. One of his fingers is bent the wrong way.

"Has anyone called the police?" asks Lindsay.

"I'll get it," says Chandler, blotting a red smear on his lip.

They hear the sound of heavy trunks being pushed aside and the door clicking open. "Oh, no, not you again," says Chandler's voice. The hero backs into view as if they're running his film in reverse.

An elderly woman has appeared. She's dressed in her lavender outfit, plastic flowers decking her hat. "Hey, fatso," she snarls at Uncle Alfred. "The meter's still running." Sylvia looks around at the crowded living room. "What's this, a goddamn prayer meeting?" In her hand she waves a tire iron. "Anybody know that guy who came out the window?"

"I hope he's gone," says Wally.

"Nope," declares Sylvia. "He's still out there. I cold-cocked him before he hit the grass. He's laid out pretty stiff. You want I should bring him in?"

28

Harold and two other men wrestle Toby's unconscious body through the front door. They heave him onto the couch and bind his arms and legs with shoestrings, belts, and neckties. In his pockets they find a .45 automatic, three clips of ammunition, a length of thin wire, and a straight-edged razor. He carries no wallet and no identification. The crowd mills around in the living room, gawking at the big body on the couch, waiting for the police to arrive. Harold has yanked Garth's finger into line and taped on a splint. Wally has swept up broken glass from the rug and tacked a blanket over the shattered living room window.

All the noise woke Alex, but not his father or Gina. They sprawl on the love seat in each other's arms. The boy comes in, rubbing his eyes, and looks down at Toby. "He's awake," says Alex.

Toby's eyes open slyly. "Hi there, little cricket," he whispers.

The room's chatter falls silent.

"Nobody told me your name," complains Alex.

"My name? It's 'Toe-bee.' "

"Are you from another country?"

"No. I'm from New York."

Lindsay is hovering nearby. She kneels next to the couch and puts an arm around her son. "This is Toby Morton," she explains. "When I was a little girl, he was a little boy, just about your age. Someone is going to come and take

Toby away. He's sick, and they're going to make him better. Understand?"

Alex nods, then spots the black album on the coffee table. "Can I look at the book?" he asks his mother.

"For a little while. Then it's back to bed for you."

Wally has come over to examine Toby. He lifts his eyelids and passes a penlight over them. Something seems to puzzle him. Big Harold comes over for a look. "Concussion?" he asks.

"I can't tell. I think he's put himself into a trance."

"I knew a fullback who could do that," says Harold, then heads off to the kitchen. The neighbors are drifting off to other rooms.

Wally shrugs to himself and looks at Lindsay's uncle. "You knew Morton from somewhere else?"

"Yeah, you recognized him," says Garth. "What's the story there?"

Uncle Alfred squats down on the edge of the coffee table. "This maniac on the couch? Oh, he paid me a visit in California. I was living on the Carroll Canal in Venice, a nice little cottage except for the smell of sewage. I shared the place with an orange cat. This fellow arrived and started asking personal questions. When I clammed up, he threatened me with a gun. Can you believe it? Needless to say, the cat and I refused to say another word. The next morning what do you think? He's back, going through my garbage. I chased the rat off. You can imagine how surprised I was to see him walk out of Lindsay's laundry room."

Lindsay's not listening. She's picturing a lake and hearing the slap of water against the dock and a woman's hoarse voice calling her son to dinner. She shudders again. Her house, her body, still feel invaded. Someone wants to go all the way with her and—oh, God—she wishes it were over. She forces herself to look at Toby. His face is calm, the hint of a smile at his lips. Is he dead? Alex has dozed off against the couch with the album open in his lap.

"The lake," she says aloud, looking to her uncle for help. "Do you know what I'm talking about? A summer vacation. Please. *What happened at the lake?*"

"The lake?" says Uncle Alfred. "That's a sordid story. You don't want to hear it." He looks at his watch. "The police ought to have arrived by now."

"Tell me," she begs, bracing herself.

"A story?" says Wally, easing himself down on the rug next to Garth. "Lindsay claims that you're a terrific story-teller." From the other rooms it sounds like the party is winding down into murmurs.

Uncle Alfred gets up and drags the wing-back chair closer to the couch. He settles into it, delighted to have three attentive adults sitting at his feet.

How long, worries Lindsay, will her uncle drag this story out?

"In the 1950s," Alfred begins, "my younger brother, John, committed adultery, and Lindsay's mother caught him at it. She never forgave him."

"You mean she walked in on them?" asks Wally.

"Yes," muses Alfred. "I imagine it was a hot afternoon. Flies buzzed at the screen. They lay entangled in each other's arms. And then—" Alfred raps his fist in the air. "A knock at the door. Next, a frenzied scramble for garments!"

"Or maybe no knock?" suggests Garth.

Alfred throws a glance at him. He's not accustomed to having his performances interrupted. And Lindsay looks impatient for answers.

"What if they look up slowly?" Garth is saying. "The wife has sneaked in."

Alfred considers this. "That's possible. But picture this—" Uncle Alfred seems to part curtains in the air. "What does the woman look like?" he demands.

Garth and Wally peer into space, but imagination fails them.

"Ah ha. You see, John had chosen the most unlikely creature as the object of his lust. If we can trust the somewhat hysterical memory of Lindsay's mother, the other

woman was a physical wreck. A semi-invalid suffering
from tuberculosis. A mousey little woman coughing up
phlegm. Can you imagine it?"

"Kiss a TB patient?" says Wally. "Actually, some cases
aren't contagious."

"The look used to turn men on," remarks Garth.

"Ah," whispers Alfred, "the deathbed pallor." His
hushed tone draws his listeners in close. "Picture the white
neck of a frail young woman. Under the bed clothes, her
shallow chest pants weakly—"

"Get to the point," says Lindsay. "What happened at the
lake?"

"Doesn't she look pale? We'd better make this brief. All
this happened at the lake, my dear. You see, this pitiful
woman had rented a cabin adjacent to the one your family
occupied. You were just a girl. I doubt you even recall that
summer trip. Why dredge it up now? As I said, your
mother put an end to it. Your family packed up and left the
next day. The whole sick affair lasted less than a week. And
that, my dear, is what happened at the lake."

Garth and Wally seem disappointed.

"But who was she?" asks Lindsay.

"*Je t'adore*," says Alex. They all glance at the boy. He's
sitting up, flipping pages in the photo album. From a hidden place he pulls out a yellowed sheet of paper, unfolds
it, and hands it to Lindsay's uncle.

Alfred glances at the letter from Paris dated 1945. "It's
from a woman," he says and flings it away. He doesn't need
a kid handing him storylines.

"What woman?" demands Lindsay.

"Forget it. Why dredge another musty romance out of
the past?"

On the couch, Toby stirs and says, "*Elle est morte*," in
apparent delirium.

Lindsay snatches the old letter and scans it. The chill is
back, rushing in. Her eyes are wild, but she looks pale, as
if the blood is being siphoned out of her to be replaced by
something else. "What is this letter?"

"Another woman. I don't know the details. It happened before you were born—before John was even married. He asked my advice when he came back from Europe. I gathered that he'd fallen in love in Paris."

"Ah," says Garth, sitting up. "A story about love in Paris?"

Uncle Alfred holds up a hand. "Sorry, that's all I know. Look, Lindsay is upset. And you, young man." He takes Alex in his arms. "Why aren't you in bed?" He gives Alex a hug and hands him to Helen. "No story for this fellow either."

Lindsay watches her son being carried off. She shudders, recalling the voice of Toby's mother calling her son to dinner at the lake: *Toe-bee. Toe-bee.* She seems miffed at her uncle. "Oh, you're so *dumb* sometimes. Don't you see? *It was the same woman.* I remember her voice. The woman at the lake was *French.*"

Alfred looks at her suspiciously. "You remember the lake?"

"Don't you see?" Lindsay explains. "She and my dad *arranged* to have adjoining cabins."

"Sure," says Garth. "Why make a pass at an invalid? They must have been seeing each other since the war."

"Or what if they *hadn't* seen each other?" suggests Wally. "Since the war and Paris. At the lake, they're finally reunited. And she turns out to be sick."

Uncle Alfred is rubbing his hands, considering the possibilities. "We may have something here. The two lovers reunited after a decade. But goodness." His face turns serious. "Imagine my brother aghast at what he sees: her face lined by time's injurious hand, the former blush upon her cheek o'ersnowed and barren, and her lovely breast now wracked by the gusty wind of foul disease!"

"But don't forget." Garth holds up a bandaged hand. "They're still in love."

"Of course they are!" bellows Alfred, outdoing Garth's gesture by dramatically raising both arms. "The ashes of that flame still glow warm within, and at the breath of a

single sigh, the old fire blazes up. John takes her in his arms.
But she averts her face from his sweet kisses. Pressing her
to his breast, he understands the awful truth. She's dying.
What terrible joy must they endure as their garments fall
away. What urgency must heave them to the brink, again,
and again! Is this the last rich moment of their pleasure's
bliss?"

"Listen, you guys," Lindsay interrupts. "I'm not in wonderful shape. We've got an unconscious crazy person on the
couch. The police are about to arrive. And I'm trying to
find out about my father. Who *is* this guy on the couch?"

"She's right," nods her uncle, glancing at the old letter
from Paris. "Lindsay's memory of a woman's French accent hardly amounts to evidence. We have no proof that the
two women were the same."

Lindsay's hands seek Toby's arm. Finding it, they grip
hard. There's no tenderness in her gesture. "Come on,
wake up," she says. "Tell them."

His eyelids lift half-open. "Sure," he says. His voice
sounds pained. He must have quite a headache.

"Yeah, where'd you get the name 'Morton'?" asks Garth.
"Tell us about your father, Toby."

Uncle Alfred glares at the figure on the couch. He's
never been upstaged by someone lying flat on his back.
"Forget this nitwit. He doesn't know anything about this
story. Leave him out of it."

"Morton?" says Toby. "I never saw him. *Robert Morton.*
His name is on some papers. They certify that he married
my mother in Paris. Some GI, I guess. The documents got
her on the ship to the States. I was born six months later
in New York. March 1946. She died when I was eleven.
They put me in a foster home, then trade school." Toby's
face strains for an instant. "At the end, when she was dying
of TB, I had to carry her to the bathroom. I was just a kid.
What a lousy deal." Toby shuts his eyes. "Oh," he smiles,
"I eventually enlisted in the Army. Like Morton, right?"
His eyes shut again.

"Well, now we're getting somewhere," announces Uncle

Alfred. "Toby is the *son* of a French woman with TB! And she came over on a ship."

Garth looks at him in dismay. Uncle Alfred hasn't caught on yet.

"Lindsay could be right!" cries Alfred. "Now, if only we had one scrap of evidence. Something that would place this son of hers—Toby was just a boy, remember, ten or eleven —at the lake cottage in the mid-1950s." Alfred rubs his brow in furious thought. He grimaces at this puzzle that won't fall into place.

Garth pats his arm. "Hey, take it easy. We already figured that out."

Alfred looks up dumbfounded. "You did?"

"We'll show you the snapshot later. Go back to the part about the ship. We want to hear you tell the part about coming over on the ship."

"Yeah," says Wally eagerly.

"Well," remarks Alfred, "there's no suspense in that part of the story. Unless—" Slowly he elevates one finger all the way overhead. Alfred might be stalling, searching for words. But Garth and Wally love it. They watch his finger ascend with the same attention they'd give to a crew hoisting a grand piano into a ten-story window. "UNLESS!" They wince at the word. "Unless—at the end of her crossing—she expected someone. In New York. To meet her!"

"But who?" Garth and Wally ask in unison.

"I'll get to that. Be patient. First picture the ship docking in England. Hundreds come up the unsteady gangplank. Tramp, tramp, tramp. All women, of course. A whole ship full of brides. They drag children along. It's crowded, the seas are rough, and then—disease breaks out."

"Dysentery," says Wally. "They'd be dehydrated. It's a real kid killer."

Alfred goes on. "Now—imagine New York harbor hoving into view. Then the Statue of Liberty. And at the docks the grinning GIs are waving up at their war brides." He grins upward and waves. "Some women on board scan the sea of faces, but there's no one there to meet them. The unmarried ones will be sent back like illegal aliens. Now here's Toby's pregnant mother passing through the crowd. Her eyes search for someone."

"She's looking for the guy she married," breaks in Wally, who can't stand the suspense. "But Morton's a no-show."

"Naw," objects Garth. "It's Lindsay's father who's going to meet her. He's the one she loves. But there's no sign of him." Garth shades his eyes with his hand and scans the crowded wharf.

"You think my brother would stand a woman up like that?" asks Alfred.

"Oh, not on purpose," explains Garth. "Letters get lost in the mails. It's a mix-up. But does she know that?"

"Nope." Wally has a melancholy look on his face. "Ten long years go by before she learns the truth."

"Hold it." Uncle Alfred stands up. "How about this? See, he doesn't know she's gotten herself pregnant. Meanwhile he's engaged to Harriet, the girl back home. But Toby's mother embarks for America anyway. And once here, she's so honorable that she never informs him that she's arrived, living alone, available, on this side of the wild and stormy Atlantic!" Alfred sits down again.

"Okay. Okay!" Wally looks impatient. "As I was saying—" He looks to see if the other two are listening. "Ten long years go by. In the meantime, she makes a life for herself and Toby in Brooklyn."

"Doing what?" asks Garth.

"I don't know," says Wally. "She works in the garment district. And brings work home at night. She's got a sewing machine in the bedroom."

"What if she's really desperate?" asks Alfred.

"Oh, boy. Now you've done it." Garth shakes his head sadly. "That would be a shame. She sells herself, huh? Night work, the kid in the next room?"

"I bet she was good looking," says Wally.

"Maybe she's had experience," says Alfred. "In Paris, during the German occupation—what if she had a German lover?"

"A Nazi?" Garth looks indignant. "Come on, give her a break."

"She worked in a bakery," states Wally, as if this will settle the matter.

"She got married!" says Garth.

"Wrong." Wally raises his voice. "She got a job in a dry cleaners!"

Uncle Alfred gets to his feet again. "Just whose story is this? ANYWAY!" he declares, all red in the face. "You two have made a mess of this woman's life."

Lindsay hears the men's voices far away. She feels numb. Nobody is helping her. It may be too late now. She feels herself giving up. They've punctured her, infused her cells with something alien, and hung her up to drain. Now she feels slipped out of herself. Next they'll slide her into a different life. What if her eyes don't line up with the holes they've cut in her new face? She watches her mannikin's hand reach out to this strange man flopped on the couch. They're two of a kind now, she decides. We're puppets— a string goes up through our heads. Lindsay taps Toby's arm and his eyes click open.

She asks him, "When did you figure all this out?"

"When I was a kid. At the lake, I guess. Your dad wanted us to meet."

"And your mother. Did she tell you for sure?"

"Not exactly. But the next year, in the spring, she was out of the hospital, but her cough was worse. She told me to call your father."

"And you did?"

"Yeah. He said he'd come right away. But he never showed up. She died."

"So you were the one. Who made him rush off in the rainstorm, I mean."

"I'd never made a long-distance call before."

"But you know what happened?"

"I figured it out a few years ago."

"Then you know he tried to get to New York before she died. But he had an accident. A bridge washed out."

"Yeah. Things like that happen. That's why I have to watch out for you."

"I wish you wouldn't."

"No. I can tell that's what you need."

"What's this talk?" Uncle Alfred is leaning into the conversation. "Who's going to watch out for whom?"

Lindsay sighs. Her voice comes out hollow, as if it belongs to someone else. "You'd better tell him, Toby."

"I have to watch out for Lindsay. After all, she is my sister."

29

THE HOUSE IS quiet and the night is dark. Lindsay kneels next to the couch. It feels right that Toby has said it aloud, mouthed the words that make it true.

"Wait just a minute," says Garth.

"Hush!" scolds Uncle Alfred, glaring down at his niece. "So, it's finally come out. Shame on you for swallowing such a flimsy story. Oh, I saw what this idiot was up to an hour ago. Now he's actually convinced you that he's your brother. Or at least, that you share a father in common. It's preposterous!"

"But that's how he died," insists Lindsay. "Toby called to say his mother was dying. That's why Daddy drove off in the storm."

Alfred considers this for a moment. "Well, that was admirable of him. But it doesn't make this muscle-bound lunatic your brother."

Her uncle is jealous, she decides. He no longer wholly possesses her, nor is he the sole keeper of her past. Now that the facts have fallen into place, she feels how smoothly they fit against her hollow interior, bracing her from within. Her father had conceived Toby in Paris. Then, ten years later, he recklessly drove off to be with the dying woman he loved. He just never made it. The real story is so simple, she thinks.

"You're confusing love with biology!" sputters Uncle Alfred. "This rotten apple here isn't from our barrel!"

There he goes again, thinks Lindsay, trying to protect

the family genes. What exactly was she so anxious about all evening? Everything makes sense. And she feels safe—almost warm. Someone is finally looking out for her.

"How could you believe this fool?" demands her uncle.

Wouldn't anyone? she thinks, frowning and biting her lip so hard that it bleeds. Toby is up on one elbow staring at her. She feels it now—coming off him: a cold wind blowing out of a lonely region in the mind. Or is it her mind? She can't decide. The chill isn't so bad now. You get used to it.

"Look at me!" orders Uncle Alfred. "I'm not a tall man. Your father, John, was an inch shorter and dark. His hair was quite black. If this fair-haired screwball is my nephew, then his mother must have been an Amazon, a Dagmar, a seven-foot Mae West." Alfred hovers over Toby, who has lain back, eyes shut. "And you know that an eleven-year-old didn't carry a woman-giant to the bathroom. It was a shock, wasn't it, Morton? To see Lindsay for the first time? After the years you spent tracking her down, she turned out too small, too dark, too much an image of your own mother. Well, I'm sorry. I'm truly sorry. You made a mistake."

Toby opens his eyes and stares blankly at the ceiling. "What you say doesn't matter. The important thing is to get Lindsay out of here. This is a dangerous place. And there isn't much time. I sense these things, and I've seen the signs. I'm in touch with certain currents. They run in the air and under the earth. The earth is afraid for itself. Did you know that? Listen sometime in the night."

Lindsay feels his words whistling past her, drawing off the heat. In her mouth she tastes the iron and salt of her own hot blood. But she sits still, chilled by otherness. If her father were here, none of this would have happened.

Maybe he is. She glances out of the corner of her eye. If things really get bad, a watchful father will intervene—for all of them. The only trouble with her father is he doesn't have a beard. What kind of patriarch is that? *Is.* That's a goof. *Was.* Her father is dead. How many years has she been making that mistake—thinking of her father in the present tense? *Thinking him present.* Oh dear, she thinks. Daddy is dead. She's never felt so cold and alone as she does now, knowing how empty the sky really is. Nobody's up there.

She sits, motionless. The old feeling of a spell coming on has lofted her up, to view herself at a distance. Far below, at the center of a glittering and spacious interior, she sits: a thirty-four-year-old housewife with auburn hair grown out. This small distant stranger has suffered breakage and loss, has burrowed out of darkness to embrace her own feelings, her own body. She's knelt before new altars where the flame still burns. But has she learned anything? She may, if left to herself. For one thing, her posture is still good. If she keeps still now, she'll understand that every-thing leads here. To this hollow instant. And oddly, *someone is watching.* But it's not conscience, and it's not a ghost. All this time, the loftiest observer has been Lindsay herself— a higher version of Self, one so refined and clear-sighted that it's beyond dealing out advice or blame. She can't count on this presence to tell her what to do. But it's there. She has even glimpsed what's about to occur through its eyes. And that knowledge is all she needs.

She looks at Toby. "My uncle is right. Your father was someone else."

"Forget about that!" It's the first time Toby has raised his voice. "Think about the danger, the peril of this place. Think of the fire storms and acres of debris. The stench of the dead and the barren land. I can save you from that. I know things, techniques for staying alive. Think about what's going to happen!"

"It's not in me to think that," she says.

"You know it is."

Lindsay stands up. "No. *You're* not in me. Maybe you want to be the last one on earth. I don't know. Look, I'm just an ordinary person."

Toby sits up, glaring at her. "You're my sister!" he hisses.

"No," she says, hearing the terrible desperation in his voice, the fear of being a small boy alone and abandoned in the world, the ache of emptiness that has made her—and the promise of possessing her—the most precious commodity in the world. She takes a breath, wondering whether she'll have to shout, or else the old word is going to sound corny. "Sorry," she says quietly. "But you're no *kin* to me."

"No!" cries Toby. His shout rings, echoing, in the house. Lindsay slumps, exhausted. But she's okay. She feels pretty good, and she wonders who decided to tie him up with neckties. What a funny idea.

From the hallway, people step in to see what the shouting is about. Garth gazes at Lindsay and then brings his palms together: *Clap clap clap.* More than once tonight he's had to hold himself back from interfering in whatever ordeal she was passing through. What if he lost her, let her slip out of reach? Now Lindsay comes over and sits down next to him. He grips her hand and whispers, "I admire you terribly."

"I love you," she says. "Gosh, it's been a long night."

Toby is moving his head from side to side. Now he takes a deep breath and lies still. Perhaps there's a reservoir in the man into which he drains his power and gathers it for abrupt release.

There's a knock at the front door. "Police," says a voice. "Open the door."

At this, Toby writhes on the couch. People step back. The man is about to erupt. Suddenly necktie fabric bursts in a loud snap. You can see the dust of threads in the air. Wrenching leather belts from his ankles, Toby springs up. He scans the room for a way out. A cluster of neighbors have shoved and edged their way into the living room. Now they stand as a barrier, blocking the route of his first midair escape. Over the piano another window pane glitters. Seeing him glance at it, people push back. They clear a runway for another spectacular leap. Someone readies the piano bench that Toby will require for the vault. He plants his feet. The police are coming in the front door. But at the last instant, Toby must reconsider another skull-rattling flight through wood and glass. Because he turns to the crowd, politely says, "Excuse me," and then sidesteps past people to reach up and yank down the tacked-up blanket. There he easily steps out through the broken window frame. Silently he trots off into shadows.

"Aw, phooey," mutters a neighbor.

"What's the problem here?" demands a police officer.

"Oh, no!" A shriek slices in from the next room. More anxious faces peer into the already packed living room. It's Wally's wife, Helen, coming in from the dining room. She presses her palms to her cheeks in agony. "Oh, how terrible!" she wails. "It's Uncle Fred. She—" Helen blinks once and stares into space. "Oh, what's the word?"

"Which one is Uncle Fred?" whispers a neighbor.

Helen wags her head, then beams with a giddy illumination and declares, "Uncle Fred *pooped* on the dining room rug!"

30

Sgt. KOWOLSKI and Patrolman Angini spend an hour cir-
culating through the crowd taking down names and state-
ments. They find Gray Chandler asleep upstairs hugging
Lindsay's pillow. In the den they shake Richard, who's
slept through everything. "What day is it?" he asks, bewildered.

"Happy Father's Day," jokes Angini.

"Naw, that was yesterday," says Kowolski. "It's past
midnight. It's Monday."

"Wrong," says Uncle Alfred, stepping forward. "It's
June 22." He checks his watch. "And just about now the
sun is crossing over from Gemini into Cancer. I always
arrive in time for the summer solstice."

"Solstice?" asks the patrolman. "The longest day—or
something. We've had calls from all over town. People are
going crazy tonight, whooping it up."

"And some," adds Alfred, "are bored to tears, confused,
or bound to wheels of fire. Such are the dreams," he sighs,
laying a hand on his breast, "this stuff is made of."

Everyone mulls this over in silence, apparently grateful
that Linsay's uncle has finally talked himself out.

Once the police leave and the neighbors have bid their
good-byes, Lindsay takes Gina aside and asks her to get
Richard upstairs to bed. "Just change the sheets in the
morning, okay? He likes toast and juice for breakfast."

Garth and Alex are waiting at the front door. "I'm coming with you in Wally's truck," says her son. In his arms

he holds his sleeping bag. A compass is strung around his neck.

"Okay," she says. Stepping over the threshold is easier than she expected. Outside, Chandler is helping Harold nail plywood over the broken front window.

"Thanks for coming by," she tells Gray.

"Yeah," he sighs.

"How's your nose?"

"It'll heal."

"You're sure you'll be okay?"

"Fine. Your uncle and I are going out to see if any bars are still open."

She gives him a kiss on the cheek and then walks out to the curb, where the pickup truck is waiting.

"Alex wanted to sit up front," explains Garth, helping her climb into the back of the truck. "Wally's taking the Interstate downtown."

They sit propped against the cab window and open the sleeping bag over their outstretched legs. Lindsay gazes at her house as Wally drives off. All the lights are on. It looks like the most glittering home on the block. She laces her fingers into Garth's under the sleeping bag. The ride is a little rough, and the wind threatens to flap the sleeping bag off into the path of headlights that glare in their eyes.

"Back at the house," says Garth, "Alex asked me if this was the end."

"I hope you told him the right answer."

"I think so."

Lindsay grips his hand. "Let's sing," she says.

"I'd rather hum."

"Good idea," she says, and presses her temple against his cheek.

Overhead, the streetlights sweep past. Finally the neon signs of Commercial Drive go out of sight behind a dark grove of trees. Out on the Interstate there are no lights. They look up together at a sky too dark for stars. But toward the east, the night takes flight, and the morning seems to dawn.